ALSO BY JAMES W. HALL

Paper Products

Tropical Freeze

Under Cover of Daylight

BONES OF
CORAL

James W. Hall

BONES OF CORAL

Alfred A. Knopf   New York

1 9 9 1

Hal
C 1

THIS IS A BORZOI BOOK
PUBLISHED BY ALFRED A. KNOPF, INC.

Library of Congress Cataloging-in-Publication Data
Hall, James W., [date]
Bones of coral : a novel / by James W. Hall.
p. cm.
"A Borzoi book"—T.p. verso.
ISBN 0-679-40017-6
I. Title.
PS3558.A369B6 1991
813'.54—dc20   90-52866 CIP

Manufactured in the United States of America
First Edition

For Evelyn

Full fathom five thy father lies;
Of his bones are coral made;
Those are pearls that were his eyes;
Nothing of him that doth fade
But doth suffer a sea-change
Into something rich and strange.

SHAKESPEARE, *The Tempest*

BONES OF
CORAL

I

Cassie Raintree was dying of brain cancer every afternoon at two-thirty. She had been dying all through January, and Shaw Chandler thought she was becoming more beautiful every day.

She wore a turban of bandages, and her cheekbones seemed to have risen to the surface. A halo of diffused light surrounded her hospital bed—that strange phosphorescence of the dying that Shaw had witnessed so often.

He knew it was goofy, but there it was. A thirty-eight-year-old paramedic who'd spent almost half his adult life wheeling the bloody, the broken and the dead to the ER or the morgue, and he'd let himself get involved in a soap opera.

Oh, he knew "Hidden Hours" was hokum, and that it was being written by some rich housewife in a Park Avenue apartment, all by formula: dark man sweeps woman away from cheese spread for intense romantic interlude. But he watched anyway, because Cassie Raintree was better than the worn-out story. She acted her way beyond it. She could draw in a breath as she stared down some bitchy accusation and then absolutely nail the sucker with a tilt of her head and a change of light in her eyes. It was art.

Everybody went on about the Meryl Streeps, but those Hollywood hotshots took a year to make a picture. They got takes, retakes, time to learn their lines, millions of dollars to make them glow. But hell, Shaw believed the real artists were the ones doing it every day. Out on the edge, cameras rolling, get it right the first time, or get out.

Dr. Cassie Raintree was the chief psychiatrist at Leewood Hospital in Oakbridge. In that position she'd gotten the lowdown on a lot of the citizens of Oakbridge. But she'd never abused her power.

She had her standards and upheld them. Like the time she'd risked her career rather than reveal intimate details about one of her patients. Shaw was with her on that one. He'd been with her, in fact, on every problem that had come her way in the year he'd been watching "Hidden Hours."

Even during the weeks Cassie Raintree had fallen for Malden Aimes, an undercover cop, Shaw had been on her side. Malden was a renegade and a dark hombre. He wasn't but half a cut above the scum he was hunting. But he burned with a passion that had electrified Cassie Raintree and lured her away from her fiancé, Dr. Barton Donaldson. And though she had broken faith with Barton, Shaw believed she'd done the right thing. Barton didn't have the sizzle this woman needed. It never would have worked.

Cassie's real name was Trula Montoya. Trula Marie Montoya. She'd been two years behind Shaw at Key West High School twenty years ago. Running with a different crowd, the arty set, but he'd known her, everyone had. She was the poised daughter of a doctor at the navy base, the talented girl with the easy smile who was headed somewhere.

Shaw Chandler had noticed her, watched her walk the high school corridors, talk to her friends. This pretty, dark-haired sophomore with the large blue eyes. His buddies catching him a couple of times and making remarks. Finally, around Halloween his senior year, he'd asked her out. She was a bright, funny girl, her eyes alive.

She wasn't the least bit in awe of him like other sophomores would have been. Talked to him from the first moment like her equal, as if perhaps she didn't know that Shaw's photograph was on the sports page of the *Key West Citizen* almost every week. Eventually Shaw had trouble explaining her to his friends, why he'd bother with a kook like her, some airy-fairy actress who never even came to the games.

After a month of movies and dances and cheap restaurants, Shaw and Trula had begun to park beside the ocean at Smathers Beach, scoot close in his Chevy pickup and kiss for hours. Then between the kissing, gaze off at the glitter of moonlight on the Atlantic. He remembered her talking at moments like that, talking about plays, about people they knew, characters around the island or in school. She was excited by all kinds of odd things. People, the way they moved, their little mannerisms. She could mimic his friends' voices, their pigeon-toed walks, how they slouched against their lockers.

She was funny and smart. He remembered her using the word *nuance* one night, and he had asked her what it meant.

Then one humid evening near Christmas, they had spread a towel across the sand, drunk beer from a quart bottle, and in a panic of laughter, stripped off their clothes and splashed into the water and held each other and kissed. But neither of them wanted to go farther than that. Nothing was said, but it was clear they were both embarrassed, unprepared for what came next. They toweled off and dressed, and afterward they kissed some more in the truck, but there was no heat in it anymore. And when he drove away from her father's house that night, he knew it was over. Though they dated for a few more weeks, it was never the same again. They had become, in that one night of sudden intimacy, merely friends.

After Shaw graduated and moved three hours north to Miami, he'd heard from his mother that Trula Montoya had dropped out of high school in her junior year and had gone to New York. And from time to time over the years, she'd mentioned Trula, appearing in this or that TV commercial, acting in some off-Broadway play.

Then about a year ago his mother had informed him that Trula Montoya had joined the cast of "Hidden Hours." He should watch the show, she said. See one of our own who made it.

So he'd sat down with the boob-tube addicts one afternoon last winter and started watching, not telling the guys he'd known Trula. And instantly he'd seen it. Trula Montoya was the only real thing on the silly show. A three-dimensional person ambling through a cardboard forest.

After that he'd begun watching "Hidden Hours" every afternoon he wasn't out on a call, waiting for her scenes, studying her, trying to separate the acting from the woman, prying around her mask for a glimpse of the island girl he remembered so clearly from that other life.

Then a couple of weeks ago, after only a year on the show, Cassie Raintree was diagnosed with brain cancer. And her vital signs began to grow weaker every day. It was clear that Trula Montoya was being written out of the show, and Shaw was vaguely depressed, walking around feeling heavy and slow. His one bright moment every afternoon at two-thirty was about to go dim.

———

One Wednesday afternoon, the second week in January, his partners, Jorge Benito and Buzz Sullivan, were watching the show. Buzz at a card table sipping a Diet Coke, and Jorge sunk into his recliner. Shaw was standing up, leaning against the rear wall. Three guys from the engine crew were scattered about the Spartan room—concrete block walls, glossy white linoleum—all in their identical recliners. Cassie Raintree was with her oncologist, and things looked bleak. Her doctor had suspended all treatment. He'd asked her if her business affairs were in order, if there was somebody she wanted him to call. No, she'd said, nobody.

A commercial came on, a deodorant soap that made people sing and smile when they used it. Buzz, watching the actors lathering up, said, "She's the star. They won't kill her off."

"What? They going to find a cure for brain cancer, huh, Buzz? Announce it right on this show?" Jorge looked around for approval from the other firemen.

"Maybe it was a bad diagnosis," said Buzz.

"She'll be gone by next week," Jorge said. "You don't survive shit like that. You get a tumor in there, it's fast growing, forget it, you're over with, a month tops."

"Dr. Jorge Benito," Buzz said. "Fresh in from Walter Reed to give his lecture on brain cancer."

"You heard what her doctor said. It's inoperable, man. I say just bury the bitch, let's get on to the sex scenes."

"I never liked her anyway," one of the engine guys said. "She's got a king-size corncob up her ass, you ask me."

"She's an actress," Shaw said. "She's playing a part."

"She's a dry sandwich," Jorge said. "You can tell the way she walks around, the woman has no lubrication."

Some of the engine guys laughed.

Shaw walked to the john and took a leak, and when he returned the show was back on and it had moved on to another part of the plot. But he wasn't interested in the rest of the characters. Without Cassie Raintree moving among these people, who gave a shit about them?

Shaw believed that Trula must have had herself written out. It'd gotten too easy for her. She wanted to test herself on some other stage, see what else she had inside her. That had to be it.

When the show was over that day, everybody standing up, stretching, Jorge said, "But I got to say it, man. Dry sandwich or not, I'm going to miss that babe. Her eyebrows, shit, they get me very hot."

"What eyebrows?" someone said.

"Man, that lady's eyebrows are so bushy, she's got to blow-dry them," Jorge said.

"You like hairy women, huh, Jorge?" Shaw said.

"So what if I do?" he said. "The thicker the eyebrows, you know, the hairier the bush. And this Cassie bitch, man, she's got to have a bush up to her navel and down to her knees."

Shaw stared at Jorge. The kid was sitting at a card table, working on his nails, digging the dirt out with the blade of his knife. A couple of the other firemen rocked up from their recliners, made some bored noises and headed back into the engine room.

"You know why you like hairy women, Jorge?" said Shaw. He felt the tightness in his throat, but wasn't sure if anyone else could hear it in his voice.

"I like hair," he said. "No reason for it. I like to get in there and smush my face in it."

Shaw said, "It's because you got homosexual tendencies."

Jorge stood up, put his knife down. Shaw moved out onto the open floor.

"Hey, hey," Buzz said. "What're you two idiots getting worked up about? It's a goddamn soap opera."

"But you're too chickenshit to admit you want to suck cock," Shaw said, going on with it, feeling the heat spreading through him. "So you get off on hairy women."

Buzz jumped up and stepped in front of Jorge, blocked him with his wide chest.

"Goddamn it, Shaw, shut up," Buzz said. He muscled Jorge back to the card table. And the boy sat down, still giving Shaw as hard a look as he could fashion.

Shaw Chandler went outside and sat down with some of the engine guys, looking out at the traffic on Bird Road, waiting for an alarm bell so they could go out and press the electric paddles to some obese, cigarette-smoking heart attack victim, resuscitate a cocaine mother, straighten up somebody's bloody mess.

———

At nine-thirty that night the three of them were in their cubicles. Shaw in his bed reading a Western, Buzz snoring, and Jorge singing along to his Walkman. When the claxon sounded, Shaw folded the corner of the page. The wall speakers came on, the female dispatcher saying, Rescue Seven respond on a Three Forty-four, a possible suicide, result of gunshot. She gave an address three blocks from the station house. Code Three, get cooking. Police were on their way.

Buzz pulled the rescue van out onto Bird, took the second left onto Seventy-fourth, a street full of warehouses and auto repair shops, and wheeled hard into the dirt driveway of a small white frame house.

A white-haired woman in a white sack dress waited for them behind the screen door. She was about sixty. Breathing hard and blinking her reddened eyes. She took a long look at Shaw, then said to follow her please, the victim was in the back bedroom. She believed he was already dead. Trying to be polite but having trouble keeping her legs under her.

She led them through a living room cramped with furniture. Big, primitive wood things, rockers and chests of drawers and tables, a secretary, a cedar coffee table, and a sofa with a jumble of bright, quilted pillows.

She walked down the narrow hallway, Jorge close behind her, rocking his head in time with her wide hips. Buzz punched him lightly on the shoulder to cut it the hell out.

In the bedroom the victim was wearing striped pajama bottoms and a white undershirt, his left arm slung over a pillow, holding it to his face. In the other hand he held a Colt .38. His heart blown out the back of his undershirt.

Buzz bent over him, checked for a pulse at his throat, while Shaw opened the equipment bag. Buzz rolled up the T-shirt, took the Life-Pak Five from Shaw and pressed the paddles to the victim's chest. Jorge and Shaw watched the tape printing out a straight line.

"I was out at the Seven-Eleven," the woman said, gazing at a blank wall. "I wasn't gone but fifteen minutes."

Buzz handed the paddles back to Shaw. He leaned over the victim and lifted the lifeless arm from his face. Shaw glanced at the man, then staggered a step backward.

"What?" Jorge peered at the guy, then back at Shaw. "What?"

"Jesus Christ," Shaw said, leaning forward for another look. He turned away, working for breath.

The man was close to sixty. A light touch of gray in his close-cropped beard. He'd gotten soft in the face and the middle. But his shoulders were still wide, his hands as thick and rough as they had been when this same man had lifted Shaw above his head to touch the ceiling of their house on Olivia Street in Key West. And his eyes, even without their shine, staring at the ceiling, they were his father's eyes. Hanson Chandler's eyes. Though it had been twenty years since Shaw had stared into them, there was no doubt. It was him. His square jaw, his heavy brow, those full, almost girlish lips. Hanson Chandler.

Shaw sat down heavily in a rocker, glanced over at the woman who was watching him quietly in the doorway.

"What's wrong, man?" said Buzz.

"It's only a gunshot," Jorge said.

"He's seen ten thousand gunshots," said Buzz.

Shaw stared at the blue rag rug. The light swam out of his eyes, the room yellowed, narrowing to a groggy slit. He lowered his head to bring some blood back to his brain.

"He looks like somebody I used to know. That's all," Shaw said, taking another slow breath. "It's okay. I'm okay."

"That'll shake you up," Buzz said.

"People look like other people," said Jorge. "What's the big deal?"

The woman was watching Shaw.

"I had it happen once," Buzz said, putting the paddles back in the plastic case. "Five, six years ago. I'm doing CPR on this lady, and it strikes me this girl looks like a girl I went out with in college. Sally something. I was actually considering marriage. Then it hits me, this girl doesn't just look like her, it *is* her. And there I am blowing into her mouth, trying like hell to revive her from an over-dose of something. I had to stop, hand her over to my partner."

"Bunch of wimps," Jorge said.

The woman, standing in the doorway, looking at Shaw, said, "Can I talk to you? When you feel better."

Shaw lifted his head. "Yeah," he said. "Sure."

She led him into the kitchen and Shaw took the chair opposite her. The room was no wider than a hallway, painted bright white, the windowsill full of violets and herbs. Muffin tins and copper colanders and kitchen gadgets hung from the walls, a collection of porcelain pitchers on one counter. Someone had emptied a farm-house and carted it here among the transmission shops and beer warehouses.

At one end of the room, a green parrot in a white cage hopped from its swing to a water trough, ruffling and shaking its feathers. It squawked and said, "Hey, sailor, hey, sailor."

The woman's eyes were faded green, the whites stained the color of weak whiskey. But her mouth was tight and resolved, as if per-haps she'd seen this night coming from a long way off and had hardened part of herself for it, even measured out her grief already for this moment.

A twitch had come into Shaw's heart. The tremors before a quake.

"I know it must be a shock," she said. "Finding him like this after so much time."

"Who are you?" he asked.

"Just somebody," she said. "Somebody helping your father get by."

"How do you know who I am?"

"Your father pointed you out to me. He watched you." She gave him a look at her eyes. "He watched you a lot."

There was a heavy knock and a voice at the front door. She frowned and rose wearily to let the police in. Shaw waited, staring at the swirl of grain in the oak tabletop, unable to summon a thought, a sharp clot forming in his throat.

The parrot gripped the cage door with its beak, gave it a rattle. "Who's a good boy?" it sang. "Who's being a good boy?"

When the woman came back into the kitchen, Shaw was focused on the bird, watching its frantic circuit of the cage. She took her chair, her eyes drifting to the wall above Shaw's head.

"I told him he shouldn't have gone down there," she said. "Of all places, Key West, where so many people knew him."

"Key West!"

She said, "He went down there again this morning, just got back tonight. And he just lay there all evening, staring at the ceiling. Wouldn't say a thing."

Her eyes drifted back, lit on Shaw and she said, "I know you had no way of knowing about it, but your daddy'd been keeping up with you. He was proud of your career, everything you did. Mighty proud."

"This is crazy," Shaw said. He fought off an impulse to push the table over, break dishes, anything to keep this woman from giving words to what was in her eyes.

The woman said, "Whenever we'd go out, he had to drive by the firehouse. Station Thirty-seven, right around the corner on Bird, that's where you work at, isn't it?"

Shaw said, Yeah, Thirty-seven.

"And you been there now, it's been almost ten years?"

He nodded.

"See? I'm telling you truly," she said. "It's why he picked this house. It's so nearby. Living here, talking about you all the time. He knew what shifts you worked, your days off. Where you were living over in South Miami. He'd park down the street sometimes, spend part of an afternoon just watching the station, on the off chance he'd see you. Sit there and watch the trucks coming and going. It was always Shaw this and Shaw that. He knew if something ever happened to him, chances were fifty-fifty it'd be you finding him." She looked down at the dark spots on the back of her hands. "He liked that idea."

"Jesus Christ," Shaw said, his eyes fogging. "Jesus Christ."

"I would say to him, 'Quit your spying, Hanson. Just go up to your boy, explain things to him. He'll forgive you. There isn't a son alive who wouldn't want to see his father again.' But he wouldn't do it."

"Oh, he damn well knew if he'd come up to me," Shaw said, "I would've turned him over to the police in a second. Made the gutless bastard serve his time."

She warned him with her eyes. She had managed her grief to this point, but don't push her.

Shaw shook his head, staring at this woman. Her face bloated by age or drink or both. Shaw was feeling the rage, twenty years of it, the acid backing up in his throat, all the hours he'd thought about the man in the bedroom, wondering where the hell he'd gone, what objects he'd surrounded himself with. Wondering what life he'd chosen to replace the one he'd abandoned. And now suddenly, here it was. This woman, this house.

Shaw glanced up. Lieutenant Dwyer was standing just beyond the kitchen door, scribbling on his pad, scuffing his shoes on the rug, waiting for them to finish. Maybe getting a little curious what their talk was about. Dwyer had to step aside for the medical examiner, whistling as he walked down the hall.

The parrot shrieked, "Hey, sailor! Who's being good?"

The woman closed her eyes and lowered her face into her hands as if another surge of shock was just then streaming into her veins. She kept her face covered, not crying, not moving, not doing anything he could see. Maybe she was searching her mind for a prayer that would work.

———

While Buzz and Jorge chatted with one of the cops and the medical examiner checked over the body, Shaw kept his back to them, prowled the room. A man's black comb lay on the varnished pine dresser, beside it a brush tangled with white hair. A thick glass box full of pennies. Two gold-framed photographs of people from another century. Her people, grizzled pioneers. Bright quilts covered the cedar chest and a bedside table, another quilt at the foot of the bed, all of them with flowery designs.

Jorge, looking over his shoulder, said, "The lady's got a nice ass on her, huh?"

Shaw whirled around and grabbed the front of Jorge's fatigues, lifted him onto his toes.

"If you could lose your goddamn hard-on for half a minute, maybe you could get some blood in your brain."

"Jesus Christ, Chandler, who put a cockroach up your ass?" Jorge struggled but couldn't break Shaw's grasp.

Shaw gave Jorge a hard rattle and let him go. He turned around and took hold of the Life-Pak and, with a quick final look at his father, walked from the room.

He was almost out the front door when the woman called him back into the kitchen.

"I almost forgot," she said, when Shaw came through the kitchen door. "He said if anything bad ever happened to him, I should see you got this." She hefted up a twisted piece of silvery metal, using both hands to hold it before her as if it were a cake she'd labored over for days. "Your father said you'd know what to do with it."

2

Dougie Barnes sat alone at a table for six in the front window of a restaurant at the corner of Seventy-fourth and Bird. Dougie couldn't tell if the place was Cuban or Chinese. He didn't read, so the menu was no help, and the people were all speaking some other language, it could've been spic or chink or Martian for all he could tell. They were all dark and greasy.

He sat there, thinking how glad he was he didn't live in this screwed-up town. You never knew which country you were in. Go a block this way, you were in Haiti, a block that way it was Nicaragua or Costa Rica, or whichever country was having a famine or a revolution at the moment. You could drive all day in Miami and not run over a single English-speaking American.

But Dougie liked his window seat. Holding his head steady and changing the focus and angle of his eyes, he could look out into the crazy Miami traffic, cars swerving and cutting each other off, or he could stare at his reflection, admire the sharp lines of his face, the gold staple in his ear, his long curly hair, or he could see over his shoulder, backward into the restaurant, and watch all the people stuff themselves with french fries and roast pig, steaming things in silver dishes.

Most important, though, he could look down half a block and see the little white house where all the police lights were flashing, the guys in blue jumpsuits coming and going. A bunch of them had gathered in the yard, under one of those trees that dropped its roots like strings from the branches. The guys smoking and joking. Police, fire rescue. All these guys knowing each other from all the dead bodies they'd pulled out of places.

The short waitress with the tilted-up nose was standing beside Dougie again, talking to him a hundred miles a minute, waving her hands like she was trying to catch flies. She motioned to a bunch of people waiting in the doorway. It was ten-thirty at night and the place was crawling with fat, hungry foreigners, everybody having a grease attack at the same time. Just smelling the foreign food was making Dougie queasy. And all those people staring at him, alone at a table for six.

"Another Coke," he said to her. Looking up at her, then back down the street.

"No, no," she said. Then a string of Cuban or Chinese he didn't understand.

"Okay, okay," Dougie said, *"ocho Cokos, ocho Cokos."* Holding up both hands with the right number of fingers. Dougie was willing to be fair, pay for his table with Coca-Colas. *Ocho* being one of the only foreign words he knew.

A hefty dark-skinned guy who'd been waiting in the doorway, maybe twenty-five or thirty, with a round face and wearing a white polo shirt and Miami Dolphins hat, came over. Brought his belly up close to Dougie and looked down on him.

The guy might have been black or Cuban, Dougie couldn't tell, but definitely a mutt of some kind. The mutt said, "She wants you to pay up and leave, so she can serve some dinners here, man. That's what the fuck she's been saying to you for twenty minutes."

Dougie looked down the street again at the flashing lights. Things were breaking up down there. There was no reason to hang around, but this guy was leaning over him, breathing spices on him and getting a hot squinty look in his face. And shaking his head the way that people did when they were pissed off at Dougie but thought he might be too weird to mess with.

Dougie said, "She wants to tell me something, she should speak English. Or one of the languages I know."

"I'm talking English to you," the big guy said. "You understand what I'm saying?"

Dougie said, "Spic spac, paddy-whack, throw the dog a bone." Put the guy off balance with a little poetry.

Dougie was wearing loose clothes. A dark sweatshirt, baggy jeans. He might be anybody under the clothes, a flab like this guy, or Mr. Universe. Only he knew for sure.

He turned to look at this guy. Little squinty eyes, close together, and crooked teeth in his moon-pie face. Dougie raised his pointing finger into the air like he was checking the direction of the wind in here. Then he lowered it slowly till it pointed like a pistol at the guy, and sank it into his flabby belly, testing its depth. Looking for the muscles holding this slob up.

The guy brushed Dougie's hand away.

Dougie said, "You haven't prepared yourself well enough to fuck with me." He gave the guy a sporting smile.

"Man, there's people waiting for this table," the guy said, not listening to Dougie, not even making eye contact "You been hogging it now for half an hour at least. The lady, there, she's asking you polite. So you should just be polite back and leave."

Dougie was running his eyes over the window again, short focus, long, medium. The fire rescue truck and the cop cars down the street, the fat guy behind him, Dougie's own face. It was like firing the TV gun at the screen, making one picture splash into another. You could see some weird shit that way, make up your own stories, a second here, two seconds there. Hear people talking across the airwaves, having conversations with people from different universes.

"Fucking look at me, man, when I talk to you." The blubber-belly pressed up against the table.

Dougie didn't know if he could manage it or not, sitting in the position he was. The guy had to be near two hundred pounds. But it was worth a shot. It'd give these bean-breaths something to jabber about for a while. So he turned in his seat, got his tennis shoes planted good on the floor and grabbed two handfuls of the guy's polo shirt just above his belt, got two good hunks of belly too, dug his thumbs and fingers in deep. He twisted and lunged and threw the guy face first across the table into the big window.

Glass glittered the air. The people in the restaurant froze for a second, then a woman screamed and some of them started running down the sidewalk. The guy lay there, feet still in the restaurant, but the rest of him outside on the sidewalk, a nice slice across his face, a few more on his arms. He was on his stomach, his face turned to the side, groaning. Mumbling in his own language, whatever the hell that was. Dougie stood up, stepped out the window. He looked back into the restaurant at the old woman on the phone.

He squatted down next to the guy and said, "Ting, tang, walla-walla-bing-bang." Consoling him with a golden oldie.

Dougie leaned back in the window, and took his glass off the table and shook some crushed ice into his mouth and set it back. He turned and crunched across the glass toward the parking lot, watching the cop cars and the rescue truck pull out of the yard of the little house down the street, come slowly up Seventy-fourth, everybody in both cars and the rescue van taking a long look at the restaurant, at this guy lying on the sidewalk, then slamming on their brakes. Dougie got in his father's Jaguar XJ-6, started it, and pulled out around the trucks and the flashing lights. He wanted to stop and watch how they handled this, but the light was green and he was rolling now, into the main street, so he had to keep his eyes forward and begin trying to read the goddamn road signs for Key West.

———

It was close to two in the morning and Shaw hadn't calmed down enough to lie on his bed. He'd spent the last two hours pacing his cubicle, sitting at his bare desk, tapping his foot, listening to the snores of the other firemen. Holding the metal fragment up, one hand, both hands. Touching it, bringing his nose to its surface, but smelling only a remote metallic scent. *U.S. Navy* was etched near its base in neat Roman letters. Another line of words was inscribed just above that. But the canister had broken apart right there, the ragged seam running through the middle of that upper line of words.

The thing looked like a milk canister with a wide, flat base. It was lined with some gray material, Teflon or something like it. It was about a foot in diameter, eight or ten inches deep, and must have weighed ten pounds.

Shaw put the canister down. No words coming into his head, just a faint noise like the buzz of a high-tension wire. He lay down on his bunk, staring at the ceiling, considering who he could talk with. But there didn't seem to be anybody.

Buzz was his closest friend. He was a good man, a man Shaw would trust with his life. But Shaw had stiff-armed Buzz for years, kept him two feet away emotionally. They fished together, spent whole days side by side out in the Everglades hauling in grouper and tarpon and snook. They hung out at bars together, went to Heat games and Dolphin games together. Buzz had Shaw over for barbecues with his pretty wife and three beautiful daughters, but always, every time the least hint of anything personal came into the conversation, Shaw would go quiet. He had built the wall high and solid between them, and now it was his own goddamned fault there was no way to scale it.

He supposed he could always call up one of the Metro shrinks, go in and tell them the whole story. But he'd get to the part about his father being the main suspect in two murders twenty years ago, and the doctor would be there reaching for the phone to call Homicide, no two ways about it. And he didn't want that. The police wore thick, heavy shoes. And they'd take as long as they liked, stamping around on that tender terrain till Shaw and his mother both were good and bruised.

Then there was Stacy, his lover for the last two months. He knew she'd make the right responses, letting him get it all out. Helping him along with it if he stalled. She'd take the day off from work, stay with him. Being as soft or strong as he needed. It would probably even make her happy if he told her.

She'd been after him lately to open up to her more. I don't have anything to open up about, he'd say. She'd say, All right, then just tell me what happened to you today, the bad shit you saw. It's boring. Boring? How could it be boring, emergencies, mayhem like that? Okay, okay, here's one. A guy was going seventy along I-95 during rush hour. He rams five other cars. Monster pileup. We go out, lean into the guy's car, and there's gray matter sticking all over the roof. The guy with no face, without a complete head. Then we see the shotgun. It's there between his legs, braced against the floor, the barrels under his chin. He wanted to do himself, but he wanted to take some assholes with him. Had an apparent thing against drivers, the highways too crammed. So anyway, he was successful. He got two little girls and their grandmother. You look at that, you register it, pry the body free, and then what? You going to meditate on it all day, try to figure it out, put your mind into that guy's mind? No, you forget about it. You get real good at forgetting about things. And so that's the kind of thing you want me to entertain you with?

That quieted her. She gave him a sympathetic look, a kiss.

But this was different. He knew he could tell Stacy this, and that he should tell her. It would make him feel better. It would make *them* feel better. But the truth was, he was afraid. If he told her about his father, finding him dead like that, and all that led up to this moment, it'd just be that much harder when it came time to break it off with her. And it *would* come time, soon, just as it had with all the rest of them.

————

When he chose to, he could remember it all with stunning clarity. It had been baseball season, a month before Shaw's high school graduation. He'd broken off with Trula months before. He was in his room, middle of the week, nine, ten o'clock, working on a project for the school science fair. With plans he'd gotten from *Life* magazine, he was building a scale-model bomb shelter.

He'd used the slats of discarded lobster traps for the shell, and cut a section away to reveal the modeling-clay family, sitting on their cots of kitchen matches and pieces of white canvas. He'd carved neat smiles onto their faces with a razor.

When his mother screamed from the kitchen downstairs, Shaw was painting the inside walls of the shelter. His brush stuttered at her voice, and again at the crash that followed. But he got control of his hand and continued his careful stroke along the back wall.

Life recommended using yellow or light blue on the inside walls. A color to lift the spirit or at least pacify it. Definitely not red, a reminder of the blood flowing outside, or any of the dark, depressing colors.

From the kitchen his father shouted, and glass shattered. And Shaw dabbed the brush into the small bottle and tried to still the tremble in his hand. Downstairs something heavy overturned. Probably his mother's round oak table with the claw feet. He heard both their voices at once. His father's bass climbing over his mother's sharp soprano. More scuffling.

It was no use. He put the brush down, rose from his chair, took a long, slow breath, and walked over to his desk and sat down. He looked up at his trophy shelf. Batting awards, a handful of smaller plaques and awards he'd won in junior high. A pennant from the Milwaukee Braves where Warren Spahn was moving to the threshold of immortality.

In the kitchen Hanson Chandler roared and Millie answered him in slow words Shaw could not decipher, and when she was finished, more furniture overturned.

Shaw's bat was a Louisville Slugger. He'd gotten it for his fifteenth birthday and had gone .325 with it his junior year. He rose from his seat, took it down from his fishing-rod rack. His hands were shaking when he put the bat on his shoulder. He turned and took two quick steps, raising the bat over his head. He hammered the bomb shelter.

His mother screamed again, louder. Shaw cocked the bat over his right shoulder, went up on his toes and came down hard, flattening the ridiculous construction against the tabletop.

Maybe it was her scream, more shrill than he'd ever heard it. Or maybe something in Shaw had suddenly switched on, adulthood, moral sense, something. He wasn't sure what had made him pick that night to turn and heft the bat to his shoulder and march out of the room.

When he entered the bright kitchen, he had the bat poised in front of his body, a bunt if necessary, a full swing if possible. In the harsh fluorescent light, he saw the round oak table on its side, two of its legs broken, aluminum pans on the floor. A jar of honey lay cracked and oozing near the back door. On the Formica countertop, a vase of bougainvillea sprigs was still safe.

His mother was sprawled behind the table. A thread of blood ran from her ear. He lifted her, carried her to her bedroom. Her eyes dim and drifting. He told her she would be all right and kissed her forehead. Then he called Dr. Figueroa, told him he would find the kitchen door open. Come quick.

Shaw went back to the kitchen, stepped over the bat, and went outside onto the porch. He looked up at the brisk stars, breathing the life back into his body.

At Captain Tony's, he found his father sitting on a barstool between two sailors. Hanson was only a few inches taller than Shaw, but heavier by forty pounds. Muscled by his navy work and by years of alley brawls. Shaw stood beside his father, waiting until finally he put down the bottle and turned.

"Why do you beat her up, Dad?" Shaw said.

Hanson appraised Shaw with a long, smoldering look.

"Since when do you ask me goddamn questions like that?"

"Since now."

"So what is this, big man? I tell you what it was about, and you're going to stand there, decide if I did the right goddamn thing?"

People hushing around them, giving them the distance they might need to settle this. Shaw said, Yes, maybe he was going to do just that.

Hanson shook his head and turned back to his beer. Shaw stood there a moment more, looking at the broad, sweaty back of this man who had taken his faultless boyish love and returned nothing. Then he took hold of the collar of his father's navy work shirt, and dragged him backward onto the floor. Hanson lay on his back for a moment and shook the blear from his eyes. Then he rolled over, coming up in a crouch.

He licked his lips, and a crazy smile possessed him. Before Shaw even raised his fists, his father threw a quick right hand that clipped Shaw's cheek and hit him another glancing shot to the chin as he was falling unconscious to the distant floor.

The next morning when Shaw woke in his bed, the house was quiet. His jaw ached and his eyes wouldn't focus. He lay there for a few minutes, listening. After some of their fights, Shaw would find his mother and father nuzzling and teasing, using their pet names. Flowers would appear on the kitchen table. Or he might find their bedroom door locked, their sweet vibrations humming through the planks of that old house. It was as if their brawls were simply a part of the peculiar shape of their love, the glue that held the family together. Just the natural stage of their passion, like the rough foreplay of cats or dogs.

This possibility tormented him, because only a few weeks before the night his father knocked him out, Shaw Chandler had also punched a girl. He and Sheila McDaniels had been sitting in his pickup at the drive-in. Shaw was trying to watch a newsreel about Ted Williams before the movie began, and Sheila was chattering about all their high school friends who were engaged, and how she and Shaw were practically the last two graduating seniors in all of Key West who weren't going to be married before the summer was over.

Shaw, concentrating on Ted Williams's swing, said nothing, and she poked him in the ribs to make him look at her, and poked him again, and although he'd given her his class ring the weekend before and told Sheila that he loved her, he found himself shouting at her to shut the hell up. Sheila pouted and then began to complain that Shaw didn't care about her at all, that he was still in love with that kooky, snooty Trula Montoya, and Sheila should never have gone out with him in the first place.

He kept his eyes on the screen, but when she poked him in the ribs again, he snapped a backhanded punch into her face, and it bloodied her nose. She screamed and bolted from the pickup, and he chased her across the drive-in and calmed her down, cleaned her up with paper towels from the bathroom. Both of them shaking hard. And Sheila had said, "This is all my fault, Shaw." He said, No, no, it wasn't, not at all. "No, it is, it is," she'd said. "I haven't been giving you enough good loving, and you've developed a violent sex frustration."

They left the drive-in, parked at Smathers Beach and made mechanical love for an hour, and afterward Shaw had felt such shame and revulsion that he could barely speak to her again.

So his night of violence with Sheila and his parents' regular brawls had made him begin to fear his own inherited blood, what might be ticking there. Afraid that in some biological way love and rage were twined deep inside his body. And if he were to survive, he would have to learn to keep his passions cool, or else some night the fractional heating in his chemistry could ignite his blood, make him draw back his fist again and drive it into a woman's body. And this time, perhaps he would not be able to stop.

———

That morning twenty years ago, Shaw had lain in his bed, rubbed his swollen jaw, stared at the bedroom ceiling. Finally he rose, splashed water on his face, dressed. As he went cautiously down the stairs, he listened for his father's morning noises, sniffed for the smell of coffee. His fists clenched, ready to meet the man, in a doorway, around a corner, take a good swing at him. Get off fast this time, determined to land at least one solid punch.

In the kitchen, his mother was sitting in her nightgown staring at the letter spread before her. She turned her bruised and lumpy face to him and handed him the letter.

"I done a bad thing," it said in his father's ragged scrawl. "I don't know what made me do it. I murdered Pinkney and Chiles and hid their bodies. Don't even bother looking, cause you'll never find them. Now I'm gone from here forever. I don't know what in hell made me do it."

Lying in his bed in Station Thirty-seven in Miami, Shaw Chandler said, "Neither do I, old man. Neither do I."

3

Dougie Barnes was an hour down the road, already on the dark strip of highway between Homestead and Key Largo, when he remembered the parrot. The bird screeching and babbling in the kitchen as he'd sat there having a conversation with the old fellow. The same old fellow who a little while later he'd shot in the chest.

The man had said he knew Dougie, knew his father too.

"Big deal, lemon peel," Dougie said.

The old man tried talking Dougie out of killing him. But Dougie hadn't given it too much attention. He watched the parrot flutter and primp, peck at seeds, toss them onto the floor of its cage. First time Dougie had been that close to a parrot. The bird looked over at the two of them at the table and squawked once and said, "Who's being a good boy? Who's being good?" Dougie couldn't believe it. A bird talking to him.

———

Dougie Barnes pulled the Jaguar off the road, onto the shoulder of that empty two-lane. No moon, a few stars. The black Everglades on both sides. A few big trucks blew past. He sat there and thought about that bird. Shit, he wanted it bad. Yeah, sure, he could wait till tomorrow, go find a pet store in Key West and buy one, but that wouldn't be the same. This particular bird and Dougie had a bond.

The parrot had screamed when Dougie stood the old man up, aiming the Colt .38 at him, screamed again when he turned him around and prodded him out into the hallway, that bird rooting him on. And when Dougie came back to the kitchen after killing the man and stood right in front of the cage, the bird said, "You're a little devil. You're a little devil."

Shit, like it knew. Dougie put the Jaguar in gear, U-turned onto U.S. 1, and burned about fifty yards of rubber. He was going to have that damn parrot.

He drove ninety, thinking the whole way of all the things he was going to teach the bird, all the words that would sound good coming out in that screechy bird voice. Dougie couldn't even remember much about the rest of his evening now, shoving the man onto the bed, holding the pillow over his face and sending a bullet into his chest.

It was almost four in the morning when he parked half a block from the house, alongside a lumberyard. A big dog in a spike collar came running over to the high fence, growling. One of those low, square dogs that looked like somebody carved it out of rock with a dull knife.

"Heebie-jeebie," Dougie said to the dog. "Harum-scarum."

It growled and foamed. Yeah, that's what they did in Miami. Found themselves a rabid dog to guard their worthless junk. Man, this town! Somebody should explode one of those bombs, the one that kills all the people, leaves the buildings and everything else. Let the cockroaches and rats run things. How much worse could they do?

Dougie walked down the broken sidewalk to the white frame house. All the lights off in there. Earlier that night he'd watched from the front window of that greaseball restaurant as the old woman had come home carrying a grocery bag. And later she'd walked out into the yard and stood there while the rescue truck and police cars drove away. She looked dumpy, harmless. Maybe he could get in, take the bird, get out without waking the woman up. Or maybe not. Didn't matter a whole lot either way.

Dougie went around to the kitchen door. It had a glass window in it, and behind that a white lace curtain. He knew there were ways to get into houses without keys, and without people hearing you, things he'd seen on TV, people using credit cards or little tools they carried on key rings. But he didn't know how to do any of them. He put his fist through the glass.

Now it just depended on how deep a sleeper the old lady was

whether she got out of this alive or not. He reached inside and unlocked the door. A couple of cuts on his fist were bleeding, but he didn't feel anything. He wiped the blood on his pants.

He stepped inside onto the glass and stood in the hallway and got used to the house again. Place still smelled of gunpowder. And there was the bird in its cage jumping around, tinkling the bell on its trapeze.

Dougie was about to open the cage when the woman appeared in the kitchen door. She wore a nightgown, her long white hair loose down her back, reminding Dougie of a ghost for a second, which in a way, she almost was.

"What're you doing in my house, boy?" she said.

"I'm just here for the bird."

"How'd you know I had a bird?"

Dougie said, "I'm Superman, I see through walls."

She said, "It was you came earlier tonight. Wasn't it?" She moved a little closer.

"I was here earlier, yeah," he said.

"He didn't kill himself," she said. "I never believed it for a minute."

She moved closer to him.

Shit, she had a knife in her hand. A big knife. Shit.

"This bird have a name?" he said.

She moved a couple of inches closer, Dougie holding his ground in front of the refrigerator.

He said, "You mind if I give it a new name? I thought of a couple, you know, but I don't want to mess with the bird's mind if it answers to something already."

The blade came up from below her waist, meant for his crotch. Dougie caught her forearm, brought it up chest high and held it between them. She twisted the blade around trying to slice his arm. He let her tire herself out a little, then he banged her hand against the doorframe and banged it again. He bent over and picked up the knife.

"Would it be a boy or a girl parrot, anyway?" he said.

The woman panted, not saying anything, out of conversation. Well, it didn't matter, the parrot could be a boy, a girl. He didn't want to marry it. As long as it talked.

He took the cage off its stand and dragged the lady and the cage into the living room. He shoved her down onto the couch and set the cage on the floor in front of her. Getting an idea now. He picked up a brass lamp with a yellow shade, yanked the plug out of the wall. Using the big kitchen knife, he cut the cord at the base. Six feet of cord.

The parrot screeched a rebel yell.

He came over to her with the cord, trying to see in her face if she was going to put up any kind of fight. Didn't look like it. He sat down beside her and started to tie a knot in the cord, but she grabbed hold of his right wrist and with her free hand she stuck him with a nail file. Must've been sitting there on the couch. It went less than an inch into his forearm, and he drew back from her. Smiling, he held the forearm out for her to see, right in her face. Blood had started to seep out.

"Now, was that polite?" He held the arm there an inch from her nose. "Treating a stranger in your own house like that? Sticking him with instruments."

Bringing her right hand up fast, the lady smacked the nail file with her palm, driving it an inch deeper into his arm.

Dougie just shook his head at her.

"That might work on somebody normal," he said.

He went on tying the knot in the cord, ignoring the nail file, and slipped the noose over her neck. He clenched it hard and fast. Now she didn't struggle. Completely changed her view of things.

The bird was going from its swing to its trough to the bars, round and round. Happy to see him, or scared. Or maybe both, flustered like a girl getting laid the first time.

"Last chance to tell me the bird's name." He stood up and moved around in front of her. "Come on, lady. Things'll go a lot better between me and the bird if I get its name right. Wouldn't you like that, knowing the bird was being taken care of?"

She stared at him and didn't say anything.

"Your husband, he'll be surprised when he sees you," Dougie said. "Coming to heaven so quick behind him."

The parrot squawked again, swinging on its trapeze with its back to their conversation. Dougie pulled the nail file out of his forearm and put it in his pants pocket.

"Say bye-bye to your bird," Dougie said. "Bye-bye."

He dragged the old woman to her feet with the cord. She'd had a bad night. First her husband, then her own self. He guessed he was sorry he had to kill her. That was probably what was making his stomach feel the way it did just then, hot and hollow. Maybe that was what feeling sorry felt like. Then again, he wasn't absolutely sure. Maybe he was hungry.

———

It was almost five a.m. Thursday morning when the claxon sounded again. Shaw jerked upright, put his feet on the floor automatically. The speakers announcing a house fire, on Seventy-fourth. His father's address.

By the time they got there the fire had spread to the garage and a big ficus tree. The engine crew ran their hose from a hydrant across the street at a body shop, and Buzz and Shaw scrambled into their bunker coats, their pants, boots.

Shaw finished dressing first, pulled on the air tank and the mask, grabbed an axe and ran to the front door. He tried it and it was unlocked. He dropped his axe, fell to his knees and began to crawl into the boiling smoke.

He was halfway across the living room when the hose line opened and a dense steam rose as the water began to pour into the house. He scrambled down the hallway on his knees and made it into the bedroom. Only one wall was ablaze there, and the visibility was better. The woman wasn't there.

He turned and crawled back down the hall and into a bathroom. The smoke was dense and his mask was fogging. He ripped aside the shower curtain and saw only the empty tub.

The kitchen was raging, flames writhing out of the door into the hallway. Shaw chose his moment and scooted past, taking a look as he went. He saw nothing but billows of fire.

The water poured through the roof and windows now, smoke and steam everywhere. When he made it back to the living room, Buzz was there on his knees in the middle of the room. He pointed and Shaw looked up.

She was there, hanging from the rafters, a cord running through one of the eyebolts where a plant had hung. Her neck was stretched out. Buzz shook his head and motioned for him to retreat, waving ominously at the ceiling. Shaw looked up at the woman again. He raised up into the heat, climbed onto the chair. Clasping her around the waist, he lifted her weight and slipped the cord off the eyebolt. Buzz yelling at him the whole time to get the hell out of there. But he got her down, put her over his shoulder and carried her to the door. It was the least goddamn thing he could do.

———

Captain Jackie Gawron was a District Five arson investigator. A short, stocky man with a bull neck and a pack of Camels in his pocket. Shaw had worked with him for years and liked him OK, though lately Gawron was starting to get irritated it was taking him so long to make chief. Letting people know he was sick of his job. Shaw had seen it before, a guy wanting badly to be in the air-conditioning when his heart attack happened.

The fire was dead and the woman's body had been sent to the morgue. The sun was just coming up as Gawron and Shaw and Buzz tramped through the rubble.

In the kitchen Gawron said, "So it appears we got a double suicide, a little delayed maybe, but still a double. Wife follows husband. I seen it twice this month already. These same sad old farts."

"I don't think that's what it is," Shaw said.

The smell of gasoline was strong. The deepest charring was there in the kitchen. The back door had been blown into the yard, most of the side wall was gone. The parrot's metal stand had fallen through the floor. Shaw didn't see the cage anywhere. It was probably down there in the crawl space. A twisted metal gas can lay next to the stove.

Gawron said, "You got some other kind of scenario, Chandler, let me hear it."

Shaw turned to Buzz and said, "You ever see a suicide do himself to the heart before?"

He thought about it a moment, looked at Gawron, back at Shaw. He shrugged.

"I guess not," he said. "Usually they go for the brain."

"And you notice the way the gun was?" Shaw said.

"How?"

"First finger on the trigger, like you'd fire it normally." Shaw demonstrated, bending his arm around, trying to squeeze his first finger at his heart.

"Awkward," Buzz said.

"Not how I'd do it," Shaw said. "I'd use my thumb on the trigger, hold it with both hands."

"Personally," Buzz said, "I'd go for the head. To hell with the heart. Once the head goes, if the heart keeps ticking you don't feel it. But you do yourself in the heart, you could be lying there bleeding to death, feeling every bit of it."

Gawron stood watching Shaw, shaking his weary head.

"Is that all?" he said.

"It wasn't any double suicide," Shaw said. "That's obvious."

He said, "Bullshit, Chandler. Plain unadulterated bullshit."

"And," Shaw said, "the pistol was in his right hand."

"Yeah? And what the hell difference does that make?"

"The dead man was left-handed," Shaw said.

"And how do you know that, Sherlock?"

Shaw breathed deeply. "I just know," he said.

"Whatta you, psychic?"

Shaw was silent.

Gawron said, "You got some personal interest here, Chandler?"

"No."

"Well." Gawron shook his head and scribbled something on his notebook. "What I see is we got a grieving widow. The lady is shocked and upset, nothing to live for anymore, once the old fart husband is gone. Wants to take the whole ball of wax with her when she goes, so she sets up an incendiary situation here in the kitchen. A little domestic ingenuity. Puts a saucepan of gasoline on the stove, runs a wick of some kind from it to the burner coils, turns the burner on high, and climbs up in her chair and kicks it over. I don't see where the situation calls for anything more complicated than that."

"I talked to the lady earlier tonight," Shaw said. "She was a tough woman. She wasn't any suicide."

"You talked to her," Gawron said. "You used your advanced psychology degree, gave her a suicide profile test and you deduced she was a hundred percent stable."

Buzz said, "Why would she burn the place down?"

"People do crazy shit," Gawron said. "It surprises me I have to explain that to you."

"She didn't kill herself," Shaw said. He touched the gas can with the toe of his boot.

"You see any signs of forced entry?"

"No."

"You find any physical evidence suggesting there was another person present?"

"The front door was unlocked," Shaw said.

Gawron said, "The lady's about to kill herself, she's not going to be real burglar conscious."

Shaw said nothing.

"Well, you put all your suspicions in your report then," Gawron said. "I'll see it gets filed properly."

"She didn't kill herself, and neither did the old man."

"Hey, Sullivan," Gawron said. "Could you get this moron out of my face? I got a goddamn job to do."

4

When he got back to the station at seven that Thursday morning, Shaw called his mother in Key West. She didn't answer at the bait shop or at home. He let the phone ring at least twenty times. Then called both numbers again to make sure he'd dialed correctly, sweat breaking out across his back as it rang.

He called information, got Mrs. Boisonault's number at the Breezy Palms nursing home. She was the only one of his mother's friends he could remember. When she answered, Shaw told her who he was and she said, "Is your mother any better?"

"She's sick?" he said.

"You didn't know?" she said. "Sick isn't the half of it."

"What's wrong?"

"I'd get my bottom down here if I was her only son."

Then he heard someone else's voice in her room. A nurse rolling in breakfast. The two of them chatting, then the phone clicked off.

He called his mother's number again and on the tenth ring she answered. Her hello slurry.

"Mother?"

The line was empty.

"Mother, you all right?"

"I felt worse," she said, voice thick. "Once or twice."

"What is it? What's wrong?"

"I screwed up," she said. "Bad."

"I'm coming down," he said. "Today, right now."

"Don't bother, son," she said.

"Do you need a doctor, anything?"

"I'm beyond doctors."

"I'll be there by lunchtime. You'll be okay till I get there?"

"I should've shot the weasel when I had the chance," she said.

"Three hours," Shaw said.

He slapped the receiver down and shouldered past the guys from the next shift straggling down the hallway. He hurried out to the parking lot, catching up to Buzz as he was unlocking his pickup. Jorge, one car over, glared at Shaw from across the roof of his Firebird.

"Man," Buzz said, climbing into the cab, "you got a bad case of the biorhythms today or what?"

"I need you to do something for me, Buzz."

They both turned to look at Jorge smoking his tires across the parking lot, swerving out into traffic.

"I want you to pass it on to Chief Clem I'm taking a leave."

"What?"

"I'd do it, but I go in there, shit, he'll try to talk me out of it. The way I'm feeling, I'll wind up swinging at him."

"Yeah, and what am I supposed to give as a reason?"

Shaw looked out at the traffic on Bird, commuters in their routines, listening to the morning news, drinking their coffee, good ordinary lives. Death by natural causes.

"I don't know," he said. "Tell him something. Say it's the jumpsuits. The navy blue conflicts with my aura. I'm getting headaches. Tell him I got to have the jumpsuits in a beige, say ecru. Tell him that. There's nothing they can do anyway, I got a month of leave time built up."

"Ecru?" Buzz said, staring at him across the roof of the car. "What're you, cracking up?"

"Thanks, man," Shaw said. "I appreciate it."

The half smile died on Buzz's lips.

He said, "I'm supposed to go in there and talk to Chief Clem, and you're not going to tell me the reason? You're standing there bug eyed, your mouth clamped shut like you're fifty feet underwater, you open your mouth you're going to drown."

"I'm sorry, Buzz. Just be my friend, do this for me."

"Jesus Christ, Shaw. I sure as shit tell you what's going on with me when I got a problem, need a favor, or something. You should try it sometime, check it out."

"I'm sorry, man," Shaw said. "You're right. Just not now, okay? Sometime later."

"Go ahead, get going," Buzz said. "You're in a hurry."

————

He had the El Camino packed by ten. A suitcase of clothes, mostly jeans, T-shirts, tennis shoes, and a couple of dress shirts, his fishing rods, a cooler of beer, and his Smith & Wesson .357. The rented house was full of other stuff, lawn mower, weed eater, mementos on the shelves, pots and pans and dishes. He looked around but couldn't find anything he'd miss. He wasn't sure, but it felt like he was leaving for good.

He spent fifteen minutes composing a note for Stacy. He'd written them before, stuck a few in mirrors, but that didn't seem to help with this one. He debated wording the note so she would be sure to hate him, then wound up saying something about needing time to think things over. He thumbtacked it to the front door.

It was that easy. You spent years in a place, sunk your taproot deep and wide into the earth. The root was thick, but it was very brittle, and with the right wind it could snap and you were loose again. Unhooked from the earth.

He'd seen it every working day. People broken from their comfortable lull, going from a drowse to dizzy panic in a flick. There was just no way to root yourself deep enough. He stood outside the house where he had lived for years, stood there with nothing but a bag of clothes. His rusting El Camino. A pistol he'd never fired.

By eleven-thirty he was in Key Largo, the fog in his head starting to burn off. He was seeing things now, the road taking shape before him. And he felt a slicing burn in his chest as he pictured Stacy finding the note after work, standing there to read it.

In another hour he was in Marathon. He pulled off and forced a hamburger down. He dug around in his bag and found his sandals and a pair of loose khaki shorts, went into the hamburger rest room and changed. He walked back to the El Camino, a Keys guy.

As always when he made that journey, the light seemed purer down there, no smog to filter the UV's out. And the air was thickened by the ocean, a vegetable odor with a faint trace of decay. There was a lot of traffic on U.S. 1, Yankees driving slow, getting stoned on the ocean panoramas as they crossed the long two-lane bridges. And though he didn't want to relax, it happened, just gazing around at the blue distances, his muscles loosened, his headache dissolved.

Shaw had read there was no spot in Florida more than sixty miles from the sea. Even in the rolling hills of the citrus belt, or horse country, or the phosphate pits of northern Florida, the air was spiced with scents of the sea. Even standing in what was close to the exact center of the state, he'd once seen the sky deepen to a perfect marine blue, the clouds rippling with iridescent reds and purples, a sunset only possible at the beach. For the whole state *was* a beach, nothing but an ancient sandbar, a lamination of limestone and aquifer, and sand. Ocean breezes permeating every corner of the land.

But what was true for Florida was even more true in the Keys. There was absolutely no escape from the sea. It was spread before you always. When you turned your back to it, you faced more of it. You woke with it, worked with it, played with it, made love with it, slept with it. Always the ocean. Always its pressure in the ears, its rippling light, its haunt.

And on the very end of that thin golden string of islands, stranded like a gaudy pendant, was Key West. Shaw Chandler's birthplace. A succulent bauble, dangling 150 miles from the safety of the mainland. Too far away to feel the real effects of the land. An outpost for the unstable, maladjusted, the just plain insane.

If they weren't insane when they came, they turned that way. They became islanders, devolved creatures. Creatures with both gills and opposable thumbs. Lower and higher forms intertwined. Still walking upright, but beginning to fall into a hunch. A thing with two hearts. One that beat in tune with the rhythms of the nearly forgotten land, one heart that obeyed only the primitive metronome of the ocean. It was part of the reason he'd left, part of the reason he so seldom returned. That island made you crazy.

Shaw rolled into Key West by two-thirty, past the navy base, the road finally spreading into four lanes past the golf course and the navy bars. He turned right onto Roosevelt Boulevard and drove to the public docks at Garrison Bight and parked in the lot. A few of the half-day charter boats had come back in already, their larger fish, some sail and grouper, were strung up along the dock. As he walked out to Chandler Beer, Bait and Tackle, he nodded hello to a couple of guys he remembered, kept on walking.

He halted in front of the door to the tackle shop, and stared at the big black padlock. A printed sign was tacked to the door. In a bold headline all creditors were informed that they should contact the Monroe County state attorney immediately.

Shaw jogged back to the car and drove over to the house on Olivia Street. It was a white shotgun house built almost a hundred years earlier by a rich Cuban cigar maker. The only two-story on the street. It had slat balustrades decorated with narrow strips of gingerbread. The windows were shuttered. There was a tin roof, air scuttles, and a white picket fence with some of the stakes missing. A snarl of weeds had broken through the fence and was spilling onto the sidewalk.

Millie Chandler was sitting on the porch swing, looking blankly across the street at the graveyard. She didn't seem to notice him when he got out of the El Camino. Her gaze fixed on the monuments and above-ground graves as he came up the walk.

And when he was standing in front of her, all she said was, "I have made a load of bad mistakes."

"Don't I get a kiss or anything?" said Shaw.

She looked down at her lap and muttered something to herself as if there were voices inside her speaking more loudly than his. When he saw the half empty Don Q rum bottle on the rattan table by the swing, and the glass with pebbles of ice, he sighed and sat down next to her.

"You quit going to AA, huh?"

"Isn't anything wrong with me," she said, her tongue clumsy. "I just like to drink."

Shaw made a neutral grunt. He'd heard that one, maybe even said it himself once.

"It helps me see things," she said. "How they really are."

"Yeah, it's famous for sharpening the eyesight."

"Don't mock me," she said softly.

"Is this what Mrs. Boisonault meant about you being sick? Drinking rum?"

She took hold of the bottle and swung it up to her lap. She extended it to him and he shook his head. After she poured a couple of ounces into her glass, she smacked the bottle down on the porch.

"If I'm sick," she said, "at least I'm too damn drunk to notice."

She turned her eyes on him. Even through the haze of rum, her solid blue eyes still had their sting. And her eyebrows were still dark, though the rest of her hair, tied back into a ponytail, had drained to white.

Shaw said, "I heard Dad was in Key West." Wanting to spill out the rest, but holding it for now.

"Where'd you hear that?" she said, watching the dark liquid trembling in her glass. Her hand afflicted with a sudden palsy.

"Someone I met told me."

She lifted her furious eyes to his.

"Who?"

"Mother," he said. "What's going on?"

"I told you before, Shaw Chandler, I don't want to ever hear that man's name mentioned in this house again." She spoke with the precise enunciation of the drunk. "Not even by you."

In the desolate weeks after Hanson had abandoned them, she had spoken those same words, when Shaw had invoked his father's name one time too many. And at that instant, her eyes had burned with the same rage as now.

"Okay. It's okay," Shaw said, looking away from her hurt. "I'm home now. Whatever it is, the two of us can get things turned around."

"Don't bet on it." She patted him on the hand, leaned over and pressed a kiss to his cheek. He breathed in her halo of lavender and booze, years falling away with those dizzy scents.

He looked off with her through the fading daylight to the graveyard. The cement tombs were scattered around the weedy three acres. Coffee cans of plastic flowers, a rusty tricycle overturned near the gate. In places the tombs were stacked three high above the impenetrable coral earth. Key West had never been an easy place to bury the dead.

Later, as the darkness collected in the house, drunk but still coherent, Millie told the story of the tackle shop, her eyes swimming as she went over it. How one day a year ago, Peter Salter, a smiley boy in his middle twenties, had wandered in the door, taken a long look around, and asked for a job. This was right after Shaw's last visit home, and Millie said she was feeling poorly and thought that yes, maybe it was time to hire some help.

Salter had begun working, dipping shrimp, running the cash register, sweeping up. Millie taught him to rig ballyhoo for the dolphin and marlin fishermen, and he took to it quickly. She taught him how to order weeks in advance of the changing fishing seasons, how to estimate shrimp sales based on wind and weather and holidays. Peter worked hard, gave a good appearance, talked fondly about his years in college.

"I fell for the little weasel," his mother said, staring into the dark. "Hook, line, and goddamn sinker."

After knowing him only six months, she sold him the tackle shop for nothing down, twelve hundred a month, a hundred-thousand-dollar balloon to come due in five years. She decided she was ready to retire, and since Shaw had never shown any interest in the shop, Peter Salter looked like just the boy to make a go of it. If Salter learned the business, kept it under control, then a hundred thousand dollars was a steal. The shop could gross that in six months during the season. But Salter didn't want to wait five years to steal the place.

Millie had never consulted with Shaw on any of this during their weekly phone talks. On the phone, things had always been going well at the tackle shop. She liked to tell tourist stories, about the weirdos who came in. Only a mention now and then about Peter, this wonderful boy who'd fallen from heaven to help her out.

"You should've told me," Shaw said. "I would've dropped everything, come down and helped."

"I didn't know what he was doing," she said. "Not till the place was already cleaned out."

For most of the past year, the boy had pocketed the daily cash receipts without making a single mortgage payment or paying any of their suppliers. He held off Millie with a song and a smile, and the rest of the creditors with the Chandler good name. Postdating checks, covering one bad check with another.

He'd also run down the stock from about fifty thousand dollars' worth of custom rods and big Penn reels and every manner of plug and spoon and marlin teaser, till the shelves were empty. Two or three Taiwan rods left, a box of monofilament, some rusty tools. Then he'd had the gall to file for personal bankruptcy and, according to the lawyers she'd gone to, he was free from prosecution. He was just a lousy businessman, and she had made a bad bargain. That's how the law would read it.

Shaw held her hand while she told it, and for a while afterward as they sat in silence and watched the television lights fluttering in windows across the graveyard.

"So, you're not sick, then?" he asked her.

"Sick at heart," she said. "But it's nothing a little eighty proof can't put a dent in."

Then he helped her up and into her bedroom. She leaned on his arm, and at the door of her room gave him a rummy kiss goodnight. He went to the kitchen, looked through the pantry, the refrigerator. A single can of white navy beans in the pantry, and in the refrigerator a half a stick of rancid butter.

He climbed the stairs, went into his room, and collapsed on his old bed. He stared at the same ceiling he'd memorized twenty years before. Same stains in the paint, same crack in the plaster running from one corner to another. He lay there for an hour and daydreamed, driving down the roads he saw up there. Steering into the heart of America, farther and farther from this tangle.

He listened to the sounds of the neighborhood, the shushing of an ocean breeze in the palms, wind chimes clittering down the street, the bass beat of a jukebox over on Duval. He rose and took the silver canister from the grocery sack and set it on his high school desk. He sat at the desk and held the canister up toward the window. A stream of moonlight plated it with gold.

He thumped the metal with a finger and it made a dull ping. He brought it up to his nose and could detect only the sweet empty scent of metal. Setting it back on the desk in a swatch of moonlight, he lined it up so it cast a shadow on the floor, something like an emperor's crown. Or maybe the ragged teeth of an attacking shark.

His father had believed that Shaw would know what to do with the thing. His father, who apparently in the last few years had stood in the shadows at a distance from his son, and had watched Shaw coming and going, surviving his life. His father, who was dead, who inhabited now that land of permanent shadows. Who could hover there and watch his son forever from the safety of that other place. Watch him standing at the window of his childhood room, staring out at the graves, chalky from the moon.

Perhaps, then, that was what Shaw felt at this moment. The thing that bristled on his neck frightened him, yet gave him an energy he had not known for years. The brush of his father's distant gaze.

5

"Have you ever owned a Siamese cat?" Dr. Waldorf asked her.

Trula Montoya said, "Are we almost done?"

"A couple more minutes," he said. His fingers hovered above the keyboard of his laptop computer.

"No, I never owned a Siamese. My father is allergic to cats."

"A primate, a rodent or a lagomorph?"

"A lagomorph?"

"A rabbit," the doctor said. "Did you ever own a rabbit?"

Trula glanced into the living room at her father. He was sitting in front of the stereo, listening to Mozart, reading a magazine. Richard Montoya's white hair had grown very long since she'd seen him this time last year. It was frizzy and was drawn backward as if by some field of electricity just behind him. Bushy white eyebrows. He might have been a mathematician, someone who had spent his life scribbling numbers on a blackboard. A man who lost himself daily in an endless string of equations, moving step by step out beyond the range of normal men.

"No," she said, turning to Waldorf. "No, no lagomorphs."

Waldorf typed that in, and his assistant, a young dark-haired woman named Anne Pickles, scribbled on her steno pad. She sat beside Dr. Waldorf, apparently backing up the computer with her notebook.

Trula went back to packing, emptying the mahogany chest of drawers, stacking her folded blouses, her underwear into the suitcases open on her bed. She was running way behind. She and her dad were on the three-fifteen from Kennedy to Miami and on to Key West.

The hangover was slowing her down—that, and she was feeling a tingling in her legs she didn't want to consider. Waldorf was wearing a green corduroy suit with leather patches on the elbow. He was sitting in the bamboo chair by the window that looked across at Washington Square, where homeless men sat in the shadows of the skeletal trees.

He said, "Have you ever had prolonged exposure to lead-glazed pottery or had extensive contact with lead-based paints?"

"No."

"You lived in Key West from the age of eight to the age of seventeen?" He scratched at his temple, and a mist of dandruff swirled in the light.

"Yes," she said.

"And you were diagnosed with multiple sclerosis when?"

"August, last August."

"Did you live around the city dump or walk near it regularly?"

"Mount Trashmore?"

"That's right."

"I lived in navy housing, on Key West proper. Across the bay from the dump. And we had another house, a weekend house. That was near the dump, yes."

Waldorf typed that in, humming to himself.

"Did you drink well water as a child?"

She was holding a pile of bras. Waldorf looked at her, at the bras, a loopy smile taking over his face. She set the bras in the suitcase and watched his professional expression return.

He ran through a quick set of facial tics. Two eyebrow lifts, a nose scrunch.

He said, "And when was your most recent exacerbation?"

"A month ago," she said.

"What form did it take?"

"Double vision, numbness in my lower legs."

"And your most recent magnetic resonance imaging?"

"The last MRI was in September," Trula said.

"Spinal tap?"

"October," she said.

She took a seat on the edge of the bed and tugged on the red ribbon that was tied to the helium-filled balloon. It was silver and heart-shaped and the message on it said, "We'll miss you."

She bumped it against the ceiling. It had lost buoyancy since the going-away party last night at Mercutio's. The party had been boisterous and funny. Almost everybody from the show had stopped by, cast, crew, writers. A lot of singing, show tunes, some tears at the end.

This morning she'd awakened with a dry, swollen tongue and a Sousa march behind her eyes, a vague recollection of climbing up onto the bar and giving a speech about returning to "Hidden Hours" when she'd licked this thing. Her father watching her from a booth in the rear. His sad eyes. And she had a spotty picture of her friends, all those forced smiles as they applauded her.

"Have you ever worked as a nurse?"

"Once, on a toothpaste commercial," she said.

Dr. Waldorf formed a polite smile and nodded knowingly as though he might put that down in her file, an ironic disposition. Anne was smiling, but keeping her head down, watching her pad.

"No," Trula said. "I never worked as a real nurse."

"Have you ever lived near a radiator shop?"

"Not that I know of."

"A nuclear power plant?"

"No."

Trula closed the suitcase, snapped the locks. She wrapped the balloon ribbon around a finger, looking at Waldorf. He was doing his neck yoga again, things popping in there. She caught herself storing his twitches away, freeze-framing them. It was an acting habit she'd developed, this muscle mimicry. If she wasn't careful, in a minute she would begin to play them back, mirror Waldorf. He twitches, she answers with the same twitch.

Waldorf tapped a few keys and his computer whirred. He brushed at his temple again, sending aloft another flurry of dried scalp.

Trula said, "So, are you through with me? You know I didn't play with lagomorphs, I can go now?"

"Well," Waldorf said. "I was hoping to ask you a couple of more personal questions. It occurred to me that since many people know you from your TV career, it might be interesting to highlight your case for the article. Give the piece a human dimension."

"A human dimension."

"You know," Waldorf said, leaning forward, "the emotional side, how MS feels, how it's affected your career."

"You want to know how I feel."

Waldorf slanted his head to the side, worry coming to his eyes.

"Maybe I put it the wrong way," he said. "I do that sometimes."

"No, no," Trula said. "You put it fine. Tell you how I feel. For your article, the human dimension."

"Maybe I should just go." He closed the lid of his machine.

"No, you don't get out of here that easily," she said. She stood up and moved quickly to the side of his chair. Ready to push him back down if she had to. "You want to know the personal side, and I want to tell you."

He stared at his machine, hit some keys.

Trula roamed the room, taking a minute to gather herself. It was there, a soliloquy. A hard lump of words in her chest. She'd been adding to it almost every hour since the diagnosis. Although she'd never spoken it, she'd been letting it grow sentence by sentence for these last five months. Honing it, savoring it. And now she wanted to deliver it, relieved finally to have a chance to let someone know.

"It was last July," Trula said. She took a long look out the window, standing near Waldorf, looking down at those homeless men. "I got out of bed one morning, and my legs crumpled. I got back in bed, thought it was peculiar, but it passed. Then a week later I was on the set taping, and I started seeing double. I couldn't read the script. People were very nice, they helped me sit down. Thought it was exhaustion. So did I.

"I went to my GP, and he wasn't sure. He asked questions, ran tests, sent me to specialists who slid me in and out of all their humming chrome tubes. Neurologists, cardiologists. But after all that, no one had a definite diagnosis.

"Then one morning last August, I was at work, cameras rolling, and my legs went numb again, and this time my hands too. I fell down, I was quivering. I was terribly frightened. But my GP actually seemed relieved. Now he could tell me what I had, the name for it, anyway. He explained to me, the wires that carried the current up my spine, in my brain, they were scarred. The sheaths insulating the wires were broken in places and I was short-circuiting. That's how he put it.

"He told me not to worry, I had MS, but I wasn't going to die, and I wasn't contagious, I'd have a normal life span. Beyond that they couldn't say. I could be in remission for ten years, not have another symptom, get strong again, return to acting. Or I could be a cripple next month, riding around in a golf cart. Nobody could be sure yet.

"He thought he was being consoling, not going to die, not contagious. And you want to know how I felt, Dr. Waldorf? I was murderous. This man in his white smock, he was smiling, actually smiling, he was so satisfied with himself, he'd figured it out, solved this thing. I stood there, wanted to strangle him.

"Then the next day I told my producer what I had, and he said, the Jerry Lewis thing? The thing with the kids? No, that's muscular dystrophy. Oh yeah, right. So he thought about it, discussed it with the writers and they decided they'd write an illness into the script. Multiple sclerosis? I said. No, they'd decided MS wasn't a sexy disease. Too much of a downer. We'll give Cassie cancer, he said. Cancer's sexy? Cancer's not a downer? Sexier than MS, he said. So, Cassie got cancer.

"Do I need to describe how I was feeling at this point? My career's over. Nobody wanted to talk about it. They had their jobs, their families. Lots to do. Hey, you can forget that denial-bargaining-depression bullshit. I never felt any of that. It was anger, start to finish. Anger, anger, anger."

Trula walked back to the bed, pulling the silver balloon with her. She sat. Waldorf's fingers clicked across the keys, catching up with her. She waited till they'd stopped moving. She glanced out at her father, still buried in his magazine. Mozart working to a finale.

"I lost my lover," she said. "For a couple of weeks, I was numb in my genitals. You know, Dr. Waldorf, a spastic vagina. Well, it went away, but it spooked the guy. All of a sudden I'm this leper, he's afraid to touch me. Afraid I won't respond the way I always had before. Or else he's going to touch me the wrong way and set me off. He told me one day he thought I was infecting his masculinity somehow. His goddamn masculinity."

She looked at the man in corduroy. His head bent over, hands poised, but still. Giving her a long look at his flaky scalp. Then she glanced over at Anne, who was watching her now.

"And I began to hate you people, you doctors," she said. "I'd volunteered for these tests, you know, to do my share about the disease. Then everyone started showing up with their lists of questions, blood tests, brain scans. All of you treating me the same way. I'm just this husk. I'm there in front of you, but all you really want is to speak to the disease. Communicate with it, make it slip up and confess its secrets.

"Last month I unvolunteered myself. If my dad hadn't talked me into this, I sure as hell wouldn't be talking to you now. 'Cause as it turns out, you're not any different from the others. Oh, I know you're good men and women, you work hard, and I'm sure you care about people. It's just that you seem to love the disease more."

"I care about people," Waldorf said. He closed the lid of his computer and rose from his chair, dusted himself off quickly. Trula stood up, made it to the door first. He ducked his head and tried to worm around her, but she blocked him.

"Hey," she said, "you asked for this. Just let me finish. Let me get this out, okay?"

"Really," he said, "I'm sorry if I insulted you."

"You didn't insult me," she said. "You don't have to use any of this in your precious article. Just hear me out."

She put her hands on his shoulders, turned him around and steered him back toward his chair. When he was sitting, she returned to the edge of the bed and sat down.

"I was hoping," she said. "I know it's stupid, but the reason I volunteered for all these tests was that I was hoping one of you people would tell me something, give me some kind of clue what did this to me. Because that would help, you know, it would help me cope with this thing. It's *in* me, but it's not *me*. It's rewriting the rules my body plays by, and it's not consulting with me. It's making me hate my body. And be afraid of it.

"And I thought, if one of you could just offer something, some idea for me to focus on, something that might have been what set all this off, then maybe I could dump all my anger and frustration and everything that's been growing in me for these last months. I could dump it on that thing. Whatever it is."

Dr. Waldorf's tics had subsided. He was looking down at his computer. Trula was empty, her rush over. She stood up and tugged the ribbon of the balloon back across the room. It'd lost more gas and now didn't even make it all the way to the ceiling.

Waldorf brushed off his lapels and his corduroy shoulders and stood up again. A sigh broke from him and he turned his eyes to Trula.

"I'm close to something," he said. "Very close."

She turned, leaned against the dresser and stared at him.

"You are?"

"In fact, I'm about to blow the lid off something down there," he said. "Expose some extremely shocking things in Key West."

"That's . . ." Trula shook her head. "That's exciting."

"As you probably know," Waldorf said, "we think we know the process the disease takes. How it disables your immune system. We think we understand the etiology fairly well now. But what switches on the disease, that's still a mystery.

"Well, I can tell you this much. I'm extremely close to revealing something important about what may have triggered your MS, and what also may have caused the unusually high incidence of it in Key West and is still causing it. I'm not saying I have a cure, not at all. And what I've found may not have any relevance to MS cases in general. But I found something down there, where you're from, a possible trigger."

"Christ." She took a long breath. "Okay, listen, tell me what I can do. I've got money, and I have time now, lots of time. I'll do anything. Big, small, you name it, I'll do it."

He considered it a moment, gazing out the window.

"Anything," she said. Looking at Anne. "Name it."

"All right, then," he said.

"Good," she said. "Good."

"I've identified several people in Key West with MS who have been unwilling to assist with the study. If you could cajole them, get them to answer the same questionnaire you've just answered, that would be very helpful."

"That's all?" she said. "I meant it, Doctor, I'm willing to do anything to find out about this thing. Absolutely anything."

"The questionnaires are quite important," he said. "That's the statistical basis for all the rest of it."

She said, OK, she would do that, of course.

"But you must be very circumspect, Miss Montoya," Waldorf

said. "There are people down there who are threatened by my research. They have let it be known that they consider me and anyone assisting me to be a danger to their livelihoods."

Trula smiled.

"What you've discovered," she said, "it's that good?"

"Oh, yes," Dr. Waldorf said. "Definitely. Definitely."

6

At nine o'clock on Friday morning Shaw walked into the Hair Today, Gone Today Unisex Barbershop on Duval Street. For years, the shop had been one of Hanson Chandler's hangouts. He and his navy buddies had spent hundreds of mornings sitting around the dinette table at the rear of the shop, under the grinding paddle fan, playing cards, drinking beer, looking at the girlie magazines.

When Shaw came in, Johnny Middleton was snapping his scissors around the fine halo of hair of a man about Shaw's age. Johnny was in his seventies, but had the black, wavy pompadour and sideburns of a country music singer thirty years younger. Shaw took a seat across from them, and put the grocery bag on the seat beside him.

Johnny put down his scissors and shook some scented oil into his hands and rubbed them together, then across the man's head. He glanced over at Shaw and a smile widened his narrow face.

"Well, lookee who wandered back home!"

"Johnny, how you been?"

"Clipping and shaving and combing," he said. "The Lord keepeth the hair growing."

The man was staring at Shaw, giving him the slimmest benefit of the doubt. Johnny drew his delicate fingers away from the man's head and wiped them on a towel, coming across to shake Shaw's hand. Johnny spoke over his shoulder, told the man Shaw's name.

"The bait-and-tackle Chandler?" the man said.

"Yes, sir," he said, clapping Shaw on the shoulder, keeping the grip on his hand. "I cut this boy's hair when he was a baby. Lord, he used to put up such a fuss, trying to swat me away like I was a swarm of mosquitoes."

The man twisted his head, stuck a finger down the toilet paper wrapped around his neck.

"What brings you back to the rock, Shaw?"

"What it better be," the man said, "is settling up the shop's accounts."

Shaw sat down again. Johnny moved back behind the man, a neutral expression taking over his face, his diplomatic mask. It was one of the reasons he'd survived in business for so long.

The man said, "There's a lot of people around here extended good faith to that mother of yours, and they got burned bad."

"I only got here last night," Shaw said. "Give me a minute."

Johnny said, "Well, I don't think anybody could rightly say it was Millie's fault. Not so far as I could see. She got taken in by an expert con man."

"My brother-in-law got taken too," the man said. "For five thousand dollars. Extending that woman credit at the fisheries."

"Well, I'm home," Shaw said. "I'm going to work something out."

"What I'm suggesting to you is," the man said, "if somebody don't get busy in a big damn hurry and start paying off their debts, somebody's ass is gonna wind up in a sling."

The three of them were silent while Johnny finished the man's hair, then shook out the sheet. The man stood up and paid Johnny, and paused by the door to give Shaw a five-thousand-dollar glare. When he'd gone, Shaw took his seat in the chair.

He said, "You see my father, Johnny? Day before yesterday?"

Johnny shook the sheet into place across Shaw's lap. He tightened the toilet-paper collar into place. Shaw met his eyes in the mirror across from them.

"You can tell me the truth, Johnny. It's not going to do anybody any harm at this point."

"I didn't see him, but I heard he was in town."

"Where'd you hear it?"

"Doyle Overby," Johnny said. He was combing Shaw's hair, putting a part in it where a part had never been. "Doyle saw him out by the junior college. Right out there in the middle of the afternoon, driving along pretty as you please like nothing was unusual about it."

"Never mind the haircut, Johnny." Shaw tugged at the collar and Johnny released the clip, pulled the sheet aside.

"The bait shop and all that," Johnny said. "You shouldn't blame your mother. That Salter boy used to come in here, stink up the place with his charm. It wasn't just her was fooled."

"I know," Shaw said. "She told me the story last night."

"Most likely you'll find Doyle down at the city docks, futzing with his boat. If they haven't evicted his butt by now. There or Captain Tony's."

"One other thing, Johnny." Shaw stood up out of the chair, went across and picked up the grocery bag. He handed Johnny the canister. "Ever see one of these?"

Johnny handled it for a minute. Shook his head.

"Could be some kind of shell casing, I guess," he said. "Looks almost like a howitzer or some damn thing. But I can't say I ever saw the likes of it." He handed it back. "You might ask Doyle about it. If he doesn't know, you could try Barnes. There's nothing about navy business Captain Barnes don't know."

"The base commander? That Barnes?"

"That's the Barnes, but he's been retired, eight, ten years now."

"Where would I find him?"

"He runs the dump now."

"The dump?" Shaw said. "A retired navy captain running the dump?"

"I know it sounds strange," Johnny said. "But it's not if you know Barnes. That man has a nose for money. And that goddamn garbage dump is one big money machine. One year Barnes is navy, next year he put in the lowest bid to build some kind of fancy incinerator, and like that, he was king of the dump."

Shaw thanked him. Put the canister back in the sack.

"So, you home for a while, then, are you?"

"Looks like I am," Shaw said.

———

Doyle Overby's forty-five-foot Hatteras was moored at the pricey Pier House dock. Shaw had no trouble finding it. The Hatteras was this year's model or last's. Its hull as grand and shimmering as any at the dock. But Doyle Overby had already put his stamp on it.

There were aluminum folding chairs on the deck, a rusty refrigerator standing next to the cabin door, car tires, a lawn mower, a wheelbarrow, and a half a dozen barnacle-encrusted lobster traps distributed around the decks and walkways. Glass jars, old paintings, piles of books. The deck looked like the last hours of a garage sale.

When Shaw approached, Doyle was sunning himself in a lawn chair. Wearing a stained T-shirt and cutoff corduroys. Next to him a three-legged golden Labrador struggled to its feet and hobbled over to the gangplank where Shaw stood. The dog made a low, uncertain growl and Doyle opened his eyes, an unlit cigarette stuck to his bottom lip.

"Shaw Chandler?"

"The same."

The dog kept growling.

"Well, come on aboard, boy," Doyle said.

Shaw hesitated, nodding at the dog.

"Nostrils, shut the hell up, you old fishface. Don't you recognize Shaw Chandler?"

The dog backed off and Shaw climbed over to the Hatteras.

"Beautiful boat, Doyle."

"Yeah, yeah," he said. "Well, it's what I got when I cashed out of my house over on Elizabeth. Remember that place?"

Shaw said of course he did.

Doyle waved him into an aluminum chair, and Shaw sat.

"Well, I couldn't afford the damn taxes no more, so I sold it. Bought this thing. But goddamn my ass, I forgot to set aside enough money for gas. I just been docked here ever since."

Doyle took the unlit cigarette off his lip, sailed it overboard, and dug another one out of the pack in his back pocket.

"You still giving the white belts a hard time, I see."

Doyle winked at Shaw and waved howdy at the man in pastel golf clothes on the Bertram across the dock. The man scowled and turned away.

"They think 'cause they made a ton of money, they don't ever have to look at the sorry likes of people like me no more. Well, they're wrong on that one."

"I heard you saw my father, Doyle."

"Oh, Johnny told you, did he?" Doyle looked up at a blue heron standing on a nearby piling. "Yeah, well, I saw him Wednesday around noon. Strangest damn thing. As I was walking back from the hospital, he came riding along, window rolled down, serious look on his face. He tried to duck his head away, but I got a good look anyway. It took me five minutes after he'd passed before I even thought who he was."

"Where exactly was this?"

"Right out there between the hospital and the junior college."

"Which way was he headed?" Shaw said.

"What's this all about, Shaw? Your daddy showing up like that after all this time? He giving himself up?"

"I'm trying to find out," Shaw said. "It's why I'm here."

"Well, all I can tell you is he was coming in from the highway, poking along. Like he didn't know just where he was going."

"You hear of anybody else around town who saw him?" Shaw said.

"How 'bout your mother?"

"No," Shaw said.

Doyle said, "Well, there isn't anybody left in town your daddy was friends with but me and Johnny Middleton. All of them either died or moved off."

"There anybody out there on Stock Island he could've been visiting? Any old navy people, maybe?"

"There's ex-navy people all over the place. Too many to keep track of. Out there, on Stock Island, like I say, I don't know anybody your daddy was particularly friends with. But there's people he knew, yeah. Captain Barnes, you remember him. And there's Randy Offsteader, teaches biology at the junior college. A couple more old-timers like me. There's Montoya, the doctor. But none of them were close to Hanson, far as I knew."

"Montoya? He lives out there now?"

"Yeah," he said. "Has some kind of run-down old petting zoo or a bird sanctuary, or something out there. I never seen it, to tell you the truth. But I heard it's there."

Shaw looked over at where Nostrils had settled down next to a washtub full of tools. The dog had lifted its head up and was taking long sniffs of the offshore breeze.

Shaw opened the grocery bag, handed Doyle the canister.

"U.S. Navy," Doyle said, running his hands over it.

"Recognize it?"

"It ain't nothing I ever dealt with," he said. "But it was a big navy. There's a whole hell of a lot I never saw, so that doesn't mean nothing just cause I never came across it."

"You think of anything, let me know, okay?"

Doyle said, Yeah, sure. He fondled the the canister a few seconds more and handed it back. "You know what, Shaw? Your daddy might've just wanted to take a look at the island again, like for old times' sake. Just cruise around, remember how things used to be. He did have an awful wide sentimental streak."

"He did?" Shaw said.

Doyle scratched his armpit and flicked his cigarette overboard.

"Oh, yeah, yeah. Hanson could get awful weepy late at night. At the bar, sitting there, singing one of those mournful Irish tunes he knew. The man had a voice, he could get it going sad and mellow and there'd be tears all along the bar."

"I never heard that," Shaw said quietly.

"Hell," Doyle said. "A boy never gets to know his old man, not till it's too late."

———

Shaw sat on a bench on Duval Street trying to figure out his next move. He watched the tourists trudge toward the outdoor cafés, the bars, for their first cold one of the day. Tourists, tourists everywhere. He knew it was fashionable to hate them, these outsiders, coming down to dirty the water, break off chunks of coral, pilfer the resources. But he'd always liked having them around. They brought a spark of liveliness with them.

With only a few days on the island, they were usually damned determined to wring some nectar out of every moment, have a few deep gulps of the perfect life. He thought of them as being like those monks he'd heard of. The ones who lifted a shovelful of dirt out of their grave every morning. Made them devote the rest of their waking time to seizing the day by the lapels.

Shaw sat on the bench for a half hour watching the tourists coming and going in that mild January sun, nothing new coming to him. Then he hauled himself up and walked over to Simonton and followed it south to United, looking at nothing as he went, just moving. He turned around and came back up, trying to claw loose a thought, the next step he should take. The hospital, the dump, the junior college. Barnes, Montoya.

Still nothing came to him, so he cut back toward the cemetery, walked home. In the kitchen he made a sandwich, and as he started to eat, he heard his mother switch on the TV in the Florida room. He got up and wandered in there with his plate. She was sipping rum and Coke from a tall glass. He sat on the frayed couch beside her. A wad of batting had worked out of a tear in the cover and Shaw poked it back in. The opening theme song for "Hidden Hours" was playing. The voice-over intoned the sappy prologue.

A minute into the show people were dressing in their formal, dark clothes, having petty confrontations, squabbling about the same tired problems as they put on their funeral suits. Shaw felt a frown take hold of his face.

Then there was a long row of black cars in a grainy outdoor shot, driving to the Leewood Cemetery. The entire cast, it seemed, climbed out of the cars, assembled around the grave in a mist of snow. A white casket was suspended over the grave.

A minister, one of the regulars, began to speak about Cassie Raintree, what a powerful influence she'd had on all who had known her. A woman of integrity and charm, a woman taken too soon. The clichés of burial. He read the Twenty-third Psalm.

When he was finished, he clapped his Bible shut and looked up at the cloudy sky. His voice was harsh and dark when he spoke.

"Why?" he said, glaring up at the heavens. "Why?" he called out again to the sky. His voice coming back in a faint echo.

"Why, oh God? Why Cassie? I demand to know!"

He spoke with an earnestness Shaw had never heard from him before, as if the script had fluttered from his mind and he was forced to speak from the heart. It seemed that even from the grave Cassie was working her power on these actors, challenging them to be better than they were.

His voice dropped half a step.

"Cassie Raintree was as full of the richness and energy of the human spirit as any person I've ever known. Yet she was ripped from our lives. Stolen from us in her prime."

He scanned the heavens, reaching up an open hand. Then slowly closing it to a fist.

"I do not accept this, Lord," he said. "I refuse to accept this travesty. I do not call on you to show us your mysterious ways. For there simply can be no reason good enough. None."

His fist trembled.

"Cassie Raintree," he said, "was better than any of us. She, of all of us, deserved a full stay on earth. And yet . . ."

He lowered his fist, bringing his eyes back to these people standing in a circle around the grave. Everyone shifted uneasily, staring at this man in black.

"It has shaken my faith to the core, Father," he said to the ground. And without raising his eyes, he spoke his benediction with quiet rage, "Oh Lord, there is something wrong in the land. There is something horribly, horribly wrong."

Shaw looked at his mother. She had set her drink aside on the table and was staring at the wall above the television.

"Well, so much for her," his mother said. "So much for her."

7

That afternoon he drove out Junior College Road on Stock Island looking for the spot where Doyle had seen his father. Beyond the sun-bruised fairways of the Key West Golf Course, he drove along the narrow asphalt road past Mount Trashmore, the white hill of garbage that you could see from five miles at sea. The mountain had been growing there since Shaw was a boy. Now beside it was an incineration plant, its two concrete smokestacks soaring a couple of hundred feet. Beside one of the two windowless buildings a line of garbage trucks waited to dump their loads.

He parked for a few minutes outside the gates of the dump and watched the trickle of traffic going past. Pickups passing by, some tourists lost their way and U-turning in the middle of the road. He didn't know why he was out here, what he was looking for. Maybe he thought he would catch a whiff of his father's psychic trail, the fairy dust every person was supposed to leave behind them.

He waited awhile longer, but he didn't see anything, not a twinkle, so he drove on to the hospital, parked and went inside. In the lobby there were a couple of black women talking, and a young mother trying to hush her two pale girls. He stood at the registration desk, looking at the counter till a nurse came over. She asked him if she could help.

"I don't think so."

"Well, what, then?"

"I don't know," he said. "I'm completely out of ideas."

"Then you want the junior college," she said and turned back to her paperwork.

"Thanks," he said.

He circled the lobby for a minute, and then he pushed through the swinging double doors and entered the west wing. He paced slowly down the hall taking a long look into each room as he went. A leg in traction, old people sleeping in the half-light, the immaculate floor, a baby crying somewhere in the distance. When he came to the end of the hall, he turned and walked back up the other side. It could be any hospital. The same frail people, the same air seasoned with Clorox and urine.

Back in the El Camino he sat and stared at the bug-splatter on his windshield. His father's trail was scentless and cold. He considered driving back out to the highway, heading north, returning to his old life. See if Stacy could manage forgiveness. No one was asking him to stay here. His mother didn't need him. He could hang around, make a project of hiding her rum bottles from her. But he'd tried that before. It didn't work.

Shaw tapped on the steering wheel. If he tried very hard he could even imagine that Hanson Chandler had committed suicide, and that he'd come down for a final sentimental look at that life he'd abandoned twenty years ago, and then he'd gone back to Miami and pulled his own switch.

Shaw sat there for a few minutes more, trying to imagine that, but not succeeding, then trying to wish the whole goddamn thing away. But it wouldn't go. It was there, a large aching cavity where his guts had been a few days before.

He started the El Camino and headed back up Junior College Road toward the highway. But as he was passing the dump, he saw a school bus in the parking lot of the plant, a stream of young kids piling off. He pulled sharply into the visitors' lot, parked alongside the bus, got out and joined them. What the hell.

He nodded at the brown-haired woman in a cowboy shirt and blue jeans who was directing the kids off the bus, forming them into a fussing, chattering line.

"Taking the tour?" she said to him.

"Is it any good?"

"The first twenty times were okay," she said.

"Isn't that the way with everything."

She led the class beneath a steaming maze of pipes, and Shaw fell in at the rear. Some of the kids were holding their noses, going *pee-ew*. Giggling, some of them holding their guts and doing fair imitations of retches. Shaw had smelled worse.

The vapors of rot floated in from the other side of the plant, where the garbage trucks were dumping their loads, and mingled with a mist of ash that hung all about them. The air had a sweet putridness to it as if someone had set fire to a house full of ripe vegetables.

He stayed at the end of the line, following a blocky, burr-haired boy who was trying to arouse a blond girl by wiggling his finger into her armpit. It didn't seem to be working. As they filed through a set of heavy metal double doors into the main building, the clank of the plant subsided. Shaw let the doors suck closed behind him. The children gathered in the middle of the two-story room and seemed awestruck by the quiet hum of huge turbines and generators.

"Class!" the teacher called. "Class, I would like you to meet Mr. Douglas Barnes, who has taken time from his busy schedule to show us around his recycling plant."

The kids muttered their hellos to the smiling man in gray slacks, blue shirt, red bow tie. He was just under six feet and strikingly fit for someone in his sixties. His graying flattop brushed to rigid attention. He smiled at the children, nodded at Shaw and the teacher, then raised both hands for quiet.

"Welcome to my world," he said. "Now I want you to follow me and see what happens to that napkin, that apple core, that old comic book you dumped in your garbage can. This way, kids."

Barnes led them first to the receiving bin, an enormous room where the garbage was collected and sifted for dangerous materials. The floor was sunken twenty feet below ground level, a football field of garbage. The walls rose to a hundred feet. As they watched, garbage trucks backed up to the lip of the receiving bin and expelled their loads, while a crane that hung down from the ceiling lifted huge chunks of trash and dropped them onto the clattering conveyor belt.

"Can you pick out your bag of garbage in there?" he said to the group over the bray of the machinery.

A lot of the kids were still holding their noses, fanning their faces.

For the next thirty minutes Douglas Barnes led the kids around his plant. He charmed them all into utter silence by the time they were nearing the end of the tour. Even the sex-crazed boy fell under his spell.

For the last stop on the tour, Barnes halted them below a tangle of girders and pipes and explained that once the garbage was burned, the remaining superheated ash fell through the big chutes behind him from the furnace above and was cooled in the water of the quench tanks. Then the residue of black glop was retrieved from the water and trucked up to the top of the landfill.

"Isn't he amazing?" the teacher whispered to Shaw. "He's got such authority. They actually listen to him."

One of the boys raised his hand. And Barnes smiled and called on him.

"When I was a little boy, there was a million sea gulls flying around the dump. Where are they? Somebody shoot 'em all?"

"No, no, son," Barnes said, smiling. "The ash that goes onto the top of the landfill is sterile. Not like the garbage that used to be there. It smelled and rotted in the sun. The ash we put up there these days has no nutritional value." He pinched up some of the black dust from a railing near the quench tank. "You wouldn't want to eat this, now, would you, kids?"

A chorus of *yicks* and *yucks*.

"Well, see?" he said. "Neither do the birds."

A girl in thick glasses shot her hand up.

"You call this a recycling plant," she said.

"Yes."

She stared at Barnes through her underwater glasses.

"But you just burn things," she said. "You don't return anything. You burn it, that's all you do."

"That's a good question, young lady," Barnes said, some of his goodwill evaporating. "But you see, we now manage to retrieve some of the energy from the garbage, which used to simply rot in the sun. Now we take the things you throw out and return to you electricity to run your televisions and stereos and your ovens and refrigerators. You wouldn't want to do without those things, would you?"

The girl seemed unconvinced, but she shook her head. No, she didn't want to give up television.

"Well," Barnes said. "If any of you have a better idea of what to do with your garbage, just write down your name and address for me, and I'll pass them on to the city government and we'll stop picking up your garbage, and let you find something better to do with it. How's that?"

"Guy should run for office," the teacher whispered to Shaw.

"So, now, is everybody ready for the grand finale?"

They cheered.

Barnes led the group up a set of iron stairs to the second tier. The floor was a steel grating. Look down through your feet, see the huff of steam coming from below. It spooked some of the kids. They formed a nervous line and Barnes held open the three-inch peephole into the furnace. He enlisted Shaw to boost each kid up a couple of feet so they could peer into the heart of the fire, feel the rush of burning air that came from the slot.

As each of the kids was staring into the hole, Barnes bent close and whispered. "Now, that's what happens to bad little boys and girls."

Shaw looked around for help from the teacher but she just shrugged.

"Somebody put you in charge of nightmares?" said Shaw, setting down a child, a few more to go.

Barnes smiled tolerantly.

"Young man," he said. "One of the things wrong with the world these days is kids no longer have any idea of hell."

"And now they do."

"Yes," he said, "and now they most certainly do."

Barnes was holding open the peephole to hell, and studying Shaw curiously, as a big blond man in overalls came hustling up the stairway. He moved in next to Barnes and muttered something to him. Barnes nodded, patted the man on the back.

He turned to the children and said in a loud stage whisper, "Well, boys and girls, we're in luck today."

He led them back down the stairs, explaining over his shoulder that they were about to witness Lars, the large blond gentleman, perform a very dangerous task. He was going to knock loose an automobile bumper that had made its away through the furnace and had become lodged in the ash chute, creating a large buildup of superheated ash that was threatening to clog the whole operation. Now it was Lars's job to reach into the small door in the chute and knock loose the bumper and let the jam-up of ash fall into the cooling tank below. Then he had to jump back out the small doorway before the ash had time to convert a few hundred gallons of the water to steam.

"Because what would happen if he didn't make it back out in time?" Barnes asked the group. Lars stood behind him, a crowbar in his hands, waiting for their answer.

"He would be hideously burned by the steam," the sex fiend said, "permanently disfigured, and have to wear a hockey mask forever." He turned to his blond goddess and grinned.

"That's pretty close," Barnes said. He turned to the big man and nodded. "Lars," he said, "go to it."

As Lars was walking up the three metal stairs to the chute door, the teacher said, "I thought you told us that everything going through the plant was reduced in mass by ninety percent."

"Oh, that's the average," Barnes said. "Most things are reduced to ash. But a few things, the iron or steel objects, things like wet newspapers, ceramics, they make it through pretty much intact. We try to separate them out in the dumping bin, but we aren't always successful. And so sometimes, they get wedged into a corner of the chute and the ash backs up on top of it."

Lars lifted the steel latch, swung open the door and stepped one rubber-booted leg into the small, darkened chute. He began to poke with his crowbar at the bumper, which seemed to be hung up just over his head.

"Let's move back a safe distance," Barnes said, spreading his arms and herding the children a few more yards away. "This is tricky work."

Standing on the concrete apron that bordered the furnace, twenty feet from where Lars worked, the children craned to get into the line of sight of the dark compartment. The chute itself was a tarnished steel funnel with heavy rivets. The small doorway into the chute had a high step-over like the passageway between the compartments of a submarine.

Shaw watched Lars hook the end of the crowbar around something well above him in the chute, then jimmy it left and right. The creak and scream of steel on steel. Lars must have budged it a little because he dragged his leg out of the chute, hopped backward, and quickly closed the door, his hand on the latch to slide it into place. He waited for a moment and when nothing happened, he opened the door carefully, and stepped back inside the chute and began working again with his crowbar.

Barnes said, "Who can tell me how hot that ash is?

"Sixteen hundred and eighty-three degrees," the girl with the underwater glasses said.

A few in the group edged backward another respectful step.

As a heavy clang sounded inside the chute, Lars clambered back out the door. Shaw saw the bumper splash in the tank. Lars stumbled backward, his boot catching on the lip of the doorway. He got his balance, then lurched forward to latch the door. Just as Lars was swinging it shut, Shaw glimpsed a black, glowing mass of lava begin to cascade from the chute.

A blast of steam roared, then blew the door out of Lars's hands, knocking him backward down the stairway. The hot gas spewed out the door, roaring like the thrust of a jet engine. Shaw whirled his back to it, shielding four or five of the kids from the contrail of scalding air. Children screamed, and in a moment somewhere above the plant an air-raid siren sounded.

"Ice!" Shaw yelled when the rush of steam had quieted. "We need some ice, quick."

"Ice?" Barnes said, looking down at Lars writhing on the ground. Several of the children were crying, but none of them seemed to be burned. The teacher was moving among them, checking.

"Cold water, ice," Shaw said. "And call Nine-Eleven."

Barnes looked slowly up from the man in the dust, and said, "I don't believe we require your help. My people can handle this situation just fine."

But Shaw sprinted to the side of the plant, turned on a spigot there and ran back with the hose. You only had a minute or two in these cases, the flesh was still cooking, blistering on the outside, destroying cells below. Every second you stopped to argue about it, figure out what to do, was another week the victim was going to have to lie there and listen to his arm throb.

Lars was sitting up when Shaw got back with the hose. He was holding out his right arm, offering it up for Barnes's view. The big man wasn't crying, but his face was broken apart in pain. Shaw sprayed the arm with the water, soaked Lars in the process. And the big man's face eased as the water ran over him.

Barnes said something, Shaw wasn't sure what. Shaw turned to him, bringing the hose around with him as he did. It was silly, he knew, uncalled for. Firing the hard stream of water into the boss man's face, but it was awfully satisfying, the kind of thing Buzz and the other firemen would have appreciated. Some of the fourth-graders seemed to like it too.

Barnes's face twisted and darkened, and he stepped forward into the spray, and wrenched the hose from Shaw's hand, and glowered at him, his breath pumping hard, his blue shirt spattered with a darker hue.

"What the hell do you think you're doing, mister?"

"I don't know," said Shaw. "But I'm sure working on it."

8

On Monday, Shaw waited till he was sure Chief Clem had settled into his office at Miami District Seven Headquarters and gulped down his first cup of Cuban coffee. Then Shaw called Clem and told him he was still in Key West and had decided he needed another couple of weeks.

"You need two more weeks," the chief said. "Just like that. And I don't get a reason."

"My mother's business is in trouble," he said. "I don't get it back together, the lady's going to be on welfare."

Shaw could hear the chief breathe into the mouthpiece, tap his pencil point against the glass desktop. Probably looking up at his collection of fire mementos, sections of hose, a double-bladed axe, photos of famous Miami fires.

"You sure you're not down there boffing some sun bunny, Chandler, you need two more weeks to work your way through the complete *Kama Sutra*?"

"I wish it were that," Shaw said. And hung up.

Then he went to the state's attorney's office. And after convincing a young man in suspenders and granny glasses that he was going to devote the balance of his stay on earth and all his savings to paying off the tackle shop's debts and reviving the business, he got a fifteen-minute lecture on fraud and passing bad checks and the danger of making unsecured loans. The state's attorney had him sign some papers, and finally gave him the key to the padlock on the door.

For the next few days, he worked in the tackle shop fourteen hours a day, making phone calls from the pay phone down the dock to suppliers, convincing them to start deliveries again. Cash only, of course. He transferred half his savings account to a Key West bank, and began making heavy subtractions from it.

In the evenings, he drove around Stock Island, aimlessly cruising, parking. There was no listing for Montoya in the phone book, and nobody he asked seemed to have heard of a petting zoo. So Shaw had taken to slowing at every mailbox out there. But he'd seen no sign of the name.

At home at night he sat in his room and handled the silver canister, tracing the grooves of those letters with his fingertip. One night he laid a blank sheet of paper over the feet and ankles of the letters from the upper row of words. He shaded them in and experimented with words. Nonsense phrases. The letters he was fairly sure of: O, B, probably a G. Gob? Bog?

He could feel his energies dwindle. He stared at the page, tried other combinations of letters. Nothing. He wadded up the paper, tossed it. In a minute he traced the squiggles again, and came up with nothing new. He crumpled that page too. The fact was, he wasn't any damn detective. His skills, if he could call them that, were in staunching blood, resuscitating the dying, or carting them away, not in finding their killers.

By Friday, eight days after arriving in Key West, he had built up a feeble stock on the shelves of the store, and people were stopping in. There was a small layer of money in the cash drawer. Not enough to buy a week's groceries yet, but moving ahead. He had used up ten years of savings. Eight more to go.

And he had almost convinced himself that Jackie Gawron was right. His father had pressed the .38 to his own chest, never mind how awkward it was, and with the wrong hand. Then that tough farm woman he lived with had followed him as soon as she could. And now Shaw Chandler was bogged down here, trying to get his mother's business going again, selling shrimp by the dozen, beer by the can, and wondering what the hell had happened to the thread of his life.

———

"Two squid," the man said.

"They come in packages," Shaw said. "Four, five to a box."

"I just want two."

"You just want two," he said. "Two squid."

From where Shaw stood behind the counter of Chandler Beer, Bait and Tackle, he could see the *Miss Liberty* on her way out of Garrison Bight, the first mate rolling up the lines. A gang of tourists in bright shirts laughing on the rear deck. Sea gulls diving and a couple of bonefish skiffs plunging through *Miss Liberty*'s wake, a guide and an angler in each boat.

It was only seven-thirty that Friday morning, and a headache was already growing tentacles behind his eyes. And if this Canadian in the red golf hat didn't back away from the counter, Shaw knew his headache would take hold, probably last all day.

"Look," he said. "We're having a special today. Four frozen squid for the price of two."

The Canadian did some fancy math in his head and said OK.

He was wearing a T-shirt one size too small, striped Bermudas, rubber flip-flops.

"Now we got that settled," the Canadian said, "I need a fishing rod, a reel, some hooks and line, and you have to tell me where I should go to catch some fish. I'm new to this area."

Shaw laughed. He could feel the headache seep away. The guy was too goddamn helpless to strangle.

He spent twenty minutes helping the man pick out his gear. A six-foot graphite rod, a Daiwa BG 15 reel, eight-pound test, long-shank hooks. Light enough tackle so if he caught anything at all, it'd feel like a whale. His bill came to $163. Shaw took him outside the bait shop and pointed him down the dock to a spot where he'd seen some kids catching snapper. The Canadian thanked him.

"I'm recently divorced," the man said.

"Yeah," Shaw said, "I hear it's going around."

"I feel disoriented," the man said. "Gutted."

"You'll probably get over it."

"I'm trying to fish, to see if it helps."

"It's a good choice," Shaw said.

He watched the man walk down the dock. The captain on *Brenda Lee Four* looked up from some leaders he was tying and watched this man loaded down with new gear shuffle past. He glanced over at Shaw and shook his head. Yeah, Shaw nodded back. The guy was pathetic all right. Another zombie from the sex wars. Trying to fish his way out of all that pain.

He took his place again on the stool at a side counter where he'd spread out all the accounts. Now that he'd bought some stock, he'd begun trying to unscramble the books. He was getting close. The IRS people were coming tomorrow, and the state tax people were scheduled to be in next week. He already knew what ballpark their numbers were in. It was goddamn Yankee Stadium.

Near as he could figure, Chandler Beer, Bait and Tackle owed a total of fifty-eight thousand dollars. Most of that to fishing tackle suppliers in the Lower Keys, a shrimp company in Homestead, and the Key West Fishery for a year's worth of ballyhoo and mullet and frozen shrimp. Throw in the back taxes, the unpaid electric, phone and water bills and what it would cost to rebuild the inventory to where it had been a year and a half ago, you were talking another fifteen grand.

He sat on the wooden stool, choking down a package of stale Fig Newtons and a Pepsi. Leaning a little to his left, he could watch the Canadian down at the end of the dock throw spastic casts into the wind, reel them in too fast. Or he could sit there and fantasize about Peter Salter.

He'd heard from some of the local dock rats that the boy had been seen in Islamorada lately, a couple of hours up the Overseas Highway. He was said to be driving a new Italian car, eating at restaurants every night, having his nails done.

Shaw decided that when he had things straightened out a little neater at the tackle shop, paid off some of the debts with the last of his retirement money and built up a little merchandise, he'd take an afternoon off, go for a drive up to Islamorada, have a chat with the boy. Maybe the two of them could test the second law of thermodynamics, see if Peter Salter in motion would tend to remain in motion.

When the Canadian came back through the screen door, Shaw was swallowing the last sip of the Pepsi. The man slapped a monster bonefish on the counter. Had to be at least fourteen pounds. Looked like it had been out of the water at least half an hour. Twenty-five minutes dead. He asked Shaw what kind of fish it was, and Shaw told him.

"Can you eat them?" the man said.

"That particular fish, you're supposed to take a picture of it and throw it back in while it's still alive."

"You can't eat it?"

"Mister, people fish for twenty years looking for a fish that beautiful. It's a game fish, not a meat fish."

"What? It's a big deal? This fish?"

"Yeah," Shaw said. "If you care about things like that."

"You want it?" the man asked. "If I can't eat it, I don't want it."

Shaw said, Yeah, OK, he'd take it. He opened the freezer and laid the fish on top of the squid and thread herring.

The Canadian left, went back down the pier, back to his spot, in search of a fish sandwich. It must have been a brutal divorce. A fish like that, you had to be numbed deep not to get a fresh heartbeat from it.

———

It was almost sunset when Shaw looked up from the books, and the Canadian was standing at the screen door. He was holding a large brown pelican. Shaw hopped down from his stool, swung open the door and said, "Jesus Christ, now what?"

"I caught this," the man said. "It went after my shrimp, got the hook, and I reeled it in."

"What? You gonna melt some cheese on it, have it for supper?"

"I'm trying to save it," the man said. "I think I broke its wing fighting it."

"Yeah," Shaw said, coming around the counter. "Looks like you did."

"Think I could use your phone, call a vet?"

"Help yourself."

Shaw held the pelican still on the countertop while the man called three, four vets, getting the same answer each time.

"They clip poodles' nails," the man said, dialing the next number, "but they don't work on pelicans."

The Canadian got the next receptionist on the phone, went through the same routine. The pelican gave a shrug in Shaw's hands, tried feebly to walk out of his grasp.

The Canadian said, "Spell that for me, please. *M-o-n-t-o-y-a.* And you're sure he does pelicans?"

Shaw picked up the pelican, came down the aisle of lead weights and bucktails and stood close to the man.

The Canadian nodded at him, and said, "Yeah, on Stock Island? No, I don't, but I'll find it if you give me directions."

"Give me the phone," Shaw said, shifting the pelican to his right arm. "Give it to me now."

———

Shaw had passed Montoya's entrance drive a dozen times in his tours of Stock Island, mistaking it for a gravel turnaround. But through the snarl of mangrove and holly branches there was a narrow road that led out to what seemed to be a narrow peninsula. A row of white houses showed up in his headlight. Cabins with small porches. And across from them were a half dozen pens. The reflector eyes of pelicans and egrets lit for a moment before he cut his lights.

He arranged the injured pelican under his arm and walked toward the largest of the houses, the only one that was lit. On the porch he raised his hand to tap on the screen door, but held it there. The bird moved weakly under his arm, then went slack again. Shaw lowered his hand and stepped back a foot into the shadows.

In the kitchen of that small wood house, a kid in his twenties was bent over a paperback book, pointing with his finger at the words. He was wearing a muscle T-shirt and black jeans and had curly black hair to his shoulders. A diamond flashed in his right earlobe.

"Giving her no time to wrig-wriggle from him, he lowered his trou-sers and thrust his erect penis be-tween her thighs just above her stock-ing tops."

The voice was slow, fumbling with the words like a third-grader standing before his class. Moving hurriedly and without apparent recognition over the simple words, slowing for the extra syllables.

At the stove, with his back to the kid, an old man was stirring something in a frying pan. He wore a starched white shirt, creased blue chinos, shiny shoes. Glasses cocked up against his forehead. His thick white hair was blown wild around his head as if he'd just escaped a tornado. He was frail, late seventies. He resembled Trula's father, but Shaw wasn't sure. It had been a long time.

"The gentle-man pulled down her drawers," the boy read.

"Where-at the lady made great play. Of shrieking and endeav-or . . . Endeav . . ."

"Endeavoring," the old man said, his voice tired.

"Endeavoring to wig-gle, wiggle, free. I could but watch. Dry-mouthed, at my cousin's firm titties. Were brought into view while the gen-tle-man's sturd-y penis. Moved to and fro be-tween her bare thighs."

The kid looked up from the book and breathed heavily. He took a sip of his Budweiser.

"Where the fuck did the bear come from?" he asked the man.

"What bear, Dougie?"

"She had bear thighs," the kid said.

"Bare," the man said. "Naked. *B-a-r-e*. Not *b-e-a-r*. *B-e-a-r* is the animal. *B-a-r-e* is naked."

"Bare-ass naked," the boy said. "I always thought it was about a bear, you know, like a naked grizzly bear."

"The discoveries of reading," the old man said, turning a knob on the stove, then opening the oven door.

Shaw stepped back into the light from the kitchen and rapped on the wooden frame of the screen door.

The man came over, the spatula in his hand. He turned on the porch light and Shaw stepped back from the door.

"Dr. Montoya?" Shaw said.

"Yes," he said, and opened the screen.

"I was told you treat wounded birds."

He lowered his glasses and peered at the pelican. Gently, he took it from under Shaw's arm and went back into the kitchen. Shaw pushed open the screen door and entered.

The kid grinned and gave Shaw a toe-to-scalp consideration. Lingering with a sneer on Shaw's upper arms. They were puny com-pared to the kid's. Dougie had the protruding veins, the ridges and strands of muscles, of a major-league bodybuilder. He rocked back in his chair, lacing his hands behind his head, giving Shaw a private anatomy lesson.

Shaw tipped an imaginary hat at the kid. Smiled the smile of the deeply impressed.

"I was born without a pain threshold," the kid said. He broke his pose, reached out, and had another sip of his beer.

"I suppose that could be an advantage," Shaw said.

The kid said, "I sat on a nail when I was four. I didn't know it till I got up and I had blood running down my leg. Now I'm learning to read. So what do you think about that?"

"Porno novels?"

"I'm highly motivated by sex," the kid said. "Aren't you?"

"Sometimes," he said.

Montoya had the pelican on the tiled drain of the sink. He'd unfolded the wing and was feeling for damage. The bird made a quiet honk, struggled briefly and then closed its eyes and was still. Shaw moved over beside the man. He gave off the scent of whiskey and fresh laundry.

Shaw asked him if the injury was serious.

"Only if you consider losing a wing serious," Montoya said quietly.

Shaw had spent a good deal of time around doctors, felt at ease with their no-bullshit directness. It could be mistaken for callousness at times, but usually it wasn't that. If you washed your hands enough times in strangers' blood, it didn't necessarily harden you to people. But always it hardened you to blood.

"But you can save him?"

The old man turned, leaving the bird on the edge of the sink. He got closer to Shaw than he needed to and said, "Son, do I look like God to you?"

Montoya moved back to the sink. He opened a cabinet and took down a glass bottle of syringes. He chose one of them and then found a small bottle of blue liquid on a higher shelf. He slid the needle through the rubber cap of the bottle and drew some of the liquid into the syringe.

"Scantily clad, terribly bad," the kid sang.

Shaw glanced his way and the kid shifted his grin up a gear. The earring flashed in his right ear. Shaw could never remember which ear meant what thing. Whether the kid was advertising that he was gay, or just trying to be dashing.

The kid said, "Bare thighs, fur pies."

Then his eyes rolled upward and he lifted his chin like someone was tickling his neck. His mouth stayed open, and he sat there immobilized as if he were listening to a sermon from the god of muscle tissue.

Whatever condition the kid was suffering from wasn't anything

Shaw had come across on Fire Rescue. This probably had a three-piece Latin name, some exotic syndrome that involved too many Y chromosomes. Maybe one of the new ones, hot off the genetic press.

When he turned back to Montoya, the pelican was slumped on the drainboard. The old man scooped it up and headed to the kitchen door. Shaw got there just ahead of him, held the door aside and followed the man out into the dark.

Montoya led him down a rocky path toward a stand of pines. Fifty feet from the house there were several tall cages covered in chicken wire. In the full moonlight Shaw could make out herons and egrets, gulls, pelicans, walking about on the sandy floor. An owl hooted nearby, then the sharp *skreet* of something small and unhappy. The Atlantic was thirty feet away, bleached by moonlight. A warm breath of wind riffled its shine.

Montoya opened the door to one of the outbuildings. He turned on the light and went inside, Shaw following. There was a chrome operating table, a strong scent of piss and alcohol. The floor was white tile, waxed to a high gloss. A sink in the corner.

"What can you do for that wing?"

"Cut it off," he said.

Shaw said, "Then what?"

"Then I breed this cripple with another cripple, and when they produce a healthy infant, and it grows to a sufficient size, I release it. Into what's left of the wild."

Montoya had one hand on the pelican, while he gave Shaw a slow once-over through his thick glasses. A splat of dried mustard marked the front of Montoya's shirt. Now that Shaw had gotten a better look at his hair, he could see it was probably that way all the time, teased by neglect into a tangled mass of cobwebs.

"I knew you were a doctor. I didn't know you were a vet too."

"Have we met before, young man?"

"I dated Trula in high school. I used to tell you I'd have her in early, and you used to say, 'No you won't.' " He put out his hand. "Shaw Chandler."

Montoya drew a slow breath through his nose. He hesitated a moment before taking a weak grip on Shaw's hand and letting go. Turning his back to Shaw, he opened the medicine cabinet and withdrew a couple of chrome scalpels. He laid out some gauze pads and went to the sink and turned on both faucets. While he washed his hands, he looked over his shoulder at Shaw.

"What do you want with me?"

"Nothing," he said. "I just brought the bird."

"Don't be coy with me, Chandler. If you have a proposition, then go ahead, make it."

"I've apparently missed a step here somewhere," said Shaw.

Montoya turned, drying his hands on a towel, watching Shaw the way a matador might watch a bull. Shaw tried to smile, but he couldn't muster much of one.

"All right, never mind," the old man said, his voice hoarse. A valve had tightened somewhere in the old man's throat, narrowing an essential passageway. "You're going to have to leave. I've got to carve up this bird before it wakes. And I don't allow spectators at my operations."

Shaw shrugged, let himself out, ambled back to the El Camino and stood for a moment looking at the main house, then down the row of small cabins. Pines and palms silhouetted by moonlight. The sounds of those birds in their dark cages, their *jeets* and *krees*. Thirty years ago that place had probably been a fishing camp. Back when people still came to the Keys wanting as little as possible intruding between them and the night air.

He folded himself into the El Camino and slid the ignition key in. Now Trula's father had turned this place into a hospital for birds. He'd heard of places like this. He'd always thought well of them.

But Dr. Montoya bothered him. That huge swing in his anxiety level when Shaw told him his name. And the quirky kid with his porno novels. Shaw sat there for a moment more listening to the birds, wondering if maybe he should get out, go back, have a longer chat with Montoya.

————

When the muscle freak laid a moist hand on his elbow, Shaw jerked, banging his fist on the gearshift lever. The kid leaned down so his smile was even with Shaw's face.

"Want to see a naked actress?" he whispered.

Shaw looked into his dark, empty eyes.

"Not tonight." His hand moving toward the ignition key, stopped. Wavered there. Jesus, what was he saying? Trula?

"A naked actress in the flesh," the kid said. "A push in the bush, it's warm, it's wet, it's squooshy."

Shaw opened the door and the kid stepped back and put out his hand.

"I'm Dougie Barnes," he said.

Shaw extended his hand and Dougie took hold of it and tried briefly to realign Shaw's knuckles.

"She's down this way," Dougie said. "Be quiet."

9

The two of them stood shielded behind the fat, round leaves of a sea grape, looking down a small slope at a basin rimmed with coral boulders and tangles of mangroves. It looked like a small quarry three or four times larger than a backyard swimming pool. Someone had carved out enough limestone and coral for a house or two, then abandoned it.

The basin narrowed on one side to a five-foot-wide channel cutting through a bank of limestone, connecting the pool with the bay. There was a chain link fence across the mouth of the channel, making a cage for the lone dolphin that rolled in the moonlight.

Its skin shone like polished slate as it broke through the surface of the water and curled back into it, blatting and inhaling in that instant. Cruising every corner of its tank, it slowly increased its speed. Then abruptly it broke its rhythm to stay under a little longer, probably to suck down a mullet that had strayed into the pen. And in a sudden golden rush of water, it surged back to the surface, resumed its circling.

"That's Bravo," Dougie whispered. He was standing behind Shaw, his presence raising the barometric pressure in Shaw's gut.

The kid wasn't that big, really. He went five-ten, maybe. A couple of inches shorter than Shaw. But his body was sharpened to such an edge that Shaw felt flabby next to him. As the dolphin rolled and glided in the dark, Shaw thought he could feel the tickle of Dougie's glance on his back and neck, as if the kid was choosing points of attack.

"That fish's been on public television," Dougie whispered close. "On one of those education shows about retarded children."

Shaw was disappointed, but relieved. Wishing it were Trula, glad that it wasn't.

"So," Dougie whispered, "how you ever gonna thank me?"

"For what?" said Shaw. "It's a dolphin. They're about as unusual as laughing gulls."

"You blind?" Dougie said. "That's not what we're looking at."

Shaw came out from behind the sea grape into a ragged spotlight the moon was throwing. He said, "I got to get going, man."

Dougie's numbing grip on his right biceps dragged him a step back behind the branches.

"You crazy?" Dougie hissed and dropped his arm.

Then Shaw saw her. In the wavering shadow and light, she was sitting on the smooth flagstone deck that had been laid at the northern edge of the pool, dangling her bare legs in the water. Her arms were crossed beneath her small breasts. The flutter of palm-frond shadows took her face in and out of the moonlight, but he saw enough to know it was her. With her hair in an uncustomary braid, her body thinner than he remembered. Still, there was no mistaking her. Trula Marie Montoya.

She was stretching her legs out, straightening her body, her bottom edging across the rocks, as she let herself down into the water, the shadows and moonlight marbling her flesh. With her hands behind her on the rocks, she guided herself carefully down.

The coppery light shone on her hair and lit the dark swatch between her legs. Thrusting her hips forward, she pushed off and slid into the basin. The dolphin continued to circle the quarry as Trula Marie Montoya wiped her eyes, squeezed the water from the braid, then breaststroked toward the center.

Shaw turned his back on the scene, though its afterimage burned fiercely behind his eyes.

"Scantily clad," said Dougie. "Terribly bad."

"I'm going."

"So go."

"We're both going."

"Fuck you, Charlie Brown. I want to watch her skinny-swim."

Shaw hesitated. He felt himself rise out of this moment, wavering to some point above the sea-grape tree. Having a brief debate with himself but not getting anywhere with it. He was a wimp if he left, a sleaze if he stayed. He listened to the lapping of the water, the dolphin's harsh breaths, not leaving but not turning either.

"You ain't gonna turn into no pillar of salt," Dougie whispered. "It's just a naked woman. What's wrong with you?"

When Shaw sighed and turned back to the lagoon, Trula was slicing through the water in an Australian crawl. She swam with her head high out of the water, in a smooth circle along the edge of the basin. The dolphin lapped her on an inside track.

"Nipples and hips and wide creamy lips," Dougie said, moving behind Shaw again, watching the spectacle from over his shoulder.

Bravo rolled and ducked into the glazed water and surfaced again just beside Trula, riding along with her as she pulled forward. They swam side by side for one full lap and then Bravo twisted to his right and bumped her, knocking her out of the rhythm of her stroke. She sputtered and laughed and began treading water near the far wall of the basin. Bravo eased over, mirroring her position, his rounded snout almost in her face.

"Foreplay," Dougie said. "Two play at foreplay."

And it did seem that way to Shaw. The dolphin held itself half out of the water just inches from Trula, with some invisible movement of its flukes. It was like the quivering tap of a male flamenco dancer, his feet moving at such a blur that nothing seemed to be happening. Just some heat, a sexual electricity charging the air.

"Watch this," Dougie said, and Shaw had the feeling that Dougie was watching him, getting off on Shaw's reaction as much as on the scene, though Shaw wasn't able to draw his eyes away from the water long enough to be certain.

The tension went out of the dolphin and it slid under the water. As it disappeared, Trula closed her eyes, leaning her head back. Then the dolphin rose up again, its skin now a pale saffron, as it seemed to slide across her skin belly to belly.

Shaw knew almost nothing about dolphin anatomy or behavior, so he wasn't sure what he was seeing. The dolphin lifted itself up again, this time almost completely free of the water, hanging there, glistening sheets falling from it, balancing unsteadily on its powerful tail. And then it let go and eased back into the water, its flesh riding close to Trula's body.

"Up and down," Dougie said. "Up and down."

Trula laughed again when the dolphin disappeared below the surface. The water on her face sparkled. She waited, scanning the pool expectantly. Bravo must have been gliding close to the bottom because the surface was unruffled. Trula edged away from the wall, breaststroking into the center of the quarry.

"Bravo," she called. "Bravo, come on, show yourself."

She swam a circuit of the pool, looking down into the dark water. Dougie shifted his stance, peeking through another break in the branches.

"Come on, Bravo, get out here," Trula said. And there was the muscle in her voice he remembered. The tone that she'd summoned whenever the script called for her to display her power. He'd suspected it, that her strength had never been just acting. From the way she moved, from that voice, Shaw had a feel for the woman Trula Montoya had become. She had something bright and solid inside her, something that gave her an uncommon leverage on the world.

"The fish's trying to spook her," Dougie said. "Warm her up for the kill."

Trula seemed to be gazing up toward where Shaw and Dougie stood, when the dolphin erupted from the center of the pool just behind her. She swiveled around and watched it hang in the air five, six, feet above her. For a long insane second it seemed that Bravo might have enough power in his body to suspend himself indefinitely in the thick night air. But he didn't. He belly flopped hard, rocking waves into the coral edge of the basin and speckling the rocks just below them with spray.

"Jesus Christ," Shaw said.

Dougie whispered, "They do this. It's their game, hide-and-seek." Then he sang quietly, "Slip slop, hide the mop."

"This is too weird," Shaw said and turned to leave. Dougie put a rough hand on his arm, halting him.

"No, it's not."

Shaw shrugged off the arm, but Dougie refastened it. The fingers locking hard to Shaw's right elbow.

"Hey, you been getting your rocks off, don't say you haven't," Dougie said. "You're my sex brother, man. You can't just walk off."

Shaw was shifting his feet, getting set to heave the kid aside when her voice sounded from the quarry.

"Dougie!" she called out. "Are you up there again, damn it?"

Trula was holding herself steady in the water, staring at the sea-grape tree. Bravo sped halfway across the pool and leapt into a silver corkscrew behind her, slicing back down headfirst, a splashless puncture in the water.

Cursing to himself, Dougie turned and broke into a run back up the trail. Shaw feinted in that direction but caught himself. He could run well enough, but this wasn't the time for it. Putting his hands in the pockets of his cutoffs, he stepped into the full moonlight and watched her.

She struggled out of the pool, hauling herself over the edge of rock, then toweled off quickly with her back to Shaw, stooping finally for her robe. The dolphin clicked and snorted at the edge of the basin. And Shaw felt the imprint of this moment burn deep into the tissues of memory.

Trula Montoya, her motions, her body, all of it lit by the crazy light of moon and adrenaline. The craggy knobs of her spine. Her sharp shoulder bones, like the vestiges of snapped-off wings. Her narrow thighs and muscled calves. The high, tight curve of her bottom. Whorls of golden hair on her upper arms and shiny ribbons of water running down her neck. All of it fixed deep and clear.

She came up the rocky path, through wavering shadows, patting her face with a white towel. Things were happening in his chest, flight and fight playing games with his blood pressure, heart rate, the muscles in his stomach.

She stood two feet away, wrapped in a white terry-cloth robe, her braid hung over the front of her shoulder, drizzling down the lapels of her robe. She stepped forward onto the same sandy patch where Dougie had been standing, and she tightened the belt of her robe and cocked her head forward to glare at this stranger.

"Who the hell're you?" she said.

It was too big a question. Every answer that came to him blocking the other. He said nothing, swallowed. Kept his hands in his pockets.

Trula angled for a more moonlit view of Shaw's face. She said, "And what the hell are you doing on my property?"

"I was sorry you died. I hated seeing it happen."

"What?"

" 'Hidden Hours,' " Shaw said, "it *was* your idea, wasn't it, writing Cassie Raintree out of the show? That's what I thought. You needed a break, wanted to challenge yourself with harder parts."

"Oh no," she said.

"Wait, wait," he said, taking a step back. "I'm not some loony fan." He showed her his open hands. "I just brought a bird by for your father, and I happened on this place afterward. I saw you. Recognized you."

She shook her head, and a faint softening of her features came and went. "And you watched me, with Bravo, just now?"

"Yeah," he said. Trying to get into the word the fact that he wasn't at all sure what he'd seen.

"So," she said, "are you a longtime peeper, or you just trying it out?"

"You don't remember me," he said. "It's been so long, I slipped right out of your mind."

Though it was lushly warm, she crossed her arms below her breasts and hugged herself as if she were chilled. He felt his body organs sinking inside him.

"Remember you?"

"Shaw Chandler," he said. "From high school."

She stiffened, took a step sideways. Poising herself, as if she were about to sprint up the slope.

"I've given everything I can," she said. "That's it."

"What?"

"You heard me," she said.

Bravo made a thrashing run across the whole length of the pool, Trula turning to watch, as he fired himself up into the air, did one twist, two, reaching up, holding there in a fantastic suspension of gravity. Then falling, heavily and without grace to crash onto the hard bed of water, as though he were trying to splash every gallon of it back into the sea.

"Well, you've got me confused with someone else," Shaw said. "I don't want anything from you."

She eased her stance a degree but was still tense.

"Really," he said. "I'll just go. I'm sorry I bothered you."

"No, wait," Trula said. Weighing it, taking a couple of careful breaths. "Okay, maybe I do have you mixed up with somebody."

"Jesus," he said. "You had me scared. I thought maybe I'd stumbled into a 'Hidden Hours' plot there for a second."

"I'm sorry," she said.

Trula put out her right hand, holding her robe closed with the left. Shaw shook her hand. It was thin and cool, bony. Her grip firm, but not a lot of power behind it.

The dolphin made a short leap, splashed. Then another one, another splash. Then began to cruise aimlessly through the pool, dipping, rising, in an impatient series of zigzags.

"Why don't I just get my ass out of here?"

He watched her breathe through her nose, her eyes on his, her arms again crossed tightly across her chest. Her eyes seemed to be growing friendlier, or maybe that was the wash of moonlight. She was meeting his eyes, shaking her head as if she were running through her options. Those lips relaxing, parting slightly so he had a glimpse of her teeth. He was trying to slow this down. Break it into the details, so he could bring them out later and savor them. The perfect shape of her ears, the flecks of gold she wore in each lobe. Her wide-spaced, intense eyes, those incredible eyebrows, the swan curve of her neck.

"You brought a bird to my father," she said. Getting the evidence straight, going to settle on his sentence.

"A pelican," he said. "With a broken wing."

She looked down at Bravo who seemed to have lost heart, just circling half speed, sewing a seam around the edge.

"You live here still? In Key West?"

"My mother's in bad shape," he said. "I came home the other day to see what I could do."

Trula softened her stance a bit.

"Shaw Chandler," she said. "Of course I remember you."

"Good or bad?"

She considered it for an agonizing moment and said, "Good." She smiled. "Yeah, I remember you very well. We had something there, didn't we? For a month or two."

"A month or two," he said. "That's all it was?"

They turned and watched the dolphin swim lazy circles of the quarry.

He said, "You got time now to take a walk, a drive?"

"A drive?" she said, and tipped her head to the side and raised an eyebrow at him. "What? In a surrey with a fringe on top?"

"They don't take walks in New York? Get-reacquainted walks?"

"Not that I know of." Smiling, making him work.

"Well, how do they do it in Leewood? How was it you met Malden Aimes, for instance? I forget."

"You don't remember the famous sauna room scene?"

"I must've been out on a call."

She turned from him, looked down at Bravo.

"Well, you missed a good one, then," she said. "Malden Aimes was chasing a bad guy through Cassie's health club, and he lost his guy and wound up walking into the women's sauna."

"And there you were."

"Yeah."

"Wrapped in a towel," Shaw said.

"No, just me and my sweat," Trula said. "No towel. At least that's how it looked on TV."

"A walk would be enough for me," said Shaw.

"I guess so," she said. "After tonight, you don't have a lot left to see."

"It's dark," he said.

"It's a full moon."

"Maybe you forgot," Shaw said. "But I already saw everything twenty years ago."

"Well, it's not exactly the same thing, after all that time."

"No," he said, watching Bravo swim. "It's much better now."

"Shaw Chandler," she said, musing on it.

"How about tomorrow night? A regular date? Like old times."

She was still wary, but finally a small smile showed, and she nodded, there under a coconut palm with the birds screaming from their cages.

"We were just playing," Trula said. "Bravo and I."

"Yeah, I could see that."

"He's happy I'm home," she said. "We're old friends."

"I'm happy too," Shaw said.

———

When he got home, his mother was lying on the couch, watching a fifties black-and-white movie. A sixty-foot crab was threatening an isolated village along the coast of California.

When he said hello, she gazed up at him, her eyes bewildered by rum. She shushed him, holding a finger to her lips, and said, "This is the good part."

Shaw sat down in the chair beside her. The crab seemed to have chosen a blond girl as his special victim. Terrorizing her at the beach at night. Following her to her bedroom. All that in ten hectic minutes.

A chopper-dicer commercial came on. Silently, they watched carrots, boiled eggs, radishes sliced into hundreds of identical pieces. When the show came back on, the blond actress was praying in a small chapel. People in the congregation fidgeted, looking over their shoulders, whispering to their doomed friends. They could hear the giant crab's approach, sense the vibrations in their pews. The candles on the altar shook, and the long lantern chains that ran from the ceiling began to sway.

Shaw leaned forward to see into his mother's eyes. The rich blue they had always been was diluted now by the boozy froth that filled her veins. Staring at the disintegrating chapel, the sharp pincers breaking through the stained-glass windows, she smiled. A twinkle flirted at the corner of her eye.

"Those radish choppers never work," she said.

"Nothing you can buy for under twenty dollars works," Shaw said. "Except maybe a dozen shrimp."

"And they only work when the tide's right," she said. She smiled at him. It was a strain for her to do it, he could see that. But she was trying. At least she'd started to try.

"We need to talk, Mother," he said.

"I know we do." She turned her eyes back to the TV. "Soon," she said. "We'll talk soon. I'm almost ready."

And on the screen, crab claws shattered the stained-glass windows and those old church walls began to cave in. The plaster saints, the prophets, all the statues glowing with God teetered and fell, shattering to a powdery, eye-stinging dust.

10

Dougie Barnes was sitting fifteen feet up in the air, driving the Munch and Crunch, a diesel Bomag bulldozer. Its steel wheels were six feet high, orange and knobbed with blunt spikes. The wheels weighed five tons, then throw in another two tons for the dozer and there wasn't much of anything the machine couldn't destroy. It was Dougie's job to drive the crusher across couches and tables and chests of drawers, pulverize them so they'd fit into the furnace of the Key West recycling plant.

Dougie finished flattening a pile of wood chairs and ran the Bomag over to the east slope of the landfill, where somebody had dropped off a truckload of building materials, wooden forms, plywood sheets, pine planks. He revved up that big diesel to get over a little hill, somebody's radio–TV–record player combination in a big cherry cabinet. In his rearview mirror, Dougie watched it come out flat from under the Munch and Crunch, no sweat.

It was just after sunrise, Saturday. A quiet week and a half since he'd lynched the old lady and shot the old man. Over the last week he'd spent a lot of time teaching his parrot, getting laid twice by two different girls, runaways, sixteen, seventeen years old. And now out here, doing his job, munching and crunching. People were throwing out their garbage all over the island just now and Dougie was waiting for it here at the landfill.

Goosing the Bomag once or twice just out of sheer bad-ass pleasure, he turned the wheels straight ahead, downshifted into first, getting some torque to crush a broken-down four-poster bed. Picturing it with an old man lying there, an old woman lying beside him. Got the heavy, spiked wheels rolling. Yeah, rolling, rolling, rolling. Keep those dogies rolling.

Dougie had every detail of the factory memorized, every number, dash and fraction. Because he loved this place, and wanted to work here forever, and he knew goddamn well that being the boss's son wasn't any guarantee he would keep his job. His father, being the total asswipe he was, was likely to fire Dougie someday for not knowing that the ash conveyor was a Huot drag chain and screw type or the boiler had a steam flow of twenty one thousand pounds an hour.

After Dougie finished munching this trash, he'd get onto the D-7 Caterpillar with the front hoe, and scrape the garbage over to the concrete pit, twenty feet deep, two hundred across. Then he'd climb up to the crane cage two stories above the tipping floor, and he would lower his bucket to scoop and fluff up the garbage, sifting through it, looking for gasoline cans or other explosive materials that might blow up in the furnace.

When he was pretty sure it was safe, Dougie would scoop up around four tons of garbage and drop it on the conveyor belt. The conveyor ran into the two mass-burn incinerators rated at seventy-five TPD. In that furnace all the shit no one wanted anymore in Key West was roasted in a seventeen-hundred-degree fire. The char dropped through the belt of the conveyor into a quench tank.

The heat that was produced ran the big Zurn boilers, made water into steam to spin the Coppus Murray turbines at 4,478 RPMs. Those turbines cranked out a max of two thousand kilowatts of electricity an hour. The steam condensed back into water, and the extra heat was let out of the Baltimore air cooling tower at a flow rate of two hundred GPM. The smoke coming out of the towers was shot through with fifty thousand volts to purify it. From the daily combustible garbage, the plant produced 5 percent of Key West's electrical power.

He liked knowing all the numbers and showing off in front of girls. Though it'd been a terrible struggle learning them. A couple of years ago, he'd just hung around, coming out to the plant with his father and walking around gawking, shooting the shit with the guys, and generally getting in the way. Asking them over and over how this or that worked, the names for every little switch and knob.

Then little by little, he'd put it together, what all the dials on the stokers and turbines and boilers were for, getting the numbers and the right names. Until one day in the winter a year ago, when a job came open, Dougie got a guy he knew to fill out his application form and turn it in and he showed up at the interview, sitting down across from his father, smiling and giving him every goddamn correct answer to every goddamn question he asked.

At the end of the interview Douglas Barnes said, "All right, I'll hire you, but it isn't because you're my son. You're just not quite as stupid as the other six guys who applied."

That's the way the old man was to him, and had been all his life. Never cutting Dougie any special slack. Still treating everybody the same way, including his own son, like he'd treated brain-dead swabbies. The man had run the Key West Naval Base for years, lording it over two thousand men. Now at the plant, all he had were four men on each shift. Had to be tough on the old fart.

Dougie loved the garbage plant because it was big, loud and dangerous. He liked watching the needles quivering on the boilers, the steam rising up to five hundred degrees, the crank and scream of the conveyor belt carrying all that shit into a seventeen-hundred-degree hellfire. He liked the Al-Jon compactor that could crush Volkswagens into air conditioners, and all that noise and steam building up in the turbines. Dougie could sit out on the Bomag bulldozer, a hundred yards from the plant, and feel the tension of the place, the power and pressure inside all that steel. The throb of it, like the place had a twenty-four-hour-a-day hard-on.

———

Later in the waiting room of Barnes Waste Management Enterprises, Dougie Barnes sat staring at the receptionist. He had showered and changed after a long day of munching and crunching, and now was wearing a white tank top, blue stonewashed jeans and flip-flops. He had on a Panama hat with a lizardskin band and a gold staple earring in his left ear. The yellow-nape Amazon parrot rode on his right shoulder. He'd named it Jerkoff. It'd turned out to be a hell of a talker. Dougie liked talkers, he was one himself.

"Hugger-mugger," the bird croaked. "Tip-top, hotshot."

Dougie took a sunflower seed from the bag in his lap, handed it up to Jerkoff.

"I'm teaching him rhymes."

She hummed at him from behind her magazine.

"Itty bitty titty," Jerkoff said. He hopped, getting a better perch on Dougie's trapezius, bending over for another seed.

"Fuck a duck," Dougie said. "Fuck a duck."

"Please, Dougie," the receptionist said, her magazine still in front of her.

"You wouldn't believe how good this bird is at picking up girls," Dougie said. "The sunset chicks love him. I go down to Mallory Square every afternoon, stand around. Next thing, I got five teeny-boppers wanting to feed him, talk to him. Good pickings."

She put down her magazine and looked over at Dougie and made a smile. He could tell she didn't mean it.

He said, "Anybody ever tell you you were gorgeous?"

"All the time," she said. She lifted her magazine again. On its cover was a woman who looked exactly like her, only wearing a gold slinky dress.

When the receptionist took a breath, two veins stood out on her skinny neck. Dougie knew he could hook a finger behind one of them and pull it to the surface, like digging up a root or a worm.

If he did that, blood would spill down the front of her white blouse, and the blotch might form the face of Jesus Christ. Maybe people would crawl on their knees for miles to worship her bloody blouse. He could stand there and collect their dollars, get rich. Why not? Strange things happened in the world.

He said, "I want to have sex with you."

She kept the magazine in front of her face.

"Don't talk like that, Dougie."

"I want to have repeated intercourse with you," he said. "We could forge bridges to dark secret regions of ourselves."

She lowered the magazine and looked at Dougie again.

"We could discover our true beings, encounter the vast glowing centers of our reptile brains. We could fuck repeatedly."

She sighed again, and said, "Dougie, I already got a boyfriend. A jealous boyfriend."

"You ever seen anybody do this?"

He dug in his pants pocket and came out with a cherry stem, held it up for her to see. Then opened his mouth and dropped it in.

He chewed it around in there for a minute, working it hard with his tongue. The receptionist watched this spectacle, shaking her head. In a minute Dougie opened his mouth, stuck out his tongue and the cherry stem was there, tied in a tight knot.

He took it out of his mouth, stood up, brought it over to her and laid it on her empty desk.

"I can do things ordinary people can't. Extraordinary things of wit and cunning."

She touched the cherry stem with her pencil, poked it. She looked up at Dougie, her face flushed. Still shaking her head, but not negative anymore. Dougie was sure if he was stuck out here in the waiting room for ten more minutes, he'd have her sliding off her underpants.

He said, "You have magnificent breasts and a splendid tush."

"Thank you," she said.

"I could insert rubber products into you," he said. "Make you cry out the names of the lost ages. The secret codes of the universe. You'd be reborn in white light and perfect joy."

"Jesus Christ, Dougie, stop it, just stop it."

"Creepy peepie," the parrot said.

She slapped the magazine down and drew in a deep breath.

Dougie Barnes could feel the words rushing up like swarms of rabid bats from some shadowy cavern inside himself. The words swirled up toward the fresh air. Often he listened to himself talking and was amazed. He loved to talk. Skittering bats flocking out of his mouth.

"Fiddle faddle, flim-flam," his bird said. "Hanky-panky."

He fed Jerkoff a seed.

"Slip, slop, hide the mop," Dougie said. "Heebie-jeebie."

When the receptionist's buzzer sounded and she said Dougie could go in, he stood up and adjusted the white tank top. It showed off his physique better than a regular shirt. He knew she was watching his muscles. He could feel her eyes running across the ridges in his triceps. He flexed them for her. Her name was Jane. She had veins in her neck. Worms wriggling from one part of her to another part.

When Dougie snapped the rubber heels of his tennis shoes together and saluted him, Douglas Barnes bowed his head and sighed. The boy, even on a good day, was an ordeal.

"Yo, Negro," Dougie said.

"At ease, boy."

Dougie popped to parade rest.

Barnes took a deep breath and shook his head sadly.

He was standing behind his oak desk, same one he'd used as a naval officer. It wasn't anything special. Might've been the teacher's desk in an eighth-grade history class. All the same, Douglas liked it. Liked its solidness, the thrift of using it still. But he had no sentimental attachment to it, or any other thing on earth.

His office was decorated with more of his old navy furniture. An American flag on a flagstand, a black-and-white photo of the current president, a set of gunmetal gray filing cabinets. A couple of armless oak chairs. A whole wall devoted to photos of ships he'd commanded and visiting dignitaries he'd escorted around the base. He'd met his share of presidents.

On the other wall was his sword collection. Samurai swords he'd started buying forty-five years ago when he'd been just an ensign, stationed in Okinawa. It was there that he'd seen his first samurai museum, the swords, the silk robes, the gloves, wax figures of them in fighting poses, and Barnes had felt a powerful thrill, a sense of recovering something he'd lost. This was why he'd gone into the armed forces in the first place. To fight. To be a lifetime warrior.

Afterward he'd always kept a wall for the swords, to remind him how he was different from the civilian world. He walked a higher road, had a higher purpose, a more stringent moral order. His warrior code drove him still, brightened his blood, gave him a keener view: The power that his nation enjoyed in the world had been won by military men like him. It was his special mission, even in official retirement, to continue the vigil against the simpering civilian population. Those bloodless fools who were always looking for ways to emasculate the armed forces. Whatever was required to keep the military strong, he would manage. Even if it meant removing a weak sister civilian occasionally, then by God, he would keep his talons sharp for the task.

Barnes clicked his ballpoint pen and looked at his son locked into parade rest. The boy had a pair of lady-killer eyes. Green, the color of a rare French cologne. Lashes out to here. That part he got from his mother, a beautiful Brazilian lady. Last Douglas had heard, she was married to a movie star, living on the guy's ranch in Montana. Twenty-eight years ago, the lady had given birth to Dougie, taken a long look at him, taken a look at her husband, and split. Leaving Douglas Oliver Barnes to raise this aberration alone.

Besides her eyes, Dougie had her jeering smile and her thick black hair. No question about it, the boy was a beauty. Barnes had seen gorgeous women come up to the boy on the street, stutter a few words, aching to touch that hard, tanned flesh. But when they'd had a longer look, or hung around till he showed them how his brain worked, the sane ones were gone. Fast. Dougie could suppress it for an hour, maybe two, but eventually it would erupt. These word games, the sex talk. The boy's feverish libido running the show.

"Okay, Dougie. Enough of this. At ease."

Dougie came out of his pose, smiled.

"Wingtip, hotshit," he said. "Singsong, Ping-Pong."

"Let's give the vocabulary a rest, too, shall we?"

"I'm extremely fond of the word *tush,* at the moment," he said. *"Tush,* and *push, bush* and *whoosh.* Words with echoes."

"Scantily clad," the bird said. "Terribly bad."

"Hey, way to go, Jerkoff," Dougie said, and smiled. He put his finger out and the bird hopped off his shoulder onto it. It ruffled its feathers and took a white stringy shit on the carpet. Dougie turned his smile on his father.

Barnes watched the bird crane its head under its wing, preening. Barnes dropped his voice, glanced at the closed door. "I wanted to talk to you, Dougie, about our secret activities."

"I killed them," he said. "A man, and also a woman."

Douglas sat down, giving the ballpoint a workout.

"I know, Dougie."

"I shot the man, hung the woman," Dougie said. "I committed suicide on them both."

"That's one thing I wanted to discuss with you."

"Jane's veins," Dougie said. "Jane's main veins."

"The thing is, boy," Douglas said, sitting down in his chair, trying to keep his voice even, "Dougie, if I give you another secret activity to do for me, I have to know you won't go inventing extra things to do. Like you did when you killed the woman last week. I don't want you trying to use your own mind on any of this. If I give you a job to do, I want to be sure you'll do it exactly as I say, nothing more, nothing less. Is that clear?"

"Yes, sir." The boy's face getting shadowy, shoulders dropping, his mood starting to swing.

"If I ask you to drive a stake through somebody's heart, what're you going to do?"

"Drive a stake through somebody's heart."

"Good."

"This makes four corpses," Dougie said. "Four full-frontal suicides I committed on people."

Barnes said, "I want you to forget all four of these people, every single detail. I don't want you dwelling on the past. The past is meaningless, Dougie. The future too. All that counts is now. Right now, and right here, the tick of this second."

"I did the Capeletti brothers," the boy said, smiling, trying to coax some gratitude out of his father.

"Yes, you did them good."

Back in October Dougie had come into his office, walked up to Barnes's desk, his face sly and cocksure, and let the newspaper clipping flutter onto the desk. Then he stepped back, expectant and proud, a cat dropping a mouse on the doorstep.

For the previous three or four weeks, Douglas Barnes had been ranting about the Capeletti brothers. The guys had won an army contract to dispose of hazardous wastes, then discovered they didn't know what the hell they were doing. So Barnes had accepted a truckload of refrigerator coolant from the two jerks. Stuff was full of PCBs. But he'd burned it anyway, at considerable risk to his business enterprises, and dug a hole in the back of the landfill and buried the gloppy char. And then the Capelettis had refused to pay. Eight thousand dollars. They'd told him he could go cry to the EPA, the DA, whoever he wanted to. Go take a flying interstate fuck, for all they cared.

Dougie had overhead all this, his father's ranting, and somehow, the dimwit had booked himself a flight up there, located the chemical plant, and had gone in there and held the two assholes' heads down in a vat of one of their products. The newspaper article described it as a gangland slaying. The police were baffled. Douglas had looked up at his son after he read the article, and the boy was smiling. Douglas had said, "You?"

"I did it to win your love and affection."

"Well," Douglas had said, "it's a start in the right direction."

Dougie said, "I held them under till they didn't gurgle."

Amazing. The boy's IQ was in negative numbers, and he'd taken down those two big-time New Jersey punks.

But even with that, Douglas had still been afraid things would go wrong with Hanson Chandler. So a week ago Wednesday when Dougie went after Hanson, Douglas had attended the city commission meeting and had spoken on behalf of the Sierra Club that was trying to stop a swank new housing project. One of Key West's most prominent businessmen taking a radical antidevelopment stand. People in the audience murmuring. Up there at the podium he'd given it his best elocution in front of a full house while Dougie was up in Miami taking his id out for a gallop.

"Killer diller," Dougie said to the bird. "Harum-scarum, rip and tear 'em." He smiled at his father and gave the parrot another seed. "You should say how proud you are of me, killing the old lady and the old man. You should say the words."

"I am, Dougie," he said. "I'm exceedingly proud of you. Proud and amazed."

"Now you got something else for me to do, huh?"

"As a matter of fact," he said, "as a matter of fact, I do."

"Hot diggety dog diggety boom, what you do to me, it's so new to me, what you do to me."

"Take this," Douglas said, holding out a white pad of paper and the ballpoint. "I want you to write this down in your own hand, keep it with you, check yourself against it."

"What you do to me, it's so new to me." Dougie took the pad and pen, sat back down. Fed the bird another seed.

"Write Waldorf," Barnes said. *"W-a-l-d-o-r-f."*

Dougie printed that in pencil on the pad. *"D-o-r,* what?"

"F," Barnes said. *"D-o-r-f."*

"Oh," Dougie said. "Waldorf."

His father nodded his head, looking out the window of his office.

"Have you been practicing your reading, son, like you promised?"

Dougie, staring at his hand moving across the pad, said, "You want me to do the same thing to Waldorf I did to the old man and his wife?"

Barnes sighed. "You know, Dougie," he said, "I saw this program on the TV about a bunch of morons who could do things, play the violin, the piano. They hear a Beethoven symphony one time and play it back."

"Make it look like a suicide?" Dougie said. "Like that?"

"These idiots can't tie their shoes or walk across a street, but they can give you the square root of kingdom come."

"Suicide's my specialty."

"I'm starting to think you may be one of those," his father said. "Telling shit from Shinola gives you severe problems, but you seem to have a genius for killing people." Barnes came around from behind his desk and stood right in front of Dougie. "At least that's what I'm hoping," he said. "That's what I'm gambling on."

"Waldorf," Dougie said, "Waldorf." Looking like he was trying to find a rhyme for it, but not coming up with a thing.

"At least," his father said, "if you screw it up, get caught, well hell, with your mental health record, they'll probably put you away in a nice country club hospital somewhere, sit you in a rocker on a veranda, let you play croquet the rest of your damn life."

"Croquet, hooray," Dougie said. "Wicket, whack it, cricket, crack it."

———

It was after midnight. Dougie sat up in his bed in the long, dark room. The moon was lighting the room well enough, he could dress without turning on the lights, not take a chance on waking his father down the hall. He stood in front of the room's one window while he dressed and looked out at the moon behind some waving palm fronds.

As much as he liked this house built on a canal a mile from the garbage plant, it was no place to bring girls. He had to sneak them in through the garage to get them into his room. Then while he screwed them, he was worried the whole time his father would open the door on them and curse them out for being so noisy. The old man had done that a few times.

Dougie got his clothes on, opened his window, stepped out onto the wood deck, and tiptoed to the driveway. Out on the road, he jogged, the night air cool, Dougie running easy. In a while, he cut across an edge of the landfill, past the Bomag bulldozer, and into a thick stand of mangroves. He waded through some water up to his ankles, sloshed around there for a minute till he found the trail and then headed inland about two hundred yards.

It was just a shack, a hovel. That's what one of the girls had called it. Dougie's hovel. Made from lumber and plywood and scraps of tin siding he'd rescued from the garbage bin. It had an old mattress in the middle of the dirt floor, and a roof that was half open. A moon roof. There wasn't a door on it yet, and only three sides.

He had a Styrofoam cooler that he kept full of ice and Busch beer, and a table and two chairs. He had a brass candlestick, and some old calendars for decoration on the walls. There was a view of the water, and Roosevelt Boulevard over in Key West. And he'd lie there with one of his girls and they'd look over there and talk about things. And they'd screw.

Dougie came into the clearing and stood looking at his house for a minute. The white-haired girl he'd met in town yesterday was in there playing her little radio. Arlene. He could see her shadow as he approached. He'd get some nooky tonight, and they'd lie on the mattress afterward, cooling off, and Dougie would see if he could get her to cuddle him, get her to let him lay his head on her shoulder, his lips touching her naked breast. Some of them let him do that.

11

The waiter was standing beside Shaw as they looked at their plates. He was a young man with a ponytail and a European accent who'd said his name was Charles. He seemed to be lingering for their approval.

Shaw wasn't much on posh restaurants, and this one was a doozy. The food looked more painted than cooked. Lots of white space on the plate. Every strand of lobster, every flake of zucchini and curl of sauce had been painstakingly put right there. You didn't eat food like that. You discussed it, got a degree in it. Shaw wanted to look at it a little longer, pay for it and leave. Go down Simonton to the Full Moon Saloon and get a slice of fried grouper smothered in cheese and onions and mushrooms.

It was Shaw's fault they were here. He'd asked around on the docks today, What was the best restaurant in town? The best? Mira's the best. That's what they all said. But you don't want to go there. No, why not? You don't have enough jewelry for that place, they said. But Shaw called, made reservations.

"So," Shaw said, glancing at the waiter. "Which end is up?"

Trula said, "It looks beautiful, Charles."

Charles bowed and said he was extremely pleased, and should they desire anything else, anything whatsoever, he would be hovering in the next plane of existence ready to swoop down and attend their slightest whims.

The wine was affecting Shaw, heating up his face. And being this close to Trula, seeing her dressed in a simple white sundress that dipped just low enough to show the freckled tops of her breasts, a pearl necklace, her hair thick and loose down her back with a peach hibiscus blossom pinned above her right ear. He felt a soft thunder in his throat, in his gut, his hands.

All he'd brought with him to Key West were T-shirts and cutoffs. So he'd shopped that afternoon, found a pair of white ducks, a navy blue shirt with a tangle of pink flamingos on it. He'd even bought a pair of deck shoes. Now he was feeling like a teenager, sitting stiff and awkward inside these new clothes. He could smell his own cologne. And he'd even taken an extra five minutes combing his hair and a much closer look at his skin than he had in months, finding things that hadn't been there last time he'd checked, a spray of wrinkles and dark saggy places beneath his eyes.

She was raising her glass of wine, an Alsatian white she'd chosen from the thick list of wines, pronouncing the name effortlessly. And he was raising his and he said, "To great food."

"To coming home," she said.

He held his glass there, clinked hers again. "To coming home," he said. "And eating great food."

He watched her begin on her salmon, cutting a sliver off the corner, touching it to a white sauce flecked with green and red.

"I found my father dead last week," he said.

She looked at him, put her fork down.

"I've been trying to tell somebody," he said. "I tried for a week. A guy I worked with, my mother, anybody. The words get there into my throat, and they catch. I know what I want to say, but I can't bring it out. That ever happen to you?"

"Yes." Eyes on his. "All the time."

"I wasn't going to say anything to you. I mean, we were close once, but we were kids. I watched you for a year on TV, imagined who you'd become, and like that. But I don't pretend I know you. You're a stranger. Then, our dinner came out and I wasn't thinking of anything, and this wine was doing its job, and I had to say it. I was at work last week, fire rescue, a normal day, and I go into this house and there he was, my father, dead."

She closed her eyes and let go of a long breath.

"I hadn't seen him for twenty years, then there he is."

"It'll be okay," she said. She glanced around, raised her hand for Charles. "We'll go somewhere. You can talk about it."

"I was just going to take you to dinner, try some charm on you.

But it's been in there, in my throat. And I was relaxed just now, looking at you eating your salmon. And it came out."

"Your fish," Charles said from the clouds above them. "It is unsatisfactory?"

She looked up at Charles and asked him for the check, and he gave them both an imperious shrug and moved away.

Shaw said, "It was set up to look like a suicide. A fire set in the kitchen to cover things up. But it wasn't any goddamn suicide. I've tried to talk myself into believing it was, so I could let it go. My mother, she needs my help. The tackle shop is a mess. Both of us are going to starve if I don't get it making some money soon. But it wasn't a suicide. I'm positive of that. And I have to do something about it." He said, "I have to do something, but I don't know what."

Trula was staring blindly at the pink flamingos on Shaw's shirt, the light draining from her eyes.

———

Driving back to Trula's, he described the night he'd found his father dead and coming back later the same night to fight the fire. Telling her the trivial details, all the knickknacks on the walls of that house, the parrot saying, "Who's a good boy? Who's a good boy?" He heard himself rattling on, giving her a fifteen minute crash course in his recent history, but wasn't able to stop himself.

As they pulled onto the dirt road that ran between the pelican pens and the cabins, she reached over and put her hand on the back of his neck and massaged him lightly. And out in the distant latitudes of his heart, he felt those familiar clouds collecting, their slow, ominous swirl taking shape. His goddamn emotions getting away from him.

He parked the El Camino near her cabin and followed her silently down to the dolphin pool. For a few moments they stood watching Bravo cruise the quarry, stitching a flickering seam in the water. Beyond the pool, moonlight smoldered on the bay. A boat was rumbling across the water, an old wooden yacht, forty feet or so, plowing up a wake of foam. Rolls of the shining water spread slowly toward them.

Shaw was embarrassed by all his jabber now. Feeling unbalanced and foolish as he heard the echoes of his voice, the strain of self-pity in it. Now he just wanted to let the silence grow around them, blot out the words.

Standing beside her, his bare arms an inch from hers, he could make out her aroma, musky with a hint of lime. And he saw the fine glint of hair on her arms, and the narrow gold chain she wore at her wrist. A ring on her right hand, a single pearl in a raised setting.

He moved slowly behind her, hesitated, then put his arms around her waist, drew her close. She stiffened, but he kept his arms there.

"I don't know, Shaw," she said.

"What?"

"If I can anymore."

"Can what?"

"Do it," she said, "the physical part, *or* the emotional for that matter."

"Why? What's wrong?"

"Your daddy's dead," she said, "and you want some comfort. But I don't know if I have any to give."

"What're you saying, Trula?"

She stroked his hands where they were clasped at her waist.

"We tried this before, you know. It didn't work out."

"We were young," said Shaw. "We weren't ready for it."

"Are we ready for it now?"

"I think I am," he said.

She shook her head and turned in his arms, laid her head against his chest, her right ear over his heart. He breathed in her hair, a mild lime.

"Hear anything in there?" he said.

"Sounds like the Fourth of July."

"Yeah," he said. "That's how it feels." Holding her tighter. And when finally she drew back slightly and gazed up at him, he kissed her. Trula returned it, tentatively, polite, but with some curiosity, her lips thin and cool.

But as the kiss lasted, he felt her nudge deeper into the embrace, her lips loosening, softening, felt a sheen of sweat on her bare back, and he drifted deeper into that kiss, as her hands came up to his head, tangling and tugging in his hair and pressing his mouth harder against hers. And both of them shifted and leaned and pressed their bodies into each other, until he felt his fear fall away, and he lost the pull of time, the grip of gravity. Nothing but this, these mouths searching, these arms, this scent. And his hands lowered to her bottom, taking each half of it in a palm, pulling her forward, helping the thrust she was already making.

"It's been a very long time," she said, her voice hoarse and unsettled.

"For me too," Shaw said.

"Come on," she said. She stepped out of the embrace and led him down the path toward her cabin.

They made it to the end of the row of cages. He halted her with a hand on her arm and she turned. They stepped into another embrace, found the fit they'd just had, improved on it. They kissed, first a series of experimental ones that grew gradually warmer, their mouths opening. She stretched in his arms, digging deeper into the warmth, beginning to tremble. He felt himself swell against her thigh, felt her press back. The dizzy torture.

They stumbled sideways against the chain link pen, leaned there, Shaw's back to it. Both of them breathing hard and kissing. She dropped a hand between his legs, brushed him. He slid his hands over the shape of her hips, higher to her rib cage, lifting her breasts with the heels of his hands. They staggered against the wire cage walls and she pulled away from him.

"I don't know, Shaw. I don't know about this."

"Me either," he said.

He followed her into the empty pen as the pelicans in the adjoining one eyed them nervously, edging backward. A tub of water sat in the center of the pen, the moon floating in its center. Coral rocks, twists of driftwood littered the sandy floor. A bed of straw had been laid out along one side of the pen. He fought his pulse, took an extra breath, brought it in deep and slow.

Yesterday, when he had allowed himself to fantasize this moment, it had been a slow, wordless ballet. The heat rising as each button came free, each zipper lowered. A saxophone smoking to a crescendo in the background. All very dopey and theatrical, like a scene from "Hidden Hours." Not this uncertain staccato way it was unfolding.

Trula unbuttoned her dress, her eyes lowered. She stepped out of it and spread it flat against the bed of straw. She might have been at home, undressing alone in her room. While her back was to him, Shaw pried off his shoes. She turned and faced him in her white bikini panties and her string of pearls, standing there as if she were allowing him a moment to view her body, attune himself to her. She was still trembling, a candle flame in a light wind, only her eyes holding steady. Then she turned and lay down on her dress, and watched him as he drew off his flamingo shirt, his pants.

When he had pulled down his undershorts, and stood above her stiff, she hooked her thumbs into her panties and drew them down. Shaw made himself stand there, wait. Wanting to take a second to see her this way, in this light, and to let himself cool a few degrees, to get his mind back. To let the storm that was building inside him lose pressure, begin to break up.

Finally he kneeled beside her in the straw. She sighed and closed her eyes, and he slid his hand across her breasts, a finger testing each puckered nipple. Then stooped over her to taste them, lingering on the right, exploring the ridges and pebbles of the aureole, the taut stub of nipple. Moving his lips into the gully between her breasts, skimming his tongue across the brush of down on her stomach. Wanting to go faster, but fighting it.

She gripped his head, lifted it, guided his mouth upward to hers. After a breathless moment, he broke away, lowered himself again and settled his mouth onto her left breast. His hand moving down the slope of her belly, dallying briefly at her navel, deep and narrow. He slid his hand across the thin skin inside her hip points, then combed inch by inch through her abundant snarl of pubic hair, on a dazed journey to her heat and dampness.

And simultaneously she explored him, the hair on his chest, his small nipples, his belly and groin. Matching the movements of his hand, tuning her heat slowly to the same level as his.

"I don't know," she said again. "I don't know."

He moved his hand gently against her. And she opened to him.

He let go of a breath that he had been holding for years.

"There," she said. "And there."

He was silent.

"And there."

When he was embedded in her, lost to any knowledge of where they were, no longer feeling the prickle of the straw, or hearing the damaged pelicans shuffling in the nearby cage, no longer worried about keeping his feelings mild, just tangling, untangling in her arms, he felt himself sink and sink into her plush fit, her dark, narrow heat.

For the first time in his sexual life he wasn't aware of pacing or positioning himself for her maximum benefit or his own. They synchronized. His touch was hers. Her shudders his. Moans and sighs, fingernails sharp against flesh. It was effortless, and there were no words attached to anything. Together they made a wisp of flame, huddled over it, fed it and fanned it, till it began to sputter and crackle. As it moved through them, their bodies rocked with it. And when it reached their thickest parts, it became a roar, consuming them, spewing their remains upward, high into the dark atmosphere.

———

"You asleep?"

Trula's head was on his chest, her breath slow and even. Her right arm slung across his stomach.

"No," she said. "Are you?"

"Close."

He kissed her hair and she burrowed into his body. He looked across her shoulder at the line of pelicans and egrets in the adjoining cage. A half a dozen one-winged, one-legged and one-eyed creatures standing in a scruffy line staring at them.

"I think we're keeping the birds up past their bedtime."

"Shaw?" she said, her voice shaky.

"Oh, that guy? Yeah, he was around here a few minutes ago," Shaw said. "He should be back soon."

"I have to tell you something."

"Oh, God, I knew it," he said. "What's the guy's name?"

"No," she said. "There's nobody else."

He waited.

"Well?"

"Shaw," she said, "I think I know why your father was killed."

12

"He came to see me," she said. "Your father did. A couple of weeks ago in Manhattan."

"My father came to see you?"

"Hanson Chandler," she said. "Yes, your father."

"Oh, man, I love this. This is too good."

Trula lifted her head from his chest. She sat up, brushed her hair from her face. He looked up at her, at the sheen of sweat on her breasts, his sweat or hers, evaporating now.

"He wanted money," she said. "He conned his way past the security in my building, came to my door early one morning and the first thing he said when I opened it, he wanted cash."

Shaw kneaded his temple. If he could get some blood moving through there, maybe he'd wake up, this would disappear. Two pelicans still lingered a few feet away, long beaks, sad eyes. Staring at this naked couple, expecting an encore.

Trula said, "He'd seen me on 'Hidden Hours' and he came to New York to extort twenty-five thousand dollars from me. That's what he asked for, twenty-five."

She turned her hands in the light, examining them as though they had just sprouted on the ends of her arms. They were large, out of proportion to the rest of her, their backs mapped with dark veins. She lowered them and her gaze wandered off to the pelicans, and she said, "Last night when I caught you watching me, and you told me who you were, my first thought was that you were working with your father, and you were here to ask for more money. It's why I said what I did, that I'd given all I could."

"But you don't believe that now."

"No," she said, turning her face back to him, a rueful smile. "No."

"Okay," he said. "Now, my father's at your door, asking for money. Why in the hell is this happening?"

"Blackmail."

Down the row of cages a heron spoke a mournful phrase.

Trula said, "Your father claimed it was my dad, not him, who was responsible for the deaths of those two sailors, back when we were in high school. Pinkney and Chiles."

"Jesus Christ Almighty."

She nodded and said, "What he claimed was, my daddy paid him forty-eight thousand dollars to take the blame for the murders and to disappear, and he did it, sacrificed you and your mother and went into hiding for twenty years to cover up for my father's crime, and now he said it was turnabout time. He needed money for a cancer operation, and he needed it in a hurry. And the only collateral he had in the world was that crime he'd taken the blame for.

"He said if I didn't give him the whole twenty-five, he was going to have to risk coming back to Key West. He knew Dad didn't have any money anymore, but he said Dad's partner did. And he'd do whatever it took to get the money, put whatever pressure he needed to on Dad."

"Whose cancer operation did he say this was for?"

"He didn't."

"And those were his words? Sacrificed my mother and me?"

"Words to that effect."

"He have evidence of this bullshit? He show you anything?"

"If I didn't pay, he said he'd produce the evidence, and my father would spend the rest of his life in jail."

"Did you see it?"

"I believed him," she said. "I would've given him the twenty-five, but fifteen was all I could get."

"Why give him anything?"

"I had my reasons."

Trula was sitting up, snapping stalks of straw in half, setting them aside. A factory worker at her job, naked in the moonlight, getting all the straw just the right size.

A breeze was keeping the mosquitoes away, a warm current

coming from the Bahamas, or somewhere farther out, Aruba. Island air, ripe with odors, cinnamon or nutmeg, overripe bananas. Living in Miami all these years, he'd forgotten about those breezes. A perfect seventy-two degrees. Sitting across from a woman he had dreamed of, their bodies still tingling. It should have been the night of his life, the night he would measure every other night by.

"I'm sorry," he said, "but I'm having a little trouble with this, believing all this."

"What? Which part?"

"This stranger comes to you, gives you a line about your father being a murderer, and like that, you hand him fifteen thousand dollars."

"Whoa," she said. "He never said Dad murdered anybody. He said my father was responsible for their deaths. Those were his words. His exact words."

"Maybe you're leaving something out. Something big."

"I think what it is, Shaw," she said. "You're having trouble believing your father could have run off, abandoned you and your mother for cash. You'd rather think he was a murderer, did something out of passion and ran off. But cash. No, that's harder to take."

"Yeah," he said. "Maybe that's part of it."

"Well, think about it. Did your father have such a great life? I mean, people abandon their families every day, disappear, start over, and for a lot less reason than forty-eight thousand dollars. It happens all the time."

"In the soaps, maybe," he said.

She winced, took a breath.

"In real life, Shaw. In real life." She snapped a dozen stalks in half, and set them down with the others. Brushed off her hands.

"I'm sorry," he said. "I'm just . . . you know . . . confused. I'm sorry."

She nodded.

He said, "Okay, my father ran away. Nobody's arguing with that. But why the hell would he confess to a murder he didn't commit? Nobody would put themselves in that kind of jeopardy for cash. That's the part I don't see."

"I asked him that," Trula said. "And he said he didn't have a choice. It was either take the money and go into hiding, or stay here and go to prison or the electric chair. My daddy was going to make sure he got framed for the murder."

She took another slow lungful of air, and peered back through the dark at the two or three pelicans who were still hanging around. She seemed to be considering something, getting the words straight in her head before she spoke.

"That spring Pinkney and Chiles disappeared, I spent a month in the hospital with pneumonia. Totally out of it. And when I came home, something had happened to Dad. He'd started sitting out on the porch all night, embalming himself with bourbon, not sleeping, not speaking to me or anyone who stopped by.

"And when I asked him what was wrong, he would make himself another drink, bury himself in it. He kept pushing me away, and you had to know him, Shaw, how he was before, to see how terrible this was. Because he'd always been very loving, involved in everything, my acting, schoolwork, all of it. Ever since my mother died of tuberculosis when I was three, he'd been that way, very attentive, protective. Then, just like that, in a month he was changed.

"And it's haunted me, all this time, what happened to him. I worried I'd said something while I was feverish in the hospital. Maybe I'd hurt him with one of the ugly teenage speeches I was always giving back then. For years, I could drive myself crazy trying to remember it, what I'd done, how I made him that way.

"So when your father came to my door and told me his story, it snapped into focus. That spring, my dad, the way he'd been before, the way he was afterward. It explained it. Dad had done something wrong and he'd tried to cover it up, and he paid your father to take the rap. Then afterward, he had trouble living with the guilt of what he'd done."

Shaw touched her knee, trailed his fingertips down her sharp shinbone, feeling the bristle.

"It explained everything about that time, my father's depression, the land, quitting the navy when he did, everything."

"What land?"

"This land," she said. "Dad owned most of this end of Stock Island. The land the golf course is on, and the hospital. He even owned the dump. This was back when you didn't have to be a millionaire to own real estate here. His friends called it Montoya's folly, the chump's dump. But he didn't care, 'cause he had this dream, turning a big chunk of the island into a bird sanctuary. He was going to use his retirement pay from the navy and his savings, and start working on his dream."

"And?"

"And then this thing happened with Pinkney and Chiles. And that same spring Dad suddenly gave up his commission in the navy two years before retirement," she said. "He sold all the land except for these couple of acres. He moved out here. And suddenly we were poor. It was Spam instead of steaks. No new clothes. No allowance. Bill collectors coming around."

Shaw picked up a handful of straw, crumbled it and let it fall on the pile beside him.

She sighed, crossed her arms across her breasts, hugging herself against this moment.

"Some afterglow, huh?" he said.

She smiled and lowered herself and rested her head on his chest again, nuzzled for the right alignment. He felt her shiver.

"So, who is this partner of your dad's?"

"I don't know," she said. "I don't know."

In a few minutes she moved her head, sniffed. She raised up to look at him. Shaw could feel the heat in his chest, the glow. He had loved Trula Montoya once a long time ago, in the stupid and miraculous way a high school boy can love, and then he'd spent all those afternoons for the last year watching her, rekindling the feelings, adding to them. He should have known how primed he was. How difficult it would be to keep things mild this time.

He watched the pelican standing at the fence, still hanging in there, watching the two humans talking. That damned bird must have been starved for drama.

She dabbed her finger at his right nipple, teasing it stiff.

"And that's why you quit 'Hidden Hours'?" he said. "You came home to find out about all this?"

She sighed.

"No," she said. "Not exactly."

Shaw waited, but she said nothing. He could feel her slip deeper into her silence. A breeze rustled the palms. The birds rearranged themselves nearby.

"What? Is it a secret, why you quit?"

"I have trouble talking about it, so yeah, maybe it's a secret."

"Okay, that's all right," he said. "Secrets are fine. I don't mind if you have secrets."

Shaw watched the pelicans, moving around now, impatient.

"I had to quit the show," she said, "because I'm sick."

Shaw waited, touched her hair.

"I have MS. Multiple sclerosis. It's not contagious or anything, and it's not going to kill me, but it isn't going away either. That's why I came home."

He was quiet. He could hear her breathing. In the distance, the gabbling of one of the birds. Her breath against his chest. Both of them waited for the words to come from his throat. The right ones. While he waited he tightened his hold on her, and he felt something in her relax, her head went slack against his chest. He closed his eyes and held her hard.

"Tell me about it," he said.

And she did, with her ear against his chest, as if she were measuring his heart rate, pacing her words against what she heard there. Giving him only what he could stand.

Shaw had known only one person with multiple sclerosis. A guy on fire rescue who had developed it a couple of years ago. Morton White wasn't more than twenty-five when it happened. He'd dropped out of law school to be a fireman, and he'd just come on with the department for a couple of months, passing the tough physicals and written tests with no trouble.

Then within two months he had gone from peak health to hobbling with a cane. Shaw had visited him once, stopping by his house with a few of the other guys, dropping off some food and money they'd collected for him and his new wife. Morton looked at them in his living room and couldn't remember who they were at first, but by the time they were ready to leave, he was sitting there slumped in his chair, joking with them in his new slow voice, saying that he'd forgotten more in the last two months than the bunch of them had ever known. Everybody agreeing, chuckling, but angling toward the door.

Trula said hers wasn't the severe kind. She had the relapsing-remitting variety. Her immune system would be fine for a while, then something, stress or something internal, would set off an exacerbation. That's what they called it. And she'd get some new symptom, or some old symptoms would recur. The numbness in her legs, the double vision, fatigue. It might never get any worse than it was right then. Stay just there the rest of her life. Or it could get a little or a lot worse. You never knew. She had to keep going to a neurologist in Miami for tests, had to watch her diet, keep fit by swimming with Bravo. She said it wasn't going to go away, ever, but people lived with it. They had lives. They loved people, they got married, had children. Sometimes they got strong enough, they could even go back to work.

When she was finished, all the sleepy orgasm was gone from her voice. She kept her head against his chest, an arm across his rib cage, breathing against his nipple, keeping it tight.

He stared up at the patch of starry sky crisscrossed with thick wire mesh. The pelicans had left their post, accepted these newcomers and gotten back to their routines.

Shaw Chandler brought his head up, kissed the part in her dark hair, breathed in as much of her scent as he could hold.

"If you can handle it," he said, "then I can."

She made a noise in her throat. Maybe she believed him, maybe she didn't. He wasn't sure if he believed himself.

Her hand came out of the dark and found him.

Breathing carefully, closing his eyes, he leaned his head back, made some involuntary noises.

"There," he said, his voice croaking.

"You want to go back to my cabin?" she said quietly, still moving her hand. "I have a bed in there. I hear that's how humans do it."

"I don't know."

"What?"

"I don't know if I can move."

"What's wrong with you? I wear you out?"

"Your hands," he said, getting it out slowly. "Jesus, how do you do that?"

"I don't know," she said. "Right then, at that moment, I was imagining I was blind, putting everything right there. Right—" She had fingernails. Perfect length. "Right—there."

"Yeah," he said. Holding himself still. "God help me."

13

"I don't have a pain threshold," Dougie said to the girl at Club Medical. The bar was a little too neon and black velvet for Dougie, but it was near his hotel. He didn't want to stray too far, get lost and have to ask somebody for directions. Like his father told him before he left, Dougie had something memorable about him. He stuck with people.

It was Sunday morning, breakfast time, twenty-first of January. He was staying at the Hilton on Basin Street. Room 705. A suite with two double beds, a view of the Superdome and a credit card for a passkey. His father had told him to do it, stay a day or two in New Orleans before he went to Utah to do his job. Complicate his trail, put some zigs and zags in it. Dougie had just stood there, smiling his fucking head off, as his father went over every step of it, over it and over it. Finally, the old man giving him a little respect.

"At least," Dougie said to the girl at Club Medical, "my pain threshold is up there so high, I haven't found it yet."

The girl was wearing a sailor's cap on top of her chopped-off red hair. Leather blouse, matching black leather pants. She had freckles. Dougie liked freckles. He liked them a lot. You looked at them long enough, took your eyes out of focus, you started to see pictures in them.

"So if I stuck a fork in your hand," the girl said, "you're saying you wouldn't feel it?" She sipped a black drink from a glass thimble. Getting a hazy smile in her eyes.

"Wouldn't feel a thing," Dougie said. He liked this girl. Her freckles, the thing with the fork. Whatever it was she was drinking. The way her eyes kept dropping to his crotch.

"Or, if I were to spank you, you wouldn't enjoy that either?"

"You could spank me, I'd never even know you were doing it."

"You serious?"

"Speckle freckle," Dougie said. "Jeckle heckle."

"I usually get two hundred an hour," the girl said. "But if I could draw blood, hey, we could work out something cheaper."

———

Shaw lay in his bed and watched Saturday become Sunday. A blade of sunlight defined itself on his ceiling, then sliced through the shadows minute by minute toward the other wall. He pictured Trula in the moonlight last night. Her narrow body, moon pale, his hands exploring it. Her hands learning his flesh.

Holding that sensation, he tried to wake himself. Playing back the night in her bed against clean sheets, the two of them in the breathless, excruciating yoga of sex, stretching, coiling. Moonlight had angled through the window of her simple room, gilding everything with its pale silver. The rattan furniture, the deal dresser.

Then he saw her across from him at Mira's. A small round table, a single rose in a vase, her hair down, her jewelry breaking the light apart. Her large hands, her solid voice. This woman.

Shaw heard his mother retching downstairs. The toilet roared in her bathroom. More retching. Hanson Chandler had come to New York, had stood before Trula Marie Montoya and had asked her for money for an operation. He had told her secrets about himself. A confused young man who had run from his family with a box full of cash. A young man with a wretched life had taken blame for two murders he did not commit. Spent his life in hiding. Then come back twenty years later to demand more payment and had been killed for it.

His father, who that same night of his leaving had sprawled on a barroom floor and had come up firing a farewell punch into his son's face, a son who would have done any task, sweated, broken himself in half for the old man. A son who lay in his bedroom now and watched a blade of light coming out of one world, reaching into another, curving down the far wall of his room.

Thinking of the words Trula had spoken to him, the way she'd smiled. Then a tumble of images. The twisted silver canister. U.S.

Navy. A bankrupt tackle shop. A boy named Peter Salter, who had robbed Millie Chandler so that he might keep his fingernails perfect.

Cassie Raintree in her coffin lowered through the snow into videotape earth. Lord, lord. The ragged, frantic electricity that lit his mind. The reel jumped its sprocket and flapping. Her lips, her mouth. Softness and hardness, damp lips. Damp lips. Hanson Chandler in her Manhattan doorway. Blackmail, Montoya's folly. Chump's dump. Stock Island. A woman hung from her own rafters, her body twisting in the smoke and flames and steam. A pistol in the wrong hand pressed to the wrong heart fired in the wrong direction. A parrot screeching, asking, Who was being a good boy? Who was being a good boy?

Shaw mingled with seven tourists in the shade of a tamarind tree. They were gathered around the hand-painted sign nailed to the trunk. In a red wavering hand it said, "Wait here for bird lecture." He'd worn his best cutoffs and a fresh button-down shirt, running shoes.

There was an overweight father and mother wearing T-shirts with cartoon cats on them, and their two skinny teenage daughters who were pretending they belonged with someone else. The father explained to the group where Bad Axe, Michigan, was, in relation to Detroit. Then how they got so red skinned. "Like a couple of idiots," he said, "we fell asleep at the beach." Everyone nodded. The young couple in preppie gray camp shorts and polo shirts smiled ironically at each other.

A black man in tattered fatigues, madras shirt and a dirty porkpie hat who looked liked he'd wandered in from the highway to beg a handful of birdseed, turned to the preppie girl and said, "Black folks get suntans too, you know."

She smiled uncertainly.

"Want to see?" he said.

The preppie prince moved over within protection distance and the black guy slid his watch aside and showed her the light band of flesh at his wrist, then held it up for the rest of them to see.

"Well, I'll be damned," said the sunburned father. "Here I am forty-two years of age, and I didn't know Negroes could tan." His daughters tried to hide behind the tree.

Shaw turned his eyes to the green dazzle of ocean between the white cottages. There was a warm breeze out of the southeast that was putting a ruffle on the water. Dark cutouts of motorboats slid by out there, outriggers raised. And he felt a swift pang as he thought of the business he'd lost by closing the shop.

It was one-fifteen when Montoya came striding down the path in a wide straw hat, white starched shirt and navy blue shorts. Skinny bowlegs, leather sandals.

He marched up to the group, ticked off eye contact with each of the visitors, lingering for an extra beat on Shaw, then told them to follow him.

He led them down the same path he and Shaw had walked last night, speaking gruffly over his shoulder as he went. This was the operating room, this was the recuperating house, and down there were the cages.

Montoya ushered them into a chikee pavilion, oak beams holding up a thatched roof. Benches to seat twenty running around the edge. There was a picnic table in the center of the chikee, and Montoya took a seat at the head of it. Shaw sat on the bench next to the slender preppie woman. She nodded hello to him cautiously, bracing herself for whatever kookiness he might be intending. Shaw nodded back.

"Young lady, would you be so kind," Montoya said, motioning for one of the teenage girls to take a seat at the picnic table. "I need the assistance of an innocent."

"I don't know how innocent she is," her father said. "But go on, Jennifer."

The girl, giving her father a hateful glance, took the seat beside Montoya.

"You wouldn't know it," Montoya said, "living in Florida, or even just visiting, you see so many pelicans everywhere, diving for baitfish, sitting on pilings, hanging around the docks, you'd never suspect they're a federally protected endangered species." He glanced around the group, his eyes turned up high to ward off questions. "In Florida, we're the caretakers of a large percent of the world's supply of pelicans. But because they seem to be so abundant," Montoya said, "we don't give a rat's ass about them."

The father frowned, looked at his wife. Her sunburned smile had begun to sour around the edges.

"And as you'll see," Montoya said, "when we take our tour, being federally protected doesn't mean a damn thing. These birds have been mangled and starved, wrapped up in fishing line left behind in the mangroves by negligent fishermen, they've been blinded by kids with pellet guns, run over by drunks, tortured by lunatics.

"A week ago, a month ago, these harmless creatures were soaring over the ocean, independent, and were in no way in competition with man. Now take a long look at them. Every damn one of them is in need of permanent care and feeding. And as if that's not bad enough, for every cripple you see here today, twenty of its brothers and sisters have perished through the cruelty or stupidity of some human being." Montoya looked around the group.

He said, "As we sit here now, there's a man somewhere in the vicinity who through ignorance or conscious act is crippling one of these birds. He's leaving his fishing line and lure stuck to a mangrove, too lazy to retrieve it, or he's throwing overboard a plastic holder for a six-pack of beer that's more than likely going to wind up strangling a pelican or a heron or a gull. That ignorant man is a federal criminal, whether he knows it or not. As bad in the eyes of the law as an arsonist or rapist or kidnaper. And he should be caught and hurled headfirst into the darkest, foulest prison we could invent."

The fat father worked his eyes around the circle, to see if the rest of them were as shocked by this madman as he was.

"That's a little stiff, don't you think?" said the preppie, rising to his feet and clasping his bird book over his heart. Shaw had a sudden picture of him, posing in front of some judge, as he begged the court's indulgence on some slimy matter. "I mean we're in the touchy area of people's needs versus birds' needs here. It's a little more complicated than you suggest. God knows, I love birds as much as anyone." He brandished his book. "But come on. Foulest, darkest prison? I think not." He glanced at his lady for approval but she had bowed her head.

The father and his wife were whispering to each other. Their girls had perked up, sitting forward on their seats.

The black man said, "I think we should hunt down the culprits and do to them exactly what they done to the birds. An eye for an eye, fishhook for fishhook." He faced the sunburned father. "How would you like it, mister, if I tied up your pretty little girls in fishing line, left them out in the woods to see how long they could survive?"

The father stood, pulled his wife to her feet.

Montoya stared at the fat father and said, "You were expecting Disney World? It's up the highway. You want some reality, stick around."

"Come on, girls," the father said. "None of us wants to hear anything this man has to say."

"I do," sunburned Jennifer said.

"Get over here, Jen," her mother said.

The two teenagers stood reluctantly and joined their parents.

Montoya turned on the bench and reached back to one of the pillars, grabbed the rope of a small dinner bell, and yanked it twice. He looked around at the group and said, "For the next part of today's program, I'm going to introduce you to a cripple named Victor and tell you the sordid story of how I came by him."

As the Michigan family was leaving, Trula appeared on the path down by the operating cottage, standing for a moment in the deep shade of coconut palms as she shifted the pelican in her arms. The mother turned and caught sight of Trula, then put her hand on her husband's arm and said something to him. They edged back to the pavilion as Trula stepped inside. She set the bird down in the middle of the table.

"Aren't you . . ." The woman came under the chikee again, holding out one hand toward Trula, a gesture between an accusing finger and an offered handshake. "Aren't you . . . from 'Hidden Hours'?"

Trula turned to the woman and took hold of her hand, and gave it a squeeze. She said that yes, she had played Cassie Raintree. Smiling in the filtered sunlight, nodding at each member of the small group, and finally coming to Shaw. She gave him a private smile and sat.

The preppie shrugged at his girlfriend. Apparently they didn't slum with the soaps.

Montoya began to describe the appalling roundabout way that Victor had come to the rescue center, the five local vets and two pet-store owners who had turned the bird away. The bird was almost drained of blood when it arrived at the center. Then Montoya asked the teenage girl to show them how easy it was to save a pelican if they ever found one injured in the wild. What gentle creatures they were. He asked her to put her hand into the pelican's beak. She said she was frightened. "Don't be," he said. "It won't hurt you. It just tickles."

There was something in Trula's eyes he hadn't noticed last night, some shadow of weariness perhaps. As the teenage girl timidly stroked the pelican's beak, Trula smiled, but her eyes were quiet and remote, as if she were monitoring more serious matters within.

When the lecture was over, Shaw knew more about pelicans and their plight than he ever wanted to. The air was thick with guilt. He sat and watched as the group broke up. The black man walked down to the row of cages for another look at all the broken birds. The preppie led his girlfriend hurriedly toward the entrance, but she pulled away from him and walked over to the wooden donation box and folded some bills and slipped them in. The family hung around for fifteen minutes, all of them but the father getting Trula's autograph. When they'd left, Shaw rose and walked over to where Trula was sitting on the front steps of the main house. She seemed to be mildly out of breath.

Shaw gazed down the line of cages where the black man was still taking his slow tour. He was talking to the birds, seemed to be commiserating. Shaw hesitated, scratching his wrist, trying to hold himself in, certain that if she saw the size of the emotion he had dammed up inside him, she would run for cover.

She smiled faintly and said, "You want me to sign something for you too?"

"You endorse checks?"

"I'm overdrawn at the moment," she said.

They both waved good-bye to the black man, who had waved at them as he headed toward the entrance. Shaw took a seat on the step below her.

"I'm afraid I've got guano duty now," she said. "Scrubbing out the pelican cages."

"I'll be damned," Shaw said. "I was just going to suggest that."

"It usually happens," said Trula, "when Dad finishes one of his talks, either people get out of here fast, or they want to stay forever, dedicate their lives to pelicans."

"He gives good guilt," Shaw said.

"You noticed."

"It's a narcotic. Puts you in a trance, makes you want to do things you wouldn't think of doing otherwise."

"Like cleaning cages," she said.

"Guano duty."

Trula stood up, stretched her arms, and stifled a yawn with her fist. She said, "Guilt certainly seems to be the drug that keeps this place going."

"Your dad used to be a doctor, now he's a vet."

"He got sick of people. Animals don't talk so much."

Trula rose and Shaw followed her over to the row of cages.

"How does he afford to feed them all?"

"He's got a deal with Johnson's Fish Market. They deliver an ice chest of fish parts every morning. Tax write-off."

She opened the door to one of the pelican cages and stepped inside, holding it for him. The wild pelicans that roosted on top of the cages were gone, probably rubbing their bellies along the sleek seas.

As Trula and Shaw entered, a couple of the big birds edged behind twists of driftwood, eyeing them blandly. The others cast long looks their way, but didn't budge.

"They like you," she said.

"How can you tell?"

"They haven't attacked you yet."

He smiled at her and she smiled back. His veins were buzzing. All that excess current he was producing.

"Well, I'm famous for my strange power over endangered things."

"Oh," Trula said. "So that's what I'm feeling."

"I woke up this morning thinking about you."

"But that's not why you came out here, is it?"

Shaw was quiet.

"You wanted to see my father again, didn't you? Take a closer look at him. Decide if maybe he was capable of murdering your dad. That's it, isn't it?"

"Yeah," Shaw said. "I guess it is."

"Well? He the prime suspect?"

"He's no murderer," Shaw said. "I've run into a few of them on the job. They look different, they smell different. They don't give much of a shit about pelicans. Injured or otherwise."

"It's good to hear you say it."

"So now what do we do?"

"Clean guano," she said. "What else?"

14

From where Douglas Barnes stood on the catwalk two stories up, he could see around Mount Trashmore to the south. A slab of the Gulf was visible there, winking like black ice. He'd been standing out there since dusk, watching the pale blue water turn to iron. Then watching the dark take it all back, drain it.

He'd been out there for hours, figuring. And the way it looked to him now, there wasn't any choice. He'd never murdered anyone, never had to, though he had no particular moral qualm against it. You did what you had to do. You didn't critique your life. You did what you had to do in the morning, and then you ate your lunch and did what you had to do in the afternoon. You might not like your duty, but you accomplished it nonetheless. From twenty years of navy service, he'd learned that if something worked, then it was moral. That was all.

It was nine-thirty now, and Montoya had just arrived. And Barnes was stalling, making the old man wait behind him in the halo of the tower lights. Montoya was quiet as usual, probably exhausted from a long day of hauling around his moral code.

"Hey, Richard." Both of them stared into the dark. "Anybody ever tell you you look just like Albert Einstein?"

Montoya was silent.

"For twenty years I been thinking it, but I never said it. The Albert Einstein of death gas. That's you, Montoya."

Below them the conveyor was still. The whole plant was shut down because the trash supply had dipped below the level they needed to keep the turbines going. So, Monday morning the crews would run voltage checks on the stokers, clean out the ash buildup from the generating tubes, test the seams of the boilers, then when enough garbage had accumulated again in the receiving bins, they'd bring the plant back up. Tuesday they'd go carefully through the sixty-five steps, synchronize their turbines with City Electric and ease back on line.

"Man, am I ever tired," Barnes said, keeping his back turned to Montoya. "I had to waste my whole Sunday afternoon at the county building wrangling with a bunch of EPA lawyers. They can't meet me during the work week. I got to go in on Sunday, sit there and listen to this bunch of smart-ass liberals in seventy-dollar Hawaiian shirts, full of glib bullshit. Cause all of a sudden we got to get our exhaust emissions down to ninety-nine-point-seven-percent clean. Ninety-eight point seven isn't good enough all of a sudden. They tell you that, but they don't say how you're supposed to get the goddamn electrostatic precipitators working any more efficiently."

He watched Lars Mandel running the Bomag bulldozer on the western edge of the landfill, his headlights jerking and shaking. Lars was staying late to grind up some the remains of the Beach Piano Bar. Five truckloads of the old bar had come out this afternoon, pool tables, chairs, even a beat-up piano, the works. Making way for another condo. Someday, ten years from now, twenty, he'd get that condo too. Grind it up, squeeze some last bit of juice from it. He was young enough, only sixty-eight, before he was dead, he'd probably incinerate half the current contents of the island.

Barnes said, "These lawyers, they're a bunch of ex-hippies still cruising on some acid trip they took twenty years ago. They heard voices coming out of the sky telling them the air should be a hundred percent oxygen, the water, it's got to be H, two and O, and nothing else. And now the pricks aren't going to rest till they shut down every industry in America."

Montoya was quiet, standing at the railing beside Barnes and staring down at Lars running the diesel.

Barnes said, "Let me ask you, Montoya, you're a medical man. Whatever the hell happened to the idea of getting tougher from being exposed to toxins? Building up immunities. It's what the viruses do, the bacteria, fleas, mosquitoes. Adjusting, getting stronger, more ruthless from all the poisons they digest. It's goddamn counter-evolutionary what's happening. We keep making the world cleaner, and what you get eventually is, everybody's a wimp. Guy gets the flu, and all of a sudden he's looking around to sue some corporation for giving it to him."

Barnes turned and looked at him. Montoya was wearing his usual sad face. Listening, but just tolerating this. The light catching in his wild mane, making it look like fiberglass.

Barnes said, "I have this speech I'm always working on in my head. I picture myself at one of those long tables, testifying before a Senate committee. I'm telling them straight out, it's Ralph Nader that's the goddamn problem. Guy made us a nation of weaklings. Or guys like him, consumer advocates, making the average citizen think he's entitled to high-octane, hundred percent pure oxygen. If the air has even a trace of something else in it, we're all going to sputter and conk out. Well, I tell them, gentlemen, I for one am no Maserati you've got to pamper. Hell, no. I'm a Ford truck. An all-American all-terrain vehicle. Pour water in my tank, sprinkle in a dash of kerosene and I'll haul six hundred Ralph Naders up Pikes Peak."

Montoya was staring at him. Barnes said, "That'd be my speech."

"Is that what you called me out here for?"

"I like talking to you, Montoya. You get me whipped up."

Barnes gazed at the yellow lights up and down the cooling tower, all along the roofline of the plant. From a distance the place seemed to be sparkling with jewels. Some nights he parked his Jaguar down the road just to look at his plant, his diamond-studded factory.

He gazed up at the sky. A windowpane tonight. Eight million stars.

He said, "Botulism toxin, shellfish poison, dry anthracis spores, those were your specialties, right?"

"You know they were, Barnes."

"Well, see, as I think you know, I been helping out some people, finding a way to burn some garbage for them they can't get rid of any other way. They got some of these new modern liquids, things I thought you might be able help me out with. Dust off your past life, give me some details."

"I won't help you, Barnes. Don't be ridiculous."

"Ridiculous? Helping people is ridiculous now?"

"You're not set up to dispose of anything toxic. I told you a dozen times already. For one thing, you have to have a furnace temperature of at least two thousand degrees. Sixteen, seventeen hundred, that's just not enough to sterilize. The furnace has to be an autoclave, a pressure cooker. What you have, this incinerator, it can't handle anything more toxic than plywood. And you don't have the safety equipment, the secured perimeter. Your staff doesn't have the training. None of it. There's no way in hell you can handle toxic materials safely."

"So you're not going to help me, then, Albert Einstein? Is that what I hear you saying?"

The little man puffed his frail chest out, moved closer to Barnes.

"What do you really want, you bastard?"

"Hey, what I'm doing is perfectly safe. You hear of anybody in Key West bursting into flames lately, anybody's car paint suddenly start peeling off? Hell, man, I got to live on this island too. You don't see me walking around in a gas mask, do you?"

He patted the old man on the cheek, slipped his arm across his shoulders. But Montoya shrugged the arm off. The little man was hot, still jacked up like a rooster. Barnes had to chuckle.

"When they catch you, Barnes, I just hope I'm there to see them string you up."

Barnes snorted.

"You know, I got feelings for those patriots, the guy in his chemical lab cooking things up to keep the country strong. This guy spends his life doing that, then all of a sudden the goddamn politicians aren't buying what he manufactures anymore, they're so busy demilitarizing, giving away the store, shifting from low to high tech. So this businessman, he's all of a sudden hanging in the breeze, got a warehouse full of defoliants, or whatever, paraquat, you name it. And now the government's saying, no, never mind, we decided that's naughty, we're going to promise our enemies never to use that shit anymore.

"But what it really is, Montoya, and you know this as well as I do, the Joint Chiefs, they got something new cooked up. Whatever it is, it makes shellfish toxin, all that bullshit you used to play with, it makes it look harmless. They got gas now, you let it loose, wham, everything turns brown, stops breathing, every bird in the tree, fish in the sea. There isn't a gas mask made can screen this shit out. But the politicians, they smile at the TV cameras, they say, hey, we're finished with biowar. We're putting all that to sleep. Phased out of the business.

"But what happens to that entrepreneur in Miami, or in Atlanta, he's been in his lab inventing stuff to make the commies' assholes seal over and their dicks fall off, make them convert to capitalism? What's he supposed to do with all that stuff on his shelves? He can't ship it abroad. You want him to pour it down the sewer? Huh? A guy can't even do that anymore. These EPA guys were bragging today, they can trace shit back through the sewer lines. They work backward from the treatment plants, sewer main by sewer main till they nab the guy.

"I'm telling you, Montoya, Big Brother's running the show now. Big Brother Environmentalist. They got goddamn monitoring wells all over the place, they watch the hydrogeologic flow, which way the aquifer is moving. Somebody dumps something in the Everglades, way the fuck out there in the middle of nowhere, can't hurt anything but the mosquito population, but the government can tell you who it was and where. So, this businessman, he's stuck. He's got to pay somebody in the toxic disposal business large sums to haul it all away. Five hundred dollars a barrel to ship it to Alabama. The rednecks up there, they pour the shit into their ground, no problem. They need the money so bad they don't even ask what the stuff is.

"But see, I got sympathy for that guy, the defense contractor. He's been a loyal American and what's it got him? A few years of profit, yeah. But Uncle Sam's hung him out to dry. So I say to myself, shit, I got this big goddamn furnace, it's out of operation half the time, the people around here can't keep me in garbage, so what the hell, I kill two birds, I offer the guy a service he can't get so cheap anywhere else. He pays me a hundred dollars a barrel, and everybody's made out fine. I wait for a strong wind from the east and it blows all the undigested toxins over to Nicaragua, and then, hell, maybe I'm killing three birds."

The old man was trying not to show anything, but Barnes could see the icy light in his eyes. Barnes recognized it. The glow of pure righteous certainty. Informers had the look, whistle-blowers. He hated those fucks.

"See, Montoya, I'm not like you. With your goddamn pelicans

and your goddamn philosophy of life. I've never had the leisure time to develop a philosophy. Never had the time for introspection, all that bullshit. I do what's in front of me, best way I can."

Barnes sighed. It wasn't any use trying to explain himself to this self-righteous asshole. Montoya looked at you, his eyes always brimming up with spit. The man was just too good for his own good.

Barnes looked up at the cooler towers, at the splash of stars. He said, "You're right, Doc, I didn't actually think you'd help me. What I really wanted was to show you something I got in the mail this week." He drew the folded sheets from his shirt pocket and handed them to Montoya.

"This guy Waldorf went ahead with it. It's all in there. Your complete history, and mine."

Montoya spread the pages against the railing, angled for some light from the tower spotlights and read.

Barnes gave him a minute or two and said, "Can you believe this younger generation? Here I go and make a five-thousand-dollar donation to a guy's foundation, suggesting he find another subject to write about, and what does he do? This shit."

Montoya read for a minute more and handed the article back, his face blank.

"I'm curious how he found out about all this," Barnes said. "This individual uncovered some things I thought just you, me and the gatepost knew about. Now how do you suppose that happened?"

"He did it on his own," Montoya said, "if that's what you're asking me. I didn't tell him a thing."

"If you say so," Barnes said, appraising Montoya, the old man, seventy-five and counting. His skin getting so thin you could see how his mind worked.

Barnes said, "And then the guy's got the gall to send me his first draft, saying he wanted me to verify all this for accuracy, doesn't want anyone to see it till I'm satisfied he's got it all right. Me, Douglas Barnes. Rubbing my nose in it."

Barnes watched Lars working, the beam of his spotlight falling on some lawn furniture, the Munch and Crunch rolling toward it, over it. The big diesel didn't even strain.

Barnes said, "I mean, if it were some medical journal, I'd say let's just forget the whole thing. 'Cause then it's just assholes like

Waldorf reading it. But a cover story in *Time*? Christ, a month from now, we'll have people crawling over us, reporters, politicians, creeps from EPA, from all over. Month after that, we'll both be hanging by our thumbs in jail."

Barnes stepped forward and put his arm around Montoya's shoulders and guided him along the catwalk toward the furnace. Montoya resisting a little, but Barnes walked the doctor past the furnace, then up half a dozen steps to the perch that was on eye level with his office. He thought of this as the prow of his factory, plunging ahead through the rough sea of stupidity and moral principles to the promised land of extreme wealth.

Lars revved up the big diesel, rolled it up a small hill of motel furniture, giving a whoop as he came down the other side.

"You know, Montoya," Barnes said, "I'm into situation ethics. The situation changes, I change my ethics. I take what I'm dealt, extract the useful, and toss the rest. It's what we did in the navy. Take the shits of the world, and by God, wring out what portion of good is in them. Same as the garbage business."

Montoya said, "I could make one phone call, that's all it would take, and I could get you off my back forever."

Barnes chuckled.

"So why haven't you ever done it? You gave me every nickel you ever made, and never once tried to wriggle out of it." Barnes was grinning at him. "I'll tell you why you didn't. Because you fucked up. You were stupid, trying to do an idiotic good deed, and you did bad, real bad. You caused two guys to die. And if it hadn't been for me coming along, saving the whole situation, right now you'd be lying under a rock with your name on it."

Montoya dropped his eyes.

Working with that man had always been like training a dog. You had to know just how to hurt him. Barnes was going to miss that part.

Barnes slapped Montoya on the back and maneuvered him around so they were both facing the west, looking out at the dark water, the brassy glow of Key West. The old man said nothing, staring out at Lars, at the dark, at whatever it was that dead men saw in their last seconds.

"You *did* spill your guts to Waldorf, didn't you? After he was down here last time, you called the man up. You decided to splash it all over *Time* magazine, no less. Tell the whole fucking world about your ugly past, and mine."

"I did," he said quietly. "I told him everything."

"And the egghead sends me a draft." Barnes chuckled. "Can you beat that? Thinking I should get a chance to verify this and that accusation. Man doesn't want to libel me without giving me a chance to respond. And I'm thinking, libel? Jesus, this isn't libel. It's worse than that. It's the fucking truth."

"You can't stop it now," Montoya said. "You can shut me up, but you can't stop it. It's all going to come out."

"As usual, you're way off, Montoya. I've taken care of that problem already. I got an unlimited future of prosperity burning the garbage of the southernmost dimwits."

A gust of diesel noise rode the wind. Douglas Barnes took a deep breath of that marshy air. Coming from the south tonight, it brought in the smell of the mangrove swamps that bordered the landfill. A dank, breathless air that always reminded him of an excited cunt. Things fermenting in there, yeast, algae, reptiles.

"Tell me something, Montoya, just one thing. Why now? Why the fuck after all these years do you have to do it? Was it Chandler showing up like that? You're afraid the man is going to spill his guts, so you wanted to beat him to the punch? Huh?"

"My daughter has MS," Montoya said. "And we gave it to her. You and I."

"Oh, yeah," said Barnes. "Of course. You did this for her. Isn't that sweet. A real tearjerker. She comes down with some disease, and you rush in to take the blame. Throw yourself on the fucking grenade. And take me with you. Yeah, great." Barnes shook his head sorrowfully. Shook it some more.

"And now you feel better?" Barnes said. "Confessing is good for the soul?"

"Nothing I can do, even this, can make her right again."

"And you thought it would, you old fool? Telling the fucking truth, bringing pain on yourself and on me, you thought that was going to make you feel better. Jesus, what an idiot."

Still shaking his head, he moved close to Montoya.

Getting right into the old man's face, he said, "Now look, Richard. I would've had Dougie handle this for me, but I wasn't sure. You're his good Uncle Montoya, teaching the boy to read and all,

I wasn't sure if it might traumatize him too much to do it. And anyway, I figure you and I have been like partners for twenty years, I can't hand you over to somebody else. It wouldn't be right."

Another breeze shushed through the plant. The bulldozer was still now. Lars, singing to himself, came out of the boiler room, two flights below them. Barnes looked down through the grating at the big man. In the same instant, Montoya pushed past Barnes, stamped down a couple of steps and yelled, "Help!" But that was all he managed before Barnes had his hands around the old man's throat, hauling him back up to the landing.

Lars stopped, looked from side to side.

"I hear you," he called out. "But I don't see you."

"It's just me, Lars," Barnes shouted, his hands tightening hard around the old man's throat. "I'm all right. Just stumbled up here on the stairs. It's nothing."

Lars craned for a look up through the crosshatching of pipes and grating. Barnes held Montoya away from his body, gripping him hard by the throat with one hand, and leaned over the railing to show himself.

"Don't forget, Lars," Barnes called down. "We're coming back on line Tuesday at noon. Be here at ten."

"Yes, sir," Lars said, still shifting for a look up through the pipes and stairs. "Have a good night, Captain Barnes."

"Oh, I will, Lars. You do too."

When Lars had his truck started, Barnes let go of the old man's throat, and Montoya bent over and gasped, dry-heaved.

Barnes reached into his shirt pocket and came out with a small glass tube the size of a crayon.

"Take this, for instance, Montoya," Barnes said, holding the vial in front of the old man. "A gentleman in Miami had to get rid of some of this stuff. Made it for the navy, but Congress has the willies all of a sudden. And they won't let the navy have it. The shit doesn't even have a name, it's so new. Just numbers and letters. But he assured me if I diluted it just right, I could personally poison every palm tree in Florida, still have enough left over to wipe out all the grass and shrubs. I thought to myself, Hell, why should I burn up something so good? Why not keep it around, a little of it anyway? Never know when it might come in handy."

With his thumb, Barnes flicked off the small rubber lid. When the stiff hit the air, it smelled like paint remover. Made him dizzy just holding it there at arm's length.

"And you know what?" Barnes said. "I think we may have found the perfect use for it."

He held it in front of Montoya's face as the old man lifted his head, his eyes wet, still making small coughs. He waved the tube off.

"Come on now, let's make it all gone-gone."

Barnes edged behind Montoya, and with a deep grip on his tangle of hair, he tipped his head back and let a thimbleful of the liquid trickle into the old man's mouth. Montoya squirmed briefly in his grip, but his strength went fast. A second, two at the most. Swallowed it right down, a kid taking his medicine. Closed his eyes, screwed up his face, and died without a shiver.

Barnes hefted the corpse up to the railing and dumped it over. He walked downstairs to the supply shed and located the garbage bags. Silver with steel reinforcement. He'd found they were the toughest. You triple-bagged something in one of those silver ones, and cinched them closed, you had nothing to worry about. Even if the jaws of the crane closed right into it, the triple-bagging wouldn't split open. He should call the Hefty people, give them a testimonial. Forget your commercials, the guy dropping his garbage down the back stairs, it doesn't break open. Have I got a gimmick for you.

Tuesday the city trucks would start lining up to dump their loads, and the old man would be at the bottom of the heap. The bag he was in would hit the furnace probably around two, three in the afternoon. Filled with all that righteousness, the old man would probably burn a little hotter. Barnes would have to remember to watch, see if the lights fluttered when Montoya lit up in there.

15

Elmira was standing at the foot of the bed wearing only her black stockings and leather sailor's cap. The three red stripes Dougie had scraped into her belly with his fingernails shot out of her pubes like rocket flames. Her pussy hair was shaved into a heart shape. A red hairy heart with rocket flames. Wow.

It was almost midnight Sunday night and Dougie was on the phone, changing his reservation to Salt Lake City, making it two seats. The line went quiet for a minute, then the woman with the southern accent came back on and said that Dougie and Elmira Barnes were confirmed on Flight One-eleven leaving New Orleans Monday afternoon at three-fifteen.

"One-eleven, I'm in heaven," he said to her. "Three-fifteen, peachy keen." And hung up.

Earlier that evening Elmira had gotten very worked up, slapping him, spanking his butt, punching him in his stomach, Dougie not flinching or groaning or anything, just watching. Muffled up in his numb sack of flesh.

Finally she stopped, saying her hands were getting swollen, and Dougie had to get up, break off the arm of a hotel chair. Then he'd rolled over onto his stomach and let her whack his buns with the chair arm. Listening to her cussing, getting hotter and hotter as she struck him. Afterward, they'd screwed for five minutes and she'd bleated when she came. The possums mating at the dump made less noise. Dougie was, as usual, dead stone quiet during the whole deal.

"We leave tomorrow at three-fifteen," he said.

Elmira smiled and held up a gold-plated letter opener she'd found in the desk. She rubbed it against her naked belly, drawing circles, then little arrows pointing toward her red bush.

"That leaves us a lot of time to kill," she said.

"Yeah," Dougie said. "You could say that."

"I was thinking, Dougie. Maybe we could find somewhere to stick this, someplace it wouldn't open a vein or anything super serious. Wiggle it around." Her eyes full of weird fever. "Could you get into that?"

"Sure," Dougie said, throwing the covers off his naked body, arranging himself so he displayed his corrugated stomach and the little curlicue marks her long nails had made on his thighs and crotch.

"But I don't want to put it in any vital organs," she said.

"I only got one of those."

She smiled, touching a finger to the point of the letter opener.

He said, "Between the two of us, I bet we could find a place to slip it in. But we should maybe order up some Band-Aids from Room Service first."

"Jesus!" Elmira put a knee on the foot of the bed and crawled onto it. "Where you been hiding at, Dougie? I been looking high and low for you, boy."

———

"Lower," Trula said. Then, "No, you turkey, not that low."

She was squatting Indian style in bed, most of the sheets on the floor. Kneeling behind her, Shaw scratched her back, content to scratch all night if she didn't tell him to stop. Staring at her pale flesh, at the three moles that formed a pyramid between her shoulder blades. A sexual Bermuda triangle. You go in, you don't come out. Because you don't want to. His hand moved there, scratched in the middle of the moles.

"I should tell you something," he said.

She moaned.

"To the left. That way, a little more."

"I've got this thing about women."

"I'll say you do."

"No, I mean it. It's not a good thing."

She turned her head, looking at him over her shoulder, as he kept on scratching. Her smile faded as she looked, eyes dimmed.

"Never mind. It's nothing," Shaw said. "I was just being stupid, forget it."

Using both hands now, Shaw tried to scratch his way out of this, make her swoon, turn her head back around, bring her eyes back up.

"Go on," she said.

"It's nothing. Really."

"We going to start evading things now? Is this the moment we start doing that? I want to be sure, write it down in my diary. Eleven-thirty, Sunday night. Started lying to each other, withholding things. The beginning of the end of it. The short, happy life of Trula and Shaw."

"All right, all right."

She pulled herself around, still in her full lotus. All that white flesh. He had to look away.

The bedroom in her cabin was lit by a dim bulb inside a bug-filled globe in the center of the ceiling. It cast a pearly gray light across the old rattan furniture, the faded seat covers with their bamboo design. Drawn across the two windows were rubbery orange curtains, woven petroleum. A side table with a marble top. Tongue-and-groove knotty pine walls. The shellac on the boards had darkened so that now the walls nearly matched the curtains. A red bookcase stood in one corner. It had a dozen novels in it, a Sinclair Lewis, a couple of Steinbecks, some science fiction. A small bathroom next to the closet. In there was a rust-stained tub and a clear plastic shower curtain with a colorful map of the world printed on it. Trula's few beauty aids were arranged on the back of the toilet.

"Your father abandoned you," she said. "That's it, isn't it? And that gave you a thing about women."

"That's part of it."

"He abuse you?"

"No," Shaw said. "Not me, my mother. Slammed her around on a regular basis. But they had this thing, the next day, they'd make up. I'd come home and they were screwing, the whole house would be quaking."

"Quaking?"

"Well, maybe not quaking, but it was obvious what they were doing. I could hear. It's a small house."

"So then, what're your telling me, you want a woman you can hit and make up with later?"

"No."

"Well, that's good."

"But it's been my pattern," he said, staring down at the flowered comforter, "at a certain point I get nervous, back off, keep my feelings mild. Move on to the next one. Start over and do the same thing again."

"Failure to commit," she said. "Don Juan syndrome. We had a character on 'Hidden Hours' suffered from that."

"There's a name for it, then it can't be so bad, huh?"

"At what point do you get nervous?"

"A certain point, I don't know." He took a breath, looked at her full on. "It's a reflex, like I have a governor on my heart, it gets to thirty-seven miles an hour, the governor switches on and I back off."

She cleared her throat, forced the trace of a smile from her face.

"What's so damn funny?"

"I'm sorry," she said. "It's just the image. The way guys talk about themselves. Like they're cars, need to go to the shop."

"I've never talked about it before. I'll work on my metaphors, okay?"

"Okay, okay, don't get in a huff." She patted his thigh. "So," she said, "are we at thirty-seven miles an hour yet? You're ready to start decelerating? Is that what you're saying, we're at that point?"

"No," he said.

"No?"

"I think we're past it. Way past it."

"Sixty? Seventy?"

"Faster," he said. "Scary speeds."

They were quiet for a moment as a jet rumbled overhead. Shaw looking up at the ceiling. It must have been a navy fighter from Boca Chica, lower and faster than a passenger plane. Using its infrared to practice strafing runs over Key West, and the dark flats beyond. Blasting out into the empty ocean sky, tearing through layer after layer of blackness. Shaw rode for a moment in the tight cockpit, as the rumble died to the south.

"We're past it," he said. "And I've never been here before."

"That's good, then, isn't it? Being someplace new."

"Yeah," he said, a smile overcoming him. "Yeah, it is."

"Dear Diary. Eleven-thirty," she said. "Sunday night. Had a serious talk with my old-slash-new lover, Shaw Chandler. He admitted to various depravities. All of which we immediately cured. Romance continues."

He reached out for her.

"P.S." she said. "Finished scraping the epidermis from his sexual equipment. Began working on dermis."

"You're not mocking me, are you?" he said. "My problem compared to yours, it's not that serious, I know. But it's my problem."

"I'm not mocking you, Shaw," she said. "I take this very seriously. I haven't felt this way, not in a long, long time, and I don't want to screw up either. But the thing is, Shaw, I don't want you starting to think of me as some kind of medicine, some love potion. Your private home remedy that'll cure all that ails you."

He brushed her breast with the back of his hand. Let the hair on his knuckles tickle across her nipple. It twisted into a dark raisin beneath his touch. He brought his hands under her breasts, lifted them lightly.

"Is it possible?"

"What?" she said. Her hand had reached into his lap and was drawing him upward.

"A person is one way for thirty years, and then all at once, something happens, and he changes, he's another way. Can it be that simple? People pay good money, go to therapists for years, it still doesn't happen. They're the same as they were at the beginning."

"Or even worse," she said. She kept her hand moving, her dark eyes growing darker, sleepy.

"Sometimes I think about that man in a loincloth sitting on top of his mountain," said Trula. "You know the one, some mystic. He's been up there for forty years living on a single leaf of lettuce, doing nothing for twenty-four hours a day but putting his mind in his navel, trying to get to a higher plane of existence, step into the other world. Satori. What keeps him going is he believes it's possible. One minute he's one way, the next minute he's another. He believes that. That one day he'll be able to just stand up and step through this thing, like a membrane into that other place. That's why he's up there, surviving on a leaf of lettuce."

"Well then, shit," Shaw said. "If he believes it, why shouldn't I?"

"Yeah," she said. "There you go."

They kissed, and it lasted awhile, no hurry or effort, no consideration. His lips meshing with hers, their hands moving on their own.

There'd been times, sitting around the fire station, bored, shooting the shit about women with the other guys, they'd each counted it up, how many women they'd made love to, how many just fondled, how many kissed, approximately. Shaw's kissing number was somewhere under a hundred. Not the record for the station house. Not even close. Thing was, he couldn't remember any of them who'd had anything unique in the way they kissed. There were only so many ways to do it. You got to a certain level of proficiency, it was the same. Lips, tongue, teeth, only so many variations. All of them blurring together.

That's what he'd said sitting in the firehouse, shooting the shit about women with the other firemen. But it was turning out to be another of his dumb ideas about the world, about himself, about the lack of possibilities. Something else he'd believed in for a long time that had turned out suddenly to be false.

Trula lay back, putting a pillow behind her head, lifting her hips and sliding the other one under them.

Shaw said, "That guy in the loincloth."

"Yeah."

"He could've saved a lot of time."

"How?"

"He should've put his mind in *your* navel. He'd be in the next plane by now."

She smiled at him.

He lowered his head, ran his tongue in a wavering line from one hipbone to the other. Completing the triangle up to her deep navel. Then he redrew the line between her hipbones and made another slow, luxurious triangle downward.

———

Barnes was too pumped up from doing Montoya to just go back to his house, so he drove over to Polly's Palace on U.S. 1. Sailor hangout. Other assorted derelicts. Star Wars Bar.

Guys with horns coming out of their sternums, fuzzy orbs for eyes. He ordered a Miller Lite, got comfortable on the stool and looked around. Nobody he recognized. Just as well, because he didn't feel like talking to anybody.

He tried to knock the quake out of his hands by gulping the beer down fast. It bothered him that he was so wired. Surprised him too. He'd done what he had to do. Self-preservation. He'd considered other options, and there weren't any. You did what you had to do and just accepted it. It was his code. It was a samurai thing. You're ordered to lead the army down from the hill into the peaceful village and slaughter your own family, you don't waver, you don't question it, you run headlong down the hill and slash. But his hands still shook.

He'd been there twenty minutes, on his third beer, starting to come down just a little, when he saw Johnny Middleton, his long-time barber, walking over. Johnny took the stool next to him. Barnes nodded at the man.

"I saw you sitting over here," Johnny said.

Barnes nodded.

"I was just talking about you the other day."

"Is that a fact?"

"Yeah," Johnny said. "That Chandler kid ever get in touch with you?"

Barnes put down his beer, swiveled the barstool around slowly so he was facing Johnny.

"Who?"

"Shaw Chandler," Johnny said, looking up at the blond stripper shimmying down the runway in their direction, dollar bills stuffed into her garter belt. "Wild Thing" was playing loud on the speakers. The stripper was carrying a thick green python in one hand, a baby chick in the other, jiggling the chick in the face of the big snake. The python was focused on the yellow bird, keeping its mouth wide. The blond rubbed the reptile against her breasts, letting the tail hang between her legs.

Johnny said, "Shaw stopped by the shop with this thing, like an old broken shell casing, he was trying to find out what it was. Had *U.S. Navy* engraved on it, so I told him if anybody knew what the hell it was, it would be you."

Barnes studied the side of Johnny Middleton's face for a moment.

"By any chance is this Hanson Chandler's son we're discussing?"

"The same."

The blond was standing in front of Johnny thrusting her snatch in his direction. She turned and bent, pooching out her ass at Johnny and Barnes, giving them both a good look. Johnny stared into it, kept staring as he got another dollar bill from his shirt pocket and reached up and slid it under her garter, keeping his hand clear of the python's tail.

Barnes had his eyes on the side of Johnny's face, waiting for him to finish his fantasy.

"And you told Chandler he should come see me?"

"Yeah, did he ever?"

"I don't know," Barnes said. "He may have."

Johnny grinned at the blond, and she winked back at him and moved on down the runway to a couple of sailors who'd just come in. The python had the chick in its mouth now, and some of the people in the audience were clapping. The chick didn't seem to know what was happening, kept wiggling its head out of the snake's mouth. A feather circling to the stage.

"What's he look like?"

"Who?"

"What're you, going senile? Who were we talking about?"

"I don't know how to describe him," Johnny said. "He's got a good thick, healthy head of hair, that I'm sure of."

Barnes took a grip of Johnny's upper arm, dug his thumb in there among the tendons and muscles.

"Jesus!"

As Johnny turned, grimacing, Barnes backed off the pressure a little, but he didn't let go.

"Could you do me the courtesy, Middleton, look me in the face, describe this individual to me, please. The best of your ability."

"Jesus Christ, yeah, sure, whatever you want."

When Johnny had finished describing Shaw, Barnes let go. Johnny rubbed at his arm and looked off at the stripper again. The python had gulped the chick a foot down into it now, the chick was still moving inside the brown-green snake, wriggling like there might be a chance this was just a hole in the ground it had been sucked into. Maybe it could peck its way back toward the light.

"Where could a person find this Chandler kid?"

Johnny put his beer down. He gazed around the bar, rubbing his arm. He seemed to be looking for a free stool somewhere else.

"I asked you a question."

"His mother's, over on Olivia by the cemetery, I'd guess," Johnny said. "There, or I heard he's been going out with Montoya's daughter. Trula, is that her name? You might find him out there, at that bird zoo, or whatever the hell it is."

"Oh, that's great."

"Or, it wouldn't surprise me, he might be up in Islamorada, hunting down Peter Salter."

"Peter Salter?"

"The kid that bankrupted Chandler's tackle shop. Stole all the proceeds and the stock. Stole Millie Chandler's livelihood right out from under her. That's why Shaw came home, to put things right with the tackle shop."

Barnes let a few seconds go by, Middleton watching the new stripper step up on the runway. This one was a black girl in a blond wig. She wore a cowgirl outfit, a riding crop in one hand.

Barnes sipped his beer. Cleared his throat.

"Sorry about that," he said. "I'm just a little keyed up tonight."

"I'll say you are."

Calming his voice, Barnes said, "So you think Chandler has some kind of vendetta going with this Salter kid?"

"Somebody stole every nickel my mother ever made, I sure as hell would hunt the shitheel down and eat his lunch. Wouldn't you?"

Barnes thought about it. Had another sip of his beer.

"Yeah, well, maybe I would," he said. "Maybe I would at that."

16

On Monday Shaw wrote a sign in Magic Marker and tacked it on the shop door: GONE FISHING. He drove over to the Key West library and spent a half hour locating the newspaper accounts of Pinkney and Chiles's disappearance.

It hadn't been a big story. Squeezed to the back pages of the *Miami Herald* by the Berlin crisis. Pinkney and Chiles had been career navy men with exemplary records, no time in the brig. Both their wives claimed their disappearances had to be the result of foul play, because their husbands were trustworthy family men and dedicated to their navy careers. Neither had any speculations about why Hanson Chandler might have sent the sheriff a note claiming he'd murdered the two men. It was the same note, word for word, that Hanson had sent Millie. The sheriff said he would cooperate fully with navy officials on the investigation. But it puzzled the hell out of him why a man would confess to murdering two men whose bodies he'd so carefully hidden. "Why didn't the sap just keep his mouth shut, and it would've looked like three sailors going AWOL?" The last sentence in the article read, "Navy officials remain mum about the disappearance of these two dads." *Herald* reporters, even back then, trying to get their sniggers into print.

At noon Shaw stopped by the barbershop and asked Johnny Middleton if he knew the whereabouts of either of the two widows. Johnny said no, but hell, if it's important, he'd give it a shot. It's important, Shaw said. Yeah, Johnny said, I can see that now. Oh, by the way, Johnny said, I saw Captain Barnes last night out at Polly's Palace. We were tipping a few, and I mentioned you, and he got very worked up. Shaw asked him what he meant. I mean very worked up, Johnny said. Angry, upset. Johnny rubbed his arm. He heard your name, he asked me to describe you, then he went off like a stick of goddamn dynamite.

"What'd you do to that man, Shaw?"

"I sprayed him with a hose a few days ago."

"Well, you made the man's short shitlist."

"Good," Shaw said. "He's on mine too."

———

Half an hour later Johnny called the tackle shop to say he'd found a lady in Bahama Village who exchanged Christmas cards with Bertha Pinkney, and Loretta Chiles still subscribed to the *Key West Citizen.* Shaw got both addresses and called the airlines to make reservations for that afternoon.

He sat on the stool behind the tackle shop counter. He was pumped. His fingers drummed on the counter, his feet kept time to a speed freak's pulse. He stood up, paced the tackle shop. Some kind of pressure was building in his chest, swelling into his throat.

He called Buzz Sullivan in Miami. Tried him at home and got no answer, then called the station and asked to speak to him.

"Hey, guess who it is," Buzz called to the firemen. "The guy who hates the jumpsuits so much. Señor Ecru." Shaw heard them laugh. Then Buzz came back on, saying, "What's happening, buddy, you finished with the sun and fun, wanna get back to the big city?"

"I need some help, man," he said. "This is serious."

"Name it."

"Pull a couple of autopsy reports for me, the man and woman, you remember the ones. Day I left, the gunshot to the heart, and the hanging."

"You still on that?"

"Yeah," said Shaw. "Do it for me, Buzz, okay? It'd be easier than if I tried."

"Sure, all right," he said. "What're you looking for?"

"See if either of them had cancer."

"Can do."

"Call me right back, okay?"

It was four o'clock when Buzz rang him back.

"No cancer," he said.

"None?"

"No," Buzz said. "But apparently the man had a pretty bad ticker. A big aneurysm on his aorta. The thing was as thin as a soap bubble. The ME had in his report that the man had suffered at least one heart attack in the past month. You know, his heart was so bad, if he'd squeezed too hard taking a shit, the thing would've exploded."

"Thanks, Buzz."

"You, okay, man? You don't sound a hundred percent."

Shaw looked around the shop, then out at a head boat coming back in full of tourists. A swirl of gulls following it.

"Buzz," he said, "I'm not sure I'm capable of a hundred percent."

"You know," Buzz said, "I'm sorry I jumped on you the day you left. I don't know what came over me."

"You were right, Buzz."

"No, no," he said. "A man is entitled to his privacy. If he doesn't want to talk about some things, his buddy shouldn't try to pressure him into it."

Shaw said, "Things have gone to hell down here. I'm into something, I don't know what."

"You need me, I'll jump in the car this minute."

"Thanks, Buzzer," Shaw said. "I'll let you know."

Shaw made it to the county courthouse by four-fifteen. When he finally found the tax appraiser's office, the secretary was locking up her phones. She glowered up at him as she slid the cover over her typewriter. She was about fifty and he could see immediately that she wasn't going to succumb to a smile.

"You're closing early?"

"We close at four-thirty," she said, pulling the cover tight over her machine.

"I still have two and a half minutes, then," he said.

She tried to exhale him away. But he didn't move.

"As a rule, I don't like to reveal myself," Shaw said. "But you look like a lady who works hard, needs her pension."

"What?"

"I been doing this all day, playing this same little game in every office in the courthouse, and I'm just flat out of gas."

"Look, young man, I don't have the slightest idea what you're talking about."

He sat down in the chrome-and-leather chair beside her desk. She leaned away from him.

"I'm from Tallahassee," he whispered, and waited, as if that explained everything. "You know, the state capital, the governor, all that?"

Her frown withered a little around the edges.

"Franks and Jamison?" he whispered again. "The county hires us to do the yearly performance evaluations for career service personnel. You know, checking procedures. Everything. God, can you believe it, nowadays they even have me measuring the length of coffee breaks." He looked over his shoulder. "There's no one else here, is there?"

"No one," she said. She wasn't sure how full of shit he was yet, but she was on the verge of deciding. Squinting her green eyes, measuring Shaw's bureaucratic vibrations.

"Hey, you're tired, I'm tired. What say we make this the quickie version," he said. "Skip the property control numbers, you know, verifying that nobody's taken home any staplers or file cabinets. Just cut right to the finish. How's that?"

She hesitated a moment and said, "All right."

"Great," he said.

"So what's the quickie version?"

"I identify a random piece of real estate, you run back through the plat book, trace ownership, that's it. Blink, I'm out of here. We both go home, have a martini and dream about retirement."

"Give me the address," she said.

"Stock Island."

"The whole island?"

"No, just the land the dump's on."

She was quick. Maybe there was hope for the system. Maybe it wouldn't crash under the awesome weight of its inefficiency and low wages. Maybe if you just scared enough employees, woke them from their deep boredom, things would lurch forward awhile longer.

Richard Montoya had owned 280 acres of Stock Island in 1959, purchasing it over several years from different owners. In 1961, the year Pinkney and Chiles disappeared, he had been leasing 120 acres to Monroe County for the landfill. In December of that year the ownership of the landfill and the other 160 acres had passed to Douglas Barnes.

"What was the value of that transaction?" Shaw said.

"One dollar and other considerations," the secretary said, pointing to the faded print.

"It doesn't say what those considerations were?" he said.

"It never does," she said, putting the plat book back on the shelf.

"What do you make of that? In your professional judgment."

"Somebody got a pretty good deal," she said.

"Yeah," Shaw said. "A regular steal."

———

It was after five, and Trula and the two women were sitting on the cement front porch of a small concrete-block house on Staples Street a block from the high school. In the front yard, dead bicycles were buried in the high weeds, a skiff was overturned on sawhorses, and an ancient paneled van covered by a clear plastic tarp was hidden permanently under a Florida holly.

Trula was exhausted. Barbie Heyman was her third interview for the day. She was twenty-nine years old, a chronic progressive, in a wheelchair for the last seven years. Paralysis had seized up most of her body, though her face was still alive and her right hand as well. That hand had been fluttering for ten minutes as Trula went down the list of questions.

While Trula shifted positions in her chair, she watched Barbie's hand wave, a conspiratorial signal. Barbie struggled with a smile. Trula smiled and nodded back. Suddenly the hand began to knock frantically against the chair arm the way someone might hail from afar: Send help, hurry, hurry, I've drifted out into the dark, swift current, only a few breaths left.

Barbie's mother, Frieda, was sitting on the porch swing, supervising the interview. She was wearing a pair of nubby pink shorts and a T-shirt from a local barbecue restaurant. Her hair was yellow and coiled tight about her head as if she had carefully attached a handful of pork rinds to her scalp.

"If you ask me, all this is a big waste of time," Frieda said. "It was the marijuana she smoked that did this to her. Nobody ever listens to me when I say it, but she was just fine and dandy before she took to smoking that stuff every day. It was drugs killed this family, pure and simple. We were going along okay, then drugs came into it, and now look at us."

"Did you ever live near a radiator shop?" Trula asked Barbie.

Barbie considered it, her green eyes holding to Trula's.

"We always lived right where we're at," said Frieda. "Except for a year or two out on Stock Island in a trailer."

"Radiators," Barbie said in her soft, unsteady voice. "No, radiators."

"How much is that doctor paying you to do this?" Frieda said.

"I'm a volunteer," Trula said.

"Well, of course, *you* don't need the money. Psssh." She dismissed Trula with a slash of her hand. "I told him we wouldn't help him make his fortune off our misery without at least fair payment. And he said he couldn't afford to pay."

"But you let me come," Trula said.

"I wanted to see who you were," Frieda said. "I watched you on TV, and I wanted to see you. That's all there is to that."

Barbie kept her eyes on Trula, waiting for the next question.

Frieda said, "All these doctors, they're living high off the hog, in their fancy houses, and they expect us to just spend our valuable time answering their questions so they can win big prizes. We're just ignorant people, and they're all high and mighty, with their big degrees. Now is it fair I should help that doctor make his fortune without proper payment? Hell, no, you bet it isn't fair." She shook her head at Trula, then looked away and surveyed her yard. She said, "And you, what do you care about any of this?"

"I have it, too," she said. "MS."

"Well, then, you got the good kind," said Frieda, still looking off. "You got the lucky kind."

Trula turned back to Barbie.

"Did you ever work as a nurse?"

Barbie's head bobbed up and down and she beamed.

"For three years," her mother said. "The only good money this family ever saw."

"Where was that?" Trula said, departing from the list.

"Out there." Frieda cranked her head toward the east. "Florida Memorial."

"That's two out of three today," Trula said. "All nurses out there at Florida Memorial. And four out of six last week."

"Yeah," Frieda said. "All of them smoked marijuana and ran around with trash too, I'll bet you that. And does that list of questions even ask about marijuana? Hell, no. He's made up his mind, that Dr. Waldorf has, and he doesn't want to know the real truth. He probably smokes joints himself."

"I liked being a nurse," Barbie said. "I was a good nurse."

"Yeah," her mother said. She sniffed and looked out at her yard, at the clouds building dark, high mountains in the south.

17

Elmira and Dougie arrived at the Salt Lake airport at six-thirty Monday evening. He rented a white Avis Cadillac, giving the guy a Diners Club Card that had turned up at the dump one day. Man, the things that people put in their trash.

Remembering now, he'd fucked up using his own credit card number for the airplane ticket. But then figuring that, well, shit, two of them traveling together, that was enough to throw anybody off. That is, if anybody ever came looking for him. So, maybe he'd done one little thing wrong, but he'd done a bunch right. He was still way ahead.

They made a cute couple. Dougie in his black nylon jacket that had the peace symbol in little Christmas lights embedded in the back. Thing was battery operated. Dougie'd missed the sixties and never got his chance on that first go-around with peace symbols, the granny glasses, the Nehru jackets. All that Woodstock shit. To go with the jacket, he'd worn a black turtleneck, black baggy jeans that gathered at the ankle, with lots of zippered pockets. High-top Reeboks, the plaid laces loose.

On the way to the New Orleans airport, Elmira had made him stop by her apartment way the hell out by an oil refinery so she could put on her traveling clothes. A few minutes later she came swinging and swaying out of her room wearing a long brown mink coat. And a red velvet hat shaped like a Frisbee. And a slinky green dress that would have to grow two feet to hit her knees.

At the last minute in the airport in New Orleans, they'd each bought a pair of sunglasses with stars and comets on the orange reflector lenses. But when he looked through them, Dougie was disappointed, everything still looked normal.

"Why're all those Mormons staring at us?" she asked Dougie as they waited in the Salt Lake airport for the rental car to come around.

"It's your tits," Dougie said.

"What about my tits?"

"Mormons keep their tits in their shirts."

She looked down at her cleavage. About a yard of it.

"You should've told me back in New Orleans," she said, "if I wasn't dressing right."

Then they were in the Cadillac, driving off, Dougie trying to concentrate on the highway signs, reading the numbers, saying them to himself under his breath. And she started pestering him, what kind of business was he in? Why the hell were they out there with all these tight-ass Mormons? Was he trying to make fun of her, letting her dress the way she had? Come on, was he selling drugs, or what? She didn't mind if he was, although she didn't use them anymore herself.

And Dougie was struggling to pick out the right road to get into town and do his job, and thinking the whole time, uh-oh, this one was fun for a while, but she's got this other side. Pissy, pouty. Another woman he could see already he was going to have to dispose of. Like one of those throwaway razors. It works great a couple of times, then, man, stuff it in the trash quick or it'll start to nick you.

On their way past the Mormon Tabernacle, headed up a long sloping avenue, he said, "You ever kill anybody?"

After thinking a minute, she said, "No."

"What? You couldn't remember?"

"I been there," she said. "I been there when the deed was done. But it's not the same thing."

"No, it isn't," Dougie said. Deciding, what the hell, tell her. She was a Bic razor anyway. Get a last good shave.

She said, "You a killer? That your business?"

"I'm primarily a lady's man," Dougie said. "But I help out around the house when I can, you know, take out the garbage, make my bed. Shoot guys through the heart."

"Maybe you should let me out."

"This afternoon," Dougie said. "We slid our silkiness in and out. I impelled my inflamed knob into your mossy grotto, bathed you in jism." Dougie turned a toothy grin to her. "And you want to get out of my car?"

"Where do you get this shit? Silkiness, and all that?"

"I'm a reader," Dougie said. "I'm a devotee of literature."

"Books and shit?"

"Books, magazines, the things with the words."

"You're a very weird person."

Up the long dark hill, the houses changed, becoming brick with columns, two, three stories, the lawns wider and deeper, big naked trees out beside the street. Streetlamps and benches. Not fancy, but the kind of place where professors lived, and scientists.

She said, "Who is this guy we're going to see?"

"Beats the bejesus out of me," Dougie said.

"You don't even know him?" Elmira said, pouting again. She'd propped her back against the door, like she was getting ready to fend him off, kick at him with those high heels. "We're coming all this way, and you aren't sure why."

"I know exactly what I got to do," Dougie said. "I just don't know exactly why I got to do it."

"Oh, fuck, man, just let me outta this car."

"Hey, it'll be fun. We'll see some blood. We'll ask the guy questions, find out what the hell this is all about. It'll be a good time."

Elmira shifted, said, "What do you want me for? I don't have anything to do with this."

"You will before we're done," Dougie said. He smiled at her, steering them with one hand down the handsome street. He said, "You ever see anybody could do this?"

He reached into the pocket of his jacket, drew out a cherry stem, held it up for her to see. He slipped it into his mouth, chewed it around while he peered out the window, looking for the address. Fifteen forty-five Avenue B.

"I seen that trick a hundred times," she said. "Tying it in a knot. Every cheap bar I been in, some loser's doing that trick to impress you. Jesus, and I thought you were something special."

Dougie turned to her, slowly losing his smile. He held the cherry stem still in his mouth, cutting his eyes back and forth from the street to her. Then he swallowed it.

———

Dougie used the brass knocker, giving three hard raps against the heavy front door, then stepped back on the porch of the two-story brick house. The guy that opened the door wasn't more than forty. Tall and skinny with greasy black hair, a hawk beak, and dark eyes. Dougie hesitated a minute, then asked to speak to the guy's father.

"My father's been dead for ten years," the man said.

Dougie wanted to say, well, isn't that a coincidence, cause you're almost dead too. But he said instead, "Then you must be Waldorf, the scientist."

"I'm Dr. Waldorf, yes," the man said. He was wearing green corduroy pants and a red flannel shirt. Leather slippers. He opened the door another inch to see Elmira better. Ghost breaths coming from everyone's mouths.

Dougie said, "I thought scientists were all old."

The guy smiled and said, "You the kids from the *Chronicle?*"

"I'm Dougie, and this is Elmira." Dougie stepped back so the scientist could get a good view of Elmira. His eyebrows lifted, and he gave his head a quick shake like he was trying to rattle his eyes into focus.

"I thought we settled on next Friday for the interview."

Dougie glanced at Elmira, thought for a second, and said, "Well, we were just so excited, we couldn't wait."

Looking at Elmira some more, her hugging her fake mink coat to herself and walking in place on his porch to keep warm, the scientist said, "Well, okay, I suppose I can spare you an hour."

"An hour should do it," Dougie said, smiling at Elmira, "don't you think?"

"Shouldn't take anything like an hour," she said.

———

They were downstairs in the scientist's rec room, Dougie in a white beanbag chair, Elmira sitting prim, with her hands folded in her leather lap, on the green-and-yellow-plaid couch, looked like something you'd donate to the winos. Both of them were scarfing down the Heinekens the guy had brought down. A bowl of onion dip and Triscuits. The guy got to choose his last supper, so shit, if this is what he wanted, what the hell.

Dougie was pissed off at the beanbag chair. He'd picked it out because he'd never seen anything like it. Turned out it was comfortable for a couple of minutes. But as the beans shifted, Dougie scooted deeper and deeper until he was practically lying on the floor.

Waldorf kept bouncing up to change the tape in the tape deck, or get more food, fiddle with the thermostat, each time checking out Elmira, thinking he was getting away with it, but both of them catching him, and glancing at each other. Nobody had said much of anything since they'd come into the house.

Waldorf poked the fire he'd built in the fireplace, his back to the two of them. He said, "You planning to tape this? Or you doing it the old-fashioned way?"

"We're into old-fashioned," Elmira said. Dougie could see she was warming to this, some hot static in her eyes. Same look she'd had when he'd broken that chair arm off last night. Breathing through her mouth, not blinking.

"No wife or kids or dog or anything?" Elmira said.

"Just me," Waldorf said.

"You and your books," Dougie said. "And your microscope."

"I bet it's been a long time," said Elmira, "since you slid your silkiness in and out."

Waldorf didn't say anything, but Dougie could tell he was falling into stage five love with Elmira. He took a seat on the couch beside her, watched her as she brought her legs up and tucked them under her on the couch, giving him a glimpse of dark panty hose.

Dougie had decided to take his time on this one. Not how he'd done with the guy and the woman in Miami. Hurrying through it, just to get it done and get out of there. He'd always heard that killers got charged up from doing the thing, some kind of thrill. He thought, Well, then, maybe he should try it slow this time, see if that's why he hadn't felt much.

Though he bragged about the pain threshold thing, it bothered him that he never felt anything. A little irritation here and there. Some hot congestion in his belly when he was having sex, or watching Trula swim naked. But nothing like what the people in the porno books felt. All that ecstasy, all that white light. Having sex for Dougie, it had always been about equal to a good beer burp or a nice long fart. About the most fun he got was driving the Munch and Crunch, or else saying weird shit, watching people react.

"So, I guess you want to know about the Key West cluster study," Waldorf said. "The main thrust of my research."

"Yeah, the main thrust," Elmira said sweetly.

The scientist tilted his head, staring at Dougie, little gears meshing behind his eyes.

"Tell us about it," Elmira said. Her voice furry and deep, like she was slipping her hand into his Jockey shorts.

"Well, it's fascinating," he said, smiling at her. "But I have to watch out. I can't tell you too much, you know, it's still in the confidential stages. I can say this, however. When the article appears it's going to cause a major uproar."

"Come on," Dougie said, "we like uproars."

"And we love clusters," Elmira said. She smiled and said, "Love clusters." Throwing Dougie a look like, See, she could do it too, say things that were strange.

Waldorf laughed uneasily, glancing back and forth between them.

"Cluster buster," Dougie said. "Heckle jeckle."

"Yes, well," the scientist said, taking a Triscuit, breaking it in half, and scooping up some onion dip. He tried to fire a secret look up Elmira's dress. She pulled her knees apart.

Addressing himself to Elmira, he said, "The MS rate in Key West is about thirty times what it should be. It works out to around one case per thousand residents. Compare that to Atlanta, for instance, which has a rate of point three, that's three-tenths per thousand. So, you can see, things are considerably out of whack. Key West, Akron, a few other cities were on my study originally. But because Key West is the only place of such a southerly latitude with such a high rate, I began to focus just on it."

"Go on," Elmira said, shifting on the couch so she brought herself a few inches closer to the man. "This is sexy stuff."

"You don't want to write any of this down?"

"We got great memories," Elmira said.

Dougie said, "We hardly ever forget anything."

Waldorf said, "Well, I was studying some possible causes of the freakish incidence. For instance, Key West is the home of the only high-security animal quarantine center in the country. Pigs, llamas, alpacas. They come in from all over the world, China, Peru, countries in Africa, places where hoof and mouth is still rampant, or rinderpest. They stay out on Fleming Key, an adjacent island, for a few months, and if they don't develop any symptoms, they're shipped off around the U.S. So, it's not hard to imagine that with the large resident population of rodents, raccoons, other burrowing beasts living there on Fleming Key too, and with a bridge connecting Fleming Key with Key West, that it's quite possible that some rather exotic infections could just waddle across that bridge and spread to the main island."

Elmira said to Dougie, "He gets very worked up, doesn't he. You see what he does with his nose?" She said to Waldorf, "You do something with your nose. You flick it, or something."

Waldorf smiled and nodded.

"Then there's the contaminated drinking water," he said, "and the landfill, heavy metals in the food chain. For instance, until just the last couple of years, Key West pumped their raw sewage out to sea. It would wash back ashore, come up on the beach, and you had people walking around barefoot in microorganisms you wouldn't want a mile away from you. Those same bacteria could easily enter the food chain through fish or shrimp consumption." He had a sip of his clear drink from the squat glass, and said, "I approached it as a detective story. What if something is in the environment down there that triggers MS, makes the people who are genetically vulnerable to it, contract it in excessive numbers. So, I started with the sewage outfall, and that led me to some pretty shocking discoveries."

"You're cute," Elmira said. "I like your nose."

"Well, thank you." Waldorf smiled so hard his mouth quivered. Then he turned to his right and looked at Dougie slouched in the beanbag chair and said, "I must say, although I'm a freedom-of-the-press man through and through, I can't really name names for the student paper. It would steal the *Time* magazine thunder. I can give you background on multiple sclerosis, and some demographical stuff, but I can't go farther than that yet. Not even off the record."

Elmira said, "I think I got just the place to put a nose like yours."

It was just after midnight, everybody gone home except for Lars, who was loading the last of the day's garbage onto the conveyor. Stoking the furnace up good so it would burn till the morning shift came on. Barnes stood under the yellow lights, by the open storage shed, and waited till Dr. Randall Motrim positioned the five-ton panel truck just where he wanted it, flush against the concrete loading ramp.

Motrim climbed down from the truck and checked his parking job. He was a short, pudgy man, wearing his civvies tonight, an open-collar white shirt and black Bermudas, sneakers with knee-high white socks. If Barnes didn't know better he'd think Motrim was a dentist from Milwaukee down for a few days with the wife and teenagers. He had that look about him, fat and domesticated.

But what Motrim was, was Richard Montoya's replacement. Head science officer for the biolab at the Boca Chica naval base. For the last fifteen years, Motrim had consistently come up with such potent shit that Barnes had heard the navy was thinking of making him an admiral. The guy had never been to sea a day in his life, and there he was, working his way to the very top.

For the last ten years, Douglas Barnes had been adding a nice supplement to his retirement pay by assisting the navy in disposing of some of their more bothersome materials, saving the taxpayers a ton of money by burying navy toxins in various sites around the dump. Though in the last year or two, he'd been burning most of it, 'cause what with the way EPA was getting so much shit from Congress, sooner or later they'd upgrade their soil-sample testing program and maybe stumble onto some of the weird materials he'd disposed of.

Motrim reached back into the cab of the truck and came out with a gunnysack.

"You're gonna love this one, Doug. Wait'll you see."

"That a sack of cash, or what?"

Motrim walked over, smiling, jiggling the bag up and down.

"No, it's frogs."

"You people must've lost it totally. Paying me five thousand bucks a month to burn up frogs?"

"No, you dumb shit, the frogs are for demonstration purposes. Liberated them from the lab myself, just to show you my latest. I know how you love this shit. You're about the only person who truly appreciates my value to society. Come over here, big guy. You won't believe this."

Motrim opened a padlock on the truck's back door, knocked the lever open and rolled the door up its track. Tonight it was cylinders, about the size and shape of cans of Ajax, a little fatter, no markings on their brown covers.

"Check this out."

Motrim reached into the truck and came out with one of the cylinders, unscrewed the lid and held it out in front of Barnes.

"Smell it," he said.

Barnes hesitated. There'd been some nights out here with Motrim that they'd had to wear rubber gloves, breathing masks. And even then he'd had some monster headaches later.

"It's harmless to breathe, Doug. What, you think I'm trying to trick you or something? Punch your ticket?"

Barnes bent and looked. It was a clear gel. He took a very small sniff.

"Smells like toothpaste, doesn't it?"

"Not any kind I ever used," Barnes said.

Motrim smiled.

"I'm real proud of that odor. I worked a long time on that. Though, hell, the navy could care less how it smells. Still, it matters to me. The artistic content, you know."

"Yeah, right."

"It's called Seluline," Motrim said. He put the open jar on the concrete loading platform and stooped to untie the gunnysack.

"Another herbicide? Something to turn all the flora brown from here to the North Pole?"

"No, this one's a solvent," Motrim said. He was holding up a frog. The thing started to piss and Motrim held it away from him, turning it around so he could see its eyes.

"A solvent," Barnes said. He was getting impatient. Standing here watching this man, he thought of Montoya, wondered if maybe someday he'd have to do to Motrim what he had to do to Montoya, wondering if it'd be as easy. But no, Motrim wasn't the kind to get religion, start having the urge to confess to the world the horrible stuff he'd been brewing up. Motrim loved it too much.

"What's the number one maintenance problem the navy has? You should know that." Motrim brought his face in close to the frog's. "The number one expense."

"Treating gonorrhea," Barnes said.

Motrim chuckled.

"After that," he said.

"I'm not in the mood for games. You got something to show me, then show me."

Motrim turned and dropped the frog into the container of gel.

"The number one problem, Doug, is barnacles. Barnacles and algae."

"Yeah," Barnes said. "Of course."

He looked into the container and the frog wasn't there.

"So naturally it fell to me to come up with a solvent, something to use to get those little fuckers off the hulls, get the ships in and out of dry dock faster. Pressurized water, chipping by hand, all that's very time-consuming. Bottom paints only work so well. And the solvents we got currently, they aren't any stronger than vinegar. So, what I did was, I invented Seluline."

The frog was gone, but there were two round shiny things sitting on the top of the gel.

"Those are its eyeballs," Motrim said. "Don't ask me why it works that way. I don't have a clue. Everything organic I've thrown into it so far dissolves, poof like that, everything except the eyeballs of frogs."

Barnes looked at those perfect orbs sitting on top of the gel.

"Smells good, doesn't it? Minty, with a hint of lime."

"Yeah," Barnes said. The eyeballs were a lot bigger than he would've expected them to be. Marbles.

"I been dropping frogs in there all afternoon, ten, fifteen frogs in one of those containers, they disappear, the total mass in the container doesn't increase, except for the eyeballs. Can you figure that one out, Doug?"

"No."

"Here, try one of these amphibians." He held out a frog to Barnes.

Barnes took it from him, held it over the Seluline and let it go. There was no sizzle, no hiss, no gurgle, nothing. The frog just disappeared. Four eyeballs now.

"You sure it's okay to burn this stuff?"

"Well, that's your area of expertise, Doug. But I think it should be fine," Motrim said. "Burn it, bury it, just don't stick your dick in it. Know what I mean?" Motrim laughed.

"The stuff cleans the barnacles right off. No deleterious effect on the hulls, doesn't penetrate rubber gloves, so it's easy to work with. But it's too strong. They won't let me go any farther with it. I got to dump this and find something that doesn't work as well, can you believe that? Just like the fucking navy. Something that doesn't work as well. Shit."

Four eyeballs.

"And after I worked so hard on that smell." Motrim took another frog out of the gunnysack. "Want to do another one?"

"No."

"You know what kills me?" Motrim said. "Being top secret like we are, the average John Q. Taxpayer, they won't ever get a chance to appreciate all the trouble we go to, all the fucking hard work that goes into keeping them safe."

18

Elmira unbuckled Waldorf's belt. He leaned forward on the couch so she could get it free. While she pulled it from his waist, Dougie stood up from the beanbag chair and went over to Waldorf's music collection to see if he had any sixties stuff. Jefferson Airplane; Crosby, Stills and Nash. Tunes from the time when everybody was screwing and smoking dope, seeing visions of cosmic peace. Those were the years when the planets had aligned exactly right, sun, moon, stars, everything, and Dougie reached puberty.

For the last ten minutes Waldorf had been running on about bacteria. Still pretending this was an interview, though it was pretty obvious it wasn't. Guy was snockered now, his glasses off. And every time Elmira touched him on the leg or gave him one of her cute looks, he'd speed up his speech. Now that she had his belt off, and wound it around her fist, and was slapping him lightly on the thigh with the loose end, Waldorf had moved into fifth gear and was rattling on like an auctioneer.

"Here's one you'll like," he said, smiling like he didn't know what else to do with his face. "There was a famous study conducted on two thousand Swedes in 1981. Their anuses were painted with fluorescent paint, the kind that lights up under black light. Similar to the material they put on the back of your hand at a rock concert. Well, some researchers painted the Swedes' anuses with this paint. . . ."

"Their anuses," said Elmira. "Their tight little wrinklies?"

"Yes," he said, making a smile. "Their little wrinklies."

She looped his belt around his neck, held either end of it and began to saw it back and forth. Waldorf kept smiling, taking little gasps like the room didn't have enough air in it.

"Let him finish," Dougie said. "This is interesting." Dougie had found the mother lode of sixties records on a bottom shelf. Everything. The Association, things he'd never seen before, Ramsey Lewis Trio, the Kinks, the Animals, the Beatles, the Kingston Trio, Peter, Paul and Mary. The cover of that one with the two guys Peter and Paul looking like beatniks, the girl, Mary, a big blond surfer girl. He looked at them, and tried to think of what they all looked like naked. He wondered if the two guys were slipping it to her. Mary puffing their magic dragons.

Elmira said, "So, you going to tell us why they painted their assholes, Stanley?"

"It was to trace the spread of bacteria," he said. "To map migratory patterns of fecal matter, among the extremely hygienic Swedes."

"What'd they find out?" Dougie said, taking the Peter, Paul and Mary out of its cover, carrying it over to the turntable.

"Within twenty-four hours," Waldorf said, "the fluorescent paint covered every square inch of the subjects' bodies. They were all literally awash in fecal bacteria. Which, of course, naturally indicates that all of us are, as well."

"Covered in shit?" Elmira said. She'd taken the belt from around his neck and was leaning back and watching him.

"Yes."

"That's the kind of stuff you do for a living? Paint assholes, see who's covering themselves in shit?"

"I had nothing to do with that experiment," he said. "I simply offered it just now as entertainment."

"It's entertaining," Dougie said. He'd gotten the turntable going, and was trying to figure out how to switch on the amplifier, but he couldn't read the little words under the switches. Shit. He'd been neglecting his studies lately, devoting more time to teaching Jerkoff and less to his porno, and already his reading abilities were starting to slip.

"I always wash after I go potty," Elmira said.

"So did the Swedes," said Waldorf. "And very carefully."

"You're saying I got pieces of shit all over me right now?"

"It's not a pretty thought, is it?" Waldorf said.

"Harum-scarum," Dougie said. "Rip and tear 'em."

Waldorf gave Dougie a stupid smile as Elmira began to unzip the man's pants.

"Free love, deep shove. Flower power, witching hour."

He had the amp on now, and he set the needle down and Peter, Paul and Mary started moaning something about being five hundred miles away from home. Repeating it over and over, five hundred miles, five hundred miles. Like it was their first time that far away from home. Big deal. Dougie was at least a thousand miles away from home, and did anybody hear him whining?

Dougie listened to them going on about it as he went over to the beanbag chair and took out the two-shot Remington derringer he was carrying in his left front pocket.

"So, are we going to go upstairs to the bedroom or do it right here?" Elmira said.

"Are we going to do something sexual?" Waldorf said. He hadn't noticed the derringer yet.

Dougie said, "Let's do it right here."

He fired a round into the beanbag chair. Then squatted down and widened the hole the bullet had made. The thing was full of white foam pellets. Not beans at all. Wasn't that just the way with everything. Nothing was ever what it seemed to be. He tore the hole wider and poured the pellets onto the floor. Fucking chair.

Waldorf was standing up, holding his pants together, giving Dougie a wild look. His hair was messed up and his shirttail was out. Standing there gawking at Dougie as though Dougie were a ghost oozing out of the walls.

"You fired a weapon in my house," he said.

"Get used to it," Dougie said.

Elmira was standing up now, smiling at Dougie, giving him one of her sexy looks. Maybe she wasn't a disposable razor after all. Maybe she was a new kind, one that got sharper the more you used it. He'd have to find out.

Peter, Paul and the surfer girl were going on about a stick of bamboo. You throw it in the water. Ooh-oohing. A nice sound to it, but hell if he could picture what was going on.

"You're an entertaining guy, Dr. Waldorf," Dougie said, aiming the derringer at him. "I liked all that about painting assholes. I enjoy people who know weird shit. Creepy peepie."

"He likes you," Elmira said, batting her eyes at Waldorf. "He doesn't say creepy peepie to just anybody."

Dougie said, "I wish I knew why it was I got to send you off to the last roundup. It doesn't seem polite to do something so serious to somebody and not even know why."

Waldorf was swallowing, still holding his pants together, watching the derringer aimed at his face.

"It's about the MS study, isn't it?" Waldorf said, his voice fluttering.

"Maybe," Dougie said.

"Well, listen, I can drop the study just like that," he said. "I don't mind at all. If I'm threatening an individual's business enterprise in Key West, I can just stop it, go on to something else. It's no biggie."

"It's no biggie," Elmira said. "I like how this beanie-weenie talks." She was standing up close to Waldorf, her hand behind him. Dougie couldn't see what she was doing. But it looked like she might be feeling around inside his underwear. Fixing to mix a little of her bacteria with his.

"Here," Dougie said, reaching out the pistol to her. "You do it. See how it feels, then describe it to me."

"I *said* it was a rush."

"What does that mean?" Dougie said. He was maneuvering the Cadillac up the entrance ramp onto the interstate.

"A rush, a gas," Elmira said. "A blast, you know, fun."

"But how did it feel? You know, inside you, wherever it is you feel things."

"Usually I feel things in here." She patted her lap, and grinned at him. Still wearing her sunglasses even though it was four in the morning. If the state patrol happened to pull up alongside of them and saw her like that, Dougie was sure that'd be the end of things.

"You're fucking with me," Dougie said. He reached over and snatched off her sunglasses, and ran his electric window down and tossed them out onto the highway. "Just tell me straight, what'd it feel like the second you pulled the trigger?"

"It scared me, but I liked it," she said. Trying now, serious, choosing her words. "It was loud and the gun jumped in my hand, and my heart went fast."

He glanced over at her as he was accelerating up the interstate, headed south. He was going to drive to Las Vegas, stay there a few days, then drop the car off and fly to Chicago, then home. A whole lot of zigs and a whole lot of zags.

"Your heart went fast," Dougie said. "How does that feel exactly?"

"What, your heart never goes fast?" she said.

"Maybe it does," he said. "I never noticed."

"Not even when I touch you here?"

Elmira slid her hand back and forth across Dougie's crotch. Dougie looked down at her hand.

"Is that all? Your heart went fast and the pistol jumped in your hand?"

"Jesus Christ, Dougie, what do you want me to say?" she said. "I felt warm spiders marching around inside my stomach, something weird like that."

"You're fucking with me again," Dougie said.

"No, I'm not," she said. She plucked Dougie's sunglasses off the dash and ran her window down and tossed them out. While she had the window open she found a couple of beer cans on the floor at her feet and threw them out, and then reached into the backseat and took hold of his jacket with the peace symbol on it and crammed it out the window and let the wind take it.

"I wouldn't fuck with you," she said. "I wouldn't think of fucking with you."

Dougie slowed the big Cadillac, started looking for a place to pull off.

"I killed a guy tonight," she said, her voice full of shivery meanness. "I killed a guy, and now my personal fitness trainer is giving me a test. I got to say something weird to pass the test, or I'm going to get whacked too."

"You threw my jacket out," Dougie said, driving slow, but not looking for a pull-off anymore. Now that he'd had a minute to think about it, hell, he was impressed with the bitch.

"Yeah, I did." She snickered. "I threw your jacket the hell out the window." She laughed again. It was clear the lady's carburetors were tuned a little too rich.

Dougie looked over at her. He patted around on the dash till he found the inside light and he turned it on. She was laughing, stoned laughing, from down in her gut.

She caught her breath and said, "I'll throw every fucking thing in this car out on the road if you aren't careful." She reached into the backseat and picked up Dougie's nylon shaving kit and ran her window down.

Dougie used his control panel to roll it back up. While she was sending it back down, he grabbed the shaving kit from her. Elmira was laughing still, giggling and laughing.

Dougie looked at the shaving kit. He pushed the button for his window, got it all the way down, the freezing dark Utah air swirling into the car. He pitched the shaving kit out onto the highway and shot the window back up.

"Guffaw," Dougie said. "Guffaw outlaw."

"Eat it raw," she said. "Eat it raw, outlaw."

"How did it feel?" said Dougie. "When the bullet was going into him and he was falling over like that?"

She looked over at him, all the laughter gone out of her now. "It made me feel, I don't know," she said. "Powerful-like. Better than speed, than coke, better than anything I ever done."

Dougie thought about that. He looked over at her one more time. She wasn't smirking anymore. She was looking ahead out the windshield, her right hand rubbing the inside of her thigh. Her face dead. Dougie thumped the dash light off.

"From now on, when I ask you how it feels," he said, "you tell me right off, okay? No more laughing, and no more throwing shit out the window. Can you do that? Huh?"

"Okay," she said, her voice dead. "If that's what you want."

———

Monday evening as Shaw showered, he could hear his mother clanking pans in the kitchen, playing the radio. He was headed to Trula's, his pulse gunning. He was thinking about tomorrow too, flying to South Carolina and then Clearwater, on the trail of something, not sure what, and not even caring anymore. Only that he was there, a shadow disappearing around a twist in the path just ahead of him.

He toweled off, pulled on his jeans and white button-down dress shirt, rolled the sleeves halfway. Put on his watch, shook out a little after-shave and slapped himself with it. A new one he'd bought this week. He sat on the edge of the bed, listening to his mother downstairs, and he clipped his nails, then ran the nail file experimentally across his fingertips. Like a safecracker, sensitizing himself to feel the trickle of tumblers. Maybe he should buy a ream of sandpaper, wallow in it, rub himself down head to feet. Slough off all that insulation. It's what he'd heard dolphins did several times a day, shedding the dead layer of skin for a new tingling one.

Millie dropped a pan in the kitchen, and Shaw stood up, tightened his belt, stepped into his sandals and headed downstairs. He was whistling when he came into the kitchen, "Michelle, my belle, these are words that go together well." A song he connected with that fall when he'd been young and strong and fast, the fall with Trula in the seat beside him.

Millie's radio was hovering between stations, a Cuban salsa fading out and a basketball game rising behind it. She wore a pair of freshly pressed striped Bermudas and an extra large white T-shirt. Her hair pinned neatly into a bun.

He kissed her on the back of her neck, filled himself with the scent of her bath soap, and she turned and kissed him on the cheeks, as though she wanted him to smell her mint toothpaste, show him she was sober. But Shaw wasn't buying it. Maybe she hadn't had a drink all day. But there was still a woozy sway to her walk, a burr in her speech.

Pulling away, she said, "I'm making your favorite. Black beans, rice, plantains. Just you and me, sit down at the dinner table, pretend we're normal folks."

"I can't, Mother."

She turned back to the stove, lifted a lid, stirred the beans.

"Yes, you can, Shaw."

"I'm sorry, Mother. You should've told me you were going to do this. I already made plans to go over to Trula's."

She walked across to the radio, keeping her face from him. She tried to find a station, ran all the way up the dial, rejecting all the rock and roll, settling finally on a big band station.

"We need to talk," she said, turning to him, her face drawn and serious. "We haven't talked since you've been home."

"That's true," he said. "We haven't talked."

"We need to do it. There's important things we need to confront. Personal, family things. We need to talk."

"Mother," he said, "look at me. Turn around and look at me."

She hesitated, stirring the rice. Shaw sat down in one of the oak caneback chairs, scooted up to the table.

"You've been home two weeks," she said.

"Yeah, busting my ass in the tackle shop."

"I don't care a damn about the tackle shop, son. Let it go if you want."

"You don't care about it?" he said. "How were you planning on eating, buying your rum? What were you going to do?"

She stirred the rice.

"Mother, turn around, okay? Sit down for a minute, would you?"

She came to the table, carrying the spoon. A valve had shut off behind her eyes. They'd lost their supply of light. She sat down across from him, holding the spoon out between them as if she were offering him the three grains of rice stuck to it.

"Never mind," she said. "It's all right, you go ahead, go see Trula. Have your life. We can talk later. There's time."

"What is this, Mother? What's going on with you?" He heard himself, felt the dry constriction in his throat, asking himself why he was angry with her, why he'd heated up so fast. "You've been drunk the whole time I've been back. I come into the room and you're staring at the wall. I say hello, you might answer me, you might not. Then tonight, all of a sudden, you decide to put your rum bottle down, wash your face, and look at me. Now, it's suddenly time to talk. And I'm supposed to stop everything and listen and talk back."

The aluminum lid on the rice pot was rattling. A trickle of water ran over the edge and steamed on the coils.

"I'm sorry, Shaw. I'm sorry the way I've been."

"I'm sorry too," he snapped. He reached out, drew the spoon from her hand and put it down on the table.

The pot lid chattered, and water flowed over the rim of the pot, smoke rising. Shaw looked over at it but didn't move.

"Thirty-eight years, and now, tonight, I'm on the way out the door, feeling pretty good about my life for the first time in a long,

long time, and you want to have a real conversation. You want to dredge things up."

"Never mind, I said. Go on, be with Trula."

"So, what is it you wanted to talk about?" he said, hating himself, the bitterness burning his throat as he spoke, but not able to control it. "You want to talk about that night I lifted you off this floor, you had blood coming out your ear, and I carried you into the bedroom and I called the doctor? We going to talk about that, finally? Or what, maybe you want to tell me now why you stayed so long with that bastard, he beat you up once a week. You going to finally explain that to me?"

She looked down at the table, the rice overflowing now, spitting, hissing.

"The thing is, see, I think it's a little late to learn how to talk, Mother. We never practiced it, you and me. What we do, what we're good at, we sit next to each other on the couch, we watch TV and inside both of us is this anger and stored-up shit, and what do we talk about? We talk about goddamn Vegamatics. We talk about nothing, Mother. Nothing. We always have, we don't have the courage for anything else.

"And then all on your own, you decide tonight we're going to have the big conversation, the big moment. Well, great. I'm glad you're finally ready to do that. But personally, I'm not ready. I'm not ready to hear what you've got to say. And I'm not ready to talk either. At least not to you, not yet. In fact, I'm not even convinced anymore that talking about it is going to do any damn good. We're just the way we are. We're never going to get well, we just got to learn how to stumble along." He took a long breath, feeling his heart struggling to catch up.

"I'm sorry," he said.

She said nothing, looking down at the table.

"I'm going away a couple of days," he said. "When I get back . . . Look, I'm sorry, Mother."

"When you get back," she said.

"I'm really sorry."

"Don't be," she said. "You said good things. You got us started. I can put the black beans and rice in the freezer. You can have them when you get back. We can talk then if we feel like it. Give us both time to sort it out."

"Yeah."

He stood up, came around the table, and kissed her on the forehead. She lifted her eyes to his and nodded her head.

"You'll make it fine, son," she said.

"Yeah," he said. "I will. Damn right, I will."

But in the El Camino parked on Olivia Street across from the cemetery, hammering on the steering wheel, he wasn't sure. He wasn't sure at all.

19

If Trula went through the motions, set the table, chilled the wine, stirred the shrimp into a creamy sauce to cover the pasta, a meal her father loved, if she turned her back on the dark screen door, went about her ordinary business, then perhaps the driveway would fill with light and her father's Ford pickup would sputter and cough and shut off, and he would reappear at the screen door. She hadn't seen him since his pelican speech on Sunday afternoon. Thirty-six hours. And though she didn't fully believe it would work, it was all she had, this incantation of normalcy.

As she circled a wooden spoon through the sauce, Barbie Heyman came into her mind. Barbie's hand thrashing against the arm of the wheelchair. Her horrible mother. OK, all right. Maybe it was true what Frieda had said. Compared to Barbie's MS, Trula's was the lucky kind. The good kind.

Trula was sick, but still young enough to learn the new rules for her life. To learn how to carry inside her these frayed wires with their seeping voltage. She was sick, but without substantial pain. Sick, but able to stand at the stove and stir the sauce, maintain appearances. Maybe you could call that lucky.

The version Barbie Heyman had was truly devilish. Chronic progressive. Her disease had climbed aboard Barbie's back and had ridden her till she stumbled and fell and could not stand again. Then it pulled itself higher onto her shoulders, stooping her, stealing her air, her strength, the luminous burn of her eyes. It was like that, a cowardly disease. A tormentor, not a destroyer. And Trula hated it for that more than anything else.

For if she had known multiple sclerosis was to slay her, she believed she could learn to forgive it. She thought perhaps she could come to that peace she had read about, the tranquillity of the terminally ill, going gently into their own good nights. In their last days learning the slow beautiful secrets of death.

But no, this was leisurely and desultory torture. Coming at unpredictable moments to unravel her. Working silently and slowly, it stripped the wires that passed life through her body. Dissolved the buffers between one dangerous part of herself and another.

This afternoon after the questionnaire was done, Barbie had wanted to talk. She wanted to describe how she felt, see if it was the same for Trula. In her torturous mouthing, Barbie described the vague static, the same sound Trula had experienced, a mild buzzing in her head. But as Barbie's disease progressed, eating away more of the fatty sheathing of her nerves, she said the buzz in her ears had risen to a solid white noise. And finally as layer after layer of wire was opened, her head roared with it, the waterfall rumble of the current freely flowing inside her.

"My body," Barbie said, "electrocuted me."

"Well," her mother said, "it might as well have."

———

While the shrimp simmered, Trula sat at the kitchen table and read over the questionnaires. Half a dozen young women, all nurses, all under forty, all having lived on the island twenty years ago. But there was variety too. Different birthplaces, different social classes, different medical histories. Enough variations to fuzz over the comparisons. Trula knew something about the unreliability of statistics. One foot in boiling water, one foot in ice, your average temperature was supposed to be something you could stand.

But somewhere in all this, there was an answer. Dr. Waldorf had said as much. A major announcement. Collate the numbers, nudge them with just the right touch, and they would finally speak the truth. She believed that. Every second since meeting Dr. Waldorf she had believed it.

When she heard the car motor outside, the crunch of wheels on the seashell drive, Trula was picturing again Barbie's hand, fluttering like a power line snapped in a storm, sputtering its amperage into the empty air.

She hurried to the screen and watched Shaw Chandler get out

of his El Camino. She watched him hesitate as a loud squawking argument broke out in one of the cages. The pelicans probably fussing over a stick of driftwood. It was nesting time, the males courting their females, offering them tall, complicated nests.

She waited till Shaw mounted the porch, then she came outside, and when he opened his arms, she stepped into them.

"He probably got a wild hair, went off on an adventure."

"He's not like that."

Shaw said, "Maybe he has a girlfriend you don't know about."

"He would've told me if he was going to be away."

"Are you sure?"

"No, I'm not sure, damn it. But wouldn't you?"

"I would, yes. Definitely."

The kitchen phone rang and Trula was out of her chair before it made a second ring. She fumbled the phone to her ear and said hello.

She let him know with her eyes that it wasn't her father.

"Oh, hello, Captain Barnes," she said, giving Shaw a long quizzical look.

Shaw rose from the table, and adjusted the dials on the stove, cooling things. He sat at the table, watched Trula, the receiver pressed to her ear, but her eyes on him, more with him than with the voice on the phone.

"Yes," she said. "I'm doing fine, thanks."

She brushed the hair off her face, listening, watching Shaw.

"No, he's not here." Then she cut her gaze to the floor. "Back from where?"

"Utah?" she said. "What the hell's he doing in Utah?"

Lifting her eyes again to Shaw's, full of worry now.

Shaw could picture Barnes talking from his office at the dump, just half a mile away. He could hear his voice, that humorless, slightly pompous tone he had. Over the years thousands of men had been in his service, obeyed his insignia. He'd never had to learn respect for social graces.

"I don't get it," Trula said. "He told you he was going, but it slipped his mind to tell me?"

She listened for a moment and said, "A hurry? I'll say he was in a hurry. He didn't take his wallet or sunglasses."

"Yeah," she said. "Yeah, sure, okay, when he gets back I'll have him call you."

She put the phone on the hook.

"He went to Utah," Trula said. "Barnes isn't sure why."

"What's in Utah?"

She tapped the stack of questionnaires.

"The only thing I know of in Utah is Dr. Waldorf, the one who's investigating Key West."

She sat down at the table across from him. On the sink counter, the ice in the ice bucket resettled. They both looked over at it.

"I'm going away tomorrow," he said. "To talk to the widows, Pinkney and Chiles."

"What in the world could they tell you?"

"I don't know," he said. "Maybe something about what happened that night. What in the hell those two men had to do with my father."

Her eyes looked past Shaw, out the screen door into the darkness, farther out. The look of someone stranded at sea, searching the horizon.

"Barnes and your father," Shaw said. "They're close friends?"

"No."

"Were they ever?"

She brought her eyes back, looked at him closely.

"Now, what's this about?"

"I was at the courthouse this afternoon," he said. "I came across some curious facts from the past."

"My father despises Barnes," she said. "Utterly, absolutely, without reservation."

"Then I wonder," he said, "why your dad made Barnes a gift of almost three hundred acres of some pretty amazing real estate."

———

Shaw left her bed at five a.m. His flight departed at six-thirty. Trula felt his kisses on her face, her shoulders, and she reached up and drew him down for a long one on the lips. When the front door closed, she rolled over into the warmth he'd left behind, drew his pillow into her arms and plunged through the airless dark back into sleep.

———

It was almost dawn on Tuesday morning when Dougie and Elmira checked into the honeymoon suite in the Econo Lodge on the end of the Vegas strip. Red satin waterbed, drawings of fat Japanese couples screwing on the walls, and a twenty-four-hour dirty movie channel. Even a pile of fresh rubbers in a dish on the night table. Dougie stared at those Japanese people, trying to figure out just how they got that way. Near as he could tell, they had to be double jointed.

When they'd arrived in town, he'd driven up and down the main streets for half an hour, both of them gawking at the bright lights, all the neon showgirls flashing up their skirts, the cowboys whirling their lariats, and Dougie trying to read some of the marquees but not able to make out anything beyond a word here and there.

It was Elmira's idea about the Econo Lodge. She'd said whenever she went in one of the big places, the fancier ones, the bellmen and everybody else working there always treated her like shit, giving her the eye like she was about to set up a booth, hang out her shingle and start giving blowjobs in the lobby.

And at the Econo Lodge check-in counter it was her idea about the honeymoon room too. Dougie going along with her cause he was exhausted from the drive down from Salt Lake, and didn't give a big shit either way. And then they got into the suite and she lay down on the water bed and spread her legs and the short dress rode up to her thighs and she said, "I want to get married."

"What for?" Dougie said.

"I never been married," she said.

"Is that a reason?"

Dougie went into the bathroom and checked himself out in the mirror. Needed a shave, and his hair getting a little greasy, but otherwise, looking good. He rinsed his mouth out, splashed his face with water, and went back out to the bedroom and over to the TV and turned it on, fiddled with it for a minute till he found the dirty movie channel, a couple of dykes going at it in a hot tub, a black woman and a blond. The blond sitting there in the tub while the black lady went underwater and blew bubbles into her crouch.

"I want to get married, Dougie." Doing her pout again.

"So get married," he said. "Who's stopping you?"

"You mean it? You want to get married too."

"Hellfire, muck and mire," he said. "Bran muffin, brain-dead puffin."

"Come on, Dougie, we got something here. We got something going. Can't you feel it? It's hot, it's very hot between us, you know, I mean it's burning me up."

Still lying there giving him a full beaver shot if he wanted it. He did, then he looked back at the blond and the black.

"Well, shit," he said. "I guess I gotta get married sometime."

"You mean it?"

"Holy-moly, roly-poly," he said.

"Dougie," she said, "you just said it, you just said you wanted to get married. I was laying here and I heard it. You made an oral contract. Now don't yo-yo me, honey."

"All right," he said, watching the blond stand up and turn around as a big guy in an orange hard hat came walking up. Water dripped off the tips of her nipples as she pushed them up against their sag. The construction guy unzipped and let his full beef patty swing out, the blond reaching up and taking it in her mouth while the black girl got behind the blond and spread her buns and wiggled her face in there. Dougie turned up the sound so he could hear the moaning and groaning. You never knew when you might learn something new to say.

"All right," Dougie Barnes said. "I don't give a shit. Let's get married."

20

It was almost noon when Shaw stepped onto Mrs. Bertha Pinkney's sagging front porch on Drew Avenue in Charleston, South Carolina. The house was a flaking white Victorian with a wraparound porch and twin towers that jutted up into the magnolia and oak branches. The house was the only one on the block without a fresh paint job or a new Volvo out front. A last holdout against gentrification. Shaw had parked his rental behind a rusty green behemoth from the early sixties. The thing vaguely resembled a Chevrolet.

To get here from the airport, he'd driven through a mile of elegant streets with horse-drawn carriages. Except for the moss draping the oaks, Charleston might be Key West's twin. Houses built by ship's carpenters, plantation architecture with island accents. There was also the same exquisitely maintained center of town fringed by rotting mansions. The same tumor of genteel charm that Shaw had witnessed in Key West seemed to be spreading layer by layer outward, restoring everything in its path, driving the old-timers howling before it.

The door swung open as Shaw was raising his fist to knock. A short black woman stood behind the screen, her white hair frizzing out of a paisley scarf. She wore a red dress spattered with rhinestones, and around her neck were half a dozen loops of gold. Slanting her head, she peered curiously through the torn screen.

"Bertha Pinkney?"

She nodded.

"I'm Captain Peter Burke," Shaw said. "Naval Intelligence."

"No, you aren't," she said. Bertha adjusted her scarf and gave him her amused consideration. She said, "Navy Intelligence boys don't ever smile."

"Well, we've changed our style," Shaw said. "We're a lot less formal these days." He was wearing a blue dress shirt, nylon flight jacket and jeans, jogging shoes.

"Let's have a look-see at your identification, then."

"New regulations," he said, smiling helplessly. "We don't carry ID anymore."

She shook her head at him, lifting an eyebrow.

"You ought to work on that paltry story, son. At least buy yourself a black wallet with a little tin badge in it."

"Yeah, thanks," he said. "That's a good idea."

"Or even print yourself up some little cards with different business names."

She opened the screen door and stepped back into the hallway, nodding for him to come in.

"But I'm at the point these days, boy, what with all my friends either dying or deaf or can't remember their own names," she said, "I'm even happy to converse with con men."

Bertha Pinkney led him into her dark and cluttered living room. Every piece of furniture was draped with shawls, rag rugs and ratty tapestries. The lampshades dripped with tassels, and a dozen ornate brass candelabra were scattered around the room.

As he sat on the long, dipping couch, Shaw glimpsed a small anteroom off the living room with a round table and a large glass globe in the center of it. What looked like a pack of cards.

"You're a shrewd judge of people, Mrs. Pinkney."

"No, I'm a seer, Mr. Chandler," she said, seating herself across from him on a chair covered in taffeta and brocade. "That is your real name, isn't it?"

He measured out a few breaths and said, "I'm impressed, very impressed."

"I take it we're about to discuss my late husband."

Smiling to herself, she let him marinate in awe, pressing her palms flat, forming a steeple, and resting her chin on its spire.

"You've got the gift," Shaw said.

"Well, the honest truth is, Mr. Chandler, I didn't have to strain myself none," she said. "I spent enough hours back then watching you play baseball. And you ain't changed all that much. Though

I'm fairly sure you wouldn't recollect me, just an old nigger lady sitting in the stands. But my boy, Darnell, back then he couldn't get enough of watching you, copying your swing. He was just fifteen when you were a big high school star."

She rearranged herself on the sofa, showed him her gold teeth.

"You might be interested to know Darnell Junior's playing A-league ball, sending me checks regular, so I guess you could say in a roundabout way, I'm somewhat beholden to you."

Shaw shook his head.

She said, "Well, then, I expect you want me to start off telling you about the night Darnell Senior disappeared."

Bertha leaned forward and opened the lid of a wooden box on the coffee table and drew out a long cigar. She offered it to him and he declined. Leaning back into the sofa, she lit the cigar with a kitchen match, closed her eyes and took a couple of dreamy breaths of the smoke, and then proceeded to tell him what she knew.

It wasn't much. Just that Hanson had called up Darnell late in the afternoon that spring day, and told him that they had some kind of work to do that night around midnight. That was irregular, she said, both him calling up suddenly like that, and working so late. The only other unusual thing seemed to be how he was dressed when he came over.

"How was that?"

"Like one of them beekeepers, a white suit on. It was hot as a devil's picnic and he came to the door dressed up like a spaceman, going to take a stroll on the moon."

"Maybe it was a grease monkey's jumpsuit, and they were going to do some work in the motor pool."

"Oh, no," she said. "I seen plenty of those. No, sir, this thing made a hell of a racket when he moved. Sounded like it was made of wax paper or some such. It wasn't no overalls."

"Darnell was a mechanic, right?"

"He was assigned to the motor pool, yeah, and he did a little mechanicking, but mainly he drove the forklift and the tractor."

He asked her questions for another half hour and they crossed and recrossed the same territory. She had no idea what her husband and Chiles and Hanson were up to that night, and it was a subject Darnell wouldn't even discuss with her from the privacy of his grave. But it was clear as a glass bell to Bertha that Hanson hadn't ever had any kind of anger toward Darnell. Fact was, she said, on that particular night he was acting a little sheepish. More quiet than she'd ever seen him. Yeah, Shaw wanted to say, he'd just beat up his son in a bar. He might've been a little winded.

At the door, Shaw shook her small soft hand. When he let go, she held on to it, turned it over, and traced a fingernail down the fine spray of tributaries in his palm. After a moment, she let his hand go and peered up into his face, her eyes suffering with her knowledge.

"Go ahead," Shaw said. "Say it."

Bertha let him see clear into her dark eyes. She said, "A person can find the dog that bit him, but that ain't going to do nothing to cure the rabies."

He smiled at her.

"But till I find that dog," Shaw said, "I won't know exactly what brand of rabies I got."

———

Elmira was singing from the bathroom. Water running in there, the toilet flushing, the medicine cabinet opening and shutting. It was ten on Tuesday. Still in Las Vegas. Gone from Key West it seemed like a month, though it was only since last Saturday. And Dougie was looking out the window of the Econo Lodge holding a Browning automatic on his lap.

Dougie was bored with looking out the window, bored with traveling. New Orleans, Salt Lake City and Las Vegas. That was a couple places too many. Key West was all the place Dougie needed. You sat there and let the world come to you. It would, sooner or later, too. Every low-down rowdy girl in America at one time or another passed through Key West, and most every mean-ass out-of-work dude did too. All of them wanting to see the view from the edge of the world. See what they could get away with. What they had the nerve to try.

He listened to Elmira singing wedding songs in the bathroom, and he rubbed the barrel of his pistol against his chin, rasping against the stubble. He was bored of sitting in this motel and having Elmira hit him with things. Early this morning, before it was even light, she'd gone out and bought a short black whip somewhere, come back and lashed him with it, making little orgasm barks the whole time. He was bored watching dirty movies on the TV. All that oohing and aahing, all the actors starting to look alike. The only thing new on the horizon was this wedding.

"I'm still going to fuck whoever I want," he yelled in at Elmira. "I'll marry you, but I'm still going to go out and fuck teenage girls. 'Cause that's what I do."

Elmira stopped singing in the bathroom.

She stepped into the bedroom, naked except for her stockings and garter belt and red high heels. Looking very good, really smearing her face goop on today, her eyes all pink and shiny, her lips white.

"Heebie-jeebie," Dougie said. "Steamy Mimi."

"I don't want to get married this morning and have to go to no marriage counselor this afternoon," she said.

"Well, don't."

"Tell me I didn't hear you right. You didn't say anything about screwing with young girls after we're married, did you?"

"I've always done just whatever I wanted."

"Well, all that's changed," Elmira said, walking over to him. Her boobs rouged up too, with shadows painted on underneath the nipples. The woman had strange ways about her. But she looked damn good to Dougie.

"When you get married, Dougie, it's because you love somebody. I explained that to you this morning, all about love."

"I forget," he said. "Tell me again."

"Dougie."

"Go on, tell me again."

"It's a good feeling," she said. "You feel safe and scared both at once. No one can get you, 'cause you got this thing to protect you. But you like it so much, you're afraid it won't last. And it's like it's your birthday every day, so you don't give a shit if somebody's nasty to you, treats you like garbage or whatever. You don't hear anything bad, just walk around smiling, nobody knowing your secret but you and the guy you love." She came over closer to him. He could smell her, the funky vegetable odor she gave off. Squash, lima beans, with a little undertone of tuna. Elmira the casserole. "Can you remember that, Dougie?"

"Yeah, I guess."

She sat down on the bed next to his chair. She took the gun out of his hand and put it on the bedspread beside her. "When you love somebody, you don't fuck around with other people anymore, Dougie. You put everything you got into the one you love. Oh, you can still look at young girls, and you can still fuck them, but you have to do it in your head after you're married. You're lying there above the one you love, and you got your eyes closed tight, it's okay to picture that honey you saw somewhere, the one you wanted to boogie with. It's okay, 'cause you're keeping your wife happy, and your own self, and you're having your cake and eating it too. You're only screwing around in your head."

Dougie looked at Elmira, at that red patch of hair between her legs. The perfect heart it was shaped to look like. He liked Elmira. He liked her as much today in Las Vegas as he had Sunday in New Orleans. She was smart, maybe the smartest woman he'd ever been with. Somebody he could take home and show to his daddy and she'd be able to stay in the ring with the old man, no problem.

He closed his eyes hard together, and reached out his hand for that patch of red hair.

"I'm touching the pubes of Marilyn Monroe," he said, fingering her, eyes tight.

"Dougie, stop it."

"Oh, Marilyn, what a creamy, pungent pussy you got."

"Goddamn it, Dougie, stop it." She pushed his hand away.

He opened his eyes.

"What's wrong?"

"You can't imagine dead people," she said. "That's not right. That's sick."

"Oh," he said. "Okay."

Trula called the police at noon on Tuesday to report her father missing. The officer taking her call was having a conversation with someone else in the office while he was taking down Trula's information. She shouted at him to pay a little goddamn attention. Told him this was important. He hesitated, then said in a cold professional tone, "Lady, everything that comes through this office is important."

Then he went on to say they'd do what they could, a few more clichés of his profession, and Trula just set the phone down in the middle of one of them and cried.

She spent the afternoon cleaning out the pelican cages. Scrubbing the concrete floors with soapy water, scouring the feeding pans. Sweeping, hosing. Furious and in despair. The pelicans kept their distance.

It was almost six when she heard the phone ring in the main house. She slammed the pelican gate shut, raced across the yard and got it on the fourth ring.

No one answered her hello.

"Who is it?" Trula said.

In a moment a woman's voice spoke.

"He was murdered."

"What? Who is this?"

"It's Anne. Anne Pickles. I met you in New York. Dr. Waldorf. I was his assistant."

Trula said, Yes, of course, she remembered her.

Anne blew her nose. There was another long pause, a hard sigh.

"Dr. Waldorf," she said. "Someone killed him."

"Oh no."

"I'm in the hospital," she said. "My words, they aren't working right, coming out. You know? I hear what I say, it's not what I meant to say all the time. So you'll excuse me. You know this condition?"

"Yes," Trula said, "I know about it."

Anne said in a fragile voice, "I told the police. I told them upset. Dr. Waldorf was upset. The research was scaring him. And the police, they treated me like an idiot, an idiot. And when I told them it had to do with MS, they looked at me. They laughed. Who would kill somebody over MS? That's how they were, they laughed at me in my face. They say it's a suicide because they found him with . . . What do you call it? . . . A little pistol. Hide up your sleeve."

"Derringer," Trula said.

"His body was burned up inside his house. But I'm sure it wasn't a suicide. I'm sure of it. He doesn't like pistols. And he wasn't depressed or anything. I would've known if he had been. We were close. Close. Derringer, right?"

Trula asked her how the fire was set.

"What?"

"The fire, what do you know about it? Was some device used?"

"In the kitchen," Anne Pickles said. "Around the stove or something. Gasoline in a saucepan."

Anne was quiet for a moment, and Trula listened to the empty line. She could feel her own rage burn cold and deep. Months ago it had taken root and had smoldered inside her without her attending to it, and now that she needed it, the strength it gave, it was there, full blown, and her hand drumming on the kitchen stove in front of her was filled with it, the heat of her outrage.

"I'm in the hospital," Anne said. "An acute attack, seizures, everything. I'm not supposed to be. You know, I'm on this phone and I'm not supposed to be."

"I'm sorry."

"See, I called you because I couldn't think of anyone. I remembered in New York. What you'd said. You'd do anything to help. You said that in New York, in your apartment. You remember saying that?"

"I remember."

Anne said, "Someone's after his research. But I can't get anybody, my friends or anybody, they think I'm going mental. But see, I know he didn't commit suicide. I know it. And he was worried about something."

"I believe you, Anne. Dr. Waldorf didn't kill himself."

"You do? You believe me?"

"Absolutely."

"Well, listen," she said, "Somebody has to go. Somebody to his office, get his computer disks, his research. I think that's what, you know, that's what this is about. Somebody wants to keep him from his article, from publishing it. I know it."

"I'm coming out there," Trula said. "Right now."

"Are you sure? You'd do that? You'd come? All the way from Florida?"

"I'm on my way."

21

Naked, lying on the water bed, Elmira said, "I want to call your daddy, tell him we're married."

Dougie was doing push-ups beside the bed. Seventy-seven, seventy-eight. Another good thing about not having a pain threshold was that he could do push-ups or chin-ups or sit-ups till his muscles failed, not feeling any pain along the way until the moment came he just couldn't push himself away from the floor.

"Eighty, eighty-one," Dougie said.

"Dougie, come on. It's the polite thing to do, calling your relatives, telling them what you done."

"Call *your* relatives," he said. "Eighty-five, eighty-six."

"I don't have any," she said. "Not any real ones."

So she got on the phone and called another of her hooker girlfriends in New Orleans. Told this one the same thing she told the other three. He's wonderful. Good-looking, great body, grinning at Dougie as she said it all, and he's into, you know, the same things I'm into. And then a little squeal as her hooker friend must have squealed at the other end.

And you should have seen it, she said. It was the cutest little chapel with the walls painted so it looked just like you were standing inside one of those big old cathedrals in Spain or somewhere. And the organ music—they had great speakers, it sounded so good—and the Mormon Tabernacle Choir singing the wedding march. No, you dolt, she said, it was on a tape recorder. And the preacher, you won't believe this, Holly, he does impersonation acts in one of the clubs and he asked us if we wanted to be married by Wayne Newton, Richard Nixon, Eddie Murphy, or Bugs Bunny. So of course I said, Wayne. Another squeal.

Dougie had liked the idea of Bugs Bunny. Or Porky Pig, a-huh, a-huh, a-huh, that's all, folks. Might catch on as a theme song for marriage ceremonies.

Then Elmira said, Well, I can't tell you just what his profession is, but he makes good money at it. No, not drugs, she said. No, Holly, not a pimp either. All during this time she was getting that pout in her voice, firing Dougie looks, like she was trying to let him know she didn't like this, him not having a job she could brag about to her hooker girlfriends.

And she said, I just can't tell you. It's very—you know—it's very serious stuff, and I can't go into it over the phone. Then she said, Key West. In Florida, down there at the tip of it. And then she laughed, laughed some more. And when she stopped, she put her hand over the mouthpiece and said to Dougie, Holly says she always thought the Florida Keys looked like the last dribble or cum leaking out of the limp dick of America. Dougie grunted. And Elmira went back, Yeah, yeah, Key West, I know there's a lot of them there. No, he's not, for Christsakes. Yeah, he has his own beach house. And then she turned to Dougie and asked him if he'd ever been married before. And he said, no, not so you'd notice, a hundred and three, a hundred and four. And she said into the phone, No, he's practically a virgin. Then another squeal.

When she'd hung up with that one, she started whining again about calling his father. Dougie's face was down in the Econo Lodge carpet then, his nose buried in the green pile. He'd made it to one hundred and thirty-four before he collapsed, and now he had just enough muscle power to roll on his back.

"So call him, goddamn it. Call him already." Dougie's sweat stuck him to the carpet. He gave Elmira his father's number at the plant, and she dialed it. "Fuck a duck," he said. "Flim-flam, slam bam, ram a dam a ding dong."

Elmira punched out the numbers. Waited. Dougie wondering if this was such a good idea, but not able to think at the moment, all the blood that should've been in his brain was in his chest muscles.

Elmira spoke to somebody, probably Jane the receptionist, and then she waited, humming the wedding march.

"Hello," Elmira said. "This is Elmira, Elmira Barnes."

Dougie watched her listening to the voice coming back over the phone. She was smiling wide, full of herself.

"Well, Daddy Barnes," she said, "say hi to your new daughter-in-law."

She listened to the phone, the smile disappearing little by little and said, "Elmira Barnes, Dougie's new wife."

Then Dougie heard his daddy's voice chirping over the phone. All that way through the wires running from Key West to Las Vegas, his father's voice coming into the Econo Lodge and lifting a rash of goose pimples on Dougie's arms and the back of his neck. Elmira wasn't smiling anymore. She held the phone in her naked lap, looking down at it.

"What'd the old man say?"

"He wants to talk to you," she said. She picked the phone out of her lap, held it out to him, staring at Dougie's chest like she could see right through it.

Changing planes in Denver, Trula phoned her father's number in the main house. She let it ring two dozen times before she gave up. In fifteen years of calling home at every hour of the day or night, in any season, he had always been there, snapping up the receiver in five, six rings at the most. His gruff voice relaxing when he heard her speak.

It was never anything he said that steadied her. No wisdom or advice. Just the timbre of his grumble, his rich, enduring bass. No matter what New York pain had brought her to the phone, in five minutes she was drawing easy breaths again. Always he had been there, always, five, six rings. The only time he had been off the island in years was to help her move back home. So she could not persuade herself that he had gone on any sudden trip. He was not a sudden man. Something had to have wrenched him away from his birds, from his tight, austere routines. Wherever he was, he was not there by choice. She was certain of that.

She called the Monroe County sheriff again and after five minutes on hold, the officer she had spoken to before came on.

"We found his pickup truck in the airport parking lot, Miss Montoya. So it looks like he did take a trip after all."

"I don't believe it."

"It was there," he said. "Black Seventy-four Ford pickup, the plates are in his name. Parked over by the rental lot."

"Somebody put it there," she said. "My father didn't take any trip without telling me."

"You have some reason to believe that?"

"I know the man. That's my reason."

Trula listened to the electric echoes between them.

"Thanks for your help," she said, and hung up.

In a mild daze she bought a hot dog and a Coke, made herself eat it while waiting at Gate Twelve on the C Concourse. As she finished it, wadding the paper and dropping it into the ashtray beside her chair, she felt the familiar bands of numbness drawing tight around her ankles. She fixed her eyes on the people moving about the waiting room, straining to focus on them, to keep at bay what she knew was happening to her.

But the warm, tight socks continued to unroll up her ankles, higher, spreading their heat to her shins, finally to her kneecaps. Or was it ice she was sinking into, deadening cold? She knew if she tried to stand now, she would fall.

She watched a Japanese family across from her, tourists, smiling incessantly as they spoke to each other. They laughed while a teenage boy in their party filmed them, leaning in close to a giggling girl, maybe his sister. Trula watched them. She looked at their smiles, their blue jeans, down parkas, bulky sweaters. Their jewelry. Listened to their choppy patter.

The numbness rose up her legs. Already she had lost her feet, her toes. She let herself look down at her vacant leather boots, someone else's feet inside them now, the connections broken. The circuits fritzing their current into the wrong pathways. She felt the familiar panic, the desperation, a surge of helpless rage. Sweat tracked down her back.

Then it stopped. The power was restored. Like that, no warning, no reason. A loose wire jiggled back into place. Her toes moved. She breathed. Let it out. Breathed it back in. One of the Japanese girls was whispering to the boy with the camera, nodding toward Trula. The boy turned and came across the narrow aisle.

He spoke to her, but she couldn't make out what he said, his English muddy, her ears still humming with the vague echoes of her heartbeat.

He bowed to her and spoke again.

"Cassie Wanetree?" He smiled and she smiled back and nodded yes. At this moment she was happy to be Cassie Raintree again.

"Take picture?" he said. "With sister there. Just a minute, prease?"

"Of course," she said. "Of course you may."

When the Japanese girl came over, Trula rose unsteadily from the chair, put her arm across the girl's shoulder, leaned lightly on her as the boy filmed this lucky moment in America.

"I sorry you died," the girl said, smiling, and bowing her head. "I hope you come back arrive soon."

"Thank you," Trula said. "Thank you."

———

"He was nasty," Elmira said.

"He's nasty to everybody," Dougie said. It was just after sunrise, Wednesday morning. They were crossing southern Utah again, the sun just coming up, the road was empty. Boring-ass strip of road for the last two hundred miles, nothing to look at but big slick rocks, no trees. Here Dougie was, stuck in the Wild West, driving up and back this same highway between Las Vegas and Salt Lake City.

"It hurt my feelings," she said. "You should've told me he was that way, got me prepared better." She was fiddling with the ring she'd bought in a twenty-four-hour pawnshop along the Vegas strip. "All I wanted was to say hello to him, tell him I'm his new daughter-in-law, and he nearly took my head off. He called me a dumb cunt, Dougie. A dumb cunt. Your father called me that on the phone. And he doesn't even know me."

"Well, he's a pretty good guesser."

"Now you're going to start being nasty."

Dougie smiled at her and said, "I'm just joking."

"You never told me we were supposed to do something else in Salt Lake," Elmira said. "You never said anything about any papers or research or anything. So it wasn't my fault. It wasn't any of my fault."

"I forgot," Dougie said. "It's no big deal."

Elmira was quiet for a minute, then she shot her window down and back up.

"It's no biggie," she said. "No biggie. That's what that dork said, trying to sound cool. Waldorf the waldork."

Dougie looked over at her. The Cadillac doing close to ninety through red-rock canyons. Wind had rubbed the rocks smooth out there, carving tunnels and bridges in them, leaving tall, skinny chimney rocks. You could strap a woman to a rock like that, leave her for a year or two, let the wind work on her, hollow out the openings she already had in her, smooth them, widen them. You could come back later and you'd have something you could put out in your front yard. A sculpture or something, Wind Woman. Stick your head through her legs and look out the backside. He glanced over at Elmira and she was smiling at him. Her orange-red hair jutting up funny all over her head.

"No biggie," she said again, giving him a loony smile.

"Biggie wiggy," Dougie said back at her. "Piggly wiggly. Hogly woggly, piddly widdly."

"Why do you do that?" Elmira said. "Why do you say all those things?"

"Holy-moly, roly-poly."

"Why, Dougie?"

"It's what I do."

"Well, it's too fucking weird," she said. "It gives me the creeps sometimes, you talk that way."

"Creepy peepie," Dougie said, "dickle dackle, spickle spackle. Penis weenis."

"Penis weenis?" Elmira said.

"You're going in there," Dougie said. "You're going in there to Waldorkus's office, and what're you going to do?"

"I'm going to splash the place with gasoline and light a match and get the hell out of there," she said.

"Then what?"

She rolled her window down, sent it back up.

"I'm going to remember how it all felt."

———

It was eight in the morning and Trula's taxi was just inching along, following the snowplow as it opened a second lane of traffic out of the Salt Lake airport.

She was groggy. Not able to rest on the plane, staying right on the edge of sleep, listening to her body, to see if she could detect the quiet fizz of another exacerbation. Hearing nothing. Feeling all right but still anxious.

Then she had tried to picture that May twenty years ago, the night Pinkney and Chiles disappeared. Her father's face coming to the screen in her mind. She put him with the other three men, Pinkney and Chiles, and also Hanson. They were doing something at night, but the part where the two men were killed was vague. It was there, hovering behind the snow flurry, just out of view. Then seeing again the weeks afterward when her father had begun to sit for hours on the front porch, looking down into his dark drinks. Giving his land away to a man he hated, quitting the navy.

And a few lifetimes later Hanson Chandler had come to her door, filling it with his hulk, his face sad and determined. Hearing again the words he spoke, that someone had to have an operation and he had to have money to pay for it, and he would wreck her father's life if Trula didn't give it to him. And then Shaw had appeared, tall and calm and funny. He had told her about his quest, searching for his father's killer. Which jolted Trula, reminded her that she had a quest too. She'd come home looking for answers about her illness. She'd had her own belly fire, but she'd let it cool. She'd come home, started helping her father with the damaged birds, and then swimming for hours with Bravo, watching the wind tousle the palms, and she'd put it aside. Gone loose and sluggish like everyone else in the Keys. The Keys disease. But Shaw had reminded her, rekindled her fire with his.

On the plane, image swirling into image, she considered it all again from the beginning, seeing Shaw's search and her own dovetailing. Their lives had mingled even before they'd met again. Hanson Chandler's suicide that wasn't a suicide, a fire to cover it up. Dr. Waldorf's death a replica of Hanson's. Someone killing the two men the same way and not concerned about anyone seeing a pattern there, the two men so apparently disconnected from each other.

And then somewhere flying over America, she had felt a quiet shaking in her gut. The first tremors of panic. And she felt it still, hours later, riding in the backseat of the taxi, shivering, pressing her hand against the cold glass window. Her blood and her breath hot and strained.

This story she was playing in wasn't a charmed half hour of TV, where viciousness and cruelty were neatly repaid. This was the random world. No cameras, no stagehands, just this disorganized flow of people, this plotless movement forward. She had to live this without direction, speak her lines, find her place onstage. And she had to fill herself with courage. Only this time she must make it solid, make it endure beyond an hour of taping. Use the anger she'd been harboring so long and drive it deep into bone and muscle until it took hold of her, became more real than art.

———

Trula found Anne's room on the third floor of Salt Lake Memorial Hospital. A breakfast tray was propped in front of her. Anne looking up, smiling.

"You came."

"Yes."

"I'm better this morning," Anne said. "I wiggled my toes just now."

"Good."

"You're in a hurry," she said. "You want to get over there, don't you? To his office for the article."

Trula said, Yes, yes she did.

Anne said, "Well, I know it's on a computer disk. And I know every night after he was finished working, he taped it to the back of a photograph on the wall of his office. But I don't know which photograph."

"That's good enough."

"I thought he was being paranoid." Anne sniffed. "Taking all those precautions."

"He knew he was onto something big," Trula said.

Anne nodded and said, "Dr. Waldorf talked about you a lot. About all those things you said to him."

"I was really unfair to him that day," Trula said. "My big speech, dumping it all on him. I just lost it."

"No, it was a good speech." Anne looked down at the scrambled eggs, bacon, not steaming anymore. "It was a good speech and Dr. Waldorf said it made a difference to him. That it gave him new energy. He said it reminded him why he was doing all this. He respected you for it." Her eyes wandered around the room, eventually came back to Trula. "I wish I'd said that speech. I've felt a lot of those same things, but I never said them out loud. I wish I had."

"Listen, Anne," she said, "do you know what it was, this announcement he was about to make? The thing he'd discovered?"

"Some of it," she said. "Just what he'd let slip out now and then. He was keeping it secret. I think, now, he was trying to protect me."

"Can you tell me?"

Anne said, "He started off, all he wanted was to write about the MS cluster in Key West. The high incidence. But then he went down there a few times to do his questionnaires, and he came across other things. So, the article turned into an expose of something bigger, something dangerous going on there. Now and in the past too.

"It's why the article was taking him so long. He started off just looking at the MS thing, very straightforward, then all of a sudden he had me doing all this research in the library, books, pamphlets. That's what was taking him so long. He had to learn about a lot of things, fires and things."

"Fires?"

"Fires, temperatures. What burns up at what temperature, things like that." The bright tracks lit on her cheeks. "It's ironic now," she said, her voice breaking. "Studying fires, and then dying in one."

"It's okay, Anne," Trula said. "It's going to be all right."

"And nerve gas," Anne said, swallowing hard, sniffing.

"What?!"

"Nerve gas," she said. "He had me digging up things, government documents mostly, the history of chemical warfare, nerve-gas testing, things like that."

"Oh, sweet Jesus."

Trula let herself down into the chair beside Anne's bed.

"What? What'd I say?"

"Nerve gas," said Trula, "it's what my father did toward the end of his career. He worked with it, I'm not sure in what capacity. It was his last research project in the navy."

"Well, that explains it."

"What?"

"Dr. Waldorf said he owed this all to your father. That without his help, there wouldn't have been an article. Your dad put him onto this in the first place."

"Really?"

"Really."

"You haven't seen him, have you? My father, he hasn't been out here? The last few days?"

Anne frowned, held Trula's eyes. Shook her head slowly.

———

In the taxi Trula unbuttoned her coat, looked off into the white distances. Hidden behind the veil of snow were mountains, the Wasatch range, the foothills of the Rockies. As they drove slowly back to the highway, the wipers slapped but did little to improve the visibility. The one on Trula's side was torn, a loop of useless rubber whipped across the window.

Trula fidgeted with the buttons on her coat, squinting out at the dull brightness of snow. Keeping her mind blank, watching things, not letting the words form in her head, the words that might talk her out of this, reason with her, turn her around, head her back to Key West.

She watched the loop of rubber swipe uselessly at the glass. She stared out the window, as they passed through downtown Salt Lake, past the tabernacle. Accelerating away from a green light, the cab fishtailed, the driver muttered to himself as he regained control.

She saw the University Pharmacy. Campus Clothing Corner. Bookstores and pizza parlors. Mexican restaurants. A steep climb up a wide avenue with tall modern buildings at the crest. Students leaning into the snow, carrying knapsacks. Then down its steep backside, the cab going faster.

After that, it was nothing the driver did or didn't do. Just an icy patch on the road. Trula felt the tires lose their grip, watched the snowbank come slowly at them, the car turning sideways, sliding, and the driver cursing, and the tires broke completely free and the Ford began a lazy, inevitable spin toward the hill of snow.

22

Elmira said, "What if somebody's in there, in the office when I go in, what'm I supposed to do, say, excuse me while I douse you with this gasoline? Huh, Dougie-buggie?"

"Don't call me that."

"Okay, huggie-Dougie," she said, "what am I going to do if somebody's in there?"

"It's why I brought this." He bent forward and pulled the Browning automatic out from under the seat, nearly drove the Caddy off the cliff doing it. He jerked them back into the lane behind a Peterbilt and put the pistol on the seat between them.

Dougie had asked his father the same thing. What if there's somebody in the office? And his father looked doubtful at him, like he was ready to cancel the whole plan. And Dougie had said, Don't worry. Don't worry, I'm just kidding you. Then his father carefully explained to Dougie that there was a very good chance that something in Waldorf's office, never mind what it was, it could bury the whole bunch of them if they didn't burn it up, so if there's somebody in there, a secretary or whatever, you use your special skills on her and then set the rest of the place on fire.

And now, as Dougie recalled the conversation in his father's office, and the other one on the phone this morning, he shook his head. Why couldn't he remember things? His father had made him write it all down. Then he'd said it over and over, five or six times: Do Waldorf, then do his office. Dougie still had the note somewhere.

Elmira tapped him on the leg and said, "I don't want to go in there alone, Dougie. Come on, it's not right, me having to do it all by myself."

They were about forty-five miles south of Salt Lake, not making any time at all because of the snow. Just following the eighteen-wheeler in front of them, trying not to slide off the cliffs. Dougie kept quiet, squinting at the road.

"I don't think you even love me. You just married me to make me do your bad things for you. That's it, isn't it? You don't love me at all. You didn't even know what love was till I explained it to you the other day."

Just like the last time they drove into Salt Lake City, she was whining again. Utah flashback. Making her voice pouty, tilting her chin down and looking up at him through her long fake lashes. Only this time, he was married to the woman. Now, that was strange. Dougie had to say, he'd taken a bold step, marrying this whore. He hadn't even known her last name till she'd said it to the Wayne Newton minister in Las Vegas. Hemple. Elmira Hemple.

"Hemple, pimple," he said, staring into the snow. "Hairy dimple."

"Don't start," she said.

He followed the eighteen-wheeler as it pulled into the passing lane, snow swirling up all around them. Dougie said, "Hey, Hemple, you wanna unlimber my member? Put a little lipstick on my dipstick?"

"My name is Barnes, not Hemple. I'm married to you, remember?"

"How about it, wanna juice my Johnson, gulp my prick while the roads are slick, make me warm in a snowstorm?"

"Right here? Right now?"

"No, on Mars. Ten light-years from now."

"Well, I might be interested," she said, reaching her hand over and stroking the leg of his black jeans. "If you'd come in there with me, into that office."

"I guess I'd have to consider it," he said, "if you sucked it good enough."

"All right," she said. "I could do that."

"So what the hell're you waiting for, woman?"

She tipped her head down, looked up at him through her eyelashes.

"Can I bite it?" she said. "Hard?"

"I don't know why not," he said. "I can spare a couple of inches."

She made one of her smiles, the crazy, lip-licking one.
"Well, I won't bite that hard," she said. "I don't think."

———

Shaw found Loretta Chiles's house on Coral Sea Drive, a
Frisbee toss from Clearwater Beach. It was a run-down A-frame
with lots of glass that looked across a wide street through a thicket
of neon signs and telephone poles at the Gulf of Mexico. A wooden
sign at the sidewalk said THE HEALING HOUSE.

He was rumpled from a night at Tampa International Airport,
sleeping on a bench near the Delta counter. When his flight had
arrived from Charleston late last night, Shaw had intended to find
a motel in Tampa, but he'd sat down to rest for a few minutes on
the bench and had slumped into sleep almost immediately.

When he woke, he knew neither season nor city, month nor
hour. He sat for a moment finding his place in this moment, watching the travelers making their brisk good-byes, their snug reunions,
the loners hurrying across the wide floors.

———

He arrived at Loretta Chiles's front door on Coral Sea
Drive at eight-thirty after killing an hour in a Denny's down the
street, dragging the cobwebs away with three cups of strong coffee.

A girl of about seventeen drew the front door open, held it,
inserting herself into the narrow opening. She was blond and wore
a black bikini. The kind of bikini that required extensive and careful
shaving.

"I'm Peter Miller," Shaw said. "Navy Intelligence."

"Hi, Navy Intelligence," the girl said.

"Hello."

"Navy Intelligence," she said, moving her eyes over him. "That's
like a what-you-call-it. You know, an oxymoron. I studied them in
English."

She was leaning a shoulder against the backside of the door.
Ready to throw her pretty weight against it and slam it on his nose
or fall backward and suck him into the house.

Shaw didn't know what to do with his eyes.

"Is your mother home?" he said.

"Sure," she said and gazed off over his head, at the weather. Letting him have the look he'd been too shy to take. She had all the swelling dimensions of the species, the tapered waist, the taut skin, the fine angles of nose and cheekbone. A girl to pin to the wall for a month. She drew an arrow down her cleavage with a sharp pink nail. And scratched at the flesh hidden under her bikini strap.

"I want to speak to your mother," he said.

"What's an oxymoron want with my mother?" she said, her eyes drifting back from the weather to his face. Granting him the honor of her smile. Her titillating finger moving inside her bra.

"You know, sweetheart," Shaw said, "I have no doubt that if somebody cut you up for bait, they could catch a thousand Saudi princes. But at the moment, God help me, I'm immune to it."

"Lucky you," she said. Her smile twisted in on itself and she turned abruptly back into the house, leaving the door ajar. Shaw waited a few minutes, watching the traffic out on Coral Sea Drive. He waited as long as he thought Navy Intelligence officers were trained to wait. Then he pushed open the door and followed a current of frying onions into the kitchen.

"Mrs. Chiles?" he said from the doorway. She was a rangy woman with short hair a shade darker than her daughter's. She wore a loose white robe and stood at the stove over a sizzling pan.

"Yes?"

"I'm sorry to wander in like this."

"Don't be sorry. That's why we're here."

Shaw saw a man lean out for a look at him from a breakfast nook off the kitchen. Another man next to him at the round table continued to eat. They had the gaunt and bloodshot look of career hobos.

"I'm Peter Miller," he said.

"We don't use last names here," she said. "Just get a plate from the table and join the others. We already chanted the Damiyatva, but after breakfast we'll be doing the Sumivarna."

"I'm not here for breakfast," he said.

Another man came into the kitchen then, a tall man with a long gray ponytail and a beard that came to the middle of his chest. He was wearing white harem pants and no shirt. He kissed Loretta

Chiles on the cheek, nodded to Shaw and joined the other men in the breakfast nook.

"I'm not here for the chants, or any of that. I want to know some things, and I was hoping you could tell me about them."

"What things?" She stirred her spatula through the onions and peppers, lifted the lid on a deep pot of brown rice.

"About your husband," he said. "About Billy Chiles's death."

"Drummond," she called toward the breakfast nook.

The man with the beard leaned out and answered her.

"You take over here, would you please," she said, setting the spatula aside. "I have to speak privately to this gentleman."

She sat on a round cushion on the wooden deck behind the house. Locking herself easily into a full lotus position as if she were professionally double-jointed. Shaw sat on the bare boards across from her. Stretched out in the grassy backyard were two women in jeans and T-shirts. They were both sleeping on blankets, using their packs for pillows.

"We're what's left of the safety net," she said, nodding toward the women. "We share what we can with them, drifters and runaways. We teach them what we know of Christian Yoga, give them healthy vegetarian food."

"The Healing House," Shaw said.

"Yes," she said. "We think of ourselves as healers." She regarded him for a few moments, and said, "Are they finally going to do something about this?"

"What?"

"Billy's death," she said. "That's why you're here, isn't it? I've been writing letters for twenty years, and you're the first person who's ever followed up. Aren't you with the government?"

"I'm not at liberty to say," he said.

"Well, you're not what I imagined," she said. "I thought it would be blue suits, black shoes, a white Ford."

"Tell me about it," Shaw said.

"What part?"

"The night he disappeared, whatever you feel is important."

One of the girls was waking out in the backyard. She rolled over, coughed a couple of times, patted her shirt until she found a cigarette. As she was tamping it against the back of her hand, Loretta noticed her and called out, "Shred it, Linda. Shred it now."

The girl hesitated, rolled her eyes, and crumbled the cigarette in her hand, dropped it in the grass, and turned over to finish her dream.

"It was Captain Barnes, Douglas Barnes, the commander of the base who did it."

"Did what, Mrs. Chiles?"

"I'm not sure exactly what he did. But he was guilty of something, though. I'm sure of that."

"Barnes," said Shaw.

"He gave me money," she said. "He called it relocation remuneration. Those were his words. But it was a bribe, pure and simple. I knew something was wrong with it at the time, but I was a young wife, in grief over my husband's disappearance, so I took it."

"How much?"

"Ten thousand dollars."

"That was a lot of money back then."

"To some of us it's still a lot," she said. "And that ten thousand is long gone, believe me. I just drove out of Key West, looking for somewhere to plop down. I had no insides left. I had every bit of myself invested in Billy. I was young and innocent and I guess I was stupid. I never questioned it, why the navy would give me ten thousand in cash to move away."

"Why *did* they? Why do you think?"

"Barnes said it was SOP, but I talked to people afterward, and no one ever heard of anything like that."

"It does sound strange," Shaw said.

"Everything about it was strange," she said. "Billy worked as a medical technician and he had very regular hours. And he never even went to bars. But that night he and that fellow Chandler who took the blame for it, well, the two of them went off together for some drinks. And that's the last I ever heard from him."

"If your husband was a medical technician, then he must have worked with Dr. Montoya."

"Yes," she said. "That's right. Montoya."

Chanting had begun inside the house. Not the resonant kind Shaw had heard before, but something frailer and more halfhearted. The croak of the imperfect believer.

"I've spoken to congressmen, I've written to newspapers, I've called the TV help lines. I've done everything I could think of, everything a citizen can. And not a single person has ever shown any interest in the case. They don't want to look at it, don't want to know."

"What kind of work did your husband do for Montoya?"

"Everything that could come up on a navy base. Venereal diseases to whooping cough."

"Billy was a doctor?"

"My husband had a premed degree and he was going to medical school as soon as the navy got through with him." She glanced up at the empty sky for a few moments, her eyes languorous as they drifted back to earth. She said, "So, he knew what he was talking about. If he said something was wrong, then something was wrong."

"What was that, something wrong?"

"Oh," she said. "I thought you knew."

"I want to hear your version."

"I thought that's why you were here, you had something to tell me about it."

She looked unhappily at Shaw, her confidence in him seeping away. Another disappointment.

She said, "They were running tests, aerosol testing. And Billy thought it was very bad. He didn't approve of it, and neither did Dr. Montoya. Both of them were fighting Captain Barnes and the rest of the navy over it. I knew that much. He was afraid he was going to be court-martialed. But he never did tell me any details. It was all classified. But I could see then, even though I was awful innocent, I could see it was eating him up. Just eating him up."

Again, her eyes loosened from the moment, went back to revisit Billy, all that. She stayed there for a long minute, then blinked hard, and came back.

She said, "I have a pamphlet upstairs. It took me a year to get it. I had to go to Washington several times, dig around, pester the librarians. It's all been declassified now, you know, the Freedom of Information Act. But they hide it in these obscure subcommittee reports. That's the way they do things. They finally tell the truth, but you know, make it very hard to find. But I found it. Names, dates, which chemicals they sprayed. All of it. I have a few copies if you want one."

Shaw said, Yes, he'd like one very much.

Loretta got up and went into the house. In a minute or two she was back with a white booklet. *Ninety-fifth Congress, First Session. Examination of Serious Deficiencies in the Defense Department's Efforts to Protect the Human Subjects of Drug Research. Committee on Human Resources, United States Senate.*

"You could say it started in the French and Indian Wars," she said. She locked herself again into a full lotus. "We gave blankets contaminated by smallpox to hostile Indian tribes. We did things like that, even then."

Shaw nodded.

"And in Louisiana, I forget when this was, but it was the last few years," she said. "I've read so much, I remember things, but I forget the dates sometimes. In Louisiana, though, I'm sure about that, the government was doing research on leprosy, trying to figure out a way they could bottle it, spray it on our enemies. For some reason armadillos are the research animals for leprosy. Anyway, despite all the precautions they took, some of the test animals escaped, and leprosy infection got established in the wild population of armadillos in Louisiana. All those armadillos walking around carrying leprosy. That's how it works. That's how sloppy they are.

"You know, I read all about this. I studied it, made it my job. How it all started in the Dark Ages, the fourteenth century, I think it was the Tatars besieging some city, Kaffa or something. They catapulted corpses riddled with bubonic plague over the walls. And it worked. In that city, the plague killed thousands and the ships that sailed from there carried infected rats that spread the plague all over Europe."

Shaw watched her blinking back the blur in her eyes. Staring out at the girls sleeping in her yard, fighting an old battle in her head.

"You mentioned aerosol testing," Shaw said. "The navy did that in Key West?"

"That's right," she said. She sniffed, then pulled in a chestful of air. "It's all in there, in that book."

"I'm not familiar with the term. 'Aerosol testing'?"

"They spray chemicals, bacteria, or whatnot into the air," she said. "To see how it spreads itself. The military used to do it to simulate an attack, a biological attack, with nerve gas, you know. They said it was so they could figure out how many people they'd kill in a real war, or how to defend against an attack. They used a bacterium, *Serratia marcescens,* they thought was harmless, nonpathogenic. It was supposed to turn people's gums red, and they could trace it that way. But it didn't just do that. It gave people pneumonia, even killed people who were sick. They were weakened, fighting some disease. It was the straw that broke their backs. It's all in the pamphlet, but you have to read it careful, between the lines to really figure out what's being said."

"Pneumonia?" Shaw said.

"Yeah, pneumonia," said Loretta. "There was a very big rise in pneumonia cases in Key West right after they sprayed."

"They sprayed this stuff, what, over a football field or something?"

"Oh no," she said. "Over the whole island. Over unsuspecting citizens."

"Jesus."

"And it wasn't just in Key West. Oh no. Back then they did the same thing in San Francisco, in New York, I think it was in the Holland Tunnel, and in the subways. See which way the air moved. But they liked Key West the best. It was their favorite place for things like that."

Shaw was quiet.

"It was perfect for them. So far away from anything. The economy was very dependent on the military, so no one complained about them or even watched them close. You could do things there, get away with things, everybody's so laid back no one would notice. And if by some chance they did notice, nobody cared." She shook her head, looked off at the girls sleeping in her backyard. "That was Billy's mistake. The poor fool cared."

23

With her eyes closed, Trula heard only the dry squeak of car tires passing on the snow-packed avenue. Her head leaned heavily against the window, as she stayed in the dense broth of semiconsciousness, unwilling to bring herself back to the light.

Eventually there were voices. Professional, authoritative. Men practiced in the ways of emergencies. Moving quick, but not hurried. Her father's voice had been that way once, definite, with a brusque impatience for the muddlers and the dalliers. Maybe she should open her eyes and watch them approach, note the color of their uniforms, the shape of their insignia. Describe them to Shaw later. Rescuers like he was.

She let herself think about Shaw again. Doing it, running him through her memory, it was like humming an old song. A tune that brought back the scent and feel of a simpler time. High school nostalgia. A time before the ways of the world and her own body had become so complicated. Before her nerves began to fray. A ballad from high school, played now twenty years later with all the nicks and scratches and skips. Two Shaws. The long-ago one and the modern one. The song she had danced to briefly, now its familiar lyrics with a new layer of meaning.

She pictured saying this to him, wishing she'd thought of it before: I've never done that with my hands before, the blind thing, putting everything there. I've never done that before.

Smiling in her mind, she pictured Shaw as a teenager, his locker door pasted over with baseball pictures, his pigeon-toed jock walk, his friends whom he resembled but was different from. Seeing that time, the gleaming hallways of that high school where she had first learned to act, where everyone was acting, but not calling it that.

But Trula knew what it was, what she was doing, that she was fitting a smile to her lips, adjusting it up and down the range of enthusiasm, and then feeling the enthusiasm come after the smile, filling up the smile, making it authentic after the fact.

And she remembered how Shaw had looked and acted back then, though she had to admit she hadn't given him a thought in all those twenty years. Still when she tried, he came back vividly, separating himself from the haze of long ago. How the two of them had stumbled into their awkward passion. Run into the water that night, naked with each other. Burning up. Natalie Wood in *Splendor in the Grass*, Deborah Kerr rolling in the surf in *From Here to Eternity*. She'd thought of it a lot since Saturday, coming back to it to warm and calm herself. Remembering how it had been the other night to be blind, projecting everything into her fingertips. She'd never done that before. She didn't even know she could.

The car was rocking.

She should open her eyes. She could run an inventory of her body, start with her toes, wiggle upward, see what was broken, what was numb. For it was clear to her, even in this state, that she had been in a car accident. The taxi was compressed around her. But even immobilized, hearing the wrecker crew and the paramedics going about their tasks, awake behind her eyelids, Trula felt strong. Unaccountably refreshed.

Maybe it was simply love, how love was transforming her. It had scraped away the dead outer layer. Let the fresh self rise to the surface. Like the oceans did. She remembered her father telling her about it, a science bedtime story long ago, giving her an education. About currents, the Gulf Stream, and the others that coiled around the globe in their mysterious pathways, stripping away the top layer of the ocean, pushing it away, and allowing the richer water to rise. It was called upwelling.

In the lower fathoms of the sea, nutrition was created. Far from the sun, the water grew heavy with its treasure, dark as indigo. Then it was drawn to the surface, loaded with plankton and those other nutrients, colder than the rest of the ocean and weightier, but still pulled upward to the daylight, to feed the fish that waited there and, eventually, man.

Maybe that's what she'd been feeling these last few days. Upwelling, the gush, the flow of imperial blue waters, rising inside of

her, full of abundance, rising to the sunlight. Making her shiver as
it came to the surface.

The car shook again and rolled forward.

She opened her eyes to a shower of white, as if she were being
hauled slowly through a car wash of sparks, the bursting of hundreds of electrical bulbs. The wrecker dragging the taxi out of the
deep drift.

A man's face was in her window and he was rubbing a circle on
the glass, trying at the same time to open the door.

"You okay?" he said.

Trula looked at the driver, slumped forward, forehead against
the steering wheel.

Trula turned to the face in the window.

"Let me out of here," she said.

"Take it easy, lady. We're working on it, fast as we can."

"Let me out of here now."

———

"Walkie-talkie, hanky-panky, namby-pamby," Dougie said
to his reflection in the rearview mirror. He'd bent it around and was
checking himself out. Mean and grisly with two-day stubble.

Elmira was inside a 7-Eleven buying postcards. As soon as they
crossed over into the Salt Lake City limits, she'd said she wanted
some mementos of their honeymoon, the Mormon Tabernacle,
snow-covered mountain ranges, the Great Salt Lake itself. If she was
going to commit murder and arson for him, then the least he could
do was pull over, let her buy some goddamn postcards.

She said she wanted to put them up on the refrigerator door in
their apartment back in Key West. The apartment, by the way, that
she hadn't seen yet, she said.

"I got two places," Dougie said. "A regular place and a beach
place."

"I bet they're both dumps," she said.

"Not really," said Dougie. "But they're nearby."

"You do have a refrigerator, don't you?"

Dougie said, "Sure, it's where I keep the body parts, all the people I've chopped up."

"Dougie," she said, "sometimes you're not funny."

"Postcards?" he said. "What's that, interior decorating?"

"It's to remind us of our goddamn travels, Dougie. All the good times we had. All the people we set fire to."

"It's a treat to beat my meat," Dougie sang, "it's a treat to beat my meat, it's a treat to beat my meat in the Mississippi mud."

That shut her up for a while. Far as he could tell the woman had two moods. Nymphomaniac and pouty.

So he pulled up to the gas pumps of a 7-Eleven on a street full of burger joints and pizza parlors. He got out and filled up the Cadillac with gas and then filled a Clorox bottle with more gas and put it in the trunk.

Then he got back into the car and sat out there with the heater on. As Elmira paid for the postcards and the gas, she talked to the checkout girl in there. Behind her, a tall guy in a leather coat with a fur collar and a cowboy hat started checking out Elmira's ass. It took him awhile, the thing was so big.

"Nitty-gritty," Dougie said to himself. "Shitty city, itty-bitty pretty-tittie."

Finally she came out of the store with the cowboy tagging along behind her, talking to her, and Elmira was saying a word or two back over her shoulder at him, looking snippy, but the guy wasn't discouraged. He opened the door for Elmira and she got in and the cowboy walked around to Dougie's side and stood waiting till Dougie sent his window down.

"The lady said I should talk to you."

"Fiddle-faddle, sidesaddle. Teeny-weeny peenie."

"I only got twenty-five bucks," the cowboy said. "What'll that get me?"

Dougie watched the smoke their breaths were making. His and the cowboy's tangling up. He felt Elmira pushing the Browning into the side of his butt. Wanting him to scare this guy away.

Dougie said, "Twenty-five American dollars, man, that gets you the whole nine yards." He turned around and unlocked the back door. "Go on, get in."

"Dougie! Whatta you think you're doing?"

"Guy's got twenty-five dollars. Give him his money's worth."

She shook her head and watched the big guy wedge into the backseat.

"I took an instant liking to this lady's ass," the man said when he'd shut the door. "Saw her bend over, looking at them postcards, and I said to myself, I'll spend my rent money to have some of that. If I have to live out in the street for the next month, sleep on a grate, hell, it don't matter none, I can stay warm just recollecting such a fine slab of woman."

"Assault and flattery," Dougie said and put the Cadillac in reverse and rolled backward out into the street. He said over his shoulder, "You ever screwed in a professor's office?"

"Do what?"

Elmira said, "What're you doing, Dougie?"

"Barbecue, wanna screw. Confuse the issue, charcoal tissue."

"What's wrong with your friend?" the cowboy said, leaning forward over the seat. "He got a mental problem?"

"Yeah," Elmira said, "I never know what person he's going to be next." Giving Dougie a long look.

"He one of them multiple personalities?"

"Not multiple," she said. "Just two."

"How's that?"

"Two," Elmira said, "dumb and dumber."

Dougie said, "Confuse the issue, charcoal tissue. Burn it down, leave the clown."

"Name's Merle," the cowboy said, putting his hand over the front seat. "But all my friends call me Big Merle."

But Dougie didn't take the guy's hand. He looked over at Elmira. She was staring forward out of the window like she was looking for the best place to jump out.

————

Trula watched the blond paramedic climb inside and slam the ambulance door behind him. Twisting her head slightly she saw him buckle himself into his seat behind her, lift a phone to his ear and begin talking, apparently to the hospital emergency room.

The van pulled away and Trula, working her hands under the coarse white sheet, began to fumble with the safety strap over her chest, found its release button and pressed it. She tilted her head to the side and saw the blond paramedic turned away from her, shooting the shit with his friend at the hospital while the driver up in the cab slowed for something, a red light maybe.

Trula slid off the gurney, moved quickly to the rear door, un-latched it as the van was beginning to accelerate away from the light. She stumbled in the snow, and heard the paramedic call out for the driver to stop. Trula took the arm of a college kid in a red down jacket and fell into step beside him. He stopped, but Trula urged him forward, forcing out a smile, and together they headed up the steep sidewalk through a swarm of students, toward the perimeter of the unversity. Go, go.

She was woozy and again the bands had begun to tighten on her legs, numbing them. A mist of snow was blowing in her face, and young people in jeans and down jackets were hurrying past her with their knapsacks full of books.

"You okay, lady?" the boy said.

Trula said she was, kept walking very slowly, didn't look back. When they had gone a hundred yards up the slope, deeper into the campus, she let go of the boy's arm and walked on alone.

With torturous slowness she followed a path of waffle-sole foot-prints, her eyes holding hard to the sidewalk directly in front of her. She climbed the hill the way a rock climber might choose his foot-holds, settling her boot into the next footprint and putting her weight on it tentatively before bringing the other foot forward. Her feet were gone, ankles and calves going. A tingle rising higher.

Before they'd slid her into the van, the blond paramedic had taken her pulse, examined the lump on her head, declared to his partner that he knew this lady from somewhere, but he couldn't remember where. He told Trula that she had a mild concussion. Told her to just lie still while they lifted her into the van.

A mild concussion. But here, in the cold air, walking up the steep sidewalk, it felt like a second head was erupting from her forehead. And a bass string vibrated just behind her eyes, amplified in the hollow chamber of her skull. At the fringe of her sight, a red fog burned.

Trula halted, and the students streamed around her. She was out of breath, looking for somewhere to lean her weight, a bench, even a low crook of tree, when a young man in a bright yellow ski jacket appeared beside her and asked if she needed any help. He called her ma'am.

She took a breath and said, "I'm looking for Dr. Waldorf's office."

The boy asked her what department that was. She peered at his face. It was swimming behind the watery haze her eyes were making. She blinked once, twice, but it didn't clear.

"Biology, immunology," Trula said. "I'm not sure."

"Lady, do you need a doctor?"

"I need Dr. Waldorf's office," she said.

The boy gave her his arm, led her up the hill. He had to ask four students before he found one who knew Dr. Waldorf.

"That's the guy got croaked," the girl in a plaid parka said. "The one, his house burned down. You know, that guy."

"Oh," the boy said. Turning to Trula. "Did you know that?"

"His office," she said. "Where is it?"

The girl regarded Trula curiously.

"In Orson Hall," she said to the boy. "Second floor, up near the monkey lab."

The boy led her to the front door of Orson Hall.

"You sure you going to be all right?"

"I'm making it," Trula said.

As she entered the warm hallway, located a stairway, there were tremors in the floor, blue flickers in the fluorescent lights. She rested on the landing between floors, pulling in harsh breaths. The bands had loosened a notch. She could vaguely feel her feet again and her eyes had cleared somewhat. She leaned on the banister, her head floating, and wondered for a moment where she was.

Someone had pushed her out onto this stage. The lights were on her. The set was a university office building. But was this Shakespeare or Chekhov or "Hidden Hours"? Which century was it supposed to be? Was she a queen or a wretched serf? Sick or well? What passion animated her? No one had bothered to show her the script, expecting her to improvise this. Her legs ached.

24

Dougie found a spot in handicapped parking up close to Orson Hall, pulled the Cadillac in next to a white van.

"What? You some kind of sex therapist, works out of the fucking university?"

"Yeah," Dougie said. He reached over and gave Elmira a poke in the shoulder. "Professor Hemple and her highly educated hairy dimple."

"I don't know what you want me to do," Elmira said. In a deep pout now. Voice heavy and slow.

"I want you to light the man up," Dougie said. "Give him great balls of fire. You know how to do that, don't you?"

"Yeah," Merle said. "Sounds good to me." He was leaning over the seat, his hand dangling across Elmira's shoulder. He snaked it down and tweaked her breast, then took a handful. She endured it, giving Dougie a strangled look. "What a hunk of woman we got here, huh, Dougie? Great balls of fire."

"I got to draw you a diagram? You're going to do what you were planning to do, but throw this into the program."

"Shit," she said.

"Go on, Big Merle," said Dougie. "Give me a minute. Elmira'll be right out. I got to get her fully motivated."

Merle huffed and climbed out of the car, stood on the sidewalk, stamping his feet outside Orson Hall. Looking at the coeds streaming into the building. Tipped his cowboy hat at a couple of them. Going *brrr, brrr,* so loud Dougie could hear him with the Cadillac windows rolled up.

"Take this." Dougie reached into the glove compartment, found the suppressor and screwed it on the Browning. He held it out to her. She took it and slipped it into her handbag.

Dougie said, "And then go around to the trunk and get out the Clorox bottle, and go in there and do him, and then put the flames to it. It's simple, Hemple."

"Why do I have to do this alone?"

"It's your initiation," Dougie said. "You do it by yourself, then we're both in this exactly the same amount."

"Yeah, all the way up to our necks."

"Hey, I married you, right? You asked me to, I did it. And I did every other damn thing you wanted me to. I let you whack me till my butt's purple and green. And now what? I ask you to do one thing, and you get all pissy on me?"

"What room'd the directory say? Two-oh-four?"

"Two-oh-six," Dougie said. "And make it quick."

"Shit," she said, and got out of the car. She went around to the trunk, and Dougie popped it open for her from the dash. She took out the Clorox bottle, slung her purse over her shoulder, went over and took hold of Merle's arm and walked into the building.

———

Trula found 206 but it took her awhile to locate the key on Anne's big brass ring. Then she had to struggle to get the door unlocked. It was oak or maple, thick and heavy with a slot of opaque glass.

Trula stepped inside, switched on the fluorescent lights.

The office was extremely tidy. The books lined up evenly on the floor-to-ceiling shelves. A neat row of plants on the windowsill. A dozen photos of family members were arranged precisely on the walls. In one of them, three boys with identical goofy smiles posed against a white background. The oldest, a teenage Waldorf, was in back, his younger flattopped brothers stood up front, all of them in matching horn-rims and fluffy pink sweaters. As if their mother had spun them through the same cotton candy machine. My Three Nerds. The all-American anal-retentive family.

It looked like the entire Waldorf clan was nailed up there. Fathers and mothers and grandfathers and grandmothers. Babies and toddlers. She lingered on one of a thirtyish Waldorf waving from under the hood of an MG roadster, face and sweatshirt grimy. Behind him a girl in her twenties with Waldorf's eyes sat cramped in a wheelchair, one hand pressed like a twisted claw to her sternum, the other hand extending a socket wrench in his direction. His sister, or perhaps a first cousin.

There were voices in the hallway, students clomping past in their boots. Trula's legs had begun to fade again. A tourniquet was tightening around her thighs, the blood puffing up above, the feeling below growing dimmer and dimmer. She leaned against the desk, almost knocking off a stone statue of a monkey puzzling over a human skull.

Now that she was here, even with the numbness crawling up her legs, she was excited, alive. She was working the glowing center of this. There was something in the article, she was certain of it, something that cut through to the marrow of her life. And now she wasn't simply doing this for herself anymore, but on behalf of Anne, and Barbie, this wall full of people.

Trula was reaching for one of the photos, when she heard a man's voice speak in a down-home drawl just outside the door.

"So which one is it? You forget your own goddamn office?"

"I know," a woman's voice said. "Two-oh-six."

Hurriedly, she lifted the photo of Waldorf and the girl in the wheelchair off the wall. Yes! On the back of it a three-inch diskette was taped. She tore it off, jammed it in her pocket and set the photo on the floor. She was just sitting down in the swivel desk chair when the door swung open.

A cowboy entered the room. Around six-two, long blond hair curling out from under his Stetson. He was wearing a suede coat with a yellowed sheepskin collar. His face had been chewed up by acne, some of which still festered around his nose. The woman behind him was carrying a white Clorox bottle. She had metallic apricot hair, chopped short, her eyes inside dark hollows of eye shadow. She was dressed in a skimpy black skirt and knee-length green boots. A woman clearly unacquainted with ten a.m. If she'd ever been awake then, it was probably to appear before a judge.

The girl's hand went to her cheek when she saw Trula, and Trula recognized the familiar shift in expression. Another fan.

"Well, hi there, sweet thing," the cowboy said, coming up to the front of the desk. The woman shut the door and leaned against it, shaking her head. "My, oh, my, like I told Elmira here, I only got twenty-five bucks on me, but if I could have both of you, Jesus Mary and the saints, I'll run to the nearest machine, empty my bank account right now, give Dougie every last nickel I got saved."

Trula hesitated for a moment, digesting this, the cowboy's toothy grin, the garish woman at the door. Going into herself for a voice, a part.

She slapped an open palm against Waldorf's desk.

"Who the hell do you think you are, barging in my office like this?" Trula said. She couldn't remember who it was. Bette Davis, Joan Crawford? No. But somebody like them. The voice of scornful command. A woman who had gone one-on-one with the best the male kingdom could put forward, and had held her own. She felt herself sink away into the voice, its rhythms and timbre.

The cowboy turned to Elmira, jerking his thumb over his shoulder at Trula.

"She for real or what?"

Elmira was peering at Trula, her mind working hard, those enormous painted eyes unblinking.

"I know this person," Elmira said. She set the Clorox bottle on the floor.

"Well, hell, then, let's party. Let's get down and get it on. Kick back, chill out, boogy, boogy, boogy." He clapped his hands, rubbed them together, then took a quick look at Elmira's face. He said, "Hey, don't worry. I'll fix it with Dougie later, about the price. But I want the both of you. I don't care what it costs. Around the world, some lezzie stuff, rim job. The works. Whooee! Did I fall into paradise today, or what?"

Cocking her head, Elmira said, "This woman died last week." Squinting at Trula. "I saw her funeral on the TV."

"What?"

"It's true," Trula said. "I died of brain cancer."

"Yeah, uh-huh," Elmira said. "It was brain cancer."

"What the fuck?" the cowboy said. "This supposed to be a gag or something?"

Trula dropped Elmira's gaze, watched the cowboy lift his hat, run his hand across his slick head. His only hair was the yellow fringe and his muttonchop sideburns. His Stetson, a ten-gallon toupee.

Elmira slid her hand into her deep black purse and left it there.

"She's an actress," Elmira said to Merle, then turned her face to Trula and drew her hand out of her purse. She held the big black automatic steady, aiming it at Trula. The cowboy turned and took a half step toward her, and she swung to face him. He stumbled, and held fast.

"You people better watch your asses. You don't know who the fuck you're dealing with here. My cousin is the goddamn sheriff of Salt Lake County, and let me tell you, he don't like his relations having pistols aimed at them. No sir, he don't like it a bit."

"Shut up, Merle," Elmira said. "And you." She wiggled the pistol at Trula. "Stand up where I can see all of you."

Trula rose and came around the desk. Her legs were working fine now. She wasn't afraid. She had the voice, fluent in melodrama. What did they have? Props, a vague script. Maybe that was it: You acted strong, you were strong. You acted healthy, you were. Maybe that was all there was. The big answer. When she got home, she'd have to call a news conference, tell the world.

"Merle," Trula said, "who's Dougie?"

"Her pimp," he said quietly, his eyes on the gun.

Trula stared at Elmira across a silence that widened into half a minute. She was starting to get an idea about this punk-rock Cleopatra. Not so bright. Complete leopardskin wardrobe. Developed an early attachment to white lipstick and teased hair.

"We wouldn't be talking about Dougie Barnes, would we?"

"Jesus," Elmira said. "How do you know him?"

Trula felt it settle inside her, a key clicking open the lock. Dougie, her father, Waldorf, Barnes. She didn't understand the linkages, the story, the crimes. Didn't even care to consider them at the moment, just satisfied to know that it would come later. Plenty of time to open that door, walk into that room and explore it. Right now the chills were rising on her neck and back, her power flowing.

"I'm walking out that door," Merle said, reaching up with both hands and tightening his hat into place. "I don't like this one fucking bit, I'm telling you."

"You're not going anywhere," Elmira said.

"Oh, come on, pretty lady. Put down that cap gun."

Elmira kept her eyes on the cowboy.

"Yeah," he said, a big grin. "Your brain-dead boyfriend slipped you a cap gun. Put you out here holding a goddamn toy with little red tape sticking out of it. A big joke. Ha."

Elmira hesitated a moment, fighting it. She threw a helpless look at Trula, and Trula shook her head. Don't fall for it, lady. But Elmira's eyes twitched downward anyway, back up.

Finally she gave in, and turned the pistol sideways and examined it. In that instant, the cowboy lunged for her, but Elmira jerked away. She flattened herself against the door, raised the pistol and fired.

A diploma shattered on one wall. Merle jerked upright, reached with both hands to his throat as if he were trying to straighten his bow tie. He seemed to be grinning at himself in a mirror of air. Blood leaked through his fingers and he brought his hands away from his throat and studied them for a long moment, then began to bark, short explosive gutturals as he stared at his fingers. Across the room the glass from the diploma trickled to the floor.

Merle wobbled and tried to speak, and blood bubbled from his lips. He stumbled sideways against the desk, lurched, reached out and raked Waldorf's ink blotter to the floor. Then he toppled forward, grabbing the arm of Trula's coat on the way down. He left a smear on the wool sleeve.

Elmira kept her back against the door, panting. Aiming the pistol at Trula.

"Now I have to do you," she said. She began to snarl, held the pistol out farther, flinching as if she were summoning the strength for another shot.

"Put it down," Trula said. "It's just us women here. You don't have to impress anybody. You're brave, I can see that."

"You saw me kill a guy," she said. "I got no choice."

"Yeah, I saw you shoot this jerk." Trula pointed at the cowboy with her toe. "He was trying to rape you, for Christsakes. You killed him in self-defense."

As Elmira stared down at Merle, Trula took hold of the monkey statue, hid it behind her body.

"Well," Elmira said, "that's kind of true. If I hadn't killed him, he would've tried to rape me."

"Of course it's true."

"Dougie'll murder me if I screw this up."

"Put it away, Elmira. Before it goes off again. Women don't kill women."

"Christ Almighty," Elmira said. "I can't believe it's you. Cassie Raintree. Man, I've hung out with Dougie too long, now I'm having hallucinations."

"Put it in your purse," saying it pleasantly.

Elmira lowered the pistol, aiming now at the floor in front of Trula.

"Into your purse where it won't hurt anybody."

"Yeah," Elmira said. She slipped the pistol into her black hand-bag.

"Now," Trula said. "Where's Dougie?"

"He's outside, parked outside."

"Okay."

Trula walked past her, keeping her eyes hard on Elmira's. The heavy statue by her hip.

No, it wasn't Joan Crawford's voice Trula had called up, or Bette Davis's, and it wasn't Cassie Raintree's either. It was a voice she hadn't heard in years. Years and years. She'd summoned a tone as commanding as existed within her, and what had come was her own voice. Trula Montoya's outraged voice. Filling her up with its satisfying resonance.

"Now I'm going," Trula said. "And as far as Dougie Barnes is concerned, I was never here. You did everything just fine."

"Yeah," Elmira said. "That would work, I guess."

"Women have to keep some secrets from men," Trula said. "If we don't they'll just run our lives. Make us do their bidding."

"That's for damn sure."

Elmira stepped aside and Trula opened the door.

"Oh yeah, before you go," Elmira said, "by any chance, you got a match?"

Elmira slid her hand into her purse, but Trula didn't wait to see if she came out with the pistol again. She wasn't confident enough of this new voice, its hypnotic power. She lifted the monkey statue and smacked Elmira's purse from her hands. The pistol fell free, and Trula kicked it across the floor, dropped the statue and left.

She was twenty yards down the hall, turning into the stairwell, when she heard the whoosh and turned to see Elmira flat against the wall outside of Waldorf's office, a wave of fire rushing out the doorway.

Her legs worked fine all the way down the stairs. As she reached the ground floor of Orson Hall, alarm bells sounded, and the spray of the ceiling sprinklers erupted in the hallway behind her. She took a fast peek out the back doors and saw Dougie sitting in a white Cadillac, combing his long hair in the rearview mirror.

She drew in a deep breath, and left by the opposite doors.

————

When the nurse turned away, Anne said, "Did you get it?"

Trula nodded.

"I knew you would. I knew it."

Trula smiled and sat down beside Anne.

"What're you going to do with it?"

"I thought you should decide," Trula said.

Anne smiled again, closed her eyes.

"Dr. Waldorf's editor at *Time* is named Edwin White. That's who you send it to."

"You're sure? There could be a lot more trouble if it's published."

"Yeah, I'm sure," she said. "Positive."

"Well," Trula said, "I'm very glad you feel that way."

"Are you going to read it first?" Anne said.

"If something in Key West triggered my MS, of course I want to know what it is," said Trula. "Wouldn't you?"

Anne shifted slightly under the sheet.

"I'm not so sure," she said. "I'm not so sure I would."

25

Shaw made it home around two in the morning on Thursday. Too late to wake Trula, so he drove home from the airport. He stood in the foyer for a moment and considered waking his mother, laying out for her the story he knew, and the rest he had guessed, see what she might be able to add. He went to her closed door and pressed his ear to it and heard nothing. Tomorrow, he supposed, would be soon enough.

Somewhere in the last twenty-four hours he had lost his frantic pulse. His breath had slowed. His need to know was still there, hotter now than it had been before, but there was no hurry. Like one of those Zen archers, the target before him, huge, but irrelevant. What mattered now was simply drawing a perfect bead, stilling the last shiver of doubt, and letting go.

He crept up the stairs to his bedroom. The broken metal canister was on the worktable in the center of the room. It gleamed in the moonlight.

He switched on the lights, picked it up, settled himself on the edge of his bed, and ran his fingers over the cracked edge, the jags and sawteeth. Smoothed now by time, or perhaps his own father's fingers.

Shaw traced his fingertips through the grooves of the letters. *U.S. Navy.* And the bases of the other letters.

He pushed himself up and went to his desk, and took out a sheet of typing paper. He sharpened a pencil. With the canister in his lap, he pressed the paper to the fragments of letters and traced them. When he was finished, he set the casing on the floor and laid the sheet of paper in front of him on the desk, staring at the curls and straight lines, the feet and ankles of those neat Roman letters.

A rooster yodeled nearby. A car passed a block away with its radio tuned loud. He looked above his desk at the rod rack coated with a velvet layer of dust, at his Louisville Slugger leaning in the corner, the trophies. Rustling at the window, the leaves of a ficus tree were lit by the streetlight, changing them to emeralds, flat and smooth, trickling in a warm stream of air.

Slowly he filled in the upper halves of the letters. It was a formality to do it. Just something to make what he already knew into concrete fact. He drew the square letters as neatly as he could, his hand steady, his body relaxed. The night was quiet now. Everything that was going to fall asleep already had. He watched the pencil as it left its trails of graphite on the page. He knew a lot of it now. Maybe not all of it. But enough to be certain that there was a good deal left to do.

He watched his hand as it moved forward across the page, as it filled in the last of the letters: BIOLOGICAL WARFARE RESEARCH PROGRAM

He lay on his bed, closed his eyes, and saw a white-water tumble of images from the last forty-eight hours. He revisited the Healing House, saw again the Chiles girl in her bikini, heard the hoboes chanting, saw Bertha Pinkney's deck of cards, the naked magnolia branches, the horse-drawn carriages. And before that to Trula, her face, the feel of her body against his, thin but strong. The energy in her hands, her eyes. Her fingers finding places on his body that no one else had found. The warm melt of their kisses. And Barnes. Captain Barnes. Garbage-plant Barnes. Father of Dougie. A man with a ten-thousand-dollar secret. And Montoya, his damaged birds. Biology. Men in moonsuits, protecting themselves from a bacterium that on four previous occasions they had sprayed in large dosages over the unsuspecting island of Key West. Hanson Chandler extorting money from Trula and probably trying to do the same to Barnes. Pretending his blackmail was for a surgery. And a last image of Hanson Chandler lying in bed in his shabby house in Miami, looking up into the face of someone who pressed a barrel to his chest and opened a violent cavity in his heart.

————

At first light on Wednesday, he dragged himself up and over to his desk. He had a sudden need to clean his Smith & Wesson, oil it, load it. Maybe go out to the range this afternoon, hang up a silhouette of Barnes, try some quick draws.

He pulled open the desk drawer where he'd stowed the pistol. And there was only the suede holster, empty. He stared at it, pushing back the panic. He tried the drawer below it, and it was empty, and the drawer below that. All the others. He dropped to his stomach and checked under the bed, under the desk. He rolled to his feet, went to the closet, dug through his duffel, patted down the shelf, looked in all the drawers again. Nowhere.

He hurried downstairs, went to his mother's room and knocked. When there was no answer, he opened the door. The room was empty, her bed made. Turning, he called out for her but there was no reply. He walked to the kitchen and dialed Trula's number. Fifteen rings and no answer. When he turned around from the phone, he staggered against the wall.

"Jesus!"

Standing next to the kitchen table, Buzz Sullivan smiled sheepishly. He was wearing jeans and a rumpled plaid shirt. His wiry gray hair was messed, and he looked very tired.

"The hell're you doing here, man? Standing in my kitchen, six o'clock in the morning? Jesus. You scared the holy shit out of me."

"I came down from Miami yesterday," he said uncertainly. "See how you were doing, what the hell you were up to. The way you sounded on the phone, so strange, I got worried."

"Well, holy shit, sit down, man." Shaw pulled out a chair at the kitchen table. But now he had noticed the somber haze in Buzz's eyes. His shoulders stooped by some weight of air. Buzz hauled in a breath, pulled out a chair and let himself down. He picked at a callus on his thumb and stared at the tabletop.

Shaw said nothing. He knew from years of working alongside Sullivan that the man had his own pace. His rituals and sense of decorum were inviolable. Shaw kept standing, while Buzz peeled a flap of the callus off and then seemed not to know what to do with it. He rolled it in his fingers and looked up at Shaw.

"When I got in yesterday afternoon," he said, "I came by here and the front door was open, so I called through the screen for a while, then I came in."

"No problem with that."

"Your mother, she was lying in the hallway, over there." Buzz pointed with his chin. "Unconscious."

"Yeah, well, I'm sorry you got stuck with that, man. She's been pulling on the bottle pretty heavy lately. I appreciate your helping out."

"It wasn't whiskey."

Shaw said nothing.

"I called rescue," Buzz said. "Guys down here, they have a pretty good response time. Small island, I guess."

"Buzz, what're you saying?"

"You didn't know, did you? She said she hadn't told you."

"What, Buzz?"

"About the cancer. And nobody else told you."

Shaw got a breath down. He managed a no.

"Bone cancer, her doctor said, a young guy named Medoff. She was diagnosed, I don't remember exactly, some time ago. You want to hear this from me, or go on to the hospital, hear it from Medoff?"

"You."

"Okay," Buzz said. "Well, apparently it was in her legs at first, a few months ago. Now it's in her spine, all over."

"Shit." Shaw squeezed his eyes shut, pressed his fingers hard against them. He opened them, but nothing had changed. The table, the chairs, Buzz, a motorcycle blatting past on Olivia. He sank into the chair across from Buzz. "Goddamn it to hell."

"Nothing you could've done. Nothing, even if you'd known."

"I should've figured it out," he said. "She tried to tell me, and I shut her up."

Buzz said, "I stayed out there with her all night, at the hospital. She said she wasn't one of those California types that wanted to die at home. She wanted them to hook her up right away to the drug machines, mix a little Demerol with some rum and let it drip. That's how she was talking. You know, her tone. Making the best, kidding around. But she's hurting."

The mechanics of breathing had suddenly become difficult for him. It was taking a lot of his attention to pull in one breath, get it deep enough, then let it the hell out.

"She didn't know where you were. You go out of town, you don't tell your own mother where you're going?"

"Come on," Shaw said. "I got to get out there."

———

Buzz drove them through the early morning traffic. As they waited at a light across from Garrison Bight, Shaw said, "You didn't by any chance go through my room, did you, Buzz, take my pistol for some reason?"

"Huh?"

"No, I didn't think so."

When they were on Stock Island, passing the recycling plant, half a mile from the hospital, he turned and stared at the buildings. The sky above the huge smokestacks was clear. But there was a wavering distortion of light at the mouths of the stacks. The clouds in the distance rippled. As he watched, a squadron of pelicans swung wide around the stacks and slanted down a long slope of air back to the glistening bay.

———

A nurse showed them the room, said his mother was sleeping now, Dr. Medoff would be in as soon as he got out of surgery.

Shaw stepped into the room, Buzz behind him. It was a gloomy twilight in there, the blinds closed against the bright, clear January morning. He pulled a chair over beside the bed, sat, and bent his ear close to her mouth and listened to the quiet rasp of her breath. A sleep deepened by the clear solution dripping into her arm.

He took her hand in his.

Sometimes, riding with accident victims on the way to the emergency room, Shaw would grip their hands. Let them take out their adrenaline on him. Especially the children or the old ones, lost, confused. Communicate with them in squeezes and hard trembling grips. Things were going to be all right, relax, we're not going to let anything happen to you, just a few more minutes, you're doing great, fine. Hold on. You ever hear the one about . . . It was in the fingers, the hand, reassurance, courage. But his mother didn't return his pressure. He felt only the cool, boneless flesh. The papery skin, too dry. Her face was flat and empty.

Shaw listened to a mockingbird outside the window. He blinked and the dim light hazed and sparkled through the moisture on his eyelashes. Once or twice he had seen Buzz cry at an accident scene, children crushed in cars, the drunk driver still stumbling around, asking, What, what? Buzz crying because he was so angry and couldn't strangle the drunk. But Shaw, in thirty-eight years, had never shown anyone his tears. Not his mother. None of the women. A lifetime under strict control.

He laid his mother's hand on the crisp sheet, rose, and joined Buzz at the foot of the bed. Both of them looking at her still, white length. Looking at her, listening to the mocker. The bird warbling its endless tape. He knew the songs were to stake out the bird's territory, nothing romantic. The mocker's way of doing it, steal the other birds' songs, add to them, make them his own.

"This morning, Shaw, I was here, and she was mumbling," Buzz said. "I don't know if she was delirious or what, but I got my ear up next to her and she kept saying something over and over. I'm not sure what it was, sounded Greek or Latin, or something. But she kept saying it, you know, like over and over."

"Not *Serratia marcescens?*"

"Jesus," Buzz said. "How the hell'd you know that?"

"*Serratia marcescens.*" Shaw stared at the floor, trying to get a grasp on this.

"What is that?"

"A bacterium," said Shaw. "Twenty years ago they thought it was harmless, but they changed their minds."

"Who?"

"The navy, the Defense Department."

"This is going right past me, man."

"I'll explain it to you later."

"I got to say it, Shaw. You got that look, like you're about to do something that somebody's going to regret."

It cost him some pain, but he smiled at Buzz.

"I'm glad you came down, buddy."

"Yeah," Buzz said. "Looks like I got here just in time for the messy part."

———

Buzz left to track down some breakfast, and Shaw was sitting beside the bed again, watching his mother's face, when her eyelids rolled open like a doll's.

"Mother."

"Your father," she said, sighing. She gathered herself and said, "He's gone."

"I know, Mother," he said. "I know."

She shook her head, swallowed, closed her eyes briefly and opened them again. He held her hand and this time he felt the lightest pressure from her.

"He ran away," she said. "Again."

"What?"

She took a difficult breath, gulped twice.

"He tried to help me," she said. She swallowed again and her mouth smacked. Eyes milky. "Help raise money to fight my cancer, but then he left, disappeared. Ran away, like before."

Shaw said nothing.

"He came to the house." She had closed her eyes, and her hoarse voice seemed to rise from her as if she were speaking her dream aloud. "A few months ago, one night, he came to the door. Twenty years, and without warning, he's in the house we had together, and he told me he had lived his life with other people, but he had always still loved me, and you, and now he wanted our forgiveness. That's why he came. He'd had two heart attacks, and it scared him, and he wanted our forgiveness. But I wouldn't give it to him. I told him, 'Get it from God, because you aren't getting it from me.'

"But we talked, and when I told him I was sick, he said by God, he'd find money to fight the cancer. He knew some people who'd gone to Mexico and had gotten better. Eating peach pits, or something. I told him no, I didn't want his money. But he did it anyway. A few weeks later he sent me fifteen thousand dollars. I tried to call him, the number he gave me, tell him to take his money back. But it was a phony number. I sent him a letter and it came back, undeliverable. He ran away the same as before. He wanted me to forgive him and I wouldn't and he ran away."

Shaw held her hand, said nothing.

"Your father said he was coming to see you too. Ask your forgiveness too." She opened her eyes for a moment, turned her head on the pillow, looking at him now. "Did he do that, ask your forgiveness, Shaw? Did he come and ask?"

Shaw held her hand, listened to the mockingbird for a moment.

"I think he may have," Shaw said. "Yes, I think he did."

"Did you forgive him?"

Shaw looked away, took a breath.

"I couldn't."

She nodded as if she understood, neither approved nor disapproved.

"I'm going to die," she said. "But it's all right. It's not so bad, really. Not so bad as everyone says." She smiled. "They have very good drugs now."

"Yes."

"Your father said he still loved us, but I wouldn't forgive him for what he did to us. I should have forgiven him, though. You should do that. You should forgive people, Shaw. It's better for them. It's better for you."

Her grip tightened.

"Mother," he said, "I have to know something."

She made a noise in her throat.

"That night, the night with the two sailors. The *Serratia marcescens*. Do you know what happened? What Dad did that night? Did he tell you?"

"We never talked about the hitting," she said faintly, her eyes closing. "I was guilty about it. It hurt too much to talk about it. But a family should talk. About everything."

"It's okay now," Shaw said. "We're talking now, so it's okay."

"It's in the water," she said. "They hid it in the water. The sailors put it down there, and it's under the water. Your daddy told me about it all, about everything he did. He was trying to get me to forgive him, and he told me everything. About the bacteria they were spraying."

"Where? What water?"

"The quarry." She winced, opened and shut her eyes.

"Mother."

Sirens flared in the hospital parking lot and Shaw felt his stomach stiffen. Her eyes came open again, and they moved to his face.

She smiled and held him in her sight for a long moment before her eyes drifted closed again.

"It's really not so bad," she said. "Childbirth is worse. Much worse. I wouldn't wish childbirth on anyone."

She tried to smile.

"The money he gave me, it's at home in the freezer, in the Tupperware. You should have it."

"You're going to be all right," Shaw said. "You're going to be fine, Mother. I'll stay here, and you'll be fine. We'll get past this. And we'll talk. We'll talk about everything."

She opened her eyes again and smiled at him, a smile beyond amusement, the fog of pain lifting from her at that moment, a familiar glimmer coming to her eyes, mischievous, young. For a second she was the tough twenty-five-year-old island girl who had simply fallen in love with the wrong sailor.

Her grip suddenly so strong, it numbed his hand.

26

___

Shaw sat beside her bed watching the Hewlett heart monitor displaying the graph of her pulse. Weak but regular. Buzz said he was going to the lobby to take a nap, but Shaw said nothing, mesmerized by the ragged line on the monitor. A quick line, then another.

A few minutes after Buzz had left, Shaw broke away from the monitor and looked up at the man entering the room. He wore a surgical gown, his mask around his neck. Rubber gloves showing at his pocket. It had been a bloody operation.

The guy was under thirty. He had a blond flattop with a braid and four earrings in his left ear, a colorful woven bracelet. Under his drab green gown, he wore white tennis shorts and pink hightop sneakers. As if he might have come to work this morning on his skateboard.

He read Millie's chart before acknowledging Shaw with a quick nod. While he pressed the stethoscope to her chest, brought his ear to her mouth, raised her eyelids, he hummed a faint tune, supplying the bass, even following the beat with slight bounces of his shoulders.

"So," the kid said, turning from her. "You Millie's boy?"

"Yeah."

"Joey Medoff, Dr. Joey, they call me."

"Dr. Joey."

"Your mother," he said, "man, she's one tough lady."

"Yeah, she is."

Holding the chart again, doing a drum roll with the pencil tip, he said, "When she first came in to see me, I remember it, the cancer was pretty far along. Had to've been hurting. I got her into radiation that afternoon, and then for two more rounds of treatment, and that slowed things down. But nothing was going to knock this out of her, and I told her that."

"When was this?"

"That I told her?"

"Yeah."

"Month, month and a half back. Before Christmas sometime."

"That's it? There wasn't anything more to do for her?"

"Nothing more anybody could do. She could go to Mayo, NIH, it wouldn't matter. But oh, she got this wild hair there for a while," Medoff said. "I think from one of her old-lady friends. Suddenly she's all hot and bothered about cancer treatments in Mexico, coffee enemas, peach pits, all kinds of crackbrain stuff. I told her, Millie, they're rip-offs, expensive as hell, and don't do a damn thing. Money didn't matter, she said, 'cause she'd come into some money. But then, I guess she changed her mind. Haven't heard any more about it."

"And now," Shaw said. "How sick is she now?"

"Relative to what?"

"Relative to death."

Medoff drummed his pencil tip on the clipboard, picking up the pace. Shaw had a quick image of slamming him backward into the wall, knocking that tune permanently out of his head.

"Let me put it this way," the doctor said. He looked around the room, still tapping his pencil. "Considering the size and number of her tumors, and the pain she must have had the last few months, at this point your mom's way ahead of the game."

"That what this is for you, a fucking game?"

Medoff gave Shaw an appraising look while he did another drum riff.

"Okay, partner, go on, it makes you feel better, be pissed off at me if you want," he said. "You don't like me, hell, that goes with the territory. I'm used to it."

"Yeah," Shaw said. "I just bet you are."

———

When Medoff was gone, Shaw sat down beside her again. Holding her hand, he imagined it, pictured the tumors in her spine blossoming millimeter by millimeter until they spread her vertebrae past the fracture point. Connections broken. Shut down.

So that was it. Hanson had been trying to buy her forgiveness with blackmail money for a crackpot cure. He'd hit Trula for fifteen, but that wasn't enough for the Juárez doctor, so Hanson had come down here to Key West, threatened to expose Barnes, reveal whatever had happened that night. And that had been the end of him. Jesus Christ. Jesus H. Christ. For peach pits.

It was ten, maybe fifteen minutes after Medoff left the room that Millie died. Shaw was still holding her hand, but there was no final squeeze, no shudder, or last words. The room grew quieter, that was all. Just the smallest fraction quieter. A hum just beyond the range of hearing was no longer there. Her silence absorbed by a larger one.

There was not even the alarm of the Hewlett heart monitor. Earlier that afternoon Shaw had turned the signal down. Now it simply drew a green LED line, no pulse, no blood pressure, readout complete. He might've performed CPR, called for the shock plates to restart her heart. He might've tried to call her back from the edge, lure her with his voice.

But he did nothing. Sat, holding her hand, looking at her face. He knew he should get up, let someone know she was gone, that the heart monitor was out of service so they could roll it down the hall to the next one.

The mockingbird was still in the tree outside. For a while Shaw sat looking at his mother's body, listening to the bird. Inside his chest he felt spaces open up. Caves, clammy and blind.

After a while he let go of her hand and went to the window. The bird was perched in the top branches of a poinciana tree and had its back to the window, surveying its narrow domain. It twitched on its limb, whistling its repertoire, broadcasting its warning. Driven by forces out of its control.

Shaw's blood had thickened in his veins, sixty-weight oil, his heart chugging hard, barely able to force it forward. Blood he'd inherited from the two that were dead. Their blood first, then his, and now becoming sludge in his veins.

He made himself walk to the door. He brought his hand to the knob.

Elmira watched out of the window of the ten-seater prop plane as they coasted low over the Florida Keys. A spatter of teensy wooded islands, it didn't look like people could live there, or anything for that matter except maybe mosquitoes. And all that water, wrinkled and crawling somewhere, six different colors of blue and green. She watched the shadow of the plane rippling across the water, like a dark bird, some kind of sign.

"You know this word?" Dougie asked her, pointing at the page of his paperback. The thing was called *Nuns in Wetsuits*. He'd been reading it since they changed planes in Denver, mumbling the words as he ran his finger along the pages.

"Trapeze," Elmira said.

Dougie hummed, nodded at her like he'd just been testing her, see if she could read.

Here Elmira was, with her husband, of all the weird things. Coming home after murdering two men she'd never even met before. And this new husband of hers, the only thing he'd had on his mind today was his parrot, Jerkoff, and how he hoped they'd been feeding him right, and he hoped the bird hadn't forgotten all the words he'd taught it, and how he was looking forward to teaching it a bunch of new ones. Then he'd started reading the book. Leaving Elmira to consider the twisted state of her existence.

"Temple dimple, hairy berry," Dougie said. "Trapeze, striptease."

Elmira went back to the window.

She'd been nervous the whole way from Utah. Going over it all, how she'd done everything that Dougie had asked her. Being a good wife. Except she hadn't shot the actress, and then hadn't told Dougie about the actress being there at all. That was probably stupid of her. It was probably how she and Dougie were going to get caught. But in a way, deep inside her, she wouldn't mind that. Going to jail might actually be safer than hanging around Dougie much longer. Dougie and his guns. Jesus, she hated guns, how loud they were, the way they looked, everything about them. And now here she was, half of Bonnie and Clyde. Guns were her business.

Elmira Hemple Barnes, a few thousand miles from home, coasting low over all that green and blue water headed to some kind of new life. She should've been feeling wonderful, it was her honeymoon. But she didn't know if she was safe, or if there'd be a dozen cops with their guns drawn waiting at the bottom of the ramp in Key West.

She kept reminding herself, she'd done the right thing marrying him. She was in love with this guy. So what if she'd only known him a couple of days. That was long enough to know.

And Dougie was good-looking, his long, dark curly hair, those deep green eyes, and he seemed to have a lot of money, and man, he was a lifetime of dreams come true in the sex department. A guy she could whack till she was too tired to lift her arms. But then she'd start thinking about this thing he did with words, and the way his father was on the phone, what he did for a living, it was bothering her bad. Making her nervous, making her have to swallow.

She took the postcards out of her purse, the ones she'd bought in the 7-Eleven, but they didn't make her feel much better. They reminded her of the cowboy, Merle, how he'd looked when she'd shot him, coughing blood, peering at her as he died. Those noises he made, trying to curse her in blood.

As they drove away from the university, Dougie had wanted to know all the details like with Waldorf. And again she'd tried to describe how it felt. This one different from Waldorf. This one awful, ugly and messy. She'd suffered vertigo.

"Vertigo?" he'd said. "The fuck is that?"

"You never saw Alfred Hitchcock? Jesus. It's like dizzy. Your head is going round and round in circles."

"What? On your neck? Spinning around?"

"No, your brain is going around, inside your head. Whirling. Like you're going to throw up, everything is going round. Light-headed. Dizzy, like you've been sniffing glue, you know."

"You got to learn to explain things better. Everything you say, I got to go over it, and then it's still confusing."

"I'm trying, goddamn it. It's hard to do it, okay? Explaining things to such a mental midget. I'm trying the best I can."

And then Dougie had asked her a lot of other things about it, how it was to look at him when he was dead, lying on the floor.

And did she feel different at that moment from the moment she was killing him? Shit like that, breaking it up into little pieces. But by that point Elmira wouldn't give him more than a word or two, she was so pissed, and depressed, and confused and generally scared shitless she was going to get strapped into the electric chair for this.

"Whatta you care anyway, how it felt? You bug me about it, but what difference does it make to you? You got no feelings, you're not gonna learn to have them from me. It doesn't work that way. You got it or you don't, that's all there is to it. Like a big dick, you're born with it or you aren't. Isn't any kind of exercise you can do to get one later in life."

Dougie had looked at her, in the waiting room at the airport in Salt Lake. He had looked at her a long time, different expressions coming and going on his face.

Finally he said, "My father's gonna love you."

And here they were on the airplane, Dougie using her for his dictionary. Elmira couldn't account for it. The way her life was going, how she was acting. Right after she'd met Dougie, something had started to happen to her, she wasn't sure what. Like she was hypnotized, doing things she was told, but not sure why. Hating it, but getting very excited by it at the same time. She kept telling him about love, but now she wasn't sure. Maybe this is what it was, confused half the time, scared shitless the rest. Maybe she'd never felt it before, and now here it was, and it wasn't what she'd thought at all.

"Are you crazy, Dougie? Did I marry a crazy man?"

It was out there before she'd thought of saying it. It had been lying there in her head, and then there it was, spoken.

Dougie lay his head back against the headrest and turned his face to Elmira. He was looking at her hair, staring at it like he was just now noticing it was short and orange.

"What'd you say to me?"

"I believe you heard me."

"I'm pretending I didn't," he said. "That's a very personal type of question."

"Tell me, Dougie. 'Cause if you are crazy, I think we should get this marriage thing annulled."

"It's none of your goddamn beeswax if I'm crazy," he said.

"I'm your wife, Dougie. I married your ass. It *is* my business. Everything about you is, that's the way it works."

"Yeah?"

"Yeah."

"Okay, then," he said. "I used to be crazy."

"Christ, I knew it."

"When I was little, I was crazy. But I made myself better. Reading like I do, driving the Munch and Crunch, teaching my bird to talk, and now, getting married to you. I'm learning the right things to do, learning how to be normal."

She leaned close to him and whispered, "Murdering people, getting your new bride to murder people. That's a right thing to do? Huh? You consider this normal?"

"I didn't talk till I was fifteen," he said.

"You're shitting me. Fifteen?"

He smiled at her, and nodded as if he were proud of it.

"Well, I believe it," she said. "Somehow I believe it."

"I mean, I *could* talk," Dougie said. "I said things to myself in the dark at night, in my bed. But I just didn't see any point to saying things to other people. You know, I thought, like, What's it accomplish? So I was mute. A cute mute. But now I talk. Now, I enjoy talking. Things come out of my mouth, I watch them, I enjoy it. I say things. It makes people squirm. I like that. Now I talk better than other people. They never heard anything like me, you can tell how they look at me."

Elmira said, "If you were crazy, you should've told me. You should've warned me of it before we got married and everything."

"I used to be crazy is what I said. I'm teaching myself the other way, that's what I just said, isn't it? Isn't that what I just spoke out loud?"

Elmira didn't answer him.

Dougie said, "I used to be crazy, and I went to hospitals, and my mother left home because she didn't want a crazy little boy. My father, Captain Barnes, said I bit her womb. I was inside her when I was just a fetus, and I bit her and then she had me, and she left right after. I don't remember doing it, biting her womb, but that's what he said.

"And when I was younger, the people in those hospitals, they didn't know what I had, or what to call me. They gave me tests and shit, but they still couldn't come up with it, so they left me alone, and that was okay, I didn't mind it, 'cause it was like I didn't know any other way, didn't have anything to compare it to."

He said, "But then a few years ago, they had to let me go, put me out here in the mainstream with the normals, and here I am. And I been figuring it out. If I was going to get along, I'd have to learn all the shit about how it works, learn to read the dials at the factory, all that. Drive a car, screw girls."

Elmira looked around at the other seats, see if anybody was listening to this. Just a teenage kid clamped inside a Walkman. Across the aisle an old lady stared out her own window.

Dougie said, "I been learning to read. Learning about sex, about parrots, all kinds of things. You know. And my father. You'll meet him in a few minutes. I'm learning about how to be a son and all. I'm getting him to respect me. He sends me to do things. I've won his confidence and respect."

"What about that other stuff, the shit you say. Penis weenis, all that? What the hell is that about?"

"I don't know." Dougie stared down at his lap. "Probably, I don't know . . . probably, it's just some of the crazy shit still there in my head. Limbo, bimbo. Plane crash, jock rash.

"So anyway, that's who I am. That's me. Dougie Barnes. And that's my complete story." He smiled at her. A nice smile. She was married to this smile. "So now you know all about me."

"Yeah," Elmira said. "So now I know."

The plane had lowered its landing gear, and they were swooping in over the ocean, then the tops of palm trees. Elmira shut her eyes, leaned back in her seat, helping the captain set the plane down, concentrating on getting the wheels level. At the same time wondering what it meant that Dougie was starting to make sense to her. Worried about it, but storing it.

"Tell me one more time," he said. "The thing about being in love."

"I'm bored with that, Dougie. Just give it a rest, okay? Let me just sit here in peace and think about my fucked-up life."

"You're my wife, you gotta tell me."

"Jesus Christ."

"Pretty please, love squeeze."

She let go of some air, shook her head.

"You want to be with the person you love." She said it like at school with the Pledge of Allegiance, the six-jillionth time in the last two days. Her eyes shut tight, leaning her head back against the headrest, but she could feel him watching her. "It's like it's your birthday every day. You get squishy inside just thinking about the person. When you aren't with them, you think about them. Everything that might normally piss you off, it's okay, 'cause you're in love."

Elmira opened her eyes, watched the island of Key West taking shape out the window. Palm trees everywhere, greener than it was out west, and everything seemed closer, thicker, wetter.

"Say the other, the rest of it."

She sighed.

"You'll do anything for that person. Not because you think you should, but because you want to. It's like you've become two people. The person you used to be, and at the same time you're swished together with the other person."

"Yeah," Dougie said. "Yeah, I like that. That's the part I completely like."

27

Shaw walked out of Millie's room and kept on down the hallway, groggy, shuffling like a patient waking from heavy anesthesia, down the stairway, moving a little faster, past Buzz in the lobby, Buzz looking up and saying, "Hey, what's wrong? Hey," but he kept on, building steam across the parking lot, faster to the road, breaking into a trot, his legs becoming weightless and invisible beneath him, hurling himself forward into a breathless sprint, his vision a blur, hearing only his breath, following the effortless asphalt road a half mile to the open chain link gate of the recycling plant, across the gravel drive, through the generator room, and a heavy metal door, past a woman with large accounting books spread open before her, up the stairs, two at a time.

He stood in the waiting room for a moment heaving for breath, feeling the fine flush of adrenaline. The receptionist stared and asked if she could help him. He waited there for another moment, coming down, gulping air, slowing his system till he could breathe through his nose, drawing three, four good breaths, then he walked past her, swung the door open, and stepped into Barnes's office.

Barnes was on the phone, but when he looked up and saw Shaw pressing against the edge of his desk, he put the receiver down, no good-byes.

"Well, Mr. Chandler, welcome once again to my humble world."

"You goddamn son of a bitch," he said.

"Not especially original," Barnes said. "But I've always thought it had a good solid ring to it."

"You gutless fuckhead," Shaw said, "I know you killed my father, or you hired someone else to do it. And I know you blackmailed Montoya, stole his land. And I know you sprayed poison over Key West. And I'm going to find out the rest of it, every god-damn detail of it. And when I do, I'm coming back here, and I'm going to tie you down on that fucking desk, and I'm going to jam an IV into you and pump *Serratia marcescens* into you till you wither up and die."

Shaw stepped back from the desk.

"My, my," Barnes said. "Haven't we been busy. Learning Latin phrases and everything."

As his anger burned off, Shaw's vision was clarifying. Barnes was leaning forward in his chair, smiling, his gray eyes bright, his upper lip lifted into the hint of a sneer. He'd been barbered in the past few hours. His gray flattop freshly leveled, his cheeks pink and gleaming. Probably a manicure too. He wore a blue-green plaid shirt, a dark blue cotton tie. Spiffed out for another big day at the dump. Smiling at Shaw, full of ugly humor. With his elbows on his desk, he pressed his palms together and began to open and close them in front of him like a poker player sneaking looks at his straight royal flush.

"So," Barnes said, "are you sure that's all the people I killed? I didn't perhaps strangle the pope? I wasn't in on the Kennedy thing, or Martin Luther King? How'd you miss them? I'm disappointed in you, Chandler."

He drew his hands apart, let the cards scatter on his desk.

"But you know what?" Barnes said. "It just so happens, and it's very coincidental too, just this very morning I stumbled upon another murder victim you might be interested in."

Dizzy from his run, from the hollow pain ringing in his chest, Shaw was disoriented. This wasn't how he'd pictured it. Maybe he was bungling this, letting his glands rule, coming here so impulsively, leaving the sizzle of his hate on the asphalt roadway and the two flights of steps, and a few curses to the man's face. Giving Barnes the permanent advantage.

As Shaw stood there before Barnes's desk, the office seemed to drain of light and air, then began slowly refilling with some viscous fluid, thicker, heavier and more desolate than anything he had ever tried to breathe, almost too dim to see through. He was a child, standing before the principal, words failing in his throat as the man across the desk decided his punishment. He could only stare and try to find his breath, stare at this man with coppery skin, cocky smile, tough, big-boned face.

"This morning I was just ambling about my property without a care in the world. It was a spectacular morning, bright, clear, the birds trilling, butterflies, everything sparkling. And then I came on a place way off on the perimeter of my land, a little spot, very secluded. And I stopped. Because something wasn't right. I squatted down. And then I saw it. Freshly turned ground. A hump of new dirt."

His intercom buzzed and he winked at Shaw, held up a finger.

"Your son's here to see you, Mr. Barnes."

"I'm busy right now," said Barnes, his voice darkening. "Tell the boy to wait."

Shaw heard the squawk of gulls, looked out the window in time to see one veering beneath the ash chute, apparently lost in the tangle of steel girders.

"So, then," Barnes said, "I'm there beside this hump of dirt. And although it's not in my nature, I think something terrible must've happened. It looks like a fresh grave. Like somebody picked a spot, and hid something in the ground.

"You've got to get this in your mind, Chandler. I'm a retired base commander. I was the equivalent to, say, in terms of how much money and manpower I managed, maybe a vice-president of Exxon, something like that. I made a lot of friends during my tenure here, the mayor, councilmen, other people. I contributed mightily to their careers. All these people are beholden to me.

"So picture this accurately. This is the man that's out there digging, an important man, a man who people trust. Try to imagine that these are my very words to the sheriff. Just how I would tell it. I run back for a shovel, come back, start digging, and then the blade of my shovel strikes a leather shoe.

"I get down on my knees, scrape the loose dirt off the poor man's face. And who do you think I found out there? Who is this person? Have any idea?"

Shaw was sleepy. He wanted to lie down somewhere. Only the final quiver of his rage left. Very tired, just a small film clip replaying, an outtake from his imagination: He jumps across the desk and digs his thumbs into Barnes's throat, rattles the man's head till his tongue breaks off. But Shaw only stood there silently. It was as much as he could manage.

"I'm not an expert on these things," Barnes said. "I've always believed we should leave such matters to men of law. We poor citizens can't begin to fathom the complexities of innocence and guilt.

"But still, if I were forced to hazard a guess, I'd say, if this dead man was a person who had committed crimes against another individual, robbed him and his mother of their earthly goods, and if the man who was robbed had made public threats against the thief, and then if that same individual's pistol was found later somewhere else entirely, with a couple of bullets missing, bullets that match up to those recovered from the corpse, and if the fingerprints of the registered owner of that handgun were the only prints on the murder weapon, then that seems to make a very compelling case against this individual. Wouldn't you agree?"

"Peter Salter," Shaw said. "You murdered him too."

Barnes said quietly, "Salter's body is there, decomposing. But I haven't actually come upon it yet. I'm saving that, that little morning stroll with the butterflies and everything. You see, the way it works, Mr. Chandler, is this. Anyone can make wild claims about another individual, mutter their suspicions of blackmail and murder. But suspicions are simply not in the same league with an actual body. A corpse can be very persuasive."

He chuckled and showed Shaw his teeth, white and cold.

"So, I'm saving my story for the right moment. A little insurance policy against your wild ravings. I'm simply going to let Mr. Salter's body remain where it is until you give me a reason to find it. I don't have to find it, mind you. In fact, I'd rather not. But I will find it, if I'm pushed. Are we clear on this, then? Are we both on the same page now, son?"

"Why don't you just have me killed like you do everyone else? Why bother with all this?"

"Well, yes," Barnes said smiling. "I certainly may have to do that, Mr. Chandler. But till just a minute ago, till you started speaking in Latin, I didn't know how much you knew. How dangerous you truly were."

"This is my new wife," Dougie said to Jane, the receptionist. Jane was wearing blue jeans and a tight sleeveless blouse today. The veins on her neck were standing out again as she ran her eyes up and down Elmira.

Elmira's traveling clothes, black leather shorts and a white see-through shirt. Dougie could sit there, ten feet away and count the bumps on her nipples. She wore sandals with long laces that she'd crisscrossed up her legs to her thighs. She'd put on her white lipstick and her white eyeshadow. Far as Dougie knew, the woman was healthy, but she liked to paint herself, make herself look like a three-day-old corpse.

"Say hello to Elmira," Dougie said to Jane. "Be polite."

"Hello," she said.

"She's staring at me, Dougie." Elmira crossed her legs in the other direction.

"Everybody stares at you, Elmira. You never notice that?"

"I don't get it," Elmira said. "Things are so busy at the garbage dump, you bring home your new bride, and your father makes you sit in the waiting room half an hour." Elmira chewed on a cuticle. She said, "Make her stop staring at me, Dougie. Could you do that, at least, huh?"

The door to his father's office swung open and Shaw Chandler came out slowly. He looked at Dougie and then at Elmira.

"Jeepers creepers," Dougie said, "it's my long-lost sex brother."

He put out his hand, but Shaw brushed past him and out the door.

"You did what?" Barnes said.

"I shot a cowboy in Waldorf's office," Elmira said. "Then burned him up along with whatever else was in there."

"Guy by the name of Big Merle," Dougie said. "Yeah, that was my idea. Confuse the issue, charcoal tissue."

Barnes went to the office window and turned away from these two. Looking out at the plant, trying to regain some order in his thoughts, not let Dougie draw him into his whirlwind.

The woman had run through half a dozen emotional states. They'd only been in his office five minutes and she'd cried twice, cursed him for not being nicer to her, laughed to the point of hysteria, and then she'd settled in and given him a serious description of the events in Salt Lake.

Barnes had already decided on the size of her garbage bag. Hefty, double-thick. And he'd probably have to use four of them so nobody would smell her perfume. He was ten feet from her, and the stuff was burning his eyes, choking him. Jasmine blossoms.

"Tell the lady to wait outside," Barnes said.

"I'm no lady," Elmira said. "I'm your daughter-in-law."

"Put the cunt in the lobby."

Elmira stood up, gave Dougie a long gut-withering look, then swung her ass back out into the lobby.

Barnes said, "You can't be serious about this woman."

"She's my wife. I married her."

"Get rid of her, Dougie. This afternoon. Get rid of her."

"I can't do that. She's my wife."

"Are you being insubordinate?"

"I don't know," he said. "Maybe."

"Get rid of her, Dougie. Or I will."

"I love her."

"Who told you that?"

"Nobody."

"She told you, didn't she? She put that into your head."

"I'm in love with Elmira Barnes."

"Boy, you're on the verge of losing my respect and admiration. Now, you don't want that, do you?"

Dougie's eyes clouded. He sank inward, quick and deep.

"You *do* want my respect still, don't you, Dougie? Your father's respect?"

Dougie's eyes drifted up.

"Can't I have both things? Elmira and you both?"

"Son, you have to decide. You have to make a choice."

There was a commotion in the lobby. Sounded like something overturned. Jane shrieked. Dougie looked at his father.

"Stay put," Barnes said.

"Yes, sir."

"So," Barnes said. "What'll it be? Are you still my boy?"

There was more noise from the lobby, the outer door slammed.

"Slam-bam, thank you ma'am," Dougie said.

"Are you still my boy, Dougie?"

In a distant voice, Dougie said, "Yes, sir."

"Very good, then," said Barnes. "I want you to take this woman to your shack now, do her, and with a minimum of noise. And I'll come out there after dark and together we'll dispose of her body."

"She's teaching me things," Dougie said. "I'm getting better. She helps me with words, how to say things. How to describe stuff. You'll like her. Tough cookie, rough nookie."

"It's been settled, Dougie. And tonight, after we dispose of her, I've got some other work for you. A whole lot of building materials accumulated while you were gone. This evening I want you to start up the Munch and Crunch. You think you can handle that?"

"I love the Munch and Crunch," he said. "It's my favorite."

"So you see, if you do the right things, you get rewards. That's how it works in the world, Dougie. But you have to do the right things if you want my complete respect and admiration."

"I'm going to go get my bird back, too. His name is Jerkoff. I'm teaching him to talk. Trapeze, striptease, antifreeze, green peas. Things like that."

28

When Shaw came back outside, Buzz had the Bronco idling at the front gate of the dump. Shaw climbed inside, shut the door. He stared out of the windshield. His tennis shirt was glued to his back. There was a flutter in his chest. An eagle had hatched there and was trying to escape.

"I was just about to come in," Buzz said. "Cause a ruckus."

Shaw nodded.

"You okay?"

Shaw was silent. He hammered the dash. Hammered it again.

"Where to?" Buzz said quietly.

Shaw directed him the half mile up the highway to Montoya's. Buzz stayed in the Bronco while Shaw walked to the main house and found Trula's note on the kitchen table.

Gone to Utah. Be back soon as I can. Trula.

Shaw went back to the Bronco.

"Now where to?"

"The docks," Shaw said.

"Which docks?"

"Foot of Duval Street."

"What now?"

"I need to see a man about a dog."

Shaw stared out his window as Buzz drove back over to Key West, down Roosevelt, past the deep-fat fry places, the tire places.

"Your mom died," Buzz said, as they were pulling up to a light in front of Searstown. "Or did you know already?"

"Yeah, I knew."

"I'm awful sorry, buddy."

"You don't have any trouble, do you, Buzz?" he said. "Letting it go from time to time. Letting it all hang out."

"Letting what hang out?"

"My mother died," Shaw said. "My father was murdered. I fall in love with a woman, she has multiple sclerosis. A man just threatens my life. I'm just sitting here, nothing's happening inside of me. I can feel my heart bumping around, that's about all."

"You're numb, man," he said. "That's normal. Shock. You're a little pale, you probably got a feeble pulse, you're thirsty."

"I know what the hell shock is, Buzz."

"Well, that's what you got, man. That's all I'm saying."

"Whatever this thing is I've got, I've had it all my life."

Buzz drove on, turning right onto Simonton, following it down the shady tunnel of oaks and banyans. The white Conch houses on both sides, porches, verandas, tin roofs, gingerbread. He drove till he had to turn left onto Caroline. Coming up behind the Conch Train, a couple of kids sitting backward in the last car waving at the Bronco. Some kind of game, collecting waves from strangers. Buzz waved at them. The kids kept waving. Working hard for Shaw's wave. He sat there, pulse feeble, clammy, all the signs.

Over the Conch Train loudspeaker, the tour guide described Sloppy Joe's Bar, which he said claimed to be the true hangout of Ernest Hemingway but wasn't really. The tourists twisted to their left to see into the dark bar anyway. The kids in the back car kept waving. Waving.

Shaw lifted his hand, brought it above the dash, gave them a small wave.

His eyes burned, his mouth quivered. He tried to collect himself, holding hard to the door handle. And then it began, hot and wet, down his cheeks, running fast over the edge of his jaw, down his throat into his shirt. He waved again at the kids but they had turned their attention to people walking down Caroline.

"You okay?" Buzz said.

For a moment he couldn't speak.

"You want to stop? Maybe get a beer?"

Shaw shook his head.

"Or maybe something stronger," said Buzz.

He fought it as it rose from his gut. Fought it, but knew he couldn't stifle it any longer. He felt it in his chest, felt it rattle in his throat, tearing the lining. And he coughed it out, a sob, coughed it out of him like a piece of meat lodged deep in his throat. He bent forward, pressing his head to the dashboard. He cried. His forehead thumping against the dash, staring at his blurry feet, feeling Buzz's hand pat his back.

————

"Damn right, he's good. Why you think I call him Nostrils?" Doyle leaned back in the deck chair, sipping his Miller Lite.

"I was hoping you could lend him to me for the evening."

"Sure I could, Shaw."

"He can get around okay? Crippled like that?"

"He's a little slower than he was with four legs, but even like he is, once he gets a scent, you won't be able to stay up with him."

"He have a leash?"

"Don't know the meaning of the word."

"But he'll do what I tell him to."

"That dog obeys in six languages, including drunken Spanish. Just stick something in front of his nose, tell him to go find the other half of it, and stand back."

"He'll find a thing, even if it's buried?"

"Got to be buried under six feet of lead for that dog not to dig right down to it."

————

It was four o'clock by the time Buzz pulled into the lot of H. L. Chitum's, an upscale tackle shop along the highway in Islamorada. He went inside and found Tom Robertson in the stockroom smoking a joint. Robertson had guided out of Garrison Bight marina for years before moving up the highway. He told Shaw that yeah, sure, he knew Peter Salter. The kid was always trying to sell them shit, rods, reels, bucktails. I thought he might, Shaw said. But hey, Chitum's didn't do business that way, Tom said. No hot property. Shaw asked him if he knew where Salter lived. And Tom said he believed it was somewhere down on Sunshine Way, three or four blocks south on the highway, bayside. That's what Tom had heard, anyway. Concrete-block house, it says, Pair-a-Dice on a sign out front. But hey, the kid's a slick dude, he said, watch out, he'll have your wallet out of your pants and into his if you're not careful. Shaw said, Yeah, he'd heard that.

Salter's house was hidden from his neighbors and the street by tall aralia hedges, so Shaw told Buzz just to pull into the carport beneath the house. They left Nostrils in the backseat, and got out and climbed the concrete steps. From the top of the stairs they had a sweeping view of the bay, choppy and gray, the sky had dropped low and turned to slate. A strong wind from the northwest. A twenty-foot Mako was tied to the dock, bobbing in the rising chop.

With a conch shell Shaw found on the porch, he broke a pane in the kitchen door and reached through it and opened the door.

"I got dibs on the top bunk," Buzz said, "when they throw us in Raiford."

"You name it, it's yours, buddy."

"Just so you know," Buzz said.

The living room was filled with unopened cardboard boxes. VCRs, microwaves, TV sets, stereos, CD players. The Penn International reels were in a back closet, still in their cartons. Shaw dumped out the dirty clothes from a pink plastic hamper and pawed through Peter Salter's clothes. Buzz found about fifty custom rods in the spare bedroom.

"You want these?" Buzz said, holding out two handfuls.

"No," Shaw said. "We're in a hurry. All I want this trip is a couple pair of dirty underpants. The dirtier the better."

"I'll let you handle that, good buddy. I got no experience in choosing dirty underwear."

Shaw dug through the clothes until he found a couple of bikini briefs. One red, one black.

"This's the ticket."

"We're out of here," said Buzz.

"Just in case," Shaw said, picking up a black silky shirt with geometric patterns on it. He gave the armpits a careful sniff. "Jesus, this guy smells so bad, I don't think we even need the damn dog."

"You're kidding me, Dougie. This is a shack. It's only got three walls, for Christsakes. I can't live in a place like this. Christ Almighty."

"It's my beach house," he said. "Where I come sometimes."

"Call me a taxi, Dougie. I'm going back to New Orleans, forget any of this happened. I can't live like this. There's bums sleeping in alleys have nicer places than this."

She picked up the edge of the naked mattress and looked at the dirt floor under it. Let it drop. Shaking her head. Dougie could hear the Munch and Crunch working, Lars Mandel gunning it up over a hill of motel furniture over on the east side of Mount Trashmore.

"All it needs is a TV," Dougie said. "Maybe a little bookshelf too, you could put up those postcards. I like it here. It's where I come to be alone."

"Well, you can just be alone here, then." She started tugging at the diamond ring, trying to get it off her chubby finger.

"My daddy said to kill you," Dougie said, standing with his back to her, looking out the missing wall. Mangroves, a view across the bay of Key West, the pancake houses, the motels.

He turned to her. Elmira had stopped yanking on the ring. Her hand still gripping it, frozen.

"Daddy said I should kill you and then the two of us would run your dead body through the incinerator, turn you into electricity."

She backed up into a corner of the shack, and put one hand on the corrugated tin wall, the other hand on the three-quarter-inch plywood. The Munch and Crunch was in low gear now, straining. Something big over there that Lars was having a hard time getting on top of. Dougie couldn't see it from here, but it sounded like maybe an old pool table or a big couch.

"I do what my daddy says. I'm an obedient boy." Dougie took a step toward her and Elmira started to say something but couldn't make it happen. Dougie said, "To keep his respect and admiration, I've got to be a good boy."

"Dougie?"

"I told him I loved you, but he said I had to do it anyway."

"Dougie, don't do this, baby."

"We had some fun, though. Waldorf and all that. And that thing in New Orleans with the letter opener. And throwing the shit out of the rental car. We had some fun memories. I never met the likes of you before, Elmira Hemple. But he said I had to choose between the two of you, and I gotta choose him."

"You'd do that?"

"Yeah."

"And it wouldn't bother you, you wouldn't hurt inside after you did it?"

"I don't have a pain threshold," he said. "It's an advantage sometimes."

"Dougie, look at me." Elmira stepped in close to him. "Do you have sex with your father?"

"Hell, no."

"Then you made the wrong choice, Dougie. 'Cause you and me, we have great sex. That's what it's all about, hon. That's it, the sum total of what it's all about. Life in a nutshell."

"I obey my father, what he says to do."

"Dougie," she said, "you're a legal adult now. You don't have to do everything your daddy tells you to do anymore. That's how it works. You get to be twenty-one, and you're free. You do whatever you want to do from then on."

"Fiddle faddle, piddle paddle. Don't try to confuse me. A boy's daddy is always his daddy."

"It's true, Dougie. What I'm saying is the gospel truth." She took another step toward him. "Ask anybody else, and find out. Your daddy isn't your boss for the rest of your life. Especially once you get married, then it makes your wife your legal next of kin, not your daddy anymore."

"You sure?"

"You been letting your daddy pull your strings way past your twenty-first birthday. You're what, thirty, thirty-one?"

"Twenty-eight, going on twenty-nine."

"See, that makes seven years you been free of him, and you didn't even know it."

"You're lying just to save your ass."

"Dougie, what does it say on the front cover of that book you were reading today? *Nuns in Wetsuits* or whatever the hell it was."

"It says the title."

"Something else too."

"Whatta you mean?"

"You must be twenty-one to purchase this material. Doesn't it say that?"

"Yeah, I guess."

She moved up closer to him. Two feet, a foot. Ducking her head a little the way she did when she was trying to get her way. Working her eyelashes. Her nipples standing up through her shirt.

"Don't you see, Dougie? When you turn twenty-one you get to do whatever you want to do without checking it out with your daddy. You didn't have to ask him if you could buy that book, did you? No, you just went in and bought it. And it's the same way with everything else. If he tells you to do something, you still got to decide if you agree with him or not. You don't just automatically do it, whatever he says."

"You don't?"

"No, Dougie, you don't."

———

Trula called three printshops before she found one near Miami International Airport that would make copies from computer disks. She took a cab to the corner of LeJeune and Flagler and walked half a block down Flagler till she found the shop. Told the cab to wait. Jimenez Copiers.

She sat on a bench by the front window while a young woman printed the article. A tall man in a *guayabera* sat next to her. He nodded to her and smiled.

"Know what you get when you cross PMS and ESP?"

Trula looked at him for a moment and shook her head.

"A bitch who thinks she knows everything."

She nodded.

The man chuckled at his joke.

Trula rose, walked to the counter and waited there till the woman brought back her computer disk and the stack of papers. The article was almost forty pages long.

She paid, and walked out to the taxi and rode back to the airport. In the cab, she read the cover page of the article. It was titled "A Plague in Paradise." She turned the page and read the dedication:

To Dr. Richard Montoya
For bravely putting himself at risk,
so that others could know the truth.

She folded the pages in half and slid the article into her leather bag. She paid for the cab, walked through the airport in a daze. She sat in the waiting area for ten minutes, eyes disconnected from the moment. Later, as the plane lifted off for the twenty-minute flight, she took the article out again, unfolded it, looked again at the cover page.

She wasn't sure anymore if she could bring herself to read it. What difference would it make even if she did? She would still have to make her daily peace with her body. Knowing the cause of her disease might only breed more anger and frustration.

The twenty-year-old boy in the surfer shirt and baggies who took the seat beside her turned to her as the plane was leveling off.

"So, you into horror, or what?" he said.

"I'm sorry?"

He pointed to the manuscript in her lap.

" 'Plague in Paradise.' Sounds very, you know, like horror."

Trula looked down at the article. She opened it to the first page.

"Yeah," she said, starting to read. "Horror."

29

Shaw borrowed an eight-foot dinghy tied up behind one of the yachts moored near the tackle shop. He and Buzz and Nostrils puttered across the marina, beneath the bridge to Garrison Bight, and out through a narrow cut and into the bay. The sun was just sending up its final flares, and a slick of crimson was spreading before them across the gray water. The wind had slackened, but it was still rough in the small boat, and Buzz held to both gunwales as Shaw motored them toward Stock Island. Nostrils lay on his side, bouncing at Shaw's feet.

He landed the boat on a mangrove island a few hundred yards from the shoreline. They stayed there for about fifteen minutes until the darkness was complete. Then Shaw cocked the outboard out of the water, and Buzz fitted the oars into the oarlocks and began to haul them toward the shore.

A bulldozer worked on the far western slope of the landfill, its headlights on. And a dump truck bumped down the hill maybe three hundred yards from where they put ashore.

Shaw sloshed through the shallows and tied the dinghy to a stand of mangroves. Buzz handed him one of the shovels and climbed out of the boat carrying the other one.

"Get the clothes, too, Buzz."

Shaw set the shovel down on the shore, came back to the dinghy and lifted Nostrils up and set him down in the shallow water. Buzz took the freezer bag with Peter Salter's clothes out from under one of the seats. The dog stumbled sideways and fell. He pulled himself up and hobbled to the bank and shook hard, shedding a silver mist of water.

The moon was dim behind a layer of washboard clouds.

Shaw opened the freezer bag and held it in front of Nostrils.

"Go on, dog. Go on!"

"I don't know about this," Buzz said. "The mutt's a goddamn wreck. Three legs, he can barely walk. Must be fifteen years old. How could his damn nose still work, the shape he's in?"

Nostrils limped away into the dark and Shaw and Buzz followed quickly.

The ground was rocky, with patches of sandy marl, palmetto scrub, cabbage palms and rough grass. Nostrils had his nose to the earth and was sweeping it left and right as he walked. They followed after him and made a long circle, coming within two hundred yards of the base of Mount Trashmore. Shaw could hear the dozer still working on the far side of the hill.

When they were almost back to the spot where they'd begun, Nostrils dropped to the ground, panting. And Buzz sat on a limestone boulder nearby. The dog shook his head, and his ears made a hollow slap against his skull.

"This is nuts, man. That dog's cruising around in a daze."

"Have a little patience, Buzzer. I don't see we have a lot of choice here. I got to find this body before we can take care of the rest of it."

"If there is a body, you mean."

"Well, if there is a body, then we've got to find it. And the only way to find it is to look for it."

"Geometric logic," Buzz said.

Shaw opened the freezer bag again and pulled out the silky black shirt and held the armpit to Nostrils' face. The dog shook his head again and cranked himself up from the ground.

"Do it, boy. Do it."

The dog led them along the shoreline for a while, moving away from the recycling plant. Sniffing close to the water, then following a finger inlet, through the lower branches of some Florida holly trees and a couple of scraggly pines.

Shaw stopped abruptly, and hissed for Nostrils to halt.

Twenty yards ahead under a canopy of small oaks there was a lean-to, one wall tin, the others plywood. A woman stood in the opening, smoking a cigarette. Moonlight shone off her leather skirt. Nostrils kept walking toward her.

The woman must have heard him coming because she lifted her

head, looking left and right. The dog ambled a yard in front of her, and when she glanced down and saw him, she shrieked and hopped to the side. But Nostrils kept shuffling, his head down, following his nose past her into some tall grass along the inlet.

"What're we gonna do?" Buzz whispered at his back.

"What else?"

"Man, oh man. I don't believe this, Shaw."

They walked along the dog's trail.

The woman was leaning away from the shack, peering into the dark at Nostrils' path through the grass, her back to them as they approached.

"Evening, ma'am," Shaw said.

She yelped, stumbled around and flicked her cigarette savagely at Shaw. It dinged him in the chest and fell to the ground. He stubbed it out with the blade of his shovel.

"What the hell!" she yelled. "Jesus fucking Christ, you scared the *piss* out of me."

"You see a dog go by here?" Shaw said.

She was pressing her hand to her heart, breathing hard.

"That way." Tipping her head. "Down there."

"Come on," said Buzz, "before we lose the thing."

A squawk came from inside the shack, and Shaw stopped. The squawk sounded again, and something lurched in his gut. Then a short, piercing screech. Feathers rustled and the bird did an imitation of a hilarious laugh.

"Hey, sailor! Hey, sailor! Who's being a good boy? Fuck a duck. Fuck a duck. Who's being a good boy? Who's being good?"

"That goddamn parrot," the woman said. "I'm out here all night in the dark, with the thing jabbering like that, it's worse than listening to Dougie, and then you two come walking out of nowhere. Jesus Christ, here I am a thousand miles from fucking civilization, chained to a fucking shack in a goddamn son-of-a-bitching mosquito-infested garbage dump. Jesus Christ."

She lifted a leg out for them to see the handcuffs locked around her right ankle, the other cuff connected to a corner pole.

Buzz put a hand on Shaw's back and prodded him forward.

"No," Shaw said. "You go with the dog, Buzz."

"What?"

"Go on now, quick, before you lose him."

"What the hell're you doing now, Shaw?"

"I gotta have a conversation," he said, "with this bird."

"I told you, Lars, it's some kind of bullshit soap product the navy wants to get rid of."

Lars stood on the loading platform looking into the open shed, shaking his head. Barnes stood a few yards away on the pavement. No reason to risk getting near the stuff if he didn't have to. He remembered those frog eyeballs floating on the surface.

"Why I have to wear the rubber suit, Mr. Barnes, for soap?"

"It's very powerful soap, Lars. It's acid or something, I don't know. Just do what I say, okay, empty the small cans into the big can. Don't spill any or get any of it on your skin or clothes or anything. This is very potent stuff."

"Whatever you say, Mr. Barnes." But the dumb Swede was still shaking his head.

"That's right, Lars. That's right, whatever I say. And you be goddamn careful now, you hear me? Don't get in any hurry with this shit."

"Yes, sir."

"And listen, Lars. After this, you can leave early tonight."

"I just come on at six."

"So go off at eight. You'll get your whole paycheck, don't worry. Just do what I tell you, and quit shaking your fucking head, would you, for once? Would you do me the courtesy of that, huh? Stop shaking it for about a minute while I'm talking to you."

"Yes, sir."

Still shaking his head, Lars used a crowbar to pry the lid off the fifty-five-gallon drum, and he set the lid aside. He unscrewed one of the bottles of Seluline and shook it over the drum. The stuff oozed out in a single gelatinous mass.

Lars shook his head and said, "This take a long while, Mr. Barnes, to fill up one of these barrels."

"Is it reacting to the drum?" Barnes said.

"Reacting?"

"Is it giving off any fumes, smoke?"

Lars looked into the drum. Put his head down there.

"No, sir. No smoke. Just lying there in the bottom."

"All right, then. I'm going to leave you here. Just remember, work carefully, Lars. Don't worry how long it takes."

Barnes stood and watched Lars dump another container of Seluline into the barrel.

Wouldn't you know it. Just when he needed the incinerator the most, the thing was shut down. Not enough garbage again. Christ. So he'd had this idea. Instead of waiting till they brought the plant back on line, another way to get rid of things.

As soon as Dougie was finished playing on the Munch and Crunch, they'd go down to the shack and get the woman, drag her back up here. Try the frog experiment with her. Something he could share with Motrim next time he came. Bring Motrim over to the drum, flip it open, there's human eyeballs staring at him. Jesus Christ, now Barnes was starting to think like that guy, with his perverted sense of humor.

It worried him a little, things tilting off-center like they were. And then his own mind not as sharp as he'd like it. Kind of dizzy, having a hard time focusing on what exact steps to take. Finding himself making lists to himself in the last couple of days, do this, then afterward do this. No, no, do this first, then that. Hup, two, three, four. Getting nervous that he'd forgotten something, was about to bungle everything. It was probably just hanging around all this garbage for too long. He just needed a break, a vacation somewhere. Somewhere where the air was clean, he could purify his system.

Next on his list, sometime soon, maybe tonight, maybe tomorrow, depending on how tired he was, Douglas was going to have to slide Dougie into the barrel. Enough was enough. He'd given the boy chances aplenty. Spent half his life trying to educate the kid. And what does he do, he brings home this whore, a woman crazier than Dougie and just as prone to yammering. Standing there in his office giving him all the gruesome details of what happened out in Utah. He told her he didn't want to know about any of it, but she kept on reciting it for him. The guy's name was Merle. She shot him in the throat. Jesus, Barnes had no interest in that. But she'd kept it up. And Dougie standing there smiling at her the whole time.

When Douglas thought about it, it was startling that he had put up with Dougie for as long as he had. Twenty-eight years of dealing with the moron. Really kind of amazing. A deranged, demented kid like him. Barnes couldn't picture any other father with that kind of patience.

————

"Nostrils found the body," Buzz said. He stood in the opening of the shack. "So now what do we do?"

Shaw was sitting on a four-legged stool across from where El-mira sprawled on the naked mattress. The handcuff bracelet still around one of her ankles. Shaw had severed the cheap tin chain with the blade of his shovel. The other cuff was still locked around the support pole outside. Looked like some kind of gag gift, some-thing Dougie had bought over on Duval Street at one of the gay leather shops.

She lay there, and the Coleman lantern hissed on the floor beside her. In its yellow halo, she looked like a woman dead for months who'd grown hungry for a human voice and had scratched her way back to the surface.

"Where'd you find the body?"

"Shallow grave, twenty, thirty feet from the road. There was an opening snipped in the fence a few feet away. Somebody wanted it to look like the murderer parked on the road, lugged the body through the fence and down there."

"Muck and mire, fuck and fire," the parrot screeched. It was gripping a wooden dowel that had been suspended by fishing line from the roof. It twisted around and dug its beak into its shoulder feathers, swinging on its trapeze.

"So how're things going back here at the ranch?" Buzz said.

"This parrot," Shaw said. "He's very talkative."

"So?"

"He's said a few things I heard before. In fact, some of the same things that other parrot said, Buzz, from the house we were in that night. Same things exactly, plus a few new ones."

Buzz stood in the opening and watched the parrot swing.

"Then who's this lady?"

"She says she's Dougie's wife."

"I *am* his wife," Elmira moaned.

"Christ Almighty, Shaw. I thought Miami was bad, but this place, man, it's a whole 'nother dimension."

Nostrils gimped over to the mattress, stuck his nose into Elmira's face, gave her a lick. She twisted away, covered her eyes with her arm.

The woman was an emotional mess. She'd been relieved at first that Shaw had rescued her. And she'd started blathering for fifteen minutes, and she'd confessed she was a murderer, then suddenly retracted it, then told him she'd set two different guys on fire in the last two days, then said, No, no, that was a lie. Don't listen to her, she was just going crazy. Afterward, she flung herself on the mattress and sobbed, writhed around there, pounding the mattress with her fists, kicking it. The whole time the bird spewing out rhyming obscenities.

"Hey, buddy, let's get the hell out of here. Huh? How 'bout it?"

Elmira sat up suddenly on the mattress.

"You got to take me with you. They're going to kill me."

"Who's going to kill you?"

"Come on," Buzz said. "We got a body just sitting out there."

"Dougie's father," she said. "He told Dougie to murder me. I think I may have talked him out of it, but I'm not sure. I don't want to find out. It could be his father got hold of him again and changed him back. Dougie's that way, he believes whoever talked to him last."

"We might consider taking you with us," Shaw said. "If you told us the truth about these murders."

"Whatta you, cops?"

"We're just guys."

"Guys with a strange nightlife," Buzz said.

"Jesus Christ, I told you too much already."

"Leave her, then," Buzz said. "We got to get moving, man."

"One of them was named Merle," Elmira said. "But that was self-defense. He was trying to rape me."

"And the other one?"

"Some geeky doctor," she said.

"What was his name, Elmira?"

"What do you care what his name was?"

"By any chance was it Waldorf?"

"Jesus Christ, you *are* cops, aren't you?"

"Come on, Shaw, goddamn it. Leave her."

"I'm not saying another word till I talk to a lawyer," she said.

"Come on, lady," said Shaw. "We'll take you out of here."

Elmira got up, found her purse on a card table and went out the opening of the shack and stood waiting for them.

Buzz said, "How the hell we going to cram all three of us, that body, and that dog in an eight-foot boat, huh?"

"Don't worry. We'll figure a way. Use our Yankee ingenuity."

———

They made a wide circle around Stock Island, passing through Cow Key Channel. Shaw was keeping the RPMs down because the dinghy was unsteady with the three of them aboard.

Twenty feet behind them, Peter Salter's body planed just below the surface. Headfirst, on his back, the line looped under his arms and across his chest. Shaw had found the best speed to keep the body from twirling on the line, and now it bubbled along nicely, two boat-lengths behind them.

Salter hadn't been in the ground for more than a day or two, but his body had started to putrefy already. When they dragged him by his ankles out of the sandy dirt, a nest of red ants flooded from the neck of his shirt. There was no way they could've carried the body along with them in the dinghy.

"It's the way my life is going," Elmira said. "Getting saved from murderers by fucking grave robbers."

She was sitting in the bow, facing Buzz, riding uncertainly on the narrow seat. Her first time at sea.

There were some fishermen along the banks of the channel, their car doors open, music playing. Lanterns, ice chests. A couple of women sitting in folding chairs minding the kids. Shaw kept the boat going in the shadows on the far side, and no one seemed to notice Peter Salter.

As they were leaving the channel, entering a dark stretch of open water, the dinghy bounced. Shaw backed off on the throttle.

"We hit something," Buzz said.

"I knew it," Elmira said. "I knew it. We're going to sink, I'm going to drown out here in the middle of the fucking ocean."

"No," Shaw said. "Something hit us."

There was a splash behind them. A slap and rush of water, and the boat lurched. The dark water churned around the corpse and Shaw twisted the throttle, tugging against the strain of the rope. Nostrils stood up, looked back into the dark and began to bark.

"Sharks," Buzz said. "A couple of them, looks like."

Elmira moaned, and Nostrils began to howl.

A tall fin came out of the deep water ahead of them, began a lazy circle around the skiff. Shaw caught a look at its stalky eyes. A hammerhead. It was at least two feet longer than the dinghy.

Elmira followed Shaw's glance, and saw the fin swooshing past the bow. She shrieked, stood up.

"Sit the hell down," Buzz said, reaching out for her. "He doesn't want us."

She struggled for footing and the boat wobbled. Buzz got her down on her seat, and she began to let out a low, mournful wail. Nostrils turned and listened to her, tilting his head.

While the sharks feasted on Peter Salter, Shaw watched the big hammerhead circle one more time, then it raked the bottom of the dinghy, tipped it slightly sideways, and moved back to the end of the rope. When it hit what was left of the body, the boat shook and surged backward. Then abruptly the water was still.

30

"Where is she, son?"

"I don't know."

Dougie went back outside of the shack, checked the handcuff again, and called her name.

Barnes stood next to the mattress and watched the boy yell into the dark. The parrot squealed and rocked on its swing.

Dougie came back inside and started to search the shack. He picked up the stool, looked under it, lifted a corner of the mattress, held up the lantern and swung it around the small room.

"Where'd you send her, Dougie?"

"I didn't," he said. "I just went to get some clothes from my room, I get back, she's gone."

"Dougie, you're making me angry, son. You're making me angry with these games of yours."

"She cut herself loose and ran off," he said. "She was scared, and she ran off."

He set the lantern down, and dropped to his knees, stretched himself out full length on the floor and began to do push-ups.

"Holy mother of Christ," Barnes said. "This's a complete and utter fuckup. I send you to nip it in the bud, and what happens? Now this Chandler kid knows all about it. Some slut you found in the gutter, she could be anywhere at this moment, blabbing it to anybody who'll listen. This has all the earmarks, Dougie, of a god-damn catastrophe."

Dougie was counting out his push-ups, going fast, pumping.

Douglas put his finger out for the parrot and the bird looked at the finger for a moment and stepped aboard. Barnes squatted down

near Dougie, taking a grip on the bird's body with his right hand.
The thing squirming hard but not getting anywhere.

"Dougie, where is Elmira?"

The bird squealed, wriggled fiercely.

"Where is she, son?"

Douglas brought the bird next to Dougie's face and seized its
head with his left hand. Holding it like a jar with a tight lid.

Dougie stopped his push-ups, holding himself at arm's length
from the ground, looking at Barnes, at the bird. The blood seeped
from beneath his tan.

"Don't," he said.

"I will, if you don't tell me where she is."

"I don't know. I don't know where she is. She must've got scared
and left."

Barnes twisted the parrot's head. The creature bit him hard on
his ring finger, struggled in his grasp, and Barnes wrenched the head
farther around, kept cranking it around till the snap came and the
bird shivered and went limp in his hands.

"Jerkoff," Dougie said.

Barnes dropped the bird into the dirt by Dougie's right hand.
One of its claws twitched.

"Get up, Dougie, and come with me. We're going to go find
these people. Start cleaning up this mess."

———

The lights were on in the main house at Montoya's place
when Shaw and the others arrived. He led them up to the house and
knocked on the screen door, but there was no answer. He opened
it, stepped inside and called out. The ceiling fan hummed, and Trula's purse and an overnight case sat on the floor near the door to
the hallway. He tried another call, and no one responded.

Buzz came inside behind him, and went to the sink and washed
his hands.

"Now I've done it all," he said. "I thought I'd already done it
all, but I was wrong. I never trolled a dead body before."

Nostrils collapsed on the front porch and sighed and Elmira
went to the refrigerator, fished out a long-neck Budweiser, twisted
it open and bubbled half of it down without a breath.

"Be a peach, would you, and get me one of those?" Buzz said.

Shaw went out the door, stood on the porch for a moment. There were no lights on in her cabin, none at the surgery cabin, and none of the cage lights. But a dim bulb burned through the trees, down toward the pavilion where Montoya had given his pelican speeches.

Through the screen, he told Buzz he had to go do something. Just stay put, he'd be back in a while.

"Take your time," Buzz said. "Do what you gotta do. Me and Elmira'll just process this beer, won't we, darling?"

He ran along the path into the dark, and he found her there, sitting at the head of the long table. She watched him come out of the shadows, her face drawn. As he walked around the table, his pulse stirred, a surge of pleasure. But she didn't stand up, she didn't come to him, she didn't bury herself in his arms. Didn't even smile as she looked at him.

She wore a white collarless blouse, cutoffs, her face scrubbed of makeup, hair loose and thick down her back.

"You're hurt," he said, sitting on the bench to her right, touching a finger lightly to her hairline above the yellowing bruise. "What happened to you?"

She tapped the pages on the table in front of her.

"*Serratia marcescens* happened to me," she said.

He brought a leg over the bench, straddling it. One of the birds yawped from the pens. The sky had cleared, and it was cooler now. He could see a narrow strip of the Atlantic, mullet splashing there, sending ripples across the fiery surface.

"I know," Shaw said.

"You do?"

"Yeah, I read about it," he said. "Four sprayings between August and December that year. That same fall we were dating. Your dad was apparently put in charge of the whole thing, the spraying, the follow up tests."

She was staring at him. Shaw had never noticed the freckle high on her right temple. How was that possible? He had touched every centimeter of her face already. Now he would have to go back, retrace his steps, do a better job. Yes.

"Where'd you read that?" she said.

"In a pamphlet. Some Senate subcommittee investigation of scientific research. It's all there, in the public record. Anybody could find it in a half-decent library, if you knew what you were searching for."

Looking at her, at her face, that freckle, he said, "The people that ordered these experiments, all they did was sit down for a few days in front of five senators, confess to whatever they did, and they got their penance and were sent on their way."

"Dad testified?"

"About ten years ago, yeah."

"And what'd he say?"

"Well, to me he sounded pissed. You can read it, I've got it back at my house. He was the only witness who thought it was wrong, spraying civilian subjects without their consent or knowledge. Everybody else, they were just following orders. There was some debate at the time about whether *Serratia marcescens* was dangerous or not, so because of that, everybody was off the hook. But your dad said, even if there was any doubt at all, even the slightest about the safety of this spray, they shouldn't have taken the chance."

She sighed.

Shaw touched her bare arm, ran his fingers across her hands.

"Some of that's in here too," Trula said. She tapped the papers. "The *Serratia* business anyway. This's Waldorf's article. I've been out here all afternoon reading it. Sitting here, going over and over it, trying to get it into my head. Trying to make sense of it."

"Waldorf was murdered," Shaw said.

"I know," she said. "How'd *you* find out?"

"I just talked to the lady that helped Dougie do it."

"Where?"

"My friend Buzz is watching her, up at the house."

"Elmira?"

"Jesus, you know her?"

"She's dangerous, Shaw. I watched her kill a guy yesterday. Out in Utah, when I was getting the article."

Shaw shook his head, whistled in disbelief.

"I'll tell you all of it later," she said. "Right now, you better worry about your friend."

"Buzz can handle her okay," he said. "He could handle a dozen Elmiras."

"You're sure?"

"I'm sure. Just calm down. Everything's fine now."

He lifted her hand from the pages and held it.

"That freckle," he said. "Is it new?"

"What?"

"This."

Shaw touched it, and his hand slipped beyond, his fingers grazing into the hair at her temple, combing, lifting it, scratching the skin lightly.

Her eyes closed slowly, and she leaned to him.

"It's always been there," she said. "Always."

And they brought their mouths together, finding it again, and something new this time, some kind of larger heat, wider and more comfortable. They kissed, moving on the bench till they were pressing close. A groan came from deep in her throat, and he answered her in his way.

After a minute or two she drew away and rested her head against his shoulder. He breathed evenly, holding her, feeling the tight, cold place inside himself, feeling it beginning to warm, loosen, resume its slow thaw.

They looked out at the strip of ocean. He laid his hand on her bare thigh and smoothed it back and forth between her knee and the cutoffs. Feeling the razor line where silk became a sprinkle of down.

" 'A Plague in Paradise,' " he said, looking at the article.

Her gaze lingered on the ocean, and she said, "It's really pretty dry. Full of statistics, graphs, charts. I read it all, studied it all afternoon, and every chart, every statistic points to this bacterium, the spraying, as the trigger for MS, here in Key West anyway."

She pulled away from him, drew in a breath, clearing her head. She pressed both hands flat to the pages as if she were trying to draw energy from them.

She said, "Seventy percent of the current cases were sixteen or younger at the time of the spraying. A majority had a bad bout of pneumonia sometime within the next year. And because of the prevailing winds, and the flight patterns of the planes, this end of the island got a higher dose of spray, and this is where most of the people lived at the time, the ones who turned out to be the MS people.

"It's filled with things like that," she said. "But when Waldorf gets to his summation, he says, 'inconclusive,' 'needs further review,' 'strong indications, but no definite link.' "

Shaw shook his head.

She said, "But the worst thing in the article isn't the MS stuff at all, or the spraying. Not what happened to me. It's what Barnes has been doing lately."

Shaw watched her as she tapped a fingernail against the papers.

She said, "He has some kind of sweetheart deal with his old navy buddies. Whatever they want to get rid of, apparently, they ship it along to him. He gets rich, they save a lot of money. Barnes burns it or buries it, or dumps it at sea. Waldorf's got a list of some of the substances he found in soil samples he took from the dump and the immediate area. These chemicals, they're all so new, so exotic, they don't register on EPA tests. That's how Barnes has been getting away with it. But Waldorf used different tests, more subtle, soil samples, air, water. There're traces of these new chemicals everywhere on the island. From the bars to bedrooms."

Shaw heard a car with a loud muffler out on the road. Its lights panned through the trees and across the pavilion as if it were turning around at Montoya's entrance road.

She said, "And apparently it's much worse for all those nurses at Florida Memorial right across from the plant. They're sick at much higher rates than they should be. And bad sick, too. MS, a whole range of illnesses. Leukemia, cancer, liver problems, everything. There're cancer clusters all over this end of the island. Don't tell me this is inconclusive. Needs further study. That's major bullshit. Like Waldorf got right up to the brink of this, but then lost his nerve, and just wound up hinting very strongly that it was the spraying that's responsible."

"Christ."

"Yeah," she said. She closed her eyes and sighed, gripped his hand, held it against her thigh.

"You know, I was trying to picture it," Shaw said, "when you were diagnosed last summer, your dad must have suspected your MS might be linked to the spraying he'd done, he must've been . . . I don't know, devastated."

She nodded.

"What I think is," Trula said, "he couldn't bring himself to tell me about the spraying. So he found a way to expose it. He located Waldorf, put him onto all this."

She picked up the article, held it for a moment, then snapped her arm out, and scattered the paper into the dark. The breeze caught a couple of pages and swirled them down toward the water.

"Have you heard from him? Your dad?"

"No," she said.

Trula stared out at the water. Her face hardening.

She said, "If Barnes was desperate enough to send Dougie out to Salt Lake to kill Waldorf to keep all this quiet, then surely . . ." She took a breath, "You know, he wouldn't overlook Dad."

She shuddered and edged closer to him.

"Dad must have known how much danger he was in. That steering Waldorf to all this could blow up in his face. But he did it anyway."

Shaw put his arm around her shoulder.

"Listen, Trula. We aren't going to let this bastard wind up in some white-collar prison, playing badminton with junk-bond traders. I want you to know right now, I won't fucking accept that."

"Whatever we have to do," she said quietly. "Absolutely whatever it takes, it's all right by me."

He saw a shadow coming down the path, and he held a finger to his lips, rose quickly and hid himself behind one of the oak pillars.

In a moment or two, a boy, about ten years old, wearing camp shorts and a Mickey Mouse T-shirt, came up to the pavilion. He was holding a white bird wrapped in a hand towel. The bird swiveled its head and tried to peck the boy's hands.

"Are you the bird doctor?"

Trula hesitated, then said, Yes, yes, she supposed she was.

"This is Princess," the boy said. He came forward under the pavilion and held out an albatross, white with yellow eyes, a laughing gull grown huge. "I named her Princess on account of how she's white and all."

Trula waved the boy closer. Shaw stepped away from the pillar and nodded to the boy and came back to sit beside Trula.

"My daddy's waiting out on the road. He wouldn't let me keep the bird in our motel room another night. We might get a disease from it."

"What's wrong with it?" Shaw said.

"It's got tar on its wings. It can't fly. I found it on the beach where we're staying and took it up to the motel room and I tried to wipe the tar off, but I couldn't get it off. My daddy said we should just let it go, let it clean itself up. But it can't fly, so I asked at the motel where to take it and they told me to come here."

The car honked twice. One short, one long.

Trula, still sitting, took the bird from the boy and held it up to the light. The black gunk had congealed on its wings. No major spills lately, so it must have been just some tanker flushing its bilges offshore. An everyday thing.

"I got to go," the boy said. But he stood there and kept looking at the bird.

"We'll clean it up," Trula said. "We'll clean it up and let it go, and it'll be all right. You did a good thing. Your daddy should be proud of you."

The car honked, one long.

"I got to go." He waved at them and ran into the darkness. "Thank you," he called from the trail.

31

"Take me to the airport," Elmira said. "You take me right now, I'll make it worth your while."

"And how would you manage that?" Buzz said. "You don't have any idea how much my while is worth."

Buzz was sitting in a kitchen chair, working on his third Budweiser. Very cold, very good, giving Buzz a buzz. Elmira came over to him, gripped both his knees, and spread his legs apart. She knelt down between them on the floor.

"Don't."

She reached for his zipper, and he pushed her hands away.

"Aw, come on. Let me put some lipstick on your dipstick."

She reached for his zipper again, and he pushed her away again.

"Maybe some other night."

"You don't know what you're missing, Buzzy."

"I got a rough idea."

He pushed her hands away again and she began to stroke the inside of his thighs, digging her sharp nails along the seams of his blue jeans.

"I can do it so good, I've converted gay guys to the straight life."

"Yeah, I bet you have at that."

She smacked her lips, bobbed her head between his legs. That weird metallic hair, apricot colored, her eyes lit up with twisted light.

"Lady," Buzz said, "you need a checkup from the neck up."

Elmira held his hand, slipped his middle finger in her mouth, sucked it in. Slurped. He jerked it out of her grasp.

"I'll take you to the goddamn airport, okay? Just get up. You don't need to do any more of that."

"Listen to the man," Douglas Barnes said from the doorway. "Listen to the man, and get up, Elmira. And let's do it ve-ry, ve-ry slowly, shall we?"

———

Trula asked him if he would mind going to the infirmary cabin and mixing up the solution to clean the albatross. She wanted to sit here awhile longer.

He said, Sure, got up, and walked across to the small cabin, glancing through the trees at the lights of the main house, wondering about Buzz and Elmira, what those two could be talking about. Comparing recipes. Swapping fishing stories.

He found a mop bucket in the back room of the infirmary and brewed up the soapy solution in the proportions she had told him, got a box of Q-tips and two white bath towels, and when he returned to the pavilion, she was sitting on the bench in the same place. He set the stuff on the table beside her, bent and kissed the part in her hair.

Taking the albatross from her hands, he sat down beside her. And while he held the bird, she began to wipe at the oily feathers. Shaw, trying to keep his hands out of the way of its beak, got nicked anyway.

"It'll survive?" he said. "Clean it up, it flies away?"

"Fifty-fifty chance," Trula said. "Dad knows how to do it. But I've only just watched."

As she worked, Shaw told her about his mother's cancer, about their last conversation. That she had died. She stopped wiping the bird, and looked at him then, said she was very sorry, and asked him if he was OK, and he said that he was maybe still a little in shock, hadn't had much of a chance today to deal with it yet, but still he felt himself coming around. He explained why his father had blackmailed Trula, what he wanted the money for. Peach pits. Then about the moonsuits, the Healing House, about Buzz showing up like he had. He told her about Peter Salter, locating the body earlier tonight, the sharks feeding on it a little while ago. He told her what Millie had said about the remaining *Serratia* being hidden in a quarry somewhere.

She stopped, looked at him.

"You ever dive to the bottom of Bravo's pool?"

"No," she said.

"Ever see it before it was filled with water?"

She thought about that, rubbing again at the black goop on the bird's throat.

"Yeah," she said. "I believe I did."

"When was that?"

She couldn't remember.

"Think about it," Shaw said.

"My memory isn't what it used to be," she said. "The MS has been screwing around with my cognitive skills."

"The quarry," said Shaw, "it was just a big hole at one time, wasn't it?"

She nodded, clenching her forehead, working hard to retrieve the moment.

"Yeah," she said. "Yeah, sure, of course." She peered at him, but seemed to be studying something inside her head. "Yeah," she said. "It used to be just a rock pit. People came out here from town, brought their wheelbarrows and pickups, chopped out stones for their fences, walls. Then all of a sudden one day it was filled with water. That year, in the spring of that year, I think."

"The year of Pinkney and Chiles."

"Maybe it was that same spring, I'm not sure. I remember coming home from school one afternoon, it could have been that spring, and standing there, seeing it the first time with water in it. My dad was there, staring into it.

"Somebody had cut that narrow channel out to the bay and let the water flood the quarry. I remember wanting to swim in it. I was excited because it was like a swimming pool, a big private pool. I could be Esther Williams, you know. But Dad wouldn't let me. He wouldn't let me go near it. Yeah, I remember that."

"And then he put Bravo there," Shaw said.

"That's right. Pretty soon afterward."

She spread open the bird's right wing and dipped one of the Q-tips in the solution, and swabbed along the ridges of its feathers.

"You're saying he dumped canisters of this bacterium out in the quarry, then flooded it?"

"Yeah," Shaw said. "And I'm not a hundred percent sure, but I think he was using Bravo as his canary in a coal mine. He must have been fairly sure the water was safe, or he wouldn't have risked putting a dolphin in there, but he wasn't absolutely sure. I'm assuming that just doing water samples wasn't good enough. So he put Bravo in there to see if the *Serratia* was still potent. He might've been studying the dolphin, watching its reaction. When nothing happened, he knew the stuff was diluted, or neutralized, it wasn't going to do any more damage."

She was quiet for a moment, looking into the yellow eyes of the albatross.

"You know, Shaw," she said, "there's something I don't get. Why couldn't Dad just have refused to cooperate, said he wouldn't spray the stuff in the first place? Told the navy to go screw themselves. Why'd he have to do all that, go to that trouble?"

"Not in the military, Trula, especially not back then, how it was, all the Communist paranoia. People building bomb shelters, throwing pinkos in jail. Everybody gung ho, let's do whatever the military says to keep this life we have. He probably did argue, that's what Loretta Chiles said, but then when he was ordered to carry on with the project, he found a way to sabotage things, a creative solution. Dispose of the real stuff, substitute something else in the rest of the sprayings. But it backfired, a couple of men were killed. That's the one thing I want from Barnes. What happened that night."

Trula fixed her eyes on his. Her face both exhausted and tranquil as if she had run some grueling race. Not going to win, but happy to be almost to the finish.

She asked him quietly if he would put the albatross in one of the small wire cages in the back room of the infirmary. Shaw shrugged and carried the albatross across to the small cabin. It was getting chilly. The wind out of the northwest had pushed away the cloud cover. A spatter of stars. He heard a plane rumbling in the distance, but he couldn't find its lights anywhere.

When he returned to the pavilion, she was still sitting on the bench, bent forward, leaning her cheek against her arms folded on the table.

"You feel like going for a swim?" Shaw said.

She lifted her head and smiled.

"The quarry's pretty deep, thirty feet at least," she said. "And anyway, what could you see at night?"

"I don't need to see it," he said. "Feeling is enough."

"You know, I've been out here since two this afternoon," she said. "Just sitting here."

"Well, then, it's time you got up, went for a swim."

"What I'm trying to say is, Shaw, I can't."

"What?"

"I can't get up," she said. "I can't walk."

He sat down beside her.

She said, "It's been coming now for a while. All the stress. Out in Utah. The last couple of days. It's an acute attack, and it feels like a big one. I got no feeling from the hips down. Lost the pelvic sphincter."

Shaw touched her hair, her cheek.

"Jesus, Trula. You need to get to a doctor!"

"My legs could be this way a couple of days, or it might go on for a month, two. There's no way to tell, no way to know for sure. But they do know one thing about this goddamn condition. The longer this phase lasts, the less likely I'll bounce back, be the way I was."

Shaw was quiet, watching her search the distance.

"Can I do anything?"

"This is a whole new stage," she said. "I haven't been here before."

"I'll carry you," he said.

"Where?"

"Anywhere you want to go."

"You'll carry me." She smiled and turned to him. She shook her head. "You would, wouldn't you? You'd carry me."

"If you feel like it, I can carry you right now. I can take you over to the quarry, and you can watch me swim."

She kept smiling. Her eyes tired, but peaceful.

"I'd carry you anywhere," he said. "Anytime."

"Is that right?" she said, still with that smile. "You'll carry me everywhere I need to go? You think you could do that, you think you're strong enough to do that?"

The albatross made a hesitant noise, a peep. It tried to open its wings against the pressure of Shaw's hands.

"I'll get strong enough," he said. "If I'm not already, then I'll just damn well get strong enough."

———

Dougie's dad had switched off the lights. Now the room was dark, but Dougie could still see OK from the light the clock gave off. Ten-fifteen.

"They went to Miami," Buzz said, for the third time. "They left an hour ago, and they won't be back till tomorrow sometime."

"Bullshit," said Barnes. He pressed the barrel of the Browning into Buzz's throat, worked it around. "Bullshit. Where are they?"

"Miami."

Buzz strained against the electrical cord that Dougie had tied him up with, but he couldn't loosen it. Dougie had knotted it hard. Harder than hard. Buzz's forehead was bleeding from where Barnes had whacked him with the gun butt.

Dougie stood next to the refrigerator, staring at Elmira. He didn't know how to feel about her at the moment. Staring at her where she was sitting at the kitchen table, her head down. The same place Dougie had sat lots of nights, Dr. Montoya cooking him supper and teaching him to read.

The four of them were just sitting around in the dark waiting. His father with the Browning, shook his head, not saying anything out loud. Shaking his head over and over, mumbling to himself like Dougie had never heard him do. Standing beside Buzz, jamming the pistol into his throat. And Elmira was slumped over, quiet for a change. Mute. Still wearing half the handcuffs on her right ankle. Elmira, his wife, who Dougie had seen just a few minutes ago with her head in this guy's crotch.

And Dougie didn't know. Should he be mad or sad about that? Sad seemed right. A woman loves you, you marry her, then the lady deceives you. You find her on her knees in front of some other guy, sucking on his finger, you should be sad. But he wasn't sure. Maybe mad was better. Smack the bitch around. Yell at her. Call her things. Sad or mad. Elmira was the only one he could ask, and she wasn't talking.

"Elmira?" He went over, sat in the chair beside her.

His daddy shushed him.

"Tell me something," Dougie whispered. "Were you thinking

about me just now, your head in this man's crotch? Were you imagining it was me? Dougie Barnes, your husband."

Elmira wouldn't look at him. He bent down, got in her face, but she ducked her eyes away from him. Sad or mad? He decided on mad. Mad was good. He could do mad.

" 'Cause that isn't how it looked to me," Dougie hissed. "How it looked to me was, you were thinking about this guy, the guy with the crotch. That's how it looked to me."

She lifted her eyes, set them on his.

"Do something, Dougie," she said. "Can't you see what's happening here? We're all going to die unless you do something."

"All that stuff about love you were teaching me," he said. "That was a lot of Las Vegas dog shit, wasn't it? Just things you made up, to get what you wanted. Wasn't it?"

"What you saw, it didn't mean anything, Dougie. I was just scared, trying to persuade the man to rescue me."

"You sucked on his finger. I watched you."

"Fingers don't count, hon. Fingers don't mean a thing."

"They count with me."

"Are you two going to shut up, or am I going to have to tie a gag on both of you?" Barnes paced in front of the refrigerator.

"I'm going to the airport," Elmira said. She stood up, that handcuff jingling. "I'm walking out of here, and damn well going to the airport and fly back home. And nobody's going to stop me."

But she didn't move to the door.

Dougie's father let out a long sigh.

"And if you try anything, mister, I'm just going to scream my bloody head off," Elmira said. But still, she didn't move toward the door.

"Dougie."

"Yes, sir?"

Barnes walked over to Elmira, shaking his head. A look that reminded Dougie of the couple of times his father had come to visit him at one or the other of the mental hospitals, back in the old days when Dougie was crazy. His father shaking his head. Mad and sad combined. Yeah. Maybe that was it.

Dougie tried to make his face look like that. Tried to change the muscles around in his cheeks, make his eyes heavy, his mouth sag, taking long breaths. Mad and sad. The way his father looked.

"Dougie?" Barnes whispered. "I'm going to get your wife out of here, take her to the airport."

"You are?"

"Yes, son." The man was talking slow, like his batteries had run down, slower and slower. Taking Elmira's arm in his hand, squeezing it. Elmira going a little slack. His father said, "I'm going to put her on a plane back to where she came from. And afterward, I'm going to drive by Chandler's house. See if the asshole is there by any chance. But I need you to stay here in case he comes here."

"You're going? Now?"

"I'll be back, fifteen minutes, twenty at the most."

Elmira tried to squirm away from him, but Barnes held her arm tighter.

"He's not taking me to any fucking airport. This man is going to kill me, soon as he gets me out of earshot."

"When this is all over," Barnes said, "you can go and see her."

"Don't let him, Dougie. Don't."

Barnes shook Elmira by the arm. Then said, "I'm going to leave you here, son, for just a few minutes. I need you here to guard this man. And to take prisoner anybody else who comes here. Knock them over the head. No matter who it is. Can you do that for me, son?"

"He's going to kill me, Dougie."

"You sucked on that man's finger," Dougie said. "That wasn't right. Not for a married woman."

Elmira screeched, tried to wrestle her arm free, and Barnes thumped her on the back of the head with the pistol and she went quiet. He had to hold her up.

"You hit my wife," Dougie said.

"I just made her a little more comfortable, is all, son."

Barnes hauled Elmira over behind Buzz. Buzz saw what was coming and tried to duck his head away, but Barnes whacked him with the gun butt. Whacked him a second time. Buzz's head dropped forward.

"Now, you just stay here, Dougie, and if anybody comes while I'm gone, you tie them into a chair."

"Should I commit suicide on them?"

"No, son. I want to speak with them. I want to ask them some questions before we dispose of them."

"You're taking Elmira?"

"That's right, to put her on a plane," he said. "I'll be back very quick. Then later, you can go join your wife."

Dougie said OK. He guessed that was all right.

He was having trouble making his face look like his father's. Maybe after they left, Dougie would go look in a mirror, practice.

"Just sit here in the dark and wait, son. And use one of those dish towels on the stove there, to tie around this man's mouth. Keep him from shouting for help when he revives."

"Okay."

Dougie looked at Elmira. His father holding her up like that. She and his father hadn't gotten along like Dougie had imagined they would. Didn't seem to like each other at all. But maybe now, going through all this together, they were developing some things in common. That's what Dougie had always heard. You needed things in common with people if they were going to be your friends. Like Dougie and Elmira had violent sex in common. And killing Waldorf and Merle. And now maybe his father and Elmira spending time together like this, they would get something in common too. He hoped so.

"Bye-bye," Dougie said to her. "See you later, sweet meat, sugar teat."

"Now, Dougie. What're you going to do?"

"I'm just going to sit here in the dark, wait to take prisoners."

"You're a very good boy."

"You killed my parrot," he said. "That wasn't right."

"Jesus, son," Barnes said, "I'll get you another parrot. I'll get you a whole fucking flock of parrots when this is over. How's that?"

But his father didn't wait around to hear his answer, just nudged open the screen door and dragged Elmira out into the dark.

A whole flock of parrots? Man! How in hell was he going to come up with names for all of them? He was going to have to sit down somewhere and think about that. How many birds were in a flock anyway? A thousand parrots, fifty thousand?

Dougie sat down in the dark and thought about that.

"You know, Dougie, your father's going off to kill her."

Dougie jerked around. Jesus Christ. You could hardly see Buzz's face through all the blood.

"He's not taking her to any damn airport. He's going to kill that woman. Unless you get off your ass, do something to save her."

Dougie got up, went over to the stove, picked up one of the dish towels.

"I'd do anything to save my wife," Buzz said. "Doesn't matter what it took, I'd save her. Any man would do the same. You don't want to lose her, do you, Dougie?"

"He wouldn't do that," Dougie said. "She's my wife."

"You sure he wouldn't?"

He tied the dish towel across Buzz's mouth, got the knot very tight. Buzz growled, made angry noises in his throat.

"My daddy wouldn't do that," Dougie said. "I don't think."

32

Bravo circled the quarry, excited, ruffling the water into a light chop. Shaw was naked in the center of the pool, treading water, watching Trula. She sat on the stone steps at the edge of the pool. She seemed to be smiling.

"Break a leg," she said.

"I just might."

Shaw pushed his arms down, pumped himself up out of the water, almost to his navel, took a deep gulp of air, then sank feetfirst into the darkness, pushing the water upward as he dropped, waving his arms through the water as though he were urging a crowd to greater cheers.

His breath hard and tight in his chest.

He opened his eyes as he swiveled and turned his head downward, began to kick and swim. Suddenly, to his right, coming out of the murkiness, a blacker faster thing bumped him, shoved him down. Bravo helping. Bravo thumping his butt, driving him deeper into the pool.

Bubbling out a few pinches of air, he felt the water turn colder, thicker. He dug deeper with choppy breaststrokes as he fluttered his feet. Bravo released him, and he felt the pressure increase in his throat and gut. He squeezed his nose to clear his ears, dug another stroke through the black water, fighting the buoyancy and a tingle of fear. He wasn't sure anymore how far down he'd come. For all he could tell, he might still be near the surface.

Maybe he should turn, drift back up, get another breath and do it all again, maybe this time, hold on to a heavy rock, let it take him down fast. As he was considering this, his hand struck something solid. He thought instantly of the canister. To find the other half of the one his father had passed on to him, or even a whole one still intact, that would seal it. Just the grail he needed. He kicked deeper, pulled the water past him, ran his fingers along the object. Metal. Yes. With slits.

He gripped it, hooking his fingers into a corroded slit, and lifted. But it wouldn't budge. He dragged himself closer to it, his chest beating now, a rising pain. Slits. Sliding his free hand across it. He frog-kicked, once, twice. Louvers. Louvers. Air vents. A machine with cooling louvers.

As he waved his legs frantically, keeping himself in place, one of his feet brushed something behind him, hard, and colder than the water, and he coiled and turned and reached for it. Sharp blips of light filled his head like notes running up the scale of torment. He had used up his air. Now he was using up something else, but still grabbing for the cold thing, getting a finger on it, then in his grip, holding it tightly, his chest hammering, he turned, kicked up, kicking and fluttering and clawing up.

But then for a moment, confused, seeing nothing but dark, turned around, not sure if he was swimming up or sideways anymore, only a swirl of dark before him, and abruptly he was sleepy, considered simply floating back, taking his time, no hurry, maybe even swallow an experimental breath of water, a long, deep drink of it, and then, exactly as that idea was forming, a mound of slick cold flesh hooked him in the crotch and lifted him up, and he rocketed forward, the water roaring past him, a torpedo propelled up and up, broke through the surface, flicked like a rubber ring from Bravo's nose. As he somersaulted and splashed, he held to the cold thing, flailed onto his back, righted himself, and gasped.

"Jesus Christ, Shaw!" Trula had crawled to the edge of the pool, was extending her arm to him. "You all right?"

He reached out for her, extending to her the cold thing, his breath burning him. His head ached, his eyes and throat. Vision an inky blur.

She took it from him. She held it for a moment and then screamed. But did not fling it from her into the water, screaming again, holding the thing before her. As he pulled himself to the bank, heaving, nauseous, dimly aware. And she was panting now, terrified, but still with the calmness of mind, the clarity, and appreciation for what Shaw had just done to retrieve this thing, the poise, even in her fright, to set the glistening skull carefully on the rocks beside her.

———

Barnes carried Elmira over his shoulder out to the highway where he'd parked the Jaguar. Sped the half mile to the plant, and dragged her out, carried her across the sandy soil to the storage shed. Huffing, starting to sweat, his heart doing a jig.

The landfill looking like barren tundra tonight, the moon coating Mount Trashmore in its milky light. A clear sky, wind cool. Tundra. Like the empty mind of a samurai. Bleak and tough and clean.

Barnes knew he'd lost his samurai concentration. Lost his patience with this woman. Should've just knocked her unconscious, tied her up until a better time came to dispose of her. He should've just stayed at Montoya's until Chandler showed up.

But the bitch had gotten to him, her irritating whine, trying to poison Dougie against him, her skintight clothes, her ridiculous hair. She'd thrown him off balance. Just like Chandler had thrown him, coming into his office this afternoon, knowing about *Serratia marcescens*.

And good God, talk about losing his concentration, tonight Captain Douglas Barnes, retired, had gotten down on his hands and knees and strangled a goddamn parrot. What in the ever-loving fuck was happening to him? He was a navy man. A man of discipline and order.

He needed to take some good slow breaths, focus, get his mind marching in good even cadence again. He had to remind himself that he was close to cleaning this all up. Close to plugging the dike. He just had to dump this woman, get back over there, wait. Keep his breath nice and easy. Do Chandler, then his buddy. Then Dougie. Then maybe Montoya's daughter, depending on how deep she was in it.

Barnes was panting as he carried Elmira up the concrete ramp. Into the bright yellow glare of the security light. And when he dropped her on the cement beside the drum of Seluline, she moaned.

Hup, two, three, four. Dump the woman, cancel the idea of driving by Chandler's house. Just get back to Montoya's and wait in the dark. Keep Dougie in line. Keep it moving ahead.

He pried the lid off the barrel, set it aside. He lifted the woman off the ground, heaved her up into his arms, and tipped her head toward the barrel.

"This isn't the airport," Dougie said.

He was at the top of the ramp, breathing hard, coming up behind Barnes. Oh, great. Wonderful. Barnes shifted the woman in his arms and stepped back from the barrel as Dougie came alongside him.

Dougie looked into the drum, and said, "There's gook in there."

Elmira was stretching in Douglas's arms, waking from one nightmare to another one. He laid her on the cement again.

"Dougie," Barnes said. "Son, we're going to have to find you a new wife."

"A new one."

"This one talks too much, son. She talks and someday someone is going to listen to her and then everything I've worked for all my life will be gone. Would you want that to happen? Would you want that, everything, all my work, to go up in smoke?"

"What're those things on top?" Dougie said, leaning over the barrel. "Marbles?"

He reached out for them, and Douglas said, No! Hold it right there! And Dougie drew his hand away.

Elmira was stirring now, trying to sit up.

Dougie looked at her, squatted down beside her. He reached out and stroked her cheek. She groaned, touched her fingers to the back of her head. Groaned again.

"Elmira's got a low pain threshold," Dougie said.

"What happened?" she said, pulling herself up to her feet. Dougie steadied her.

"Put her in the barrel, Dougie."

"I'm going," she said hoarsely. "To the airport."

"In the barrel, Dougie. Put her in the barrel."

"There's gook in there."

"We're getting you a new wife, Dougie. A better one."

She turned her head, looked at Douglas, then at Dougie.

"Monsters," she said, her voice a rusty hinge. "Fucking monsters."

She staggered down the loading ramp.

"Stop right there." Barnes dragged in a long breath. Christ, look at him. A military man. Reduced to this.

He raised the Browning and aimed at her back. She hobbled a few feet across the tundra. He held his aim, center of the back. She was walking slow, her head to one side like she was listening over her shoulder.

Women! Christ Almighty, what good were they? Men were one thing. Men were warriors. Men came at you head-on, fought you fiercely, or they tried to outsmart you, and you had to kill them, there was no choice, that or die. But women. Women had nothing to fight with. They were all soft places and wet places. Their one and only purpose in life was to wrap their legs around a man, receive his fluids, and reproduce. They were weak and worthless in battle. Their only weapon was their backside. Sex, and walking away.

Elmira had raised her hand and was shooting them both a bird as she walked away into the dark, keeping her face forward.

Barnes squeezed off a round, and the woman fell forward, rolled to her side.

"First you killed my bird," Dougie said, "and now you killed my wife."

"Wives come and go," Barnes said. "But you have your father forever."

Dougie blinked his eyes. Pressed a hand to each temple and rubbed in circles.

Barnes told Dougie to bring the woman's body over here. Don't even consider disobeying him. Using his voice of command on the kid. And the boy lowered his eyes, took a deep breath. Then went over to her and picked her up and brought her back.

"What's done is done, son. We can't bring back your wife, we'll just have to get you a brand-new one. So, go ahead, put her inside here. In the barrel."

Dougie gazed out at the plant, took a few moments deliberating this, then he lifted Elmira up and slid her feetfirst into the Seluline. Barnes put his hand on Dougie's shoulder and drew him away from the barrel.

"You're a good boy, Dougie. You're a good obedient son, and that's what counts. That's what truly matters in life. You stay this way, we might be able to work it out between us. Carry on our life together. We'll come through all this, get all this behind us, and get back to the way things were before."

Dougie shrugged his hand off, and stepped up to the barrel and looked inside it. Barnes edged up behind him.

"Shit," Barnes said.

"I think she's still alive," Dougie said. "She's breathing."

"Goddamn it," said Barnes. Nothing was happening. She was there, wedged into the barrel, settling deep into the clear gel, but nothing was going on.

He stood there a minute, two, Dougie at his shoulder, still nothing happening to her. Maybe human hide was too tough. Or maybe Motrim had weakened the potency of the solution with one too many frogs. Shit.

He waited another minute, then reached carefully into the barrel and touched a finger to the gel. It didn't burn his fingertip, even felt a little cool. He rubbed it across his other fingertips with his thumb. Nothing. Then he scooped up a handful of it, and slung it out into the dark. Shit, just when he needed something like this, it had lost its sizzle.

He sniffed his fingers. It *did* smell good. Motrim was right about that much anyway. But it certainly wasn't a substitute for the incinerator.

"Come on, boy. Put the lid back on, and leave her. We'll take care of this later. Now we've got to move out. Take up our positions."

He wiped his hand on the leg of his blue coveralls.

"I'm upset," the kid said. "Something inside me hurts."

"Don't be stupid, son," Barnes said. "Come on, we've got a mission to execute."

———

Buzz said "Holy shit" again. It was the third time he'd said it since seeing Trula. Recognizing her and saying, "Holy shit, I know you. You're from that TV show."

Shaw had carried Trula inside, set her in a chair. Then untied

Buzz, turned the lights on in the kitchen. He'd put the skull on the kitchen table.

Barnacles were scattered across it. Their sharp puckers dotting the forehead and cranium. Green and lacy algae hung from the eye sockets. Simple creatures, gluing themselves to what was available down there, finding this white bone in the dark and colonizing it with their kind.

"What happened? Where's Elmira?"

"Barnes took the woman off. Dougie followed them a couple minutes later."

"When was that?"

Buzz leaned over the sink, pressed the wet dish towel to his forehead.

"Things broke up here, I don't know, maybe ten, fifteen minutes ago," Buzz said. "Barnes said he was coming right back."

Shaw went over to the light switch and turned it off.

"You knew each other all along, then, huh?" Buzz said, turning from the sink, holding the cloth against his forehead. "The two of you, the actress and the fireman. And you never said anything to the guys about it, just watched her show along with the rest of us."

Trula was looking at Buzz. Buzz glanced at her again and said, "Holy shit."

"Now I know why you went after Jorge that day, the things he said about her. At least that much makes sense now."

"What's this?" Trula said.

"Nothing," said Shaw.

"He was defending your honor," said Buzz, "against the remarks of a macho asshole."

"You were?"

"Nothing happened." Shaw was frowning at Buzz.

"So, would you look at this. Shaw Chandler and Cassie Raintree."

"Trula Montoya," Shaw said.

"You two are like, what, you just like each other? You're close? Or more than that?"

"Buzz," said Shaw. "Come on, knock it off."

Buzz leaned against the sink, keeping the dish towel pressed to his forehead.

"We like each other," Trula said. She reached out for Shaw's hand, and they locked fingers.

"Holy shit," he said.

"You want her autograph, Buzz? Want her to sign something for the guys?"

"Hey, Shaw, let me ask you something, man. You have any idea what the hell we're doing here? What the plan is?"

"Yeah," he said. "I got a vague plan."

"Oh, good," Buzz said. "I was worried you hadn't thought this through. That we're out here in the dark with our peckers lying full stretch on the table and Barnes is the one holding the meat cleaver. I'm glad to see I was wrong."

"Don't worry, Buzz," said Trula. "Have some faith in Shaw. He got us this far, didn't he?"

"Holy shit," Buzz said, looking at her. "Holy shit, I don't believe it's you."

33

Both hands of the luminous clock were closing in on midnight when Shaw heard the porch steps groan and a moment later heard whispering at the kitchen window. Buzz was back in his chair, the electric cord loosely looped around his arms. Stationed behind the kitchen door, Shaw held the skull in one hand, a long bread knife in the other.

Trula was sitting in a chair in the hallway, out of sight.

"Okey dokey," Dougie said, as he came through the door.

He went over to Buzz and gave him a quick look. Buzz with his chin to his chest.

"Just like we left it," Dougie said. "Except Elmira's not here anymore."

Barnes opened the screen door and stepped into the room. He panned his automatic slowly around the room, and Shaw eased out and clopped the skull against the back of his head. Hard enough to drive a tenpenny nail through an oak plank.

Barnes toppled forward onto the table, and Buzz was instantly behind Dougie, locking his arms into a choke hold, forearm against Dougie's throat, other arm hooked behind his head, pressing it forward.

Shaw flipped the lights on.

"You got him, Buzz?"

"I don't know," he grunted.

Dougie scuffled backward, his eyes rolling upward as if he were trying to peer into his own brain. Both his hands gripping convulsively at Buzz's forearm, but Buzz was winning the tug-of-war. Even a guy who didn't feel pain needed a little air to keep going.

Shaw came over, raised the skull, nailed Dougie a good one.

Then another one. The boy's eyes frosted over, lost their hold on the world.

"Better give it one more," Buzz said, still straining. "The guy's a goddamn ox."

Shaw hammered him again, and he went soft in Buzz's arms.

"Tie him in the chair, Buzzer. Very tight."

"My pleasure."

Shaw got Barnes's automatic, then went to the hallway, lifted Trula from her chair and brought her into the kitchen. She was holding another bread knife and an aluminum mallet for tenderizing meat. Kitchen warriors.

Barnes lay flat on his stomach. Squatting down beside him, Shaw pressed a knee to the middle of Barnes's back, and tied his wrists behind him with a length of clothesline that Trula had located earlier.

"Well, shit, that was easy enough," Buzz said.

"It's the next part that's going to be hard," Shaw said, as he hauled Barnes upright, dropped him in the remaining chair.

"What? Calling the police?" Buzz said.

"We're not doing that."

Buzz looked at him.

Trula said, "You're not going to fight us on this, are you, Buzz?"

"If you're planning on torturing these guys, yeah. Damn right I'll fight you on it."

Shaw held up the Browning, popped the slide out. Nine rounds left. He slid it back in.

"I just want to ask the man a few questions," Shaw said.

Buzz looked at him some more.

Shaw said, "That's not torture, is it, Buzz? Asking questions."

"What's happening to you, man? What's gotten into you? I never saw you this way."

"I've never been this way."

"It's not pretty, Shaw. It's time to bring this back to earth, man. Call in the law."

"Hey," Shaw said. "Let me ask you. If something fucked up your family, Buzz, something happened to you when you were young, before your life even got going, and you had a chance now, all of a sudden, one little chance, to see what it was, find out exactly what happened, what sent everything off in the wrong direction, wouldn't you want to do it? Wouldn't you be willing to bend the rules a little, make it a little hard on the guy that fucked you and your family over?"

"No torture," Buzz said. "I won't stand for that."

"Okay, no torture," said Shaw. "Fair enough."

Lars arrived at one-fifteen. He was driving a forty-foot crane with a bucket scoop that could lift six tons of garbage at a time, carry it from the Munch and Crunch over to the receiving bin and drop it in. Bumping along on its big tank treads. Dougie had been explaining it to them for the past half hour. Ever since Shaw had made Barnes call Lars and tell him to get the crane over here.

Dougie gave them the exact horsepower of the diesel, the top speed, the capacity of its gas tank, who manufactured it, how much it cost. How often it broke down. Barnes scowling at him the whole time. Dougie's forehead had swollen up, and there was a deep gash at his hairline. But the boy didn't seem to notice it. Rattling on about the crane, all its measurements and vital statistics.

When they heard the crane arrive, they went out onto the porch, Buzz and Shaw standing on either side of Barnes. Lars climbed out of the cab, came over, stood in the yard looking up at them, shaking his head.

"I don't get it, Mr. Barnes."

"I told you on the phone, Lars," Barnes said. "You go down to the quarry. You dredge whatever's in there out of there. It's not real fucking complicated. I think you can handle it."

"But why? Out here in the middle of the night, Mr. Barnes. If you don't mind my asking, you get me out of bed, wake my family. I'd like to tell them why it is, you know, when I go home tonight."

Barnes said nothing.

Shaw had the Browning pressed into his lumbar spine, rubbing the barrel back and forth across the knobs.

"Just do it, Lars," Barnes said. "Pull everything out of there. That's all the fuck you got to do. Put it on the bank beside the quarry, and go on back to your bed. Okay?"

Lars shook his head.

"Okay, Mr. Barnes. This is what you want, Lars will do it for you. I just tell my wife, it's more strange things I'm doing for my job."

After Lars was on his way, Shaw and Buzz took Barnes back into the kitchen.

"You coming, Trula? You want to watch this?"

"I'll stay here," she said. "Buzz and I'll entertain Dougie."

"You sure?"

"I'm sure," she said. "You can tell me later. I'm running a little low on energy. Sitting here is enough for me."

Shaw smiled, and turned to Buzz.

"Knock him out again if you have to. Keep knocking him out. He seems to enjoy it."

"Don't worry about it, man. Just go do what you gotta do. I'll do what I gotta do."

"I'd feel better," Shaw said, "you used more rope on him."

"Go," Trula said. "Go, and come back."

———

Bravo swam in the channel, hanging back near the gate out to the bay. His quarry all muddied up. Barnes stood beside the rusty shell of a front-end loader. Broken and without tires, its front scoop twisted. A pile of bones lay nearby, a second skull, a femur, pelvis, ulna, clavicle, fibula, tibia. And three or four dozen rusted-out canisters were piled on the other side of that crippled tractor.

Lars ran the scoop through the water again, bumping it along the bottom. Then he raised it, and this time it held only rocks and mud.

Shaw shook his head at Lars and waved it away, and Lars opened the jaws and let the muck splash back into the quarry.

Barnes was standing beside Shaw, his hands behind his back. Silently moving his gaze from Shaw to the pile of debris, then Lars. Measuring out a strategy.

But Shaw wasn't worried. Even without the pistol in his hand, or Barnes's hands tied, Shaw knew he could handle him. He felt the familiar jitter of adrenaline, that comforting transfusion of power.

Shaw kept the Browning out of sight as Lars took another bite out of the pool. Again, only mud and rock and some stringy sea grass. A light breeze stirred the branches and flickered through a stand of sea oats like the rush of black flames.

"Tell him that's enough," Shaw said. "He can go."

Barnes yelled for Lars to stop.

The diesel throttled down, and Lars climbed out of the cab and came over.

"Okay, now, Mr. Barnes," Lars said. "I'm digging up bones here. This is something serious you have to be telling me about."

Barnes looked at Shaw.

"So tell him," Shaw said. "Tell him about the bones."

"Jesus Christ," said Barnes. He grimaced at Shaw, gathered himself for a moment. "Okay, Lars. What we're doing here is, we're digging up an Indian burial ground."

"Indians, Mr. Barnes?"

"Seminoles, Comanches, Mohicans, some goddamn tribe or other."

"Comanches driving tractors?" Lars shaking his head.

"Yeah, yeah," Barnes said. "Indians. You never heard it, Lars, where the name Key West comes from? *Cayo Hueso.* It's Spanish, means Island of Bones. It's printed right up there on the airport wall. *Cayo Hueso.* The name Key West, it didn't come from 'western island.' But *hueso,* 'bone.' *Hueso* became 'west.' Get it? Bones. It's where Key West got its name."

"What bones?"

"The fucking bones of Indians that the Spaniards found on the beaches here. The island, it was a battleground or a burial ground. The same fucking thing, either way you look at it. Bones, Lars. And what we're doing here, we're doing archaeology."

"So late at night, Mr. Barnes?"

Shaw said, "You can go now, Lars. Go on back to bed."

"Island of Bones," Lars said. "These bones?"

"Get the fuck home, Lars," Barnes said.

Barnes sat down on a limestone boulder near the edge of the quarry. After Lars had moved the crane back up the path, Shaw took the Browning out of his pocket, jacked a round into the chamber. He moved over beside Barnes and pressed it to his temple.

"Tell me," he said. "Tell me about all this."

"You seem to have forgotten," Barnes said. "About Mr. Salter. Mr. Salter's body."

"You mean that empty grave near the road, where the fence is snipped? That what you're talking about?"

Barnes stared at him.

"Yeah, we dug the body up tonight. Buzz and I. Fed it to the big fish." He drew a slow circle on the side of Barnes's head with the barrel. Stuck it in Barnes's ear, wiggled it.

"I want to hear what happened that night. I don't want any more screwing around. I don't want any jokes. I'll kill you in a second, no guilt whatsoever. You don't tell me every little piddling detail of it. If I think you left one thing out, I'll pull this trigger till my hand cramps."

"I wasn't here," Barnes said. "How the fuck should I know what happened?"

"Montoya was here, though," Shaw said. "Wasn't he?"

"Yeah," he said. "But I wasn't."

Shaw could hear Lars in the distance, the diesel moving the half mile down the highway to the plant.

He pinched Barnes's right ear, pulled it hard away from his head, pressed the barrel of the Browning to it, aiming it off toward the bay.

"I don't want to have to hurt you, Barnes."

"I'm not going to tell you shit, Chandler. Not shit."

"Yes, you are."

Shaw fired.

Barnes fell forward on the ground, sprawled there, face in the sand, writhing, groaning. A big plug of cartilage gone. The concussion probably exploded his eardrum, tore loose the hammer, anvil and stirrup. Malleus, incus, stapes. What with all Shaw's good medical training, he could chop off little pieces of Barnes all night, give him the Latin name of every part.

Was this torture? He'd have to tell Buzz later, this was just reality therapy. Showing Barnes what a gunshot sounds like. The sound you don't usually get to hear because you're dead by then.

Shaw grabbed him by the back of his coveralls and hauled him back to the rock. Barnes's eyes squeezed tight.

Shaw said, "And Montoya came to you later, didn't he? He came to you about what had happened out here. He laid it out in front of you, the good honest naval officer he was, told it all to his superior officer. And then you decided, probably right then, you decided you had yourself a lifelong easy mark. You could hold this over Montoya forever, wring every dime, every square foot of land out of him forever. That's what happened, isn't it?"

Shaw took hold of Barnes's collar, shook him. That gunshot probably still chiming in his blood.

"Montoya confessed to you," said Shaw. "He told you the whole deal."

His voice frail, Barnes said, "Montoya was a dumb shit. A pain-in-the-ass, moralizing little dumb shit."

"What happened that night? What did Montoya tell you?"

Barnes groaned. His ear bleeding, running down his neck. He tried to scrunch up his shoulder, rub his ear.

Shaw said, "We already know Montoya sabotaged the spraying, the *Serratia marcescens*. He brought the canisters here and was trying to bury them. But something happened."

"Yeah, something happened," Barnes said.

"It was my father, wasn't it? He did something."

"A fucking hothead, your father."

Shaw pressed the pistol to the back of Barnes's head again. Slid it back and forth. The man cringed.

"All right, goddamn it," Barnes said.

Shaw took the pistol away from his head, pressed it against his spine again.

Barnes said, "Pinkney was driving the forklift. Chiles and Montoya and Chandler were standing around up here, watching."

"And what happened?"

Barnes swallowed. The ear was probably numb now, the echo of the shot dying out. The shredded cartilage wasn't bleeding enough to kill him any time soon. But hang him by his heels out here all night, maybe that would do it.

"Chandler," Barnes said. "He'd been drinking with Chiles that night before they came out here. Some bar downtown. The two of them drinking, and Chandler got in a brawl with some teenage boy."

Shaw leaned forward.

"Keep talking," he said.

"I didn't get the whole story, but Chandler punched some high school kid," Barnes said. His voice hoarse, his throat filled with ground glass.

"Yeah?"

"And Chiles was ragging him about it," Barnes said. "Keeping after him, how big and tough Chandler was, knocking out some teenage boy. Chiles was on the edge of the pit, directing Pinkney where to dump the canisters, giving Chandler shit the whole time, and Chandler lost it. Jumped on the loader, went berserk, pushed Pinkney out of the way and tried to run over Chiles, and the hothead dumped the front-end loader into the rock pit, took Chiles with it. Crushed Chiles, broke Pinkney's neck in the fall. Killed two guys, bam, like that. And he didn't even have a fucking scratch himself."

"He killed them both," Shaw said.

"It was a complete and total fucking disaster." Barnes squeezed his eyes again.

Shaw took a long breath, held it, let it go slowly.

"That was me," he said distantly. He took a breath, another one, said, "I was the high school kid. I picked a fight with my father."

"What?"

Shaw said nothing. Lowering the pistol, the blood flooding from his legs, arms. Feeling faint.

"You?" Barnes choked out a laugh. "You? Oh, great. Oh, yeah, that's beautiful. Now every-fucking-body's guilty. You, your old man, Montoya." He laughed again. "That's fucking great. All the good guys turn out to be bad guys. Ha! I love it."

The darkness was yellowing. Shaw looked around the quarry. Seeing that night again, hearing what his father had said to him at the bar, turning around on his stool. Frowning at his son. Saying it in front of everybody: *You're going to stand there, decide if I did the right goddamn thing.*

Shaw turned away from Barnes, stared at Bravo blatting back in the channel.

"My father, he took the money, just agreed to the deal," Shaw said, watching Bravo, "didn't argue, didn't question it?"

"Oh, Christ, yeah, he argued. He was a crazy man. All the problems he had with his goddamn wife, and shit, it still took some serious convincing."

"What kind of convincing?"

Shaw, inside a dense mist, watching the dolphin. Hearing himself ask the questions, the things that part of him still wanted to know, but the other part, the dazed part, didn't give a shit about anymore.

"Oh, the two of them came to my office, middle of the night. Chandler was huffing and puffing around. The asshole said he wanted to go to trial, have it all out in public. Said he could prove it was an accident. He was just following orders. And I sat him down, and told him then he should just get adjusted to the idea of living out his days in a prison for killing Pinkney and Chiles. 'Cause I would fucking well see to that. Yes, sir. And I could've done that. I had that kind of power.

"So the idiot, he had no choice, he took Montoya's money. A shitload of money too. Montoya feeling so guilty, like he'd done it himself, killed these two guys. He thought he was doing Chandler a favor. And Chandler leaves, disappears. The cops hunted for him for a while, but nothing ever came of it.

"And then what do you know, the dumb shit comes back. Twenty years later, he shows up at my office, demanding more money, and that's what started this whole goddamn thing up again. Because I wasn't about to give Hanson Chandler any of my damn money. I made that money. I put it together, dollar by dollar. And I'm not giving it to some two-bit sailor who comes up to me with some sad story. And he threatened me. Had the amazing goddamn nerve to threaten me, said he was going to expose the whole thing, the cover-up, all of it."

"So you sent Dougie to reason with him."

Barnes chuckled.

A strong breeze washed through the branches, the sound of hundreds of bats flittering for cover.

Barnes stood up from his rock, and Shaw turned to face him. Barnes staggered slightly to his left, caught himself. Then he drew his hand out from behind his back. He opened his left hand and held it out for Shaw to see, the rope still knotted around his wrist. Then he held out his right. No hand there, just the bloody remnants of flesh and bone.

Shaw blinked. Only half of him there. The other half back twenty years, walking into Captain Tony's, dragging his father down from the barstool. Taking the old man's solid punch to the jaw. Starting all this. The cause of everything.

Barnes swiveled and struck out with his good hand. Maybe it

was aikido, judo. One of those stolen treasures from the Far East. Definitely something fast and hard, not the least mystical, something that spun Shaw to his right in a lurching pirouette, sending him over the edge of the rocks and backward into the quarry, and in the same spinning motion the Browning came out of his hand.

Shaw splashed hard and breathlessly on his back in the quarry. And before he had opened his eyes, he heard the blast of the pistol. He ducked, dived back into the cold darkness. Heard the burning rip of another slug through the water. And that woke him from his daze, woke him to the harsh, cold black water. And he hauled himself down through the quarry, down into the coldest and darkest place he could find.

34

Breathless, stifling his pant, Shaw surfaced in the channel. Saw Barnes standing twenty yards away holding his bloody stub up to the moonlight, examining it. Quietly Shaw coasted forward a few yards, settled under a jut of coral and limestone, where he held himself, face out of water, breathing. Still.

In a moment or two, he heard Barnes roaming the bank, his stumbling walk. Shaw held his breath, the pitted limestone cutting his hands as he steadied himself there. Coming closer, Barnes mumbled to himself, taking both sides of an ugly argument.

Roaring fast from the north, a jet broke into the sky low overhead. Another navy training run, at less than a thousand feet, ripping away to the south. Rattling windows in Key West, putting an extra tremble in Shaw's gut.

As the rumble died, Shaw heard Barnes move to the bank just above him, stand there. Shaw didn't breathe. He saw a drop of blood fleck the stone a few inches from his face. Barnes muttered a curse, another one.

"You're a dead man, Chandler," he said quietly.

Holding his breath, Shaw pressed hard against the bank, and his small movement sent a ripple radiating outward.

"I see you," Barnes sang. "I see you."

Barnes moved on the bank above him.

"You bastard," Barnes said. "You ruined everything."

Two yards in front of Shaw, Bravo erupted in a silver geyser, shot five feet up in the air, spiraled, and came down hard on his side. Barnes fired twice. A third time.

The dolphin disappeared, stayed down, the pool shaking now. And Barnes howled. A sound at once pitiful and gruesome, wailing up from the dark crumbling center of his spirit. The howl of a man frightened for the first time, whose fear was made more intense by his own piercing expression of it.

Shaw thought he heard Barnes scramble back up the pathway, cursing to himself, making strangled grunts and moans. Shaw waited a minute. Another. He heard nothing. He waited longer.

Well, goddamn it all. The bastard could shoot him if he wanted. Shaw wasn't staying in this quarry a minute more. He'd face what he had to face. And he climbed over the edge.

He ran, slogging inside his soaking clothes, his tennis shoes heavy, past the bones, the canisters, up the path to the house, running toward the lights through the trees. Across the sandy lot, the seashell drive, past the lawn furniture, vaulting to the porch. He barged through the door, into the kitchen, water pouring from him.

Dougie's chair was broken into pieces, Buzz lashed to another chair. Unconscious. No sign of Trula.

Shaw lifted Buzz's head, pulled open a lid. Still alive. He cut Buzz free from the chair and laid him on the kitchen floor, talking to him, calling his name, asking him where Trula was, what happened, Buzz silent.

Feeling again the numb, deadened jaw that his father had given him, the weight of his mother in his arms as he had carried her to her bedroom that night, laying her out in her bed. All of it shuffling chaotically in and out of his memory as he rose from Buzz's side and went to the door and sprinted away into the dark.

———

"Boiler main steam bypass," Dougie said to Trula. "Boiler main steam bypass. Oh, yeah."

He located a red wheel on the west wall and turned it all the way to the right. Then picked up the manual again.

"I got to go down this list of numbers, do each one in the right order. But the problem is, I'm not too good with numerals," Dougie said to her. "In the porno books, sixty-nine is about it for numbers."

Trula said nothing. She was sitting on the metal stairway that led up to the offices. If Dougie would lose himself in his work a little more, maybe she could make it up there, lock the doors behind her, call Nine-Eleven.

"There's sixty-five steps to bring the plant on line," he said. "So knowing the number sixty-nine is no big help."

Dougie was moving around the boiler room, making adjustments, pulling levers, throwing switches, turning knobs. As he stooped for another one, Trula dragged herself up one stair, then another.

Dougie looked up at her, came over to the stairs.

"I saw Elmira sucking the guy's finger. And I had to decide, mad or sad? I chose mad. But you know, when my daddy killed Elmira, I didn't have to decide anything. Didn't have to ask how to feel about it. It just came, and did what it wanted to do to me."

"Dougie," she said. "Listen to me."

"Yeah."

"What're you doing? Why'd you carry me here?"

"I felt like it."

"Why, Dougie?"

"He killed my bird, then he killed my wife. And now my belly is full of wet, heavy towels. And someone is gripping my heart muscle and twisting one hand one way, the other the other way, doing an Indian burn on it. It's how I feel, how I'm feeling now. That's sad, isn't it? How sad feels?"

"Yes," Trula said. "That's sad."

"I thought so."

"Why did you bring me here, Dougie?"

"We're going to have a funeral," Dougie said. "You need people for a funeral. You know, it's like the garbage plant is the only friend I got anymore. The bulldozer, the turbines and boilers. And I'm going to put Elmira through it, her body, instead of burying her. Like if the plant was a church. And her ashes are going to be where I can see them, spread on Mount Trashmore, that's what I want. Bring the plant back alive, and burn her.

"And then whenever Daddy comes home, burn him. Put him inside the furnace and burn him dead. Because he killed my bird and my wife. And then once I'm done with that, you and me can slide our silkiness in and out. I'll disappear into your mossy grotto and send you into wordless bliss. We'll cry out the names of the lost universes, bleat our joy."

"Dougie, listen to me. This is wrong. What you're doing here, it's wrong, Dougie. Wrong. Do you hear me?"

He said, "You sure you won't read these things to me? You do that and things'll go faster here. I'm a slow reader."

Trula shook her head at him, and Dougie shrugged and held the manual up and pointed his finger to his place.

"Mud drum blow down valve," he said. "Closed."

He walked over to the orange lever on the side of a large silver vat, and yanked it down.

"Mud drum, mud drum."

Dougie pulled the lever down an extra inch or two more.

"As water in boiler heats up," he read. "As water in boiler heats up, it will ex . . . it will expand, increas-ing drum level. Knife valve, open."

Trula edged up another stair. Ten to go.

"This is the tricky part," Dougie called to her. "This is the part when the furnace temperature goes up to five hundred degrees, starts to make some steam. It's just jiggling the needles now, starting up.

"But if the temperature climbs too fast, one of the turbines by itself couldn't handle all the steam pressure and could rupture, and send a backwash into the system, and that could cause ruptures all along the hot-well lines.

"So I got to do it all just in the right order, every valve, every turbine switching on in the right sequence, follow the manual. If the lines rupture, the plant can fill with steam. Two-thousand-degree steam. And there might be an electric surge thing, shoot-ing along the lines to Key West Electric Company, and it could knock the power lines right off the poles. Set fire to downtown Key West."

He smiled over at her, showing off. She nodded her head, duly impressed, and when he turned, she went up another step.

"Step number fifty-nine," he said. "Set dump valve. At a pres-sure. Higher than plant header pressure."

Dougie got on his knees and scooted under a big copper tank. Trula could see him twist and squeeze back under there. She made it up three more stairs before he came out. Her arms getting tired, hands scraped up. Dougie stood up and tipped his head to one side.

"You hear that whistle?" he said. "That's the superheated water through the lead tubes that go to the dump tank. It's supposed to sound that way. Everything's right. Everything's thumping along like it's supposed to do. I'm doing good."

Trula watched him walk to the door of the boiler room, stand there and look up at her.

"That door up there to the offices is locked. So I wouldn't bother dragging your ass up any more steps."

Trula slumped forward.

"I got a couple more things, then I'm going to get my wife," he said. "We're going to have a funeral."

———

Dougie left the generator room, walked across the asphalt apron to the storage shed and looked in the barrel at Elmira. She wasn't there. Just those marbles, and something else. Dougie stared at it. He stared some more. He recognized it somewhere in his head, but he couldn't bring it out into words. He knew he recognized it. He kept staring, and then, yeah.

The handcuff. Yeah. The handcuff that had been around her ankle.

"Where'd she go?" Dougie said.

He leaned over the barrel, trying to angle for more light. She wasn't in there. He rolled the sleeves of his blue work shirt up to his elbow.

"Elmira?" he said, and plunged his hand into the clear goo.

Nothing in there. Nothing but goo.

"It's going to take a half hour or so," Douglas Barnes said, standing on the apron, teetering to his right, then left, like he was trying to keep his balance on a surfboard. "But, boy, you're going to lose that arm. That arm's just going to up and disappear, like this."

Barnes held his hand out, pulled a red bandanna away from his fingers, and there was nothing there but four bloody knuckles and a nub of a thumb.

"This is your arm in half an hour."

Dougie saw the pistol tucked in his father's belt, and he sprang down off the loading platform, tackled the old man and slammed him to the ground. It didn't require much effort to knock him unconscious. Three or four smacks and his head started to jelly against the pavement. Then Dougie stood up, wiped the goo onto his pants leg, and slung the old man over his shoulder and headed over to the receiving bin.

35

Shaw had done it. Caused it all. The moment he had put down his paintbrush, then crushed his bomb shelter, come downstairs, lifted his mother into her bed, tracked his father to the bar, confronted him. Everything had flowed from that moment. That decision.

But he didn't know where that moment came from. He didn't know where the original blame was. What unpredictable gland had chosen that night to function. What seepage of what hormone had triggered his doomed trip to the bar.

He was never going to understand that. He had gone as far back as he could. Now he was going to have to begin to move ahead through the murkiness, act, and live, without ever knowing the source of it all. And though he knew now he was never going to understand it, and he wasn't ever going to be free of it, he knew at the same time he was going to damn well keep trying to do both.

––––––

Shaw drove the El Camino the half mile to the recycling plant. He sped. He didn't stop for the locked gates but gunned through them, and they buckled, broke open.

His synapses red-lining, eyes straining to pick up anything out there in the yellow half-light, he slewed through the gravel, kept going around to the smokestacks, past the storage shed. Braking hard at the receiving bin.

There was Dougie, rolling a dolly with a fifty-five-gallon drum on it toward the edge of the garbage pit.

Shaw, caught in the rapids of his fear and outrage, tumbled

forward, no control. He was out the door and running. Dougie turned, a weird smile, holding the dolly handles, watching Shaw sprint, and then at the final second, he stood aside and planted a forearm in Shaw's throat.

Shaw heard a distant groan. The light went gray, his vision withered. He heard himself choke, felt something force him to the ground, a monstrous weight bearing down on his chest. Far away, he could see his hands gripping an ankle. Dougie's foot on his chest.

"I'm having a funeral," Dougie said. "And you're invited."

As the light returned to his eyes, Shaw drew back his arm and drove his right fist upward, jolted his knuckles against Dougie's kneecap. But Dougie didn't register the blow.

"You're acting inappropriately," said Dougie.

Shaw gripped the toe and heel of the boy's tennis shoe and wrenched it to the right. Dougie only ground down harder, his heel against Shaw's sternum.

"Some people are just born impolite," Dougie said. "No manners at all."

Dougie stooped over him, took him by the front of the shirt and dragged him to his feet.

"You're all wet," he said. "But I got just the place to dry you out."

Shaw swiveled and slammed his knee into Dougie's groin. The boy winced, but not in proportion to the blow. Shaw clubbed him in the jaw, gouged a finger at his eye, hit close, something wet.

"Fuck a duck," Dougie said. "Roly-poly, hot and holy."

Dougie gripped Shaw by the shoulders, twisted him around so he was facing the receiving floor. It was brimming with garbage, bags, lumber, bundles of newspapers. As Shaw struggled, Dougie locked his hands around Shaw's chest in a bear hug. He lifted him and walked him toward the edge of the pit. Bright spotlights lit the vast concrete room, a football field sunken twenty feet below the level of the ground. Garbage covering it.

The pressure Dougie was applying clouded Shaw's vision again. He stretched his arms behind him, joined his hands at the small of Dougie's back, gripped tight. He had done this as a boy, reversing a bear hug to flip and body slam. Hold your attacker tightly, bend at the waist and toss him over your back. But that was with boys his own strength. Boys who couldn't lift him so high from the ground to keep him from planting his feet, boys who couldn't squeeze his ribs so hard he could hear them snap, and make him see the dazzle of pain at the rim of his sight.

Dougie walked him forward, suspended him over the thirty-foot drop, and Shaw kicked his heels into Dougie's shin, knowing it was doing nothing, and feeling his own strength ebbing. The light dimmed. He shot an elbow back into Dougie's ear.

"You haven't prepared yourself well enough," Dougie said. "To fuck with me."

"Don't, Dougie," Shaw gasped.

"And I thought we were sex brothers," Dougie said. He dropped Shaw into the pit.

"Shaw!"

He opened his eyes. The stench dizzied him, a sweet, sickly rot of fish and flesh. The air was not air but had mass, and it seemed to vibrate with a vile dark green color. His ribs ached and his stomach was wriggling into his chest.

"Shaw!"

He was facedown in it. Eyes opening into the black plastic nightmare of roaches and rotten food, the slippery rank muck of diapers and damp mushy remains of vegetables.

He heard the roar of a motor and felt something hot and hard in his throat. Vomit rising in him. He rolled onto his back and gasped. But there was no air here, only this other thing, this thing he was mired in.

"Shaw, it's me."

Trula leaned into his sight. She was balanced on a stack of red plastic bags, five feet above him. He had fallen into a valley, lying in this dent, and was looking up at her.

"Are you okay?"

"Broken ribs," he said. "Are you?"

"Yes," she said. "He was gentle with me. Picked a soft spot and heaved me."

"What's he doing?"

"That," she said, pointing.

Shaw brought himself to his knees, grunting, and he climbed up over a wooden chair, a pile of plastic pots, a mound of garbage bags, and was beside her.

She was dirty, her cheek stained with yellow streaks, her hair matted. She was staring up at Dougie who sat in a metal cage high above the sea of garbage.

"He's cremating his wife," she said. "Then, I think, us."

From the arm of a crane, a pair of large metal jaws lowered on a long steel cable. Dougie, working the levers in the cage, jiggled the jaws left, then edged them right. When he had them in position, they squealed open and dropped from ten feet above the garbage.

Shaw saw something move to their left behind a hill of broken lobster traps and plywood sheets. A pistol lifted up, aiming unsteadily at the cage.

"Get down," he said.

Trula pressed flat beside him as the pistol fired, and a bullet ricocheted off the high concrete wall thirty feet from Dougie's cage.

The jaws lifted the fifty-five-gallon drum along with dozens of bags of garbage and brought it smoothly to the front of the heavy belt. The conveyor flowed into a curtain of asbestos strips. Beyond the curtains, as Shaw remembered from his tour of the plant, the garbage would ride on the conveyor for another five feet, then fall down a chute where a sliding door opened at controlled intervals, admitting trash to the heart of the fire.

Dougie revved the engine and opened the jaws of the scoop and set the barrel carefully on the belt. The big can wobbled, bumped against the high steel sides of the conveyor, stabilized, and began its journey toward the curtains.

Dougie's voice sounded over the loudspeakers mounted in the upper corners of the big room.

"Now we should say a prayer."

On the far wall, below Dougie's cage, Barnes was climbing slowly up the metal rungs that were mounted to the cement wall. They ended at a catwalk that led to Dougie's cage.

"Elmira Hemple Barnes," Dougie said over the loudspeaker. "Elmira and I slid our silkiness in and out of each other. And I married her, and she taught me how to say a few things. And then my daddy shot her. My daddy shot her dead, and now she's going to her funeral. Now she's dead, a dead redhead."

Barnes was still on the rungs, ten to go to the top, resting.

"Walla walla bing bang," Dougie said. "Amen."

Dougie raised the scoop and wrenched the crane to the right, and the heavy metal jaws swung hard at the wall, toward the spot where Barnes had halted.

"Jesus!" Trula said, and turned her eyes away.

Barnes saw it coming, paralyzed for a moment, then tried to climb out of its way. But the scoop slammed him against the rungs, pinning him there as the jaws bounced away. Shaw watched the pistol clatter into a pile of lumber.

"Trula, can you move?"

"Squirm a little," she said. She kept her eyes from the wall.

Dougie brought the jaws close to where Barnes was flattened against the metal rungs. Delicately, he maneuvered the jaws to his father's side.

"You stay down," Shaw said. "I'm going after him."

She gave his hand a squeeze and he tried standing, but pitched forward into a huge pile of lawn clippings, branches. He climbed over them, pushing past more plastic bags. Skidding down hills of trash, dragging himself over branches and boxes and debris of every sort.

Using the metal jaws with dexterity, Dougie pinched his father off the wall, the jaws clamping him at the waist. Barnes kicked his legs, and let go of a weak scream.

"Now it's time for my father's funeral," Dougie said from the speakers. "The lesson is . . . The lesson of my father's life is, you shouldn't kill people's birds and their wives. That's not right. You were a bad dad, so it's your turn to burn."

Shaw found a good trail across some planks and scaffolding and made it halfway to the far wall as Dougie was dropping Barnes onto the front edge of the conveyor.

Douglas Barnes raised up, his hands coated with blood. He pushed himself to his knees. The jaws hovered directly above him, keeping pace with the conveyor.

Barnes glanced up at the jaws, then staring at Dougie, he saluted. Got to his feet, still saluting, stood as tall as he could manage, blood running from his hand to his forehead and down his face. He began to march forward away from the fire, saluting a flag in the impossible distance.

"No way, Jose," Dougie said. "Flat splat, you dead rat."

With a thrust of the levers, Dougie hammered his father against the metal treads.

Shaw pulled himself over cardboard boxes, piles of clothes, palm fronds, a TV set, broken toys, lampshades, rotten flowers, a huge pile of books and magazines, slippery with food, across a pile of vinyl records, through the gamy vapors of a rotting animal, and finally to the cement wall.

He saw the pistol resting on a coil of garden hose. Beside the hose was a gap in the garbage, a fifteen-foot plunge to the floor. Shaw stepped out onto a sheet of plywood that lay next to the hose. It rocked under his feet. Its far corner teetered an inch from the pistol's butt. Shaw balanced himself across the board, tipping it neither right nor left, came to what seemed its center and kneeled down, stretched himself flat, and edged forward, reaching for the pistol.

He heard the crane working behind him, but he kept his focus on the pistol, inching forward across the rough wood. He snaked his arm out, feeling the fulcrum wobble beneath him, the sheet of plywood teetering toward the pistol, a hair away from unseating it from the hose.

Trula yelled behind him, and he took a breath and lunged. The corner of the board nicked the pistol, dumping it from the hose, and it tumbled down the hill of bags. Shaw dove after it, spreading his legs as he fell. He got it by the barrel, hanging upside down, his feet hooked in fissures in the trash.

Jamming the pistol in the waistband of his jeans, he twisted double, hauled himself back to the surface, and scrambled to the first rung of the ladder.

Trula screamed again, and Shaw pulled himself higher and saw her digging down below the surface of bags where he'd left her, trying to hide from the jaws. Dougie dipped the jaws, then raised them. His laugh echoing through the speaker.

"Slip slop, hide the mop," he said. "Boola boola, Trula."

Up the ladder, hand over hand, to the catwalk. Twenty feet from Dougie's cage. As Dougie concentrated on his work, Shaw crept down the catwalk, pulling the pistol out. He popped the slide. Barnes had left him two rounds.

Out in the sea of garbage, Trula screamed again. Not terror but outrage. The cage blocked Shaw's view as he clicked the slide closed and covered the last steps to the opening.

"Whatta you going to do now?" Dougie said, without turning. "Shoot me?"

"Yes, I am."

"I wouldn't if I were you," said Dougie. "Unless you want to turn Trula boola into a roasty toasty crispy critter. A lusty busty piece of crusty."

Shaw moved beside Dougie, the pistol aimed at his head. Dougie made a subtle adjustment in the levers, brought the jaws to the front of the conveyor. He jiggled a small handle and Shaw stepped forward to see.

The scoop had opened and Trula was gripping the lower jaw. Her legs dangled onto the conveyor, feet bouncing against the moving treads.

"That's a Huot drag chain and screw conveyor. It's rated for twelve thousand pounds. Moves at ten miles an hour. Faster than a person can walk. I'm real good at this, don't you think?"

Shaw pressed the barrel to the back of Dougie's head.

"Move her off of there, Dougie. Now!"

"All it takes is a little wiggle and she's on her way. Three funerals in one day. And you'll make four."

"I'm going to pull this trigger. Now do it, get her off of there."

A deep rumble sounded nearby and Dougie looked up.

He sat forward in his seat, craning to see out the wide opening of the receiving bin to the adjacent building, the boiler room.

"Aw, shit," he said.

An alarm bell began to ring, a red bulb flashed in the far corner of the huge room. Blinking above a set of concrete steps that led up out of the ocean of garbage to the ground level.

"Shit, fuck," Dougie said. "I must've got my numbers assbackward or something."

"Bring her down from there, Dougie. Right now."

"Guns don't scare me," he said. "I already lost an arm. But I don't have a pain threshold, so it doesn't matter."

He turned his shoulders so Shaw could see his right side. Nothing but a few strands of his shirtsleeve, drenched red. The conveyor rumbled and squealed, seemed to be picking up pace. Trula was still gripping the jaw, but her head had sagged. Shaw thumbed back the hammer.

"That's it, Dougie. Pull her back from there."

Dougie took his hand from the control panel, sat back in the chair. The cement floor was polished with blood.

"Which one gets her down? Which lever?" Shaw said, moving alongside the boy.

Dougie didn't answer. His eyes empty, a smile on his lips. He blew a bubble of blood, popped it.

Shaw watched as Trula let go, dropped onto the conveyor, knelt there, her back to the curtains. She crawled forward, looking for something to hang onto, but there were only the high steel sides.

Dougie grabbed for the pistol and Shaw knocked him away, and threw him forward onto the control panel, pinned him there, his left hand on the back of Dougie's neck, and Shaw fired both rounds into his right temple, and spun Dougie's chair aside.

He gripped one of the levers and dragged it back. The jaws rose on the steel cable. He tried pushing the lever forward and the jaws dropped. That was it. That was it. Slow it down. Focus on it. Trula saw the jaws coming back down, and crawled faster against the flow of the conveyor. She was almost to the curtains now. Another explosion came from the other building, and the violent sputter and crackle of something electrical.

Trula reached a hand out for the jaws. Shaw nudged the lever forward, easing the jaws closer to her. She got her right hand on it, then the left, and Shaw moved the lever back and helped her stand, helped her rise to her useless legs, and he lifted her, brought her forward on the conveyor, to the lip of it.

Dougie groaned, pulled himself upright, and flopped forward across Shaw's hands on the controls.

And the jaws wrenched from Trula's grasp. The big scoop flew to the ceiling, clanged against the crane arm. Shaw heaved Dougie away from the board. Got his hands on the levers again, but by then Trula was at the curtains, moving quickly through them, on her back.

For a moment the lights fluttered. Then they blacked out. The conveyor shuddered and stopped. Sparks erupted from the control panel, and Shaw tumbled backward away from it. He came to his feet, ran onto the catwalk.

He climbed over the guardrail, chose his spot, then dived into a pile of black trash bags. He landed on his side, hauled himself upright, groaning, cursing.

The enormous room was dark now, except for the single flashing red beacon, and as he fought his way across the mounds of trash, boards jabbed him, exposed nails cut his flesh.

He had learned that you could not save all of them. It was not possible. It was rookie nonsense to believe you could. But still, on every ride to every fire, to every accident, every alarm, he and Buzz and all of them always believed they would arrive soon enough and have the skills and the luck and the savvy to rescue every one of the injured. He knew it was a lie, but it was a lie that renewed itself every time the claxon sounded.

When at last Shaw reached the base of the conveyor, he saw it was eight, ten feet beyond his reach. Furiously he piled bags on top of each other, threw lumber and fragments of furniture into a hill that at last he climbed, and reached out for a grip on the conveyor.

He chinned himself up, pulled over the edge of the metal railing, and she was there. Lying on her back, looking at him.

"Some fun, huh?" she said, and smiled.

"Can you move?"

"Well, I don't think I'm up to dancing."

Shaw reached out for her, but the light flickered on, and the conveyor groaned and wrenched into gear, and surged forward, Trula moving away from him.

He dragged himself up, fell onto the heavy belted treads, got to his feet and ran to her. He hoisted her to his arms, turned and ran back down the belt. But the power was flooding the circuits. Spotlights brighter than before, the conveyor rolling at a gallop.

He ran as fast as he knew how, then shifting up a gear, he ran faster. But he didn't gain on it. The sides were steel and smooth and too high to scale. He raced forward, his ribs blazing, but concentrating on his footwork, on the rough path flowing toward them.

His breath tore his throat, and Trula held to him as the lights grew brighter, the scream of the conveyor louder. He staggered, caught himself and for a moment he thought of his mother, her final incredible hand strength, his father lying on the bed staring up into the empty eyes of Dougie Barnes, and Shaw picked a spot out in the air, a place he was headed, a good place where he'd never been, going with Trula beyond this, beyond anything he'd known he could do, and he felt the gates open inside him, and he gained a foot, another foot. Moving to within two yards of the brink, the air scalding him now, as he leaned forward dangerously, churning into the final straightaway, the ribbon at the finish.

He felt the lines of his gait purify, his legs moving easily now as he dragged down a huge breath and bellowed a wordless curse, and hurled himself forward and carried them to the edge, and launched them both beyond it and down, and as they fell, the lights shut off again, and there were explosions, one after the other, and as they landed in the hill of trash, a blast from the building next door shook the earth.

And they lay in the piles of trash, Shaw gasping, Trula cradled against him. And when his breath returned, they lay still and watched the lights of the burning plant play on the high walls of the vast concrete room.

"We should probably get out of here," he said. "Those stairs over there, under the red light."

She took a breath, nestled deeper against him.

They lay there for a while longer, watching the smoke blow past, listening to the racket outside, large structures crumbling.

"We should go," he said.

"Yes," said Trula. "Now is good."

In no hurry, he stood and lifted her easily into his arms, and carried her across that rough sea of rubbish and decay.

36

"Whatta you mean, you don't carry Twinkies anymore. I been coming in here twenty years, by God, there's always been Twinkies right here by the goddamn cash register."

Shaw said, "Try the oatmeal cookies, Ben. They're better for you."

He was rigging the last few silver mullet with double hooks, working on the oak cutting board, scales and fish slime on his hands now.

Ben said, "I don't want nothing that's better for me. I want Twinkies, goddamn it." The man was in his seventies, a burgundy baseball hat with a bonefish embossed on the front. Khaki uniform. *Ben* sewn above his pocket. He said, "Look at me, Shaw Chandler. I look like I could benefit from eating oatmeal at this time of my life?"

"It's never too late to try something new, Ben."

"The hell you say." Ben got out his wallet. "How much for the flies?"

Shaw wiped his hands on a towel and punched it into the cash register.

"That's all?"

"You come in here," Ben said, "change everything around, new shelves, new paint, everything, Jesus, I can't find a damn thing anymore. Takes me twice as long to do my shopping. And then you don't have any goddamn Twinkies."

"Eight seventy-nine, Ben," Shaw said.

"Eight seventy-nine? Christ, I used to pay half that."

"These are hand tied. You know, by that guy, up in Key Largo.

Thorn, whatever the hell his name is. He takes a half a day on every one of them."

"Eight seventy-nine, Christ."

"I still got that Taiwanese garbage, if you want it. It's back there on the far wall."

Shaw could see Trula down the dock. Leaning on the aluminum cane in her right hand. Limping along between Johnny Middleton and Doyle Overby. The early morning sun staining the sky behind them. A smear of reds against the blue. The three of them had started fishing together lately, going out on Doyle's yacht, trolling for billfish. It was too early in the year for marlin, but they'd snagged a couple of good-sized sail.

Ben counted out the money. Two quarters, and twenty-nine pennies. Eight wrinkled ones.

"I'll order some Twinkies, Ben," Shaw said. "Have 'em tomorrow maybe. Definitely by the weekend."

Ben said nothing. Put his fat black wallet away.

Shaw dropped the flies in a small paper sack, watched Trula standing twenty yards down the dock, chatting with one of the deckhands on *Miss Liberty*.

"Don't listen to me," Ben said, "going on like I do. I just get riled, I see things change. Fact is, you're doing a good job, Shaw. You are. I'm glad you're staying on."

"Thanks, Ben."

Ben smile darkly.

"But if you don't get those damn Twinkies, boy, you'll never see me on your doorstep again." He winked.

"Yes, sir."

Ben opened the door, jingling the bell above it. He held the door open for Trula and Johnny and Doyle, nodding at them, and they nodded back. Johnny dressed in a dapper gray jumpsuit, epaulets, and phony insignia. Doyle wore the same cutoff corduroys and ripped undershirt he'd been wearing for as long as Shaw had known him.

"Those Kona lures come in yet?" Doyle asked.

"No, not yet," said Shaw. "But I rigged you some silver mullet instead."

"I like them plastic jobs better," Doyle said.

"You got no taste or judgment, Doyle Overby," Johnny said.

"Yeah," Doyle said. "That's why I let you come along fishing with me."

"He lets me come along," Johnny said to Shaw, " 'cause I put three hundred dollars of high-test gasoline in his boat every time."

"I prefer those hard plastic lures," Doyle said. "The ones with the little rubber skirts. They remind me of my first wife, Cordelia. Same big eyes, flat little head. Can't dent them with a sledgehammer."

Johnny said, "If you hadn't kept trying to dent that woman, she'd still be around."

Shaw said, "I don't allow any fighting in here. You guys going to insult each other, just move on down the dock."

The two of them went down the leader aisle, needling each other, both of them as puffed up as bantam roosters.

Trula sat on one of the stools across the counter from Shaw. She was wearing a white T-shirt, denim overalls speckled with the white paint she'd been using on his mother's bedroom walls. She'd twisted her hair into an intricate bun. A little lipstick. That freckle. Those eyebrows.

"Hey."

"Hey, yourself," she said.

Shaw made a small slit in the belly of the last mullet, jabbed the pointed leader wire through the cut. Trula leaned on the counter across from him. He didn't need to kiss her yet. He didn't need to come around the counter and touch her, hold her, do anything. Not yet. He could stay where he was, finish his work, carrying on a small conversation with her. He could stay there for, say, two, three minutes. Not even reach out and touch her hand. He could do all that, but he couldn't keep his heart from shaking. That was hopeless.

"I thought we could do supper out tonight," she said. "When I get back in from fishing. Maybe take Buzz along, if he's up to it."

Buzz was staying with Shaw till he'd recovered from the concussion Dougie had given him. He was still seeing double about half the time, and still having some light-fracturing migraines, but he was improving. He was staying upstairs in Shaw's room, while Shaw and Trula stayed in the downstairs bedroom.

Trula was getting fond of Buzz, starting to know him in ways

Shaw never had. She sat by his bed and they talked and talked. Couldn't shut either of them up. Shaw got the impression they might be talking about him some of the time, but he wasn't sure.

"Buzz'll like the Full Moon Saloon," said Shaw.

"Fish sandwich, smothered in cheese and mushrooms," she said.

"Onions, fries. A pitcher of beer," Shaw said.

"Buzz tell you what Medoff said?"

Shaw said, "Yeah. He might never remember anything about that night. The blow he took. Otherwise he's fine." Shaw reached for her hand, and she stretched it out to him. "I'd say he's lucky. I could use a little selective amnesia myself."

She said, "Well, he'll be back fighting fires in no time."

She looked at him, her eyes working.

He twisted the wire carefully, setting the hooks back into the belly slit.

"Do I miss it?" Shaw said. "Is that what you're asking me? Do I miss the claxon going off at three in the morning? I'm half asleep and giving mouth-to-mouth to a six-month-old baby out in the middle of the street. Do I miss that?"

"You do, don't you?" she said. "You miss it."

"A little," he said.

"And I miss New York," she said. "The show."

"But otherwise," he said. "How's your life?"

"Oh, it has its compensations," she said. "For instance, there's nowhere in Manhattan you can find a grouper sandwich fresh as the Full Moon Saloon's."

In the back of the store Johnny and Doyle started fussing about which leader line to buy.

"You still love me?" she said. She got off her stool and edged around the counter and stood next to him. When he didn't answer her right away, she poked him in the ribs.

"I asked you a question, mister."

She poked him again.

Shaw was threading the wire out of the mullet's mouth, concentrating, feeling his way with his fingers inside the cramped, slimy body of the fish.

She poked him a little harder, made him miss the mouth, jab the wire tip into his finger. He winced.

"You don't love me. You stopped, and now you're afraid to admit it."

Another poke.

Shaw put down the mullet. He turned and reached out and held her face in his slimy hands, and kissed her. And that was the extent of Shaw Chandler's extraordinary discipline and control. That was the beginning again of this other thing, this new wordless language they were learning to speak, syllable by syllable, putting together their first phrases, the baby talk of this new life.

In the far distance, he heard the bell on the door jingling. Someone coming in for a dozen shrimp, a handful of lead sinkers, a popping cork, some leader wire, long-shank hooks. Someone coming into his tackle shop to spend their money. But they would just have to wait. He was busy. He was kissing Trula Montoya, and she was kissing him.

A Note on the Type

The text of this book was set in Sabon, a typeface designed by Jan Tschichold (1902–1974), the well-known German typographer. Because it was designed in Frankfurt, Sabon was named for the famous Frankfurt type founder Jacques Sabon, who died in 1580 while manager of the Egenolff foundry. Based loosely on the original designs of Claude Garamond (c. 1480–1561), Sabon is unique in that it was explicitly designed for hot-metal composition on both the Monotype and Linotype machines, as well as for film composition.

Composed by Creative Graphics, Inc.,
Allentown, Pennsylvania

Printed and bound by Fairfield Graphics,
Fairfield, Pennsylvania

Typography and binding design by
Dorothy S. Baker